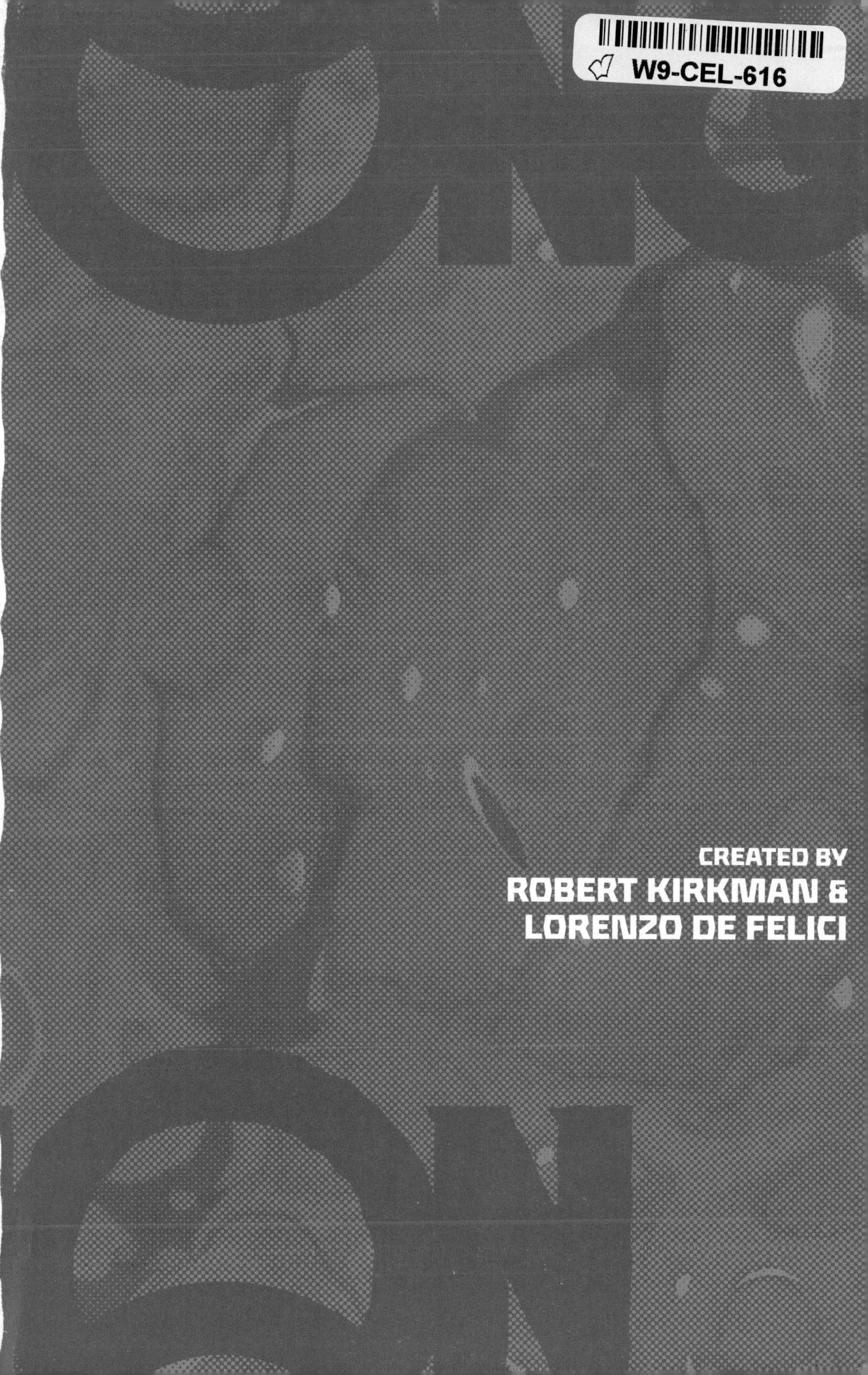

CREATED BY
ROBERT KIRKMAN &
LORENZO DE FELICI

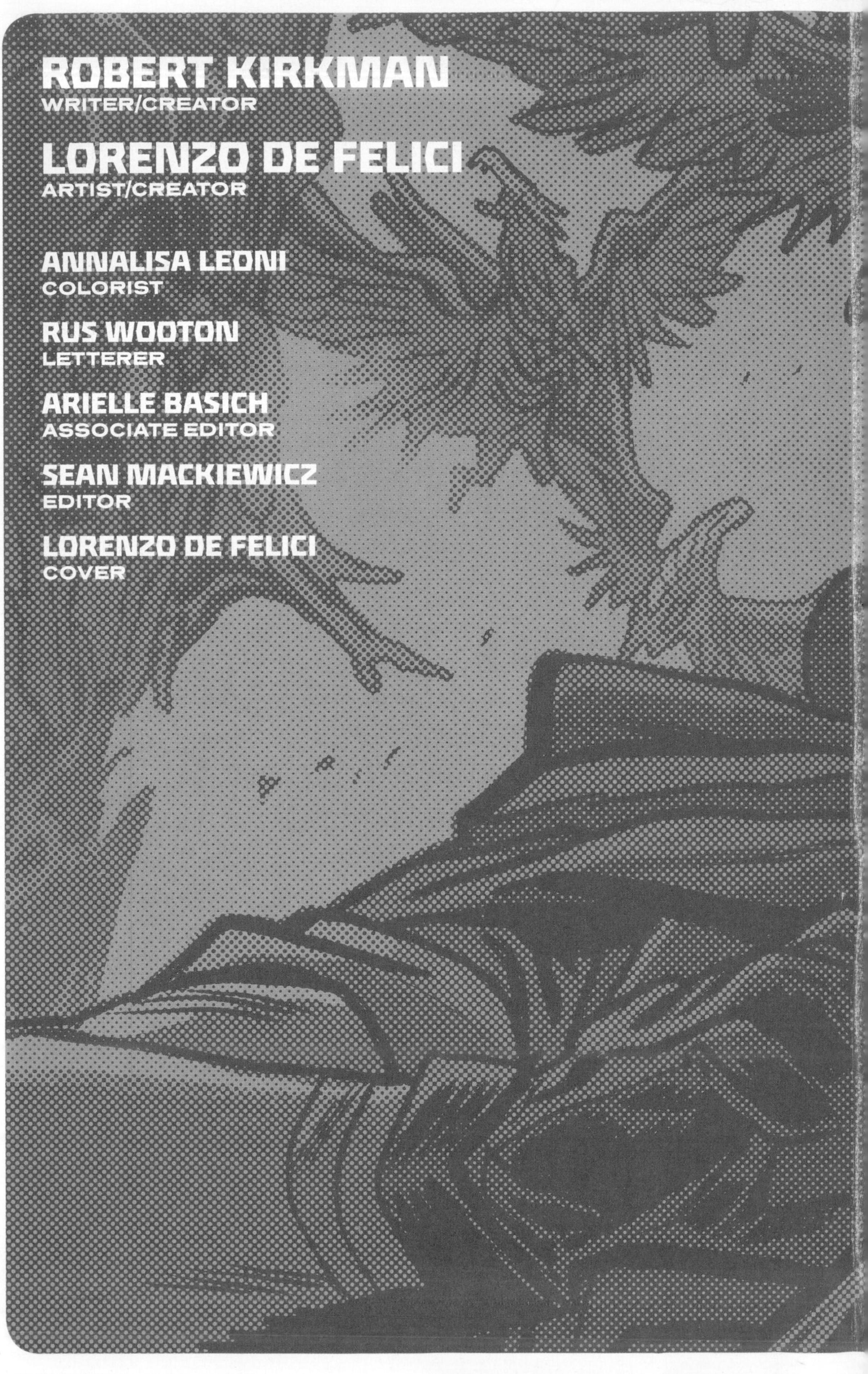

ROBERT KIRKMAN
WRITER/CREATOR

LORENZO DE FELICI
ARTIST/CREATOR

ANNALISA LEONI
COLORIST

RUS WOOTON
LETTERER

ARIELLE BASICH
ASSOCIATE EDITOR

SEAN MACKIEWICZ
EDITOR

LORENZO DE FELICI
COVER

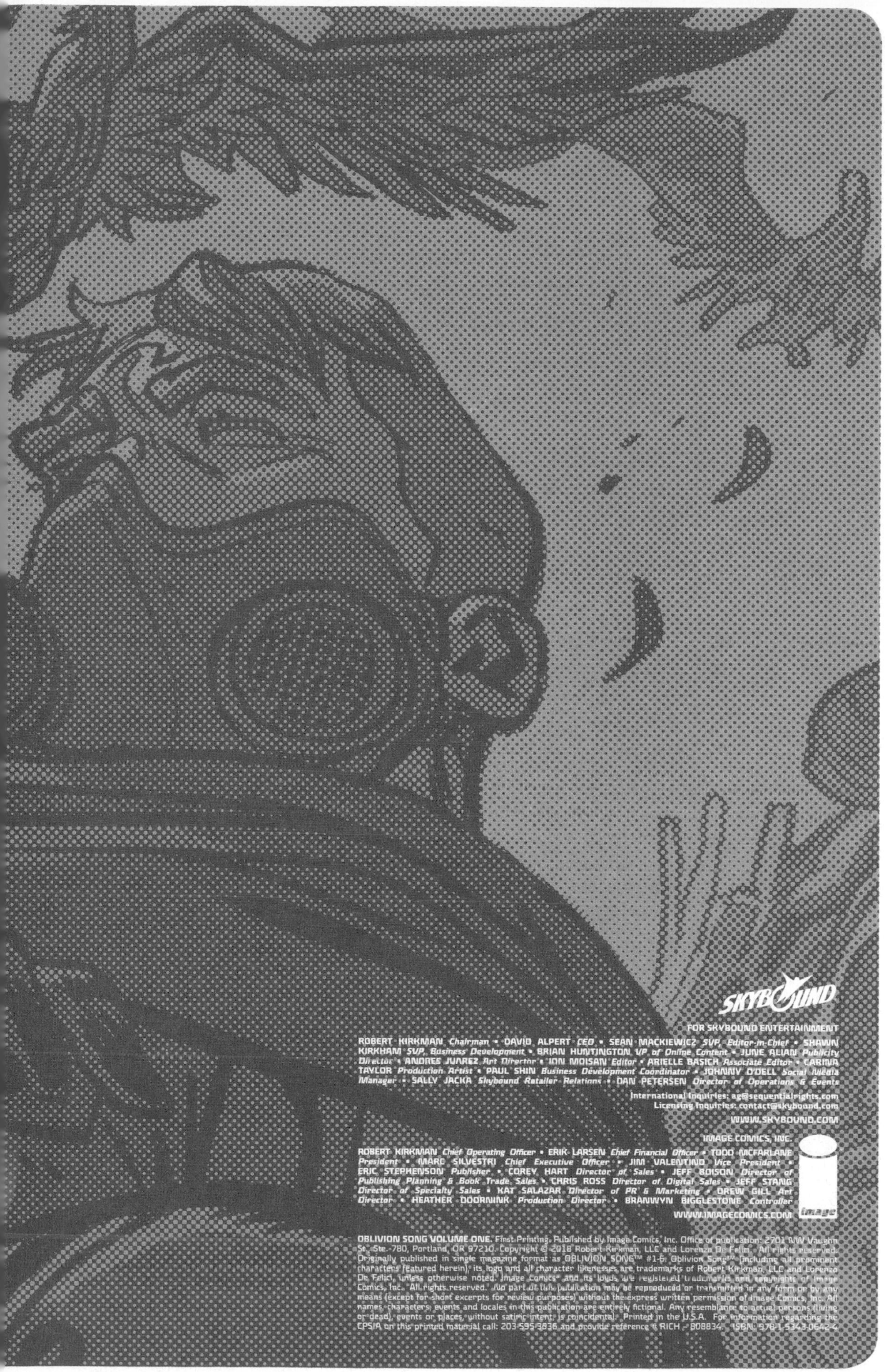

FOR SKYBOUND ENTERTAINMENT

ROBERT KIRKMAN *Chairman* • DAVID ALPERT *CEO* • SEAN MACKIEWICZ *SVP, Editor-in-Chief* • SHAWN KIRKHAM *SVP, Business Development* • BRIAN HUNTINGTON *VP of Online Content* • JUNE ALIAN *Publicity Director* • ANDRES JUAREZ *Art Director* • JON MOISAN *Editor* • ARIELLE BASICH *Associate Editor* • CARINA TAYLOR *Production Artist* • PAUL SHIN *Business Development Coordinator* • JOHNNY O'DELL *Social Media Manager* • SALLY JACKA *Skybound Retailer Relations* • DAN PETERSEN *Director of Operations & Events*

International Inquiries: ag@sequentialrights.com
Licensing Inquiries: contact@skybound.com

WWW.SKYBOUND.COM

IMAGE COMICS, INC.

ROBERT KIRKMAN *Chief Operating Officer* • ERIK LARSEN *Chief Financial Officer* • TODD MCFARLANE *President* • MARC SILVESTRI *Chief Executive Officer* • JIM VALENTINO *Vice President* • ERIC STEPHENSON *Publisher* • COREY HART *Director of Sales* • JEFF BOISON *Director of Publishing Planning & Book Trade Sales* • CHRIS ROSS *Director of Digital Sales* • JEFF STANG *Director of Specialty Sales* • KAT SALAZAR *Director of PR & Marketing* • DREW GILL *Art Director* • HEATHER DOORNINK *Production Director* • BRANWYN BIGGLESTONE *Controller*

WWW.IMAGECOMICS.COM

OBLIVION SONG VOLUME ONE. First Printing. Published by Image Comics, Inc. Office of publication: 2701 NW Vaughn St., Ste. 780, Portland, OR 97210. Printed in the U.S.A. For information regarding the CPSIA on this printed material call: 203-595-3636 and provide reference # RICH – 808834. ISBN: 978-1-5343-0642-4

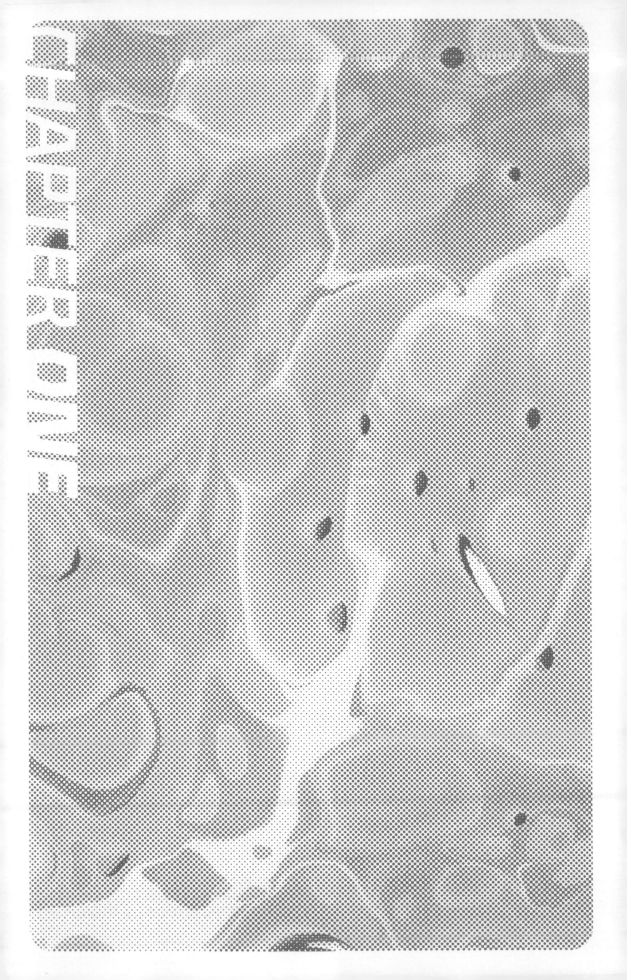

CHAPTER ONE

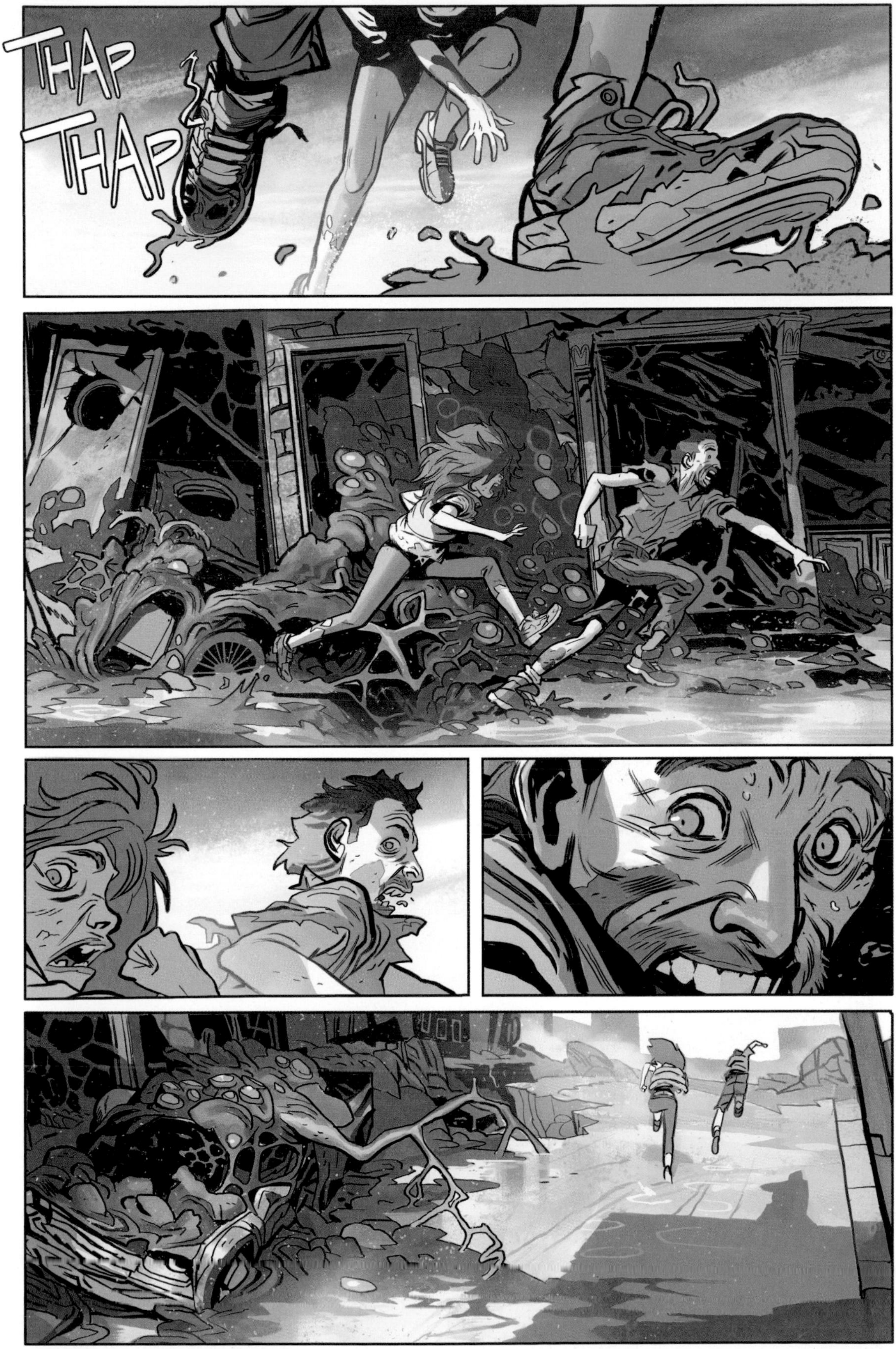
THAP
THAP

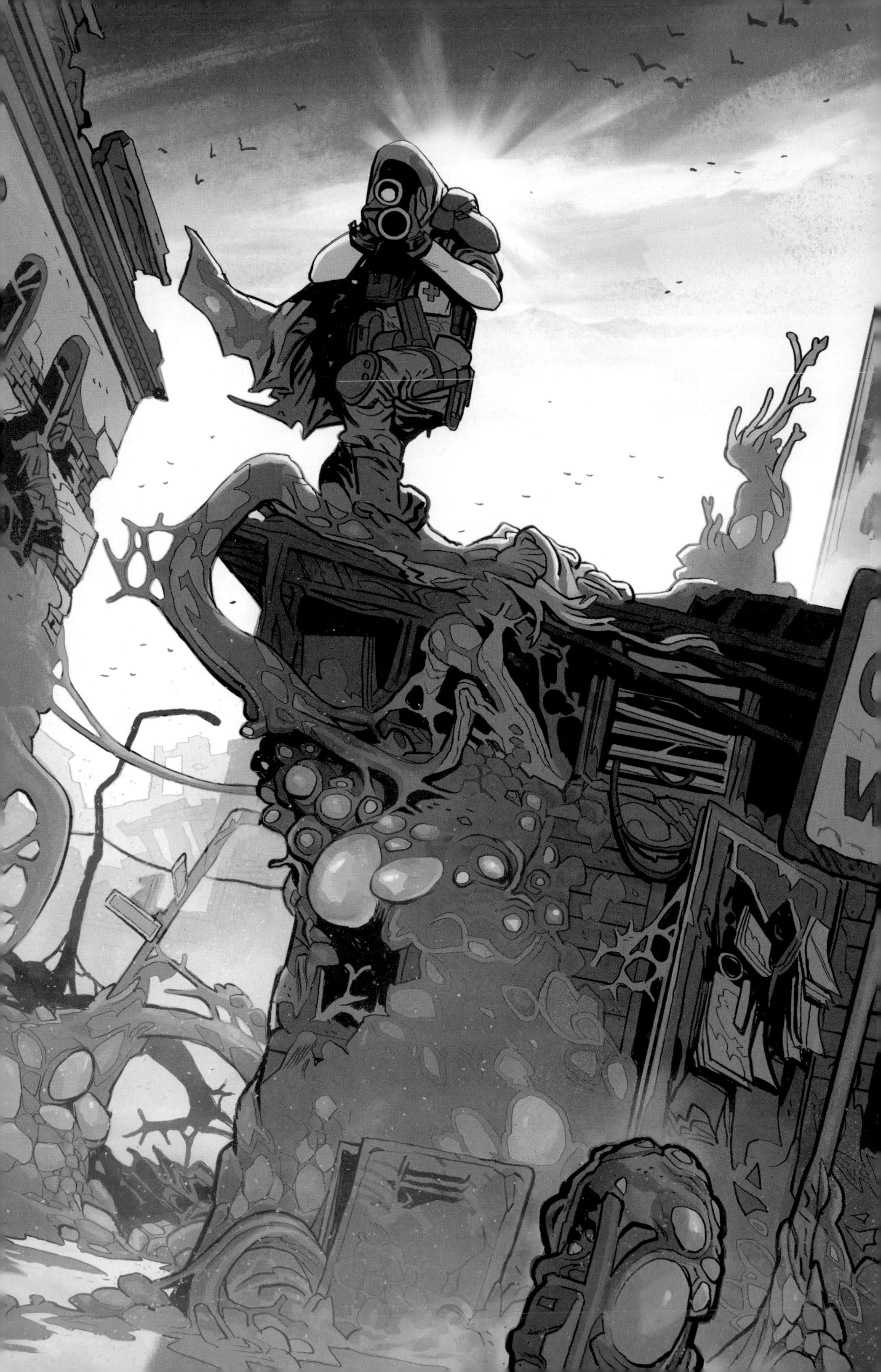

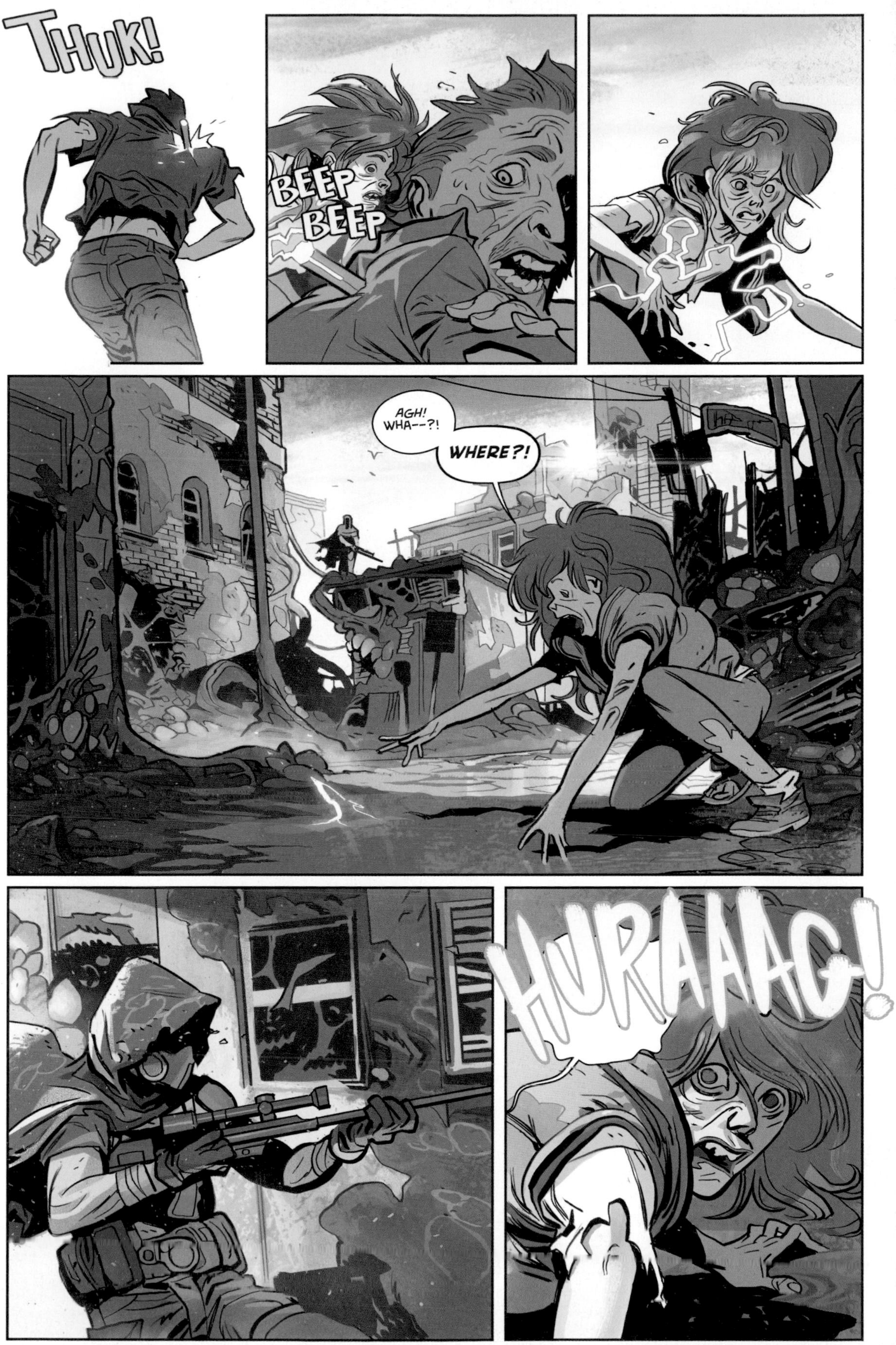
THUK!
BEEP
BEEP
AGH! WHA--?!
WHERE?!
HURAAAG!

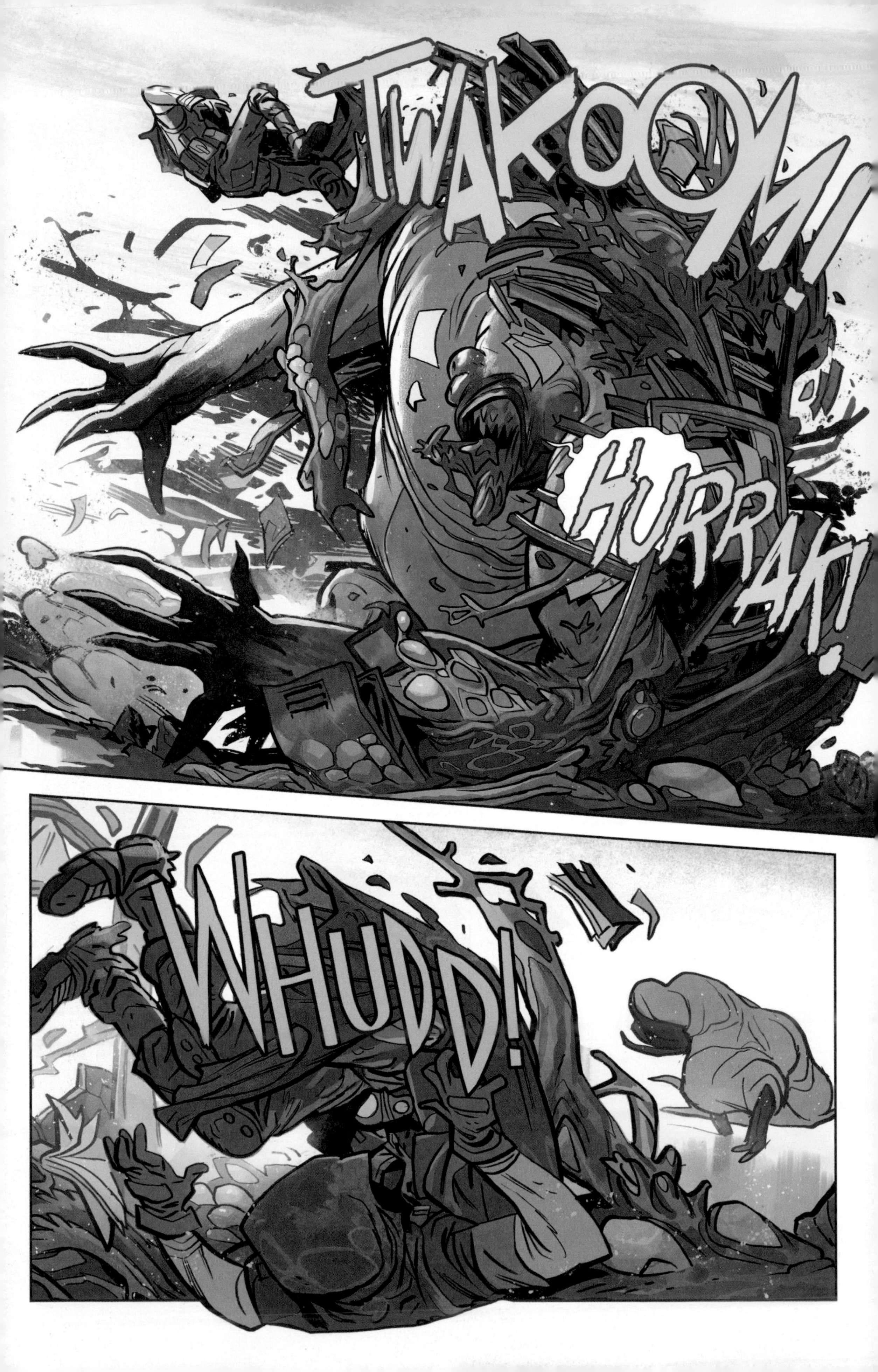
TWAKOOM!!
HURRAK!
WHUDD!

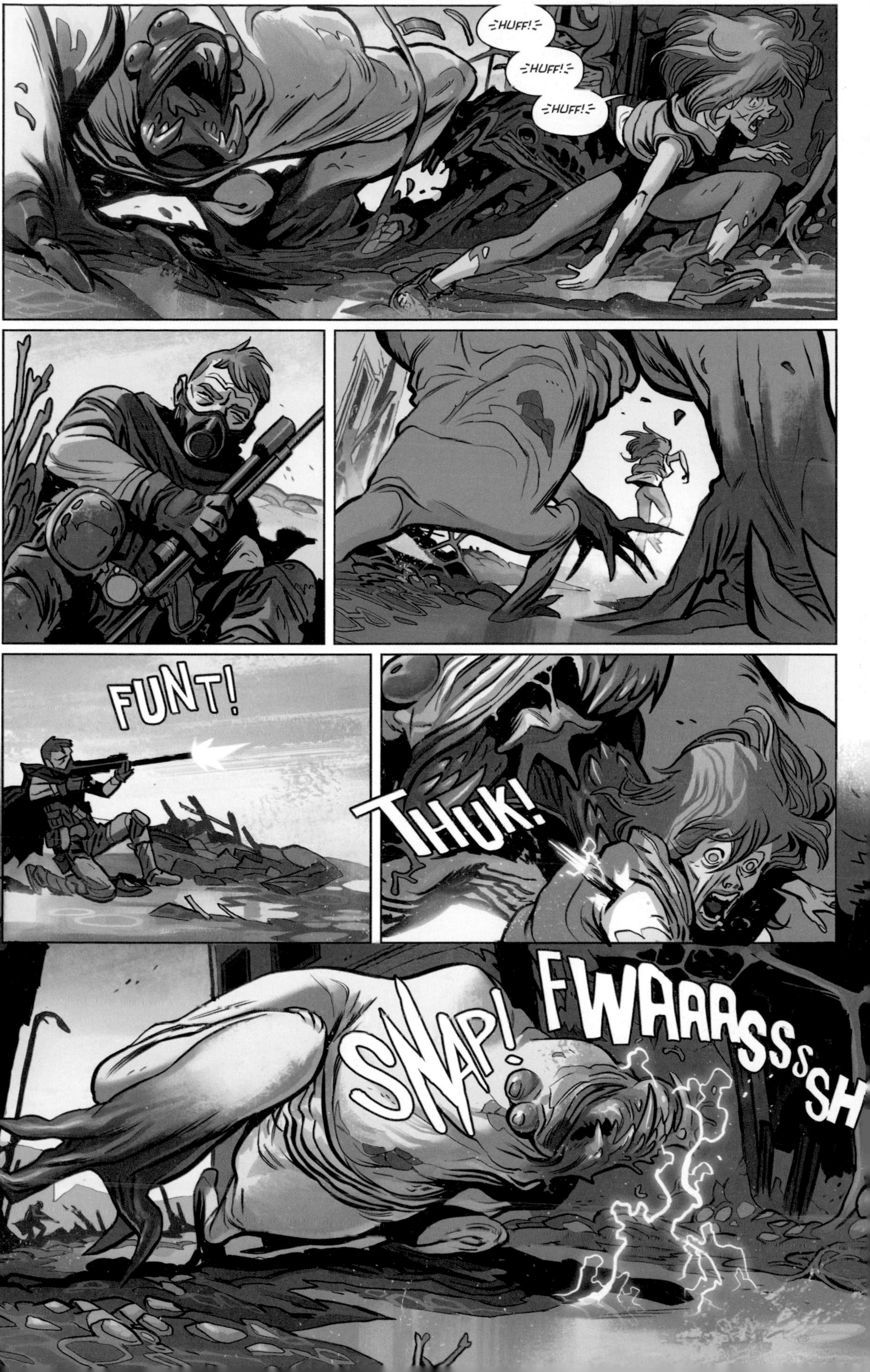
HUFF!
HUFF!
HUFF!
FUNT!
THUK!
SNAP!
FWAAASSSSH

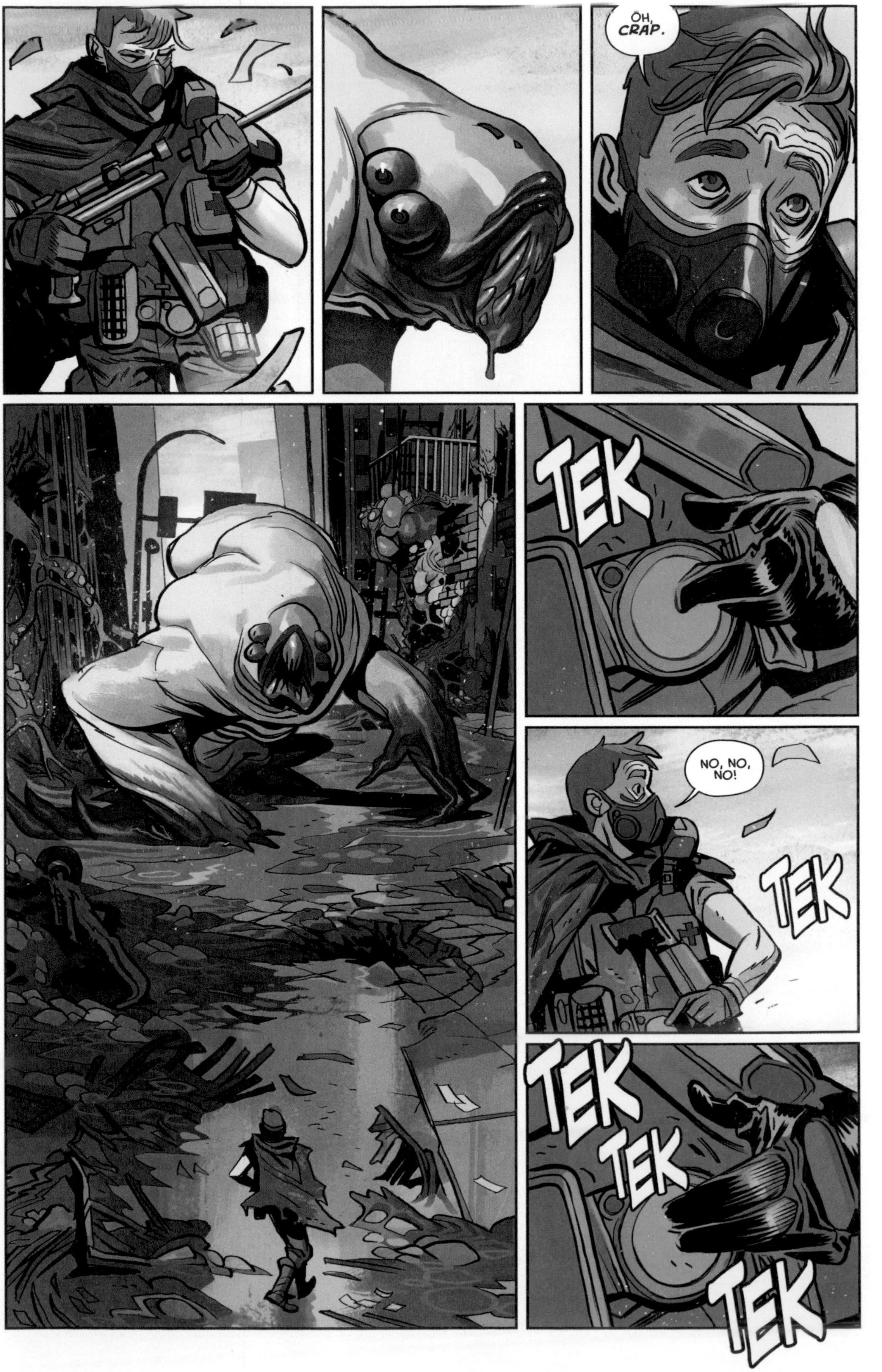
OH, CRAP.
TEK
NO, NO, NO!
TEK
TEK
TEK
TEK

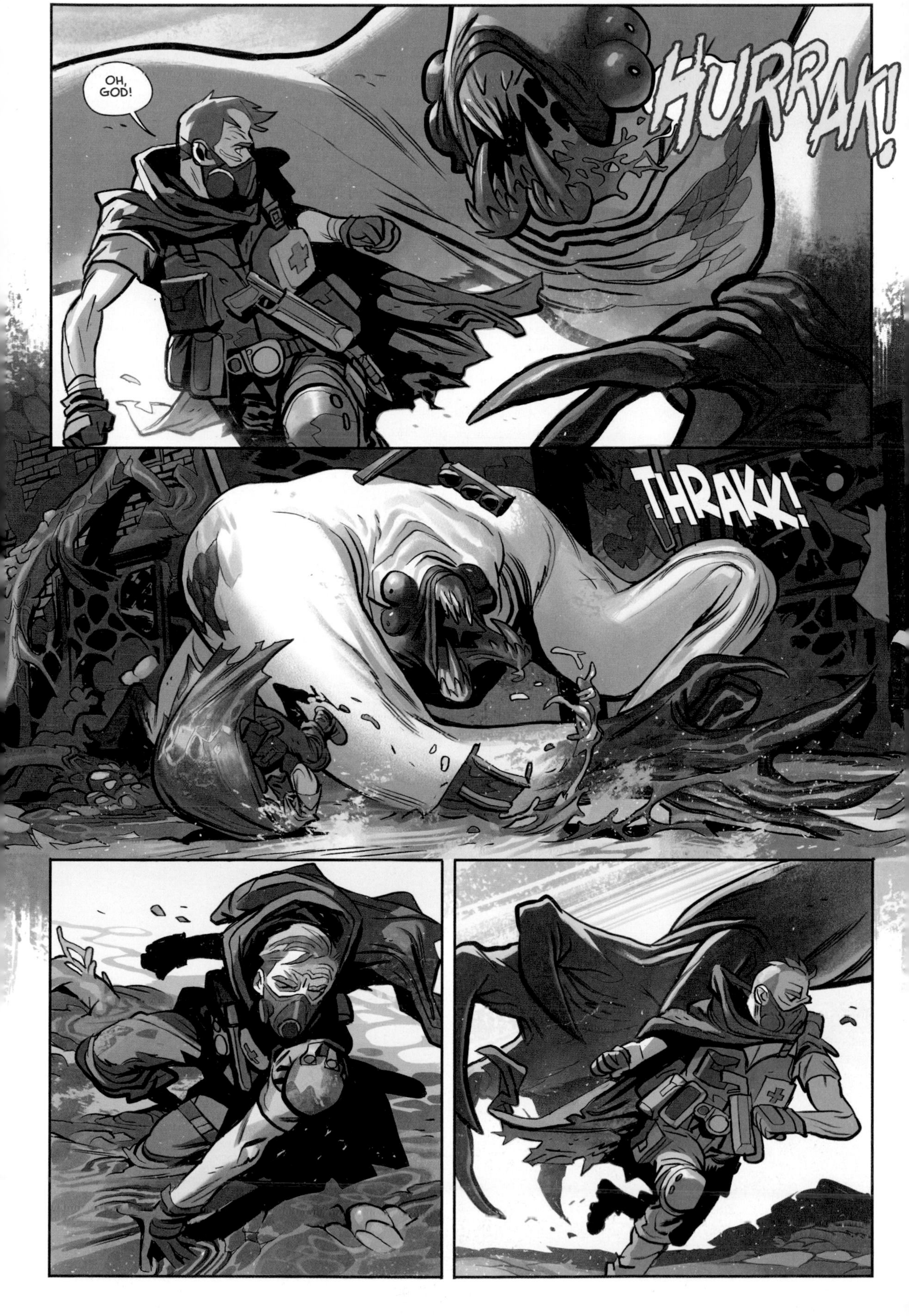
OH, GOD!
HURRAK!
THRAKK!

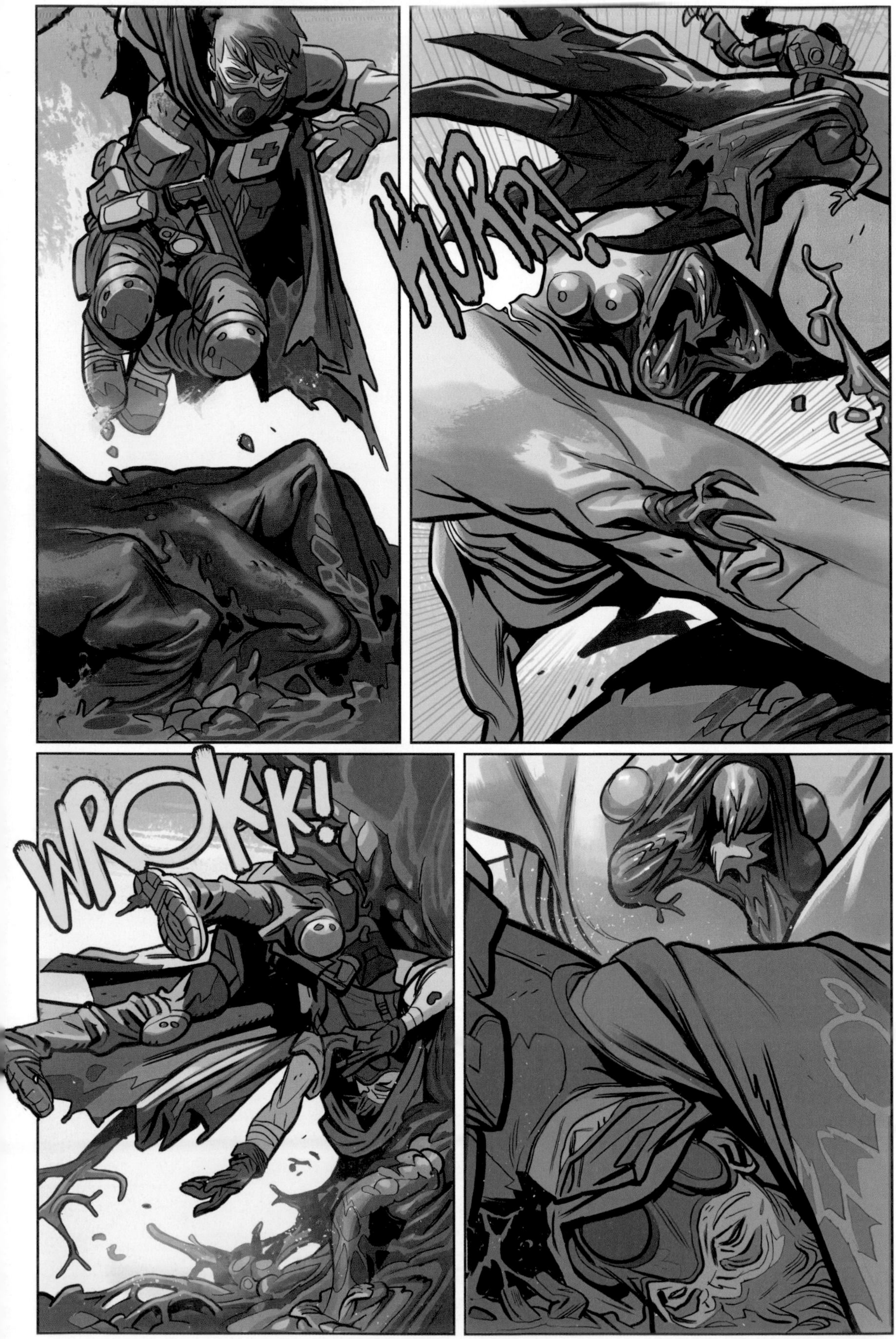
HURR!
WROKK!

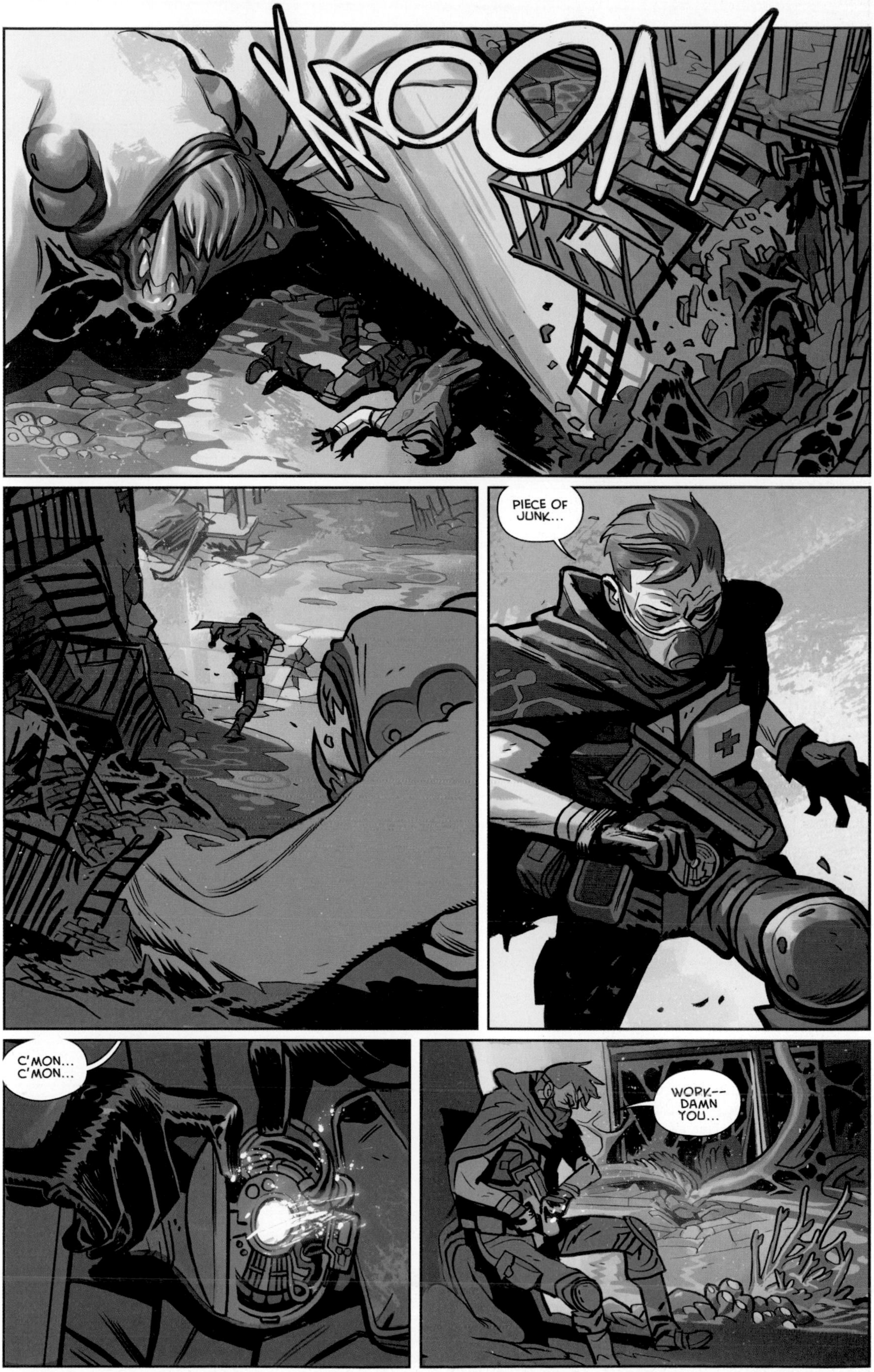
KROOM
PIECE OF JUNK...
C'MON... C'MON...
WORK--DAMN YOU...

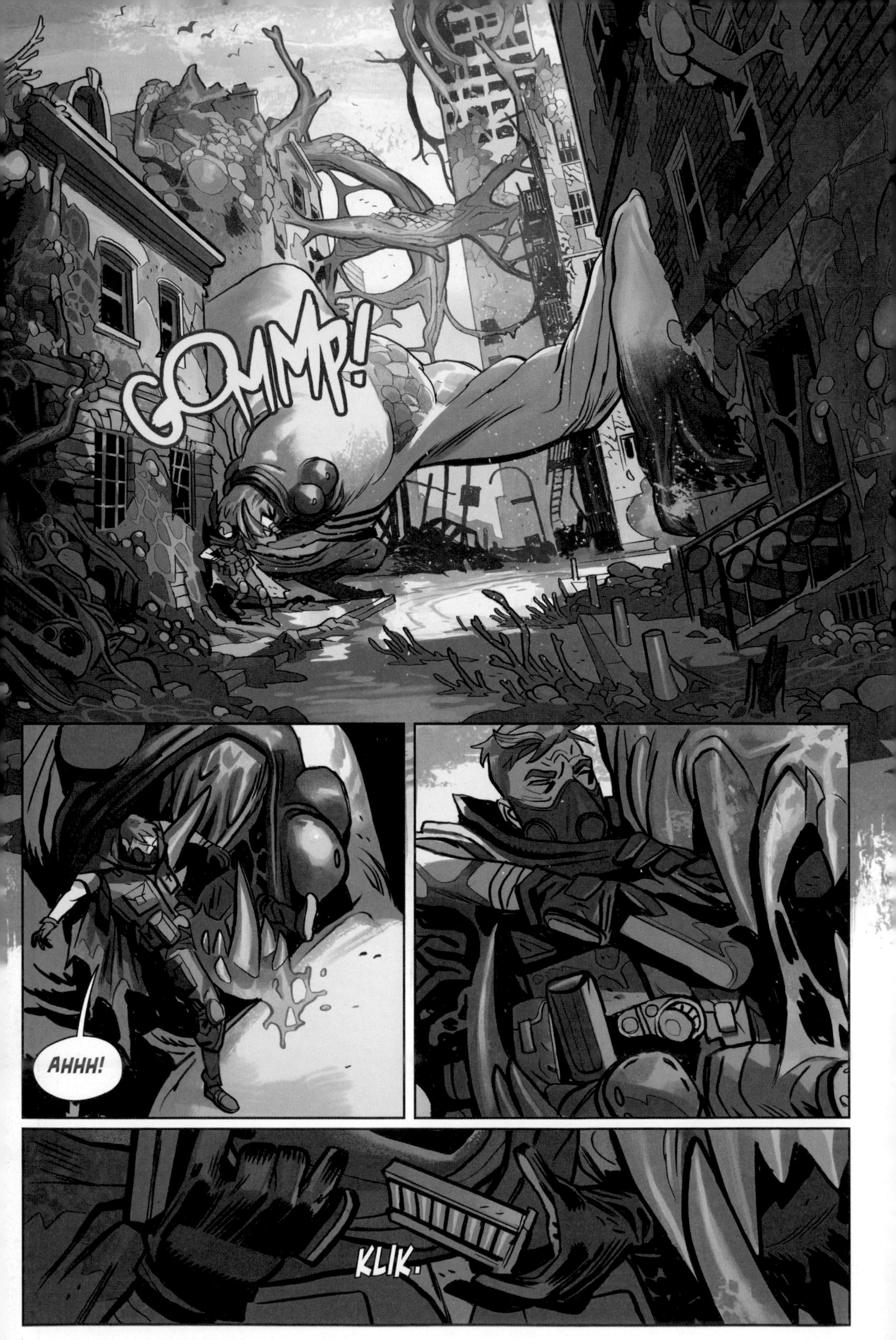
CHOMMP!
AHHH!
KLIK.

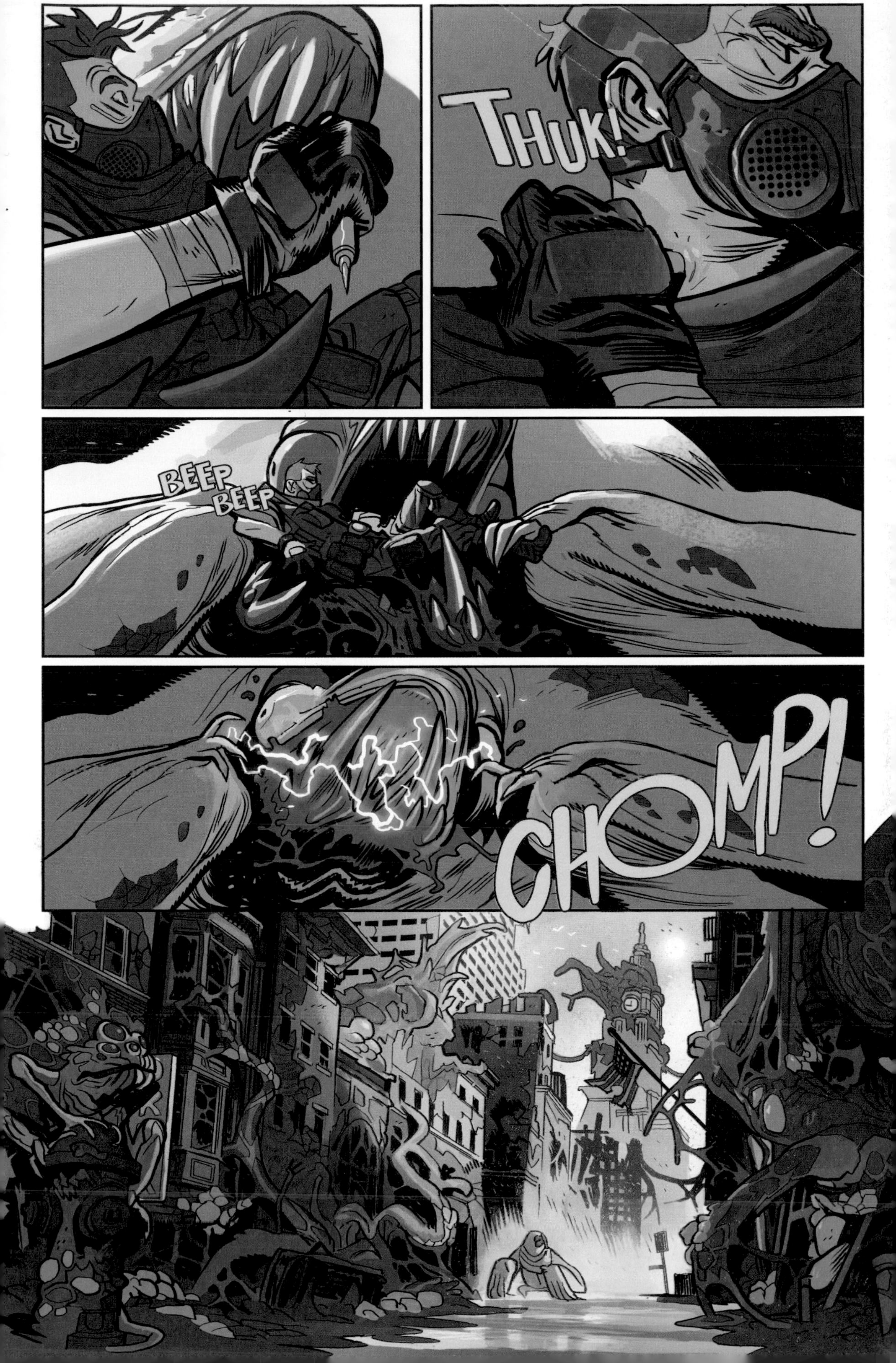
THUK!
BEEP
BEEP
CHOMP!

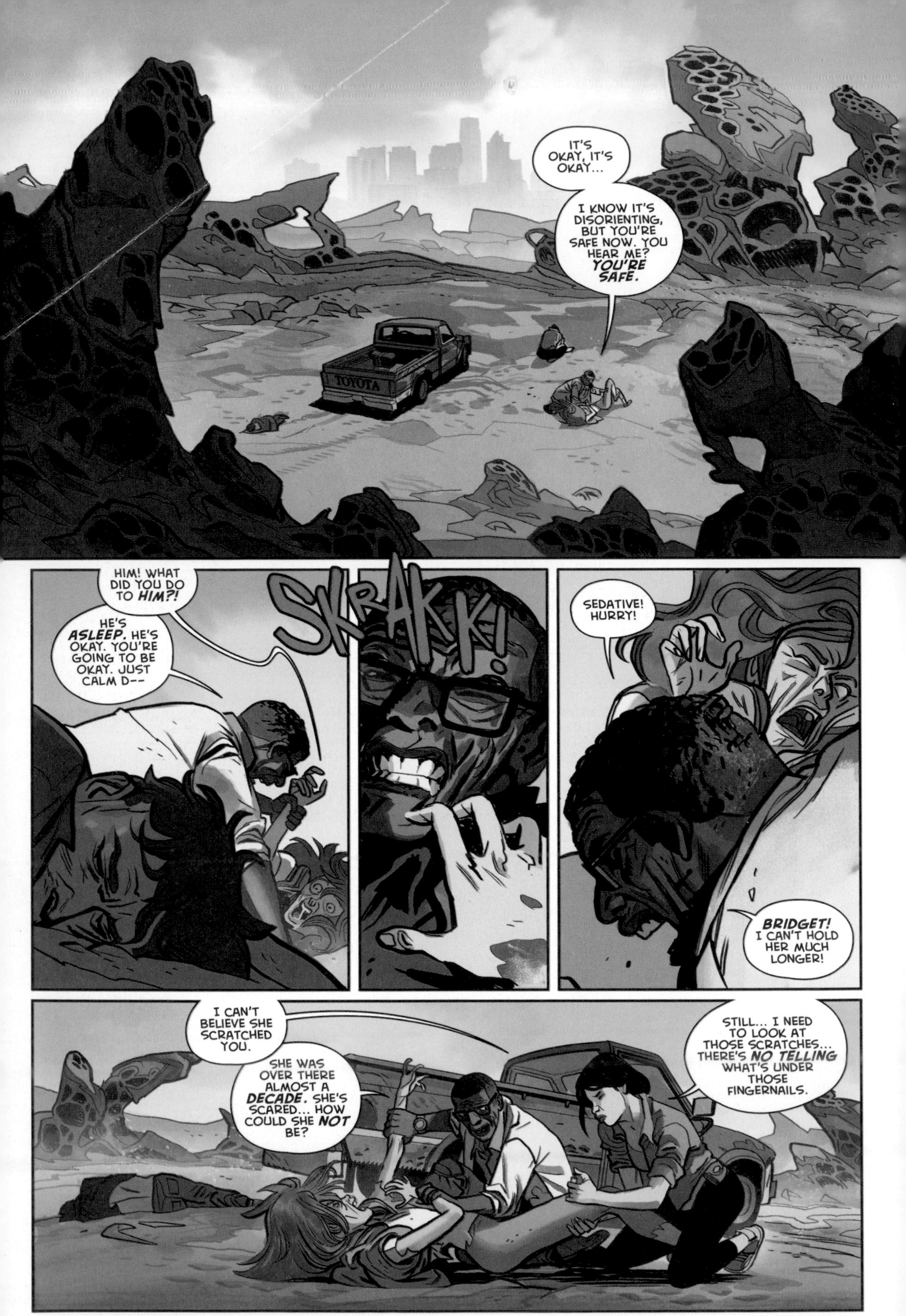
IT'S OKAY, IT'S OKAY...
I KNOW IT'S DISORIENTING, BUT YOU'RE SAFE NOW. YOU HEAR ME? YOU'RE SAFE.
TOYOTA
HIM! WHAT DID YOU DO TO HIM?!
HE'S ASLEEP. HE'S OKAY. YOU'RE GOING TO BE OKAY. JUST CALM D--
SKRAKK!
SEDATIVE! HURRY!
BRIDGET! I CAN'T HOLD HER MUCH LONGER!
I CAN'T BELIEVE SHE SCRATCHED YOU.
SHE WAS OVER THERE ALMOST A DECADE. SHE'S SCARED... HOW COULD SHE NOT BE?
STILL... I NEED TO LOOK AT THOSE SCRATCHES... THERE'S NO TELLING WHAT'S UNDER THOSE FINGERNAILS.

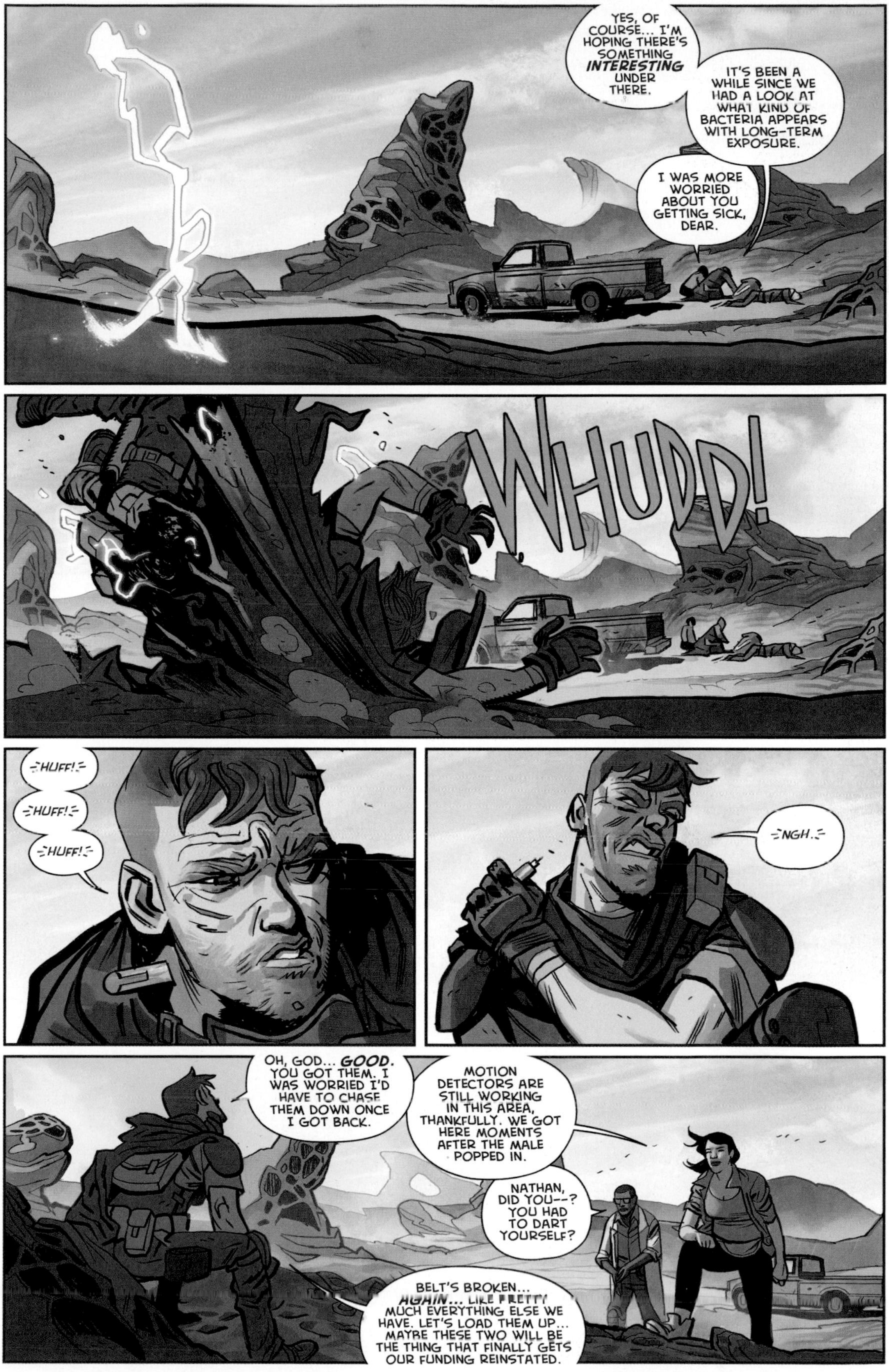

YES, OF COURSE... I'M HOPING THERE'S SOMETHING INTERESTING UNDER THERE.
IT'S BEEN A WHILE SINCE WE HAD A LOOK AT WHAT KIND OF BACTERIA APPEARS WITH LONG-TERM EXPOSURE.
I WAS MORE WORRIED ABOUT YOU GETTING SICK, DEAR.
WHUDD!
HUFF!
HUFF!
HUFF!
NGH.
OH, GOD... GOOD. YOU GOT THEM. I WAS WORRIED I'D HAVE TO CHASE THEM DOWN ONCE I GOT BACK.
MOTION DETECTORS ARE STILL WORKING IN THIS AREA, THANKFULLY. WE GOT HERE MOMENTS AFTER THE MALE POPPED IN.
NATHAN, DID YOU--? YOU HAD TO DART YOURSELF?
BELT'S BROKEN... AGAIN... LIKE PRETTY MUCH EVERYTHING ELSE WE HAVE. LET'S LOAD THEM UP... MAYBE THESE TWO WILL BE THE THING THAT FINALLY GETS OUR FUNDING REINSTATED.

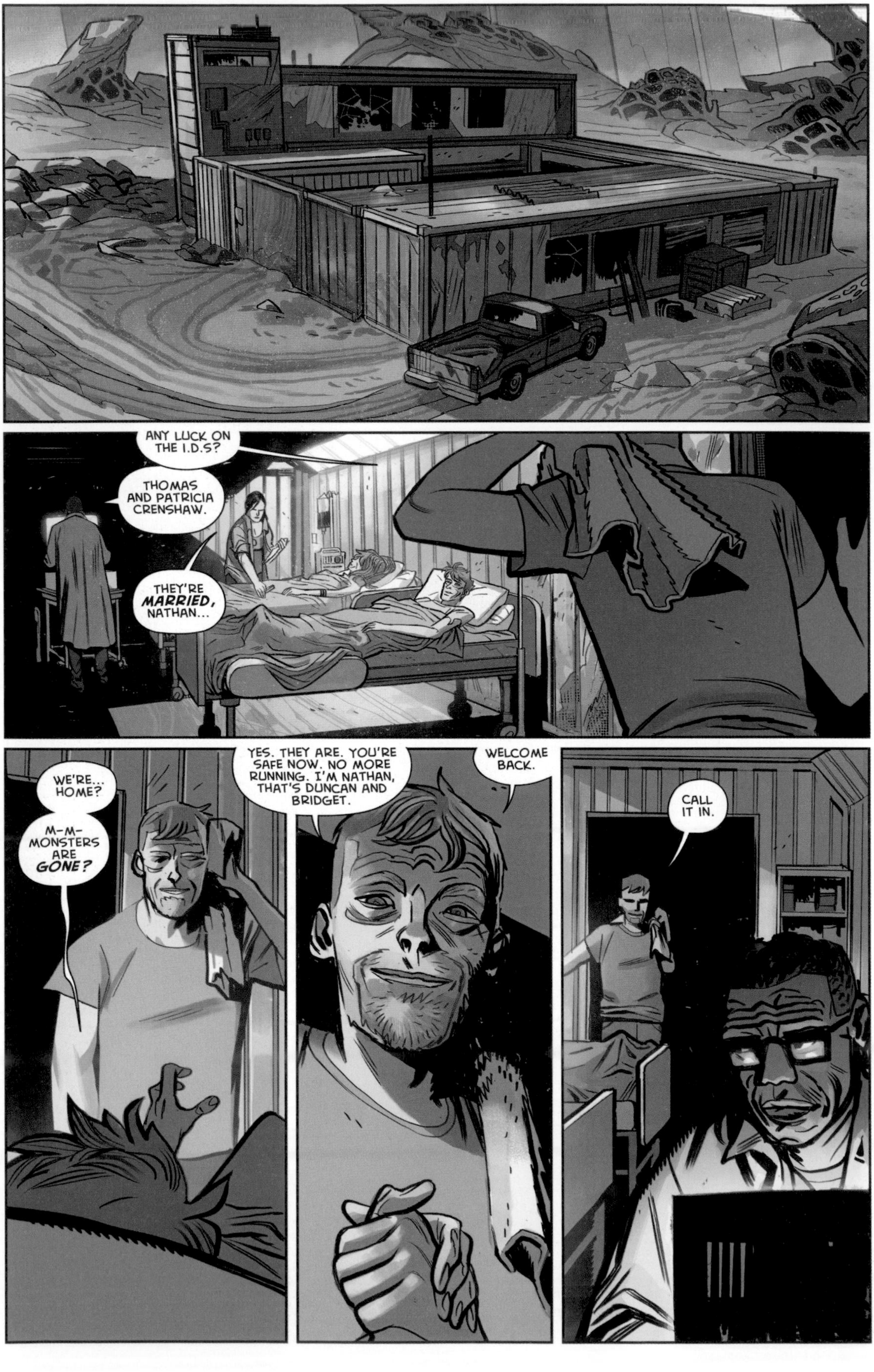
ANY LUCK ON THE I.D.S?
THOMAS AND PATRICIA CRENSHAW.
THEY'RE **MARRIED,** NATHAN...
WE'RE... HOME?
M-M-MONSTERS ARE **GONE?**
YES. THEY ARE. YOU'RE SAFE NOW. NO MORE RUNNING. I'M NATHAN, THAT'S DUNCAN AND BRIDGET.
WELCOME BACK.
CALL IT IN.

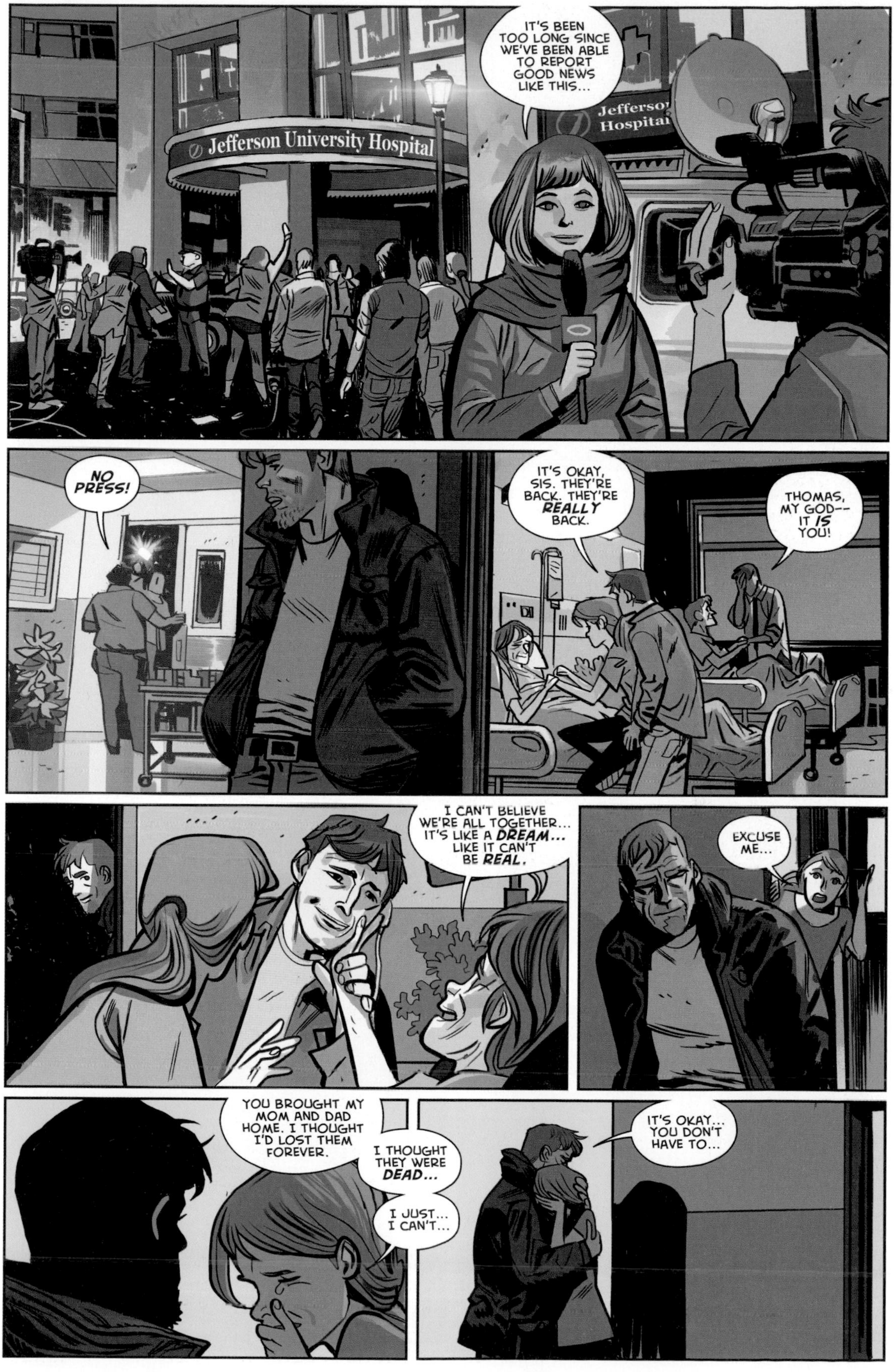
Jefferson University Hospital
IT'S BEEN TOO LONG SINCE WE'VE BEEN ABLE TO REPORT GOOD NEWS LIKE THIS...
Jefferson Hospital
NO PRESS!
IT'S OKAY, SIS. THEY'RE BACK. THEY'RE REALLY BACK.
THOMAS, MY GOD-- IT IS YOU!
I CAN'T BELIEVE WE'RE ALL TOGETHER... IT'S LIKE A DREAM... LIKE IT CAN'T BE REAL.
EXCUSE ME...
YOU BROUGHT MY MOM AND DAD HOME. I THOUGHT I'D LOST THEM FOREVER.
I THOUGHT THEY WERE DEAD...
I JUST... I CAN'T...
IT'S OKAY... YOU DON'T HAVE TO...

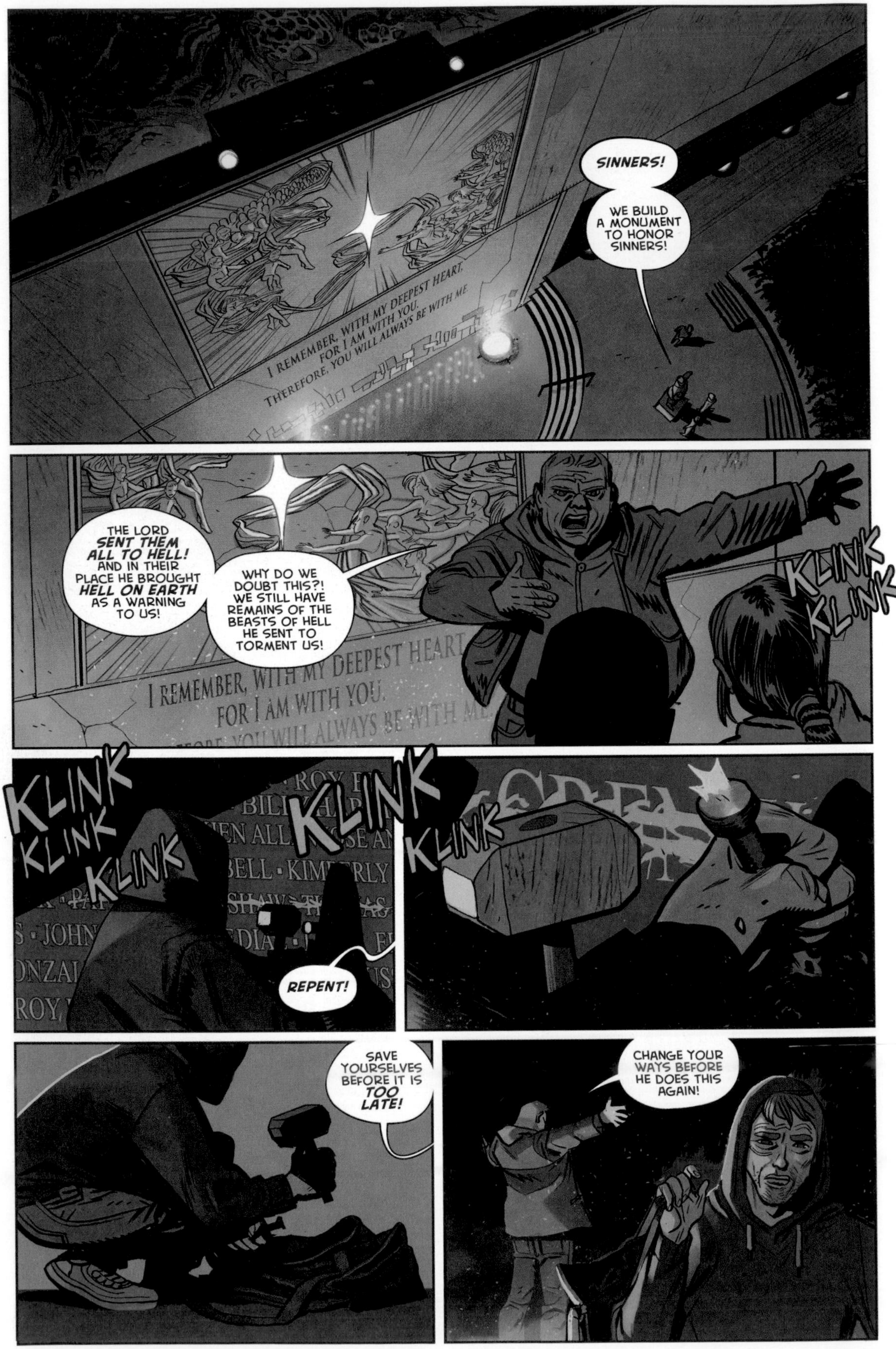

SINNERS!
WE BUILD A MONUMENT TO HONOR SINNERS!
I REMEMBER, WITH MY DEEPEST HEART, FOR I AM WITH YOU. THEREFORE, YOU WILL ALWAYS BE WITH ME.
THE LORD SENT THEM ALL TO HELL! AND IN THEIR PLACE HE BROUGHT HELL ON EARTH AS A WARNING TO US!
WHY DO WE DOUBT THIS?! WE STILL HAVE REMAINS OF THE BEASTS OF HELL HE SENT TO TORMENT US!
KLINK KLINK
KLINK KLINK KLINK
KLINK
KLINK
REPENT!
SAVE YOURSELVES BEFORE IT IS TOO LATE!
CHANGE YOUR WAYS BEFORE HE DOES THIS AGAIN!

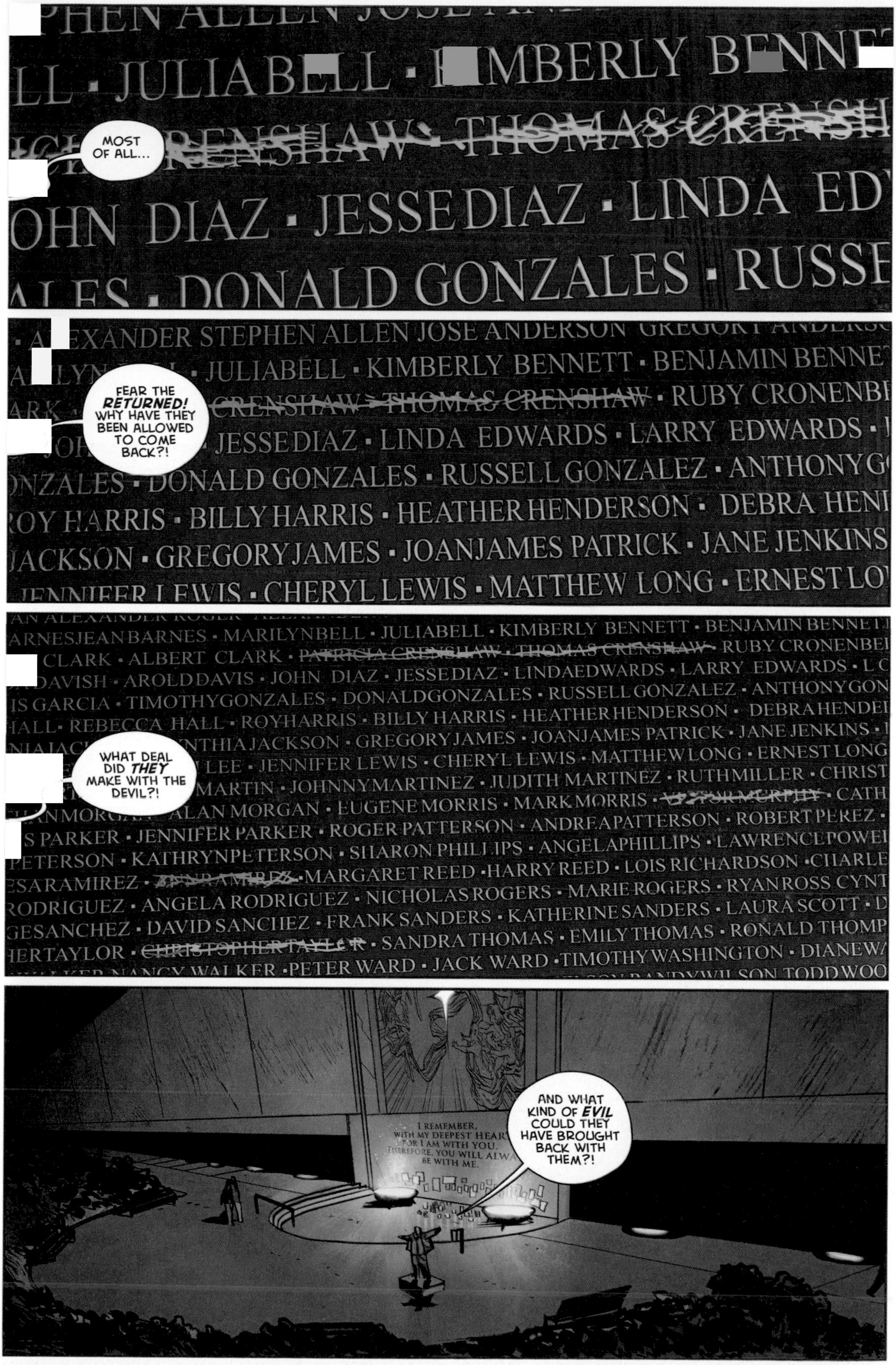
MOST OF ALL...
FEAR THE RETURNED! WHY HAVE THEY BEEN ALLOWED TO COME BACK?!
WHAT DEAL DID THEY MAKE WITH THE DEVIL?!
AND WHAT KIND OF EVIL COULD THEY HAVE BROUGHT BACK WITH THEM?!

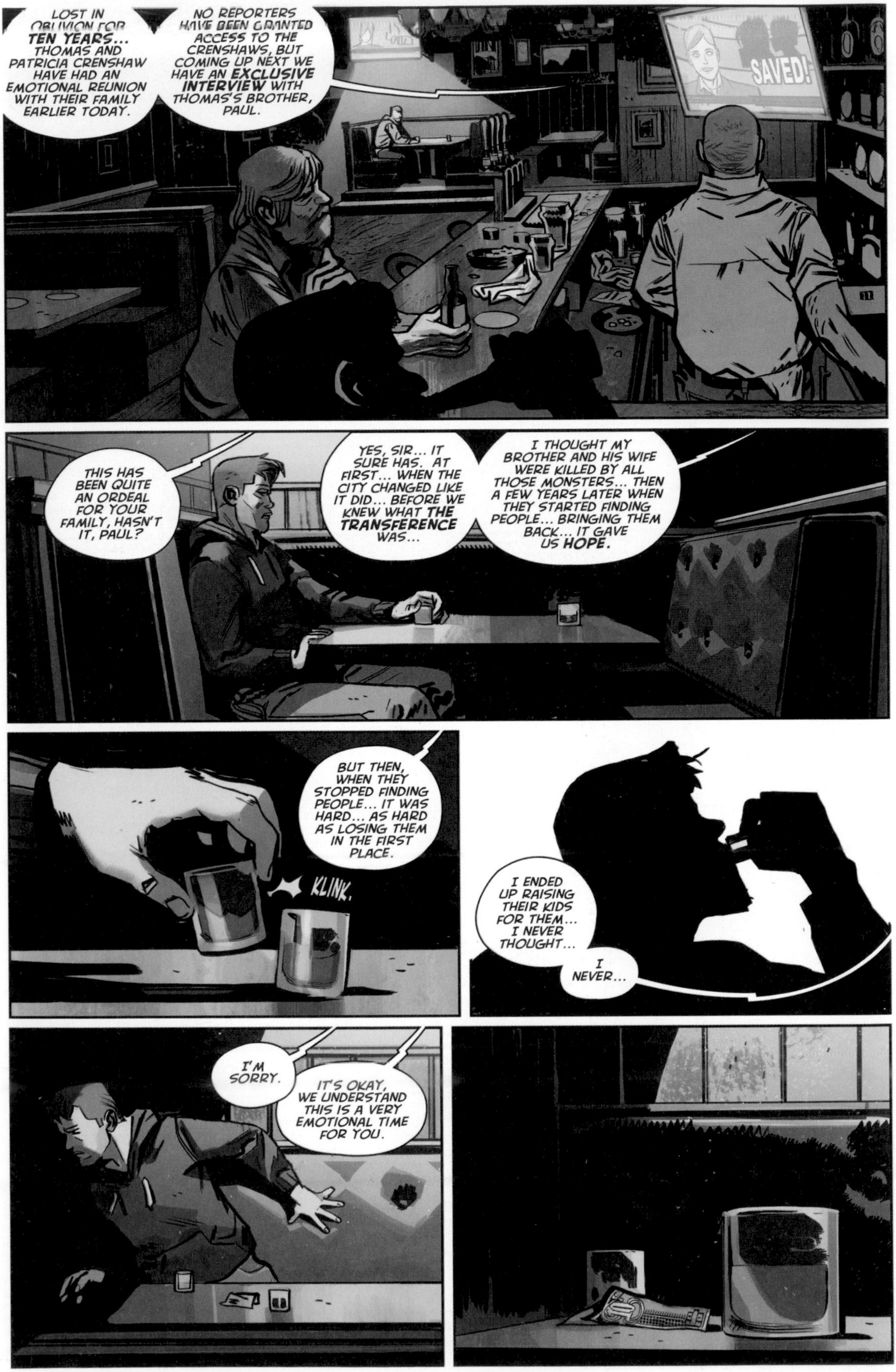
LOST IN OBLIVION FOR TEN YEARS... THOMAS AND PATRICIA CRENSHAW HAVE HAD AN EMOTIONAL REUNION WITH THEIR FAMILY EARLIER TODAY.
NO REPORTERS HAVE BEEN GRANTED ACCESS TO THE CRENSHAWS, BUT COMING UP NEXT WE HAVE AN EXCLUSIVE INTERVIEW WITH THOMAS'S BROTHER, PAUL.
SAVED!
THIS HAS BEEN QUITE AN ORDEAL FOR YOUR FAMILY, HASN'T IT, PAUL?
YES, SIR... IT SURE HAS. AT FIRST... WHEN THE CITY CHANGED LIKE IT DID... BEFORE WE KNEW WHAT THE TRANSFERENCE WAS...
I THOUGHT MY BROTHER AND HIS WIFE WERE KILLED BY ALL THOSE MONSTERS... THEN A FEW YEARS LATER WHEN THEY STARTED FINDING PEOPLE... BRINGING THEM BACK... IT GAVE US HOPE.
BUT THEN, WHEN THEY STOPPED FINDING PEOPLE... IT WAS HARD... AS HARD AS LOSING THEM IN THE FIRST PLACE.
KLINK.
I ENDED UP RAISING THEIR KIDS FOR THEM... I NEVER THOUGHT...
I NEVER...
I'M SORRY.
IT'S OKAY, WE UNDERSTAND THIS IS A VERY EMOTIONAL TIME FOR YOU.

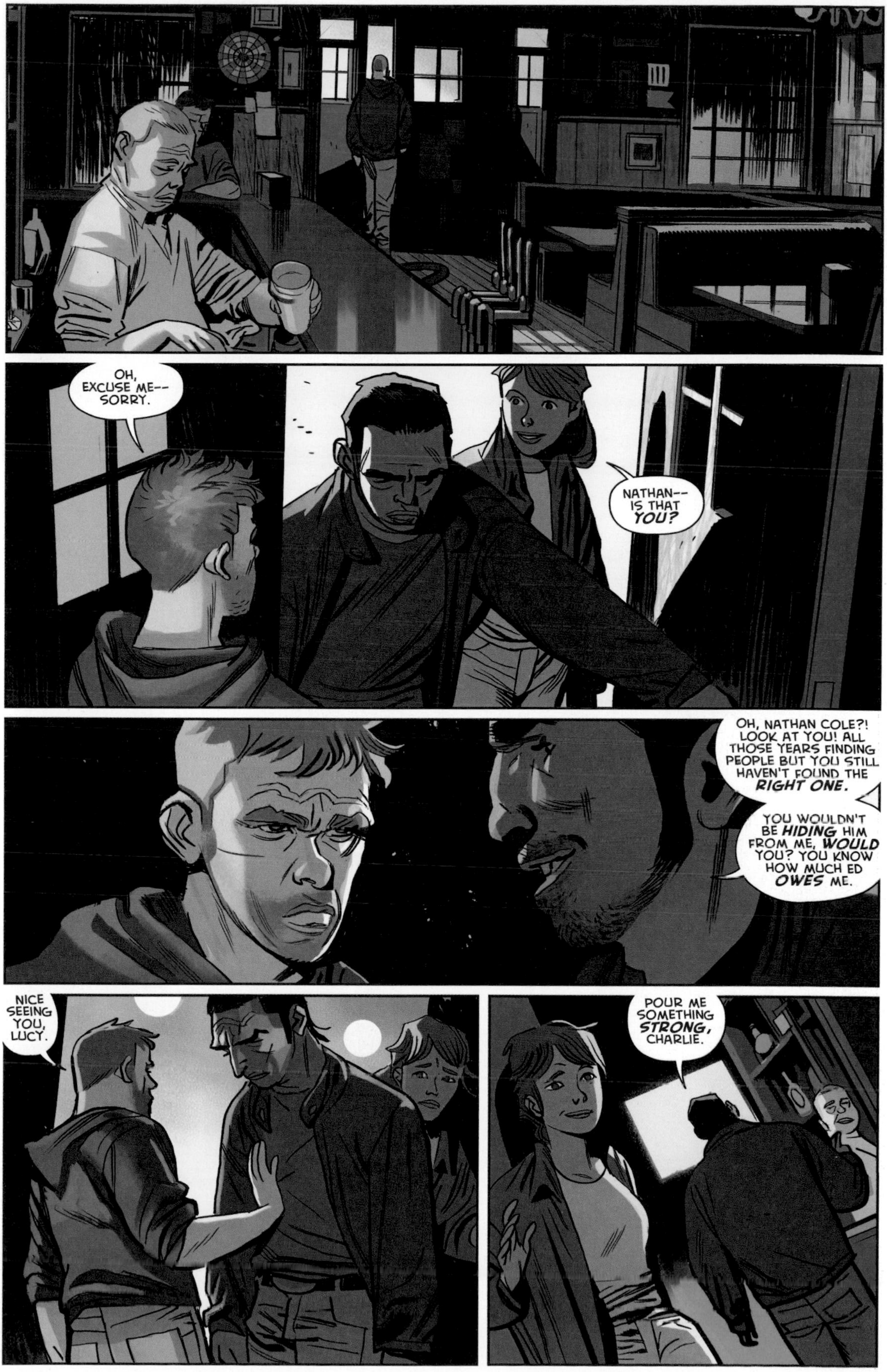
OH, EXCUSE ME-- SORRY.
NATHAN-- IS THAT YOU?
OH, NATHAN COLE?! LOOK AT YOU! ALL THOSE YEARS FINDING PEOPLE BUT YOU STILL HAVEN'T FOUND THE RIGHT ONE.
YOU WOULDN'T BE HIDING HIM FROM ME, WOULD YOU? YOU KNOW HOW MUCH ED OWES ME.
NICE SEEING YOU, LUCY.
POUR ME SOMETHING STRONG, CHARLIE.

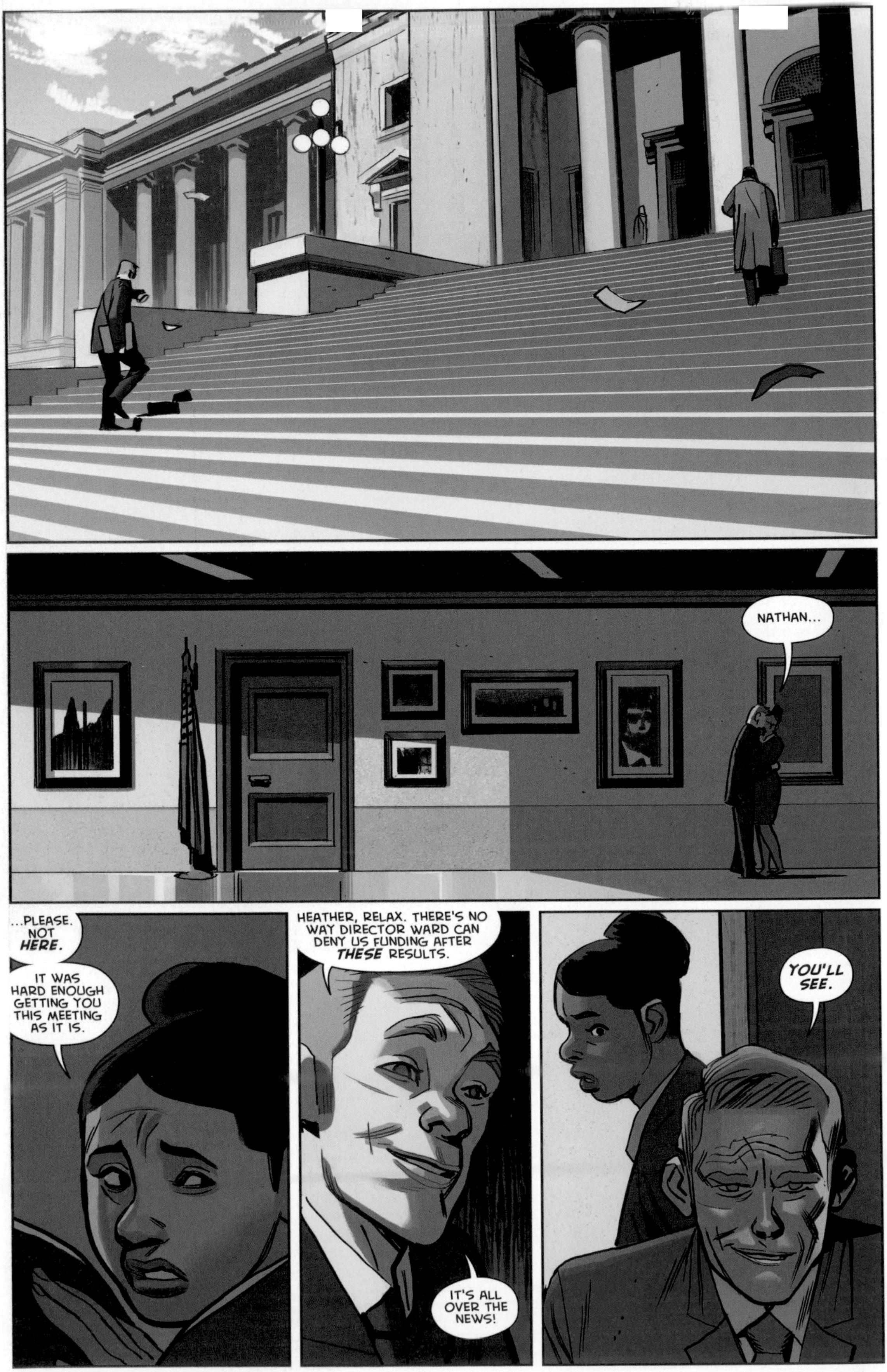
NATHAN...
...PLEASE. NOT HERE.
IT WAS HARD ENOUGH GETTING YOU THIS MEETING AS IT IS.
HEATHER, RELAX. THERE'S NO WAY DIRECTOR WARD CAN DENY US FUNDING AFTER THESE RESULTS.
IT'S ALL OVER THE NEWS!
YOU'LL SEE.

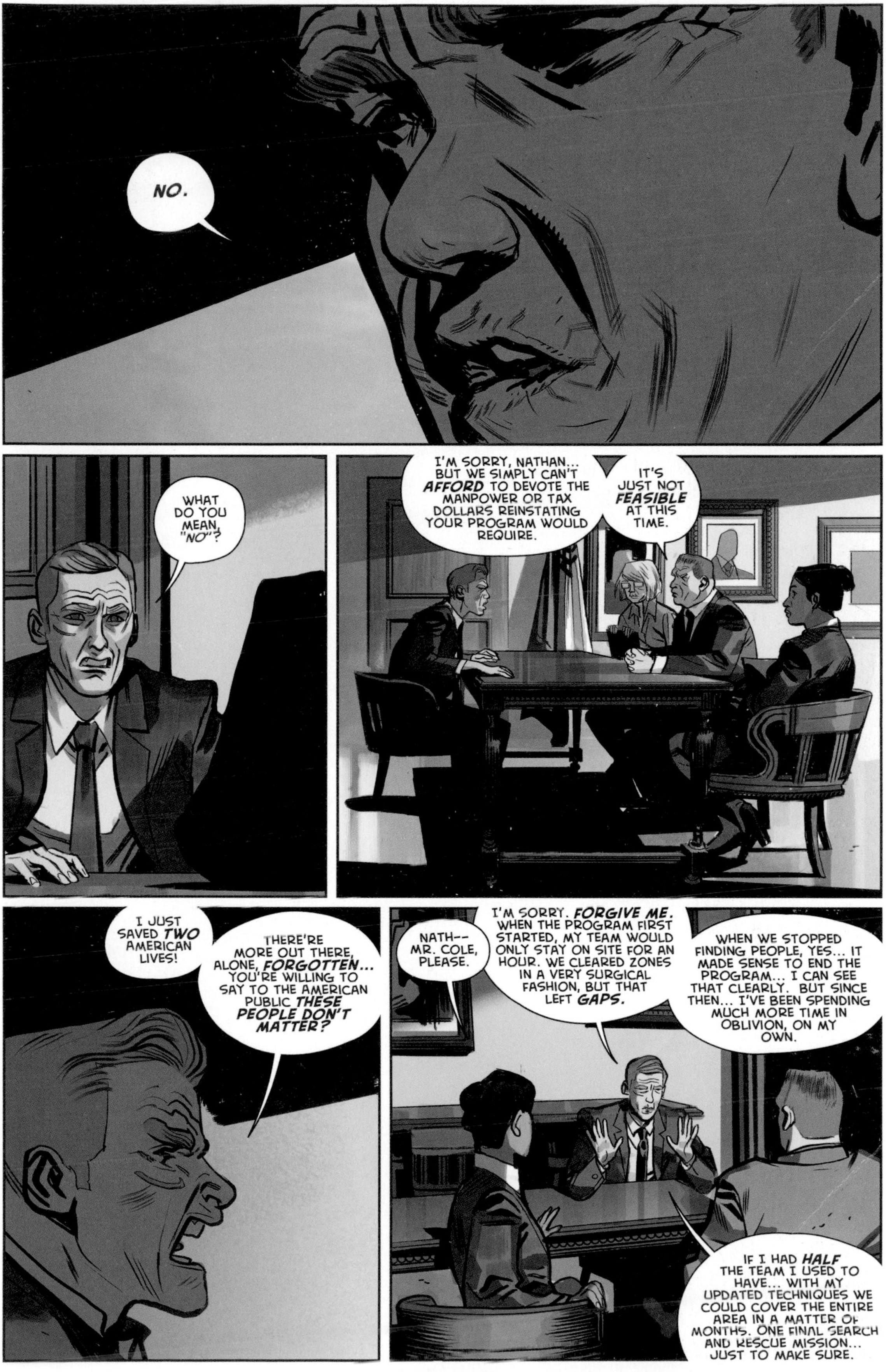
NO.
WHAT DO YOU MEAN, "NO"?
I'M SORRY, NATHAN... BUT WE SIMPLY CAN'T AFFORD TO DEVOTE THE MANPOWER OR TAX DOLLARS REINSTATING YOUR PROGRAM WOULD REQUIRE.
IT'S JUST NOT FEASIBLE AT THIS TIME.
I JUST SAVED TWO AMERICAN LIVES!
THERE'RE MORE OUT THERE, ALONE, FORGOTTEN... YOU'RE WILLING TO SAY TO THE AMERICAN PUBLIC THESE PEOPLE DON'T MATTER?
NATH-- MR. COLE, PLEASE.
I'M SORRY. FORGIVE ME. WHEN THE PROGRAM FIRST STARTED, MY TEAM WOULD ONLY STAY ON SITE FOR AN HOUR. WE CLEARED ZONES IN A VERY SURGICAL FASHION, BUT THAT LEFT GAPS.
WHEN WE STOPPED FINDING PEOPLE, YES... IT MADE SENSE TO END THE PROGRAM... I CAN SEE THAT CLEARLY. BUT SINCE THEN... I'VE BEEN SPENDING MUCH MORE TIME IN OBLIVION, ON MY OWN.
IF I HAD HALF THE TEAM I USED TO HAVE... WITH MY UPDATED TECHNIQUES WE COULD COVER THE ENTIRE AREA IN A MATTER OF MONTHS. ONE FINAL SEARCH AND RESCUE MISSION... JUST TO MAKE SURE.

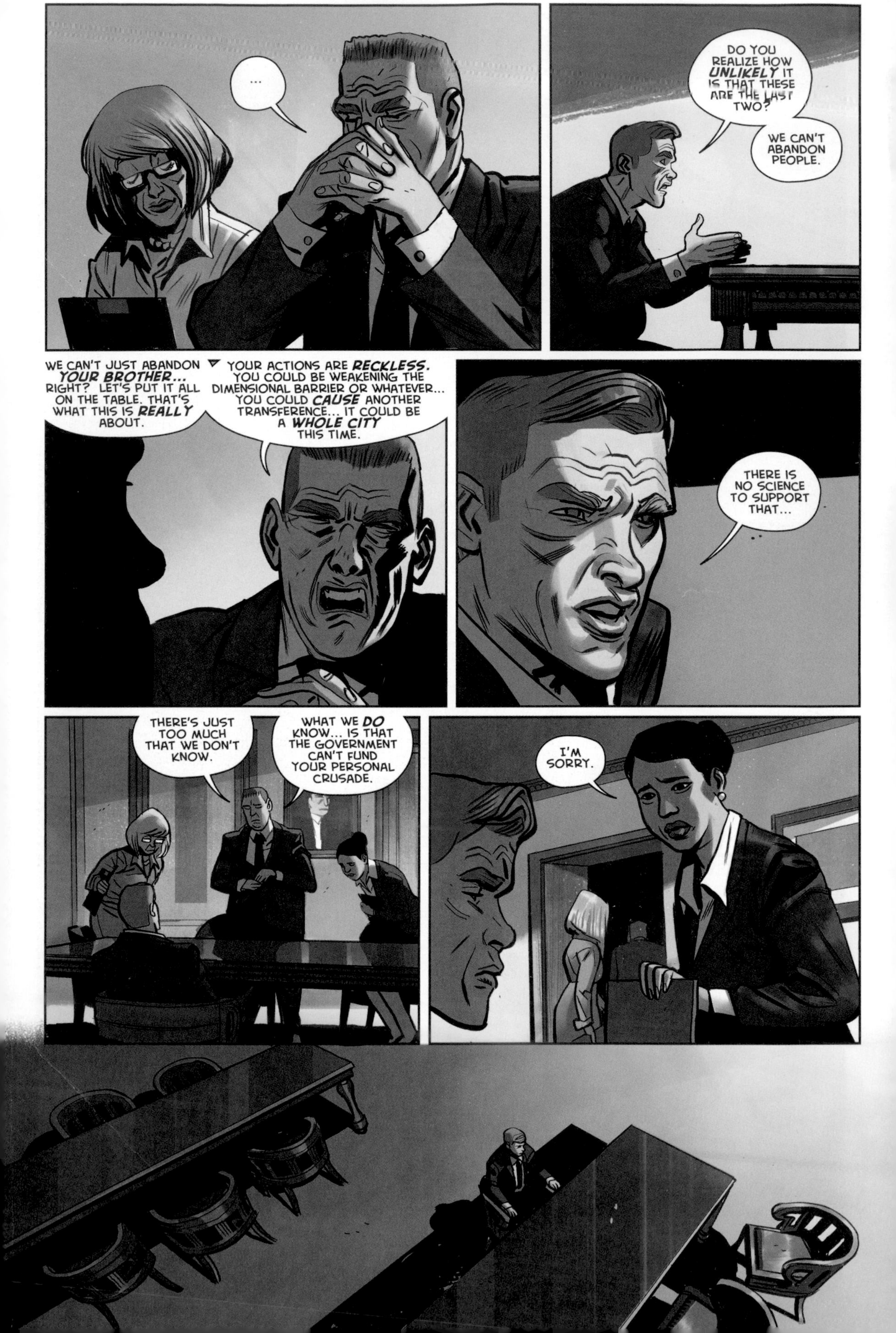
...
DO YOU REALIZE HOW UNLIKELY IT IS THAT THESE ARE THE LAST TWO?
WE CAN'T ABANDON PEOPLE.
WE CAN'T JUST ABANDON YOUR BROTHER... RIGHT? LET'S PUT IT ALL ON THE TABLE. THAT'S WHAT THIS IS REALLY ABOUT.
YOUR ACTIONS ARE RECKLESS. YOU COULD BE WEAKENING THE DIMENSIONAL BARRIER OR WHATEVER... YOU COULD CAUSE ANOTHER TRANSFERENCE... IT COULD BE A WHOLE CITY THIS TIME.
THERE IS NO SCIENCE TO SUPPORT THAT...
THERE'S JUST TOO MUCH THAT WE DON'T KNOW.
WHAT WE DO KNOW... IS THAT THE GOVERNMENT CAN'T FUND YOUR PERSONAL CRUSADE.
I'M SORRY.

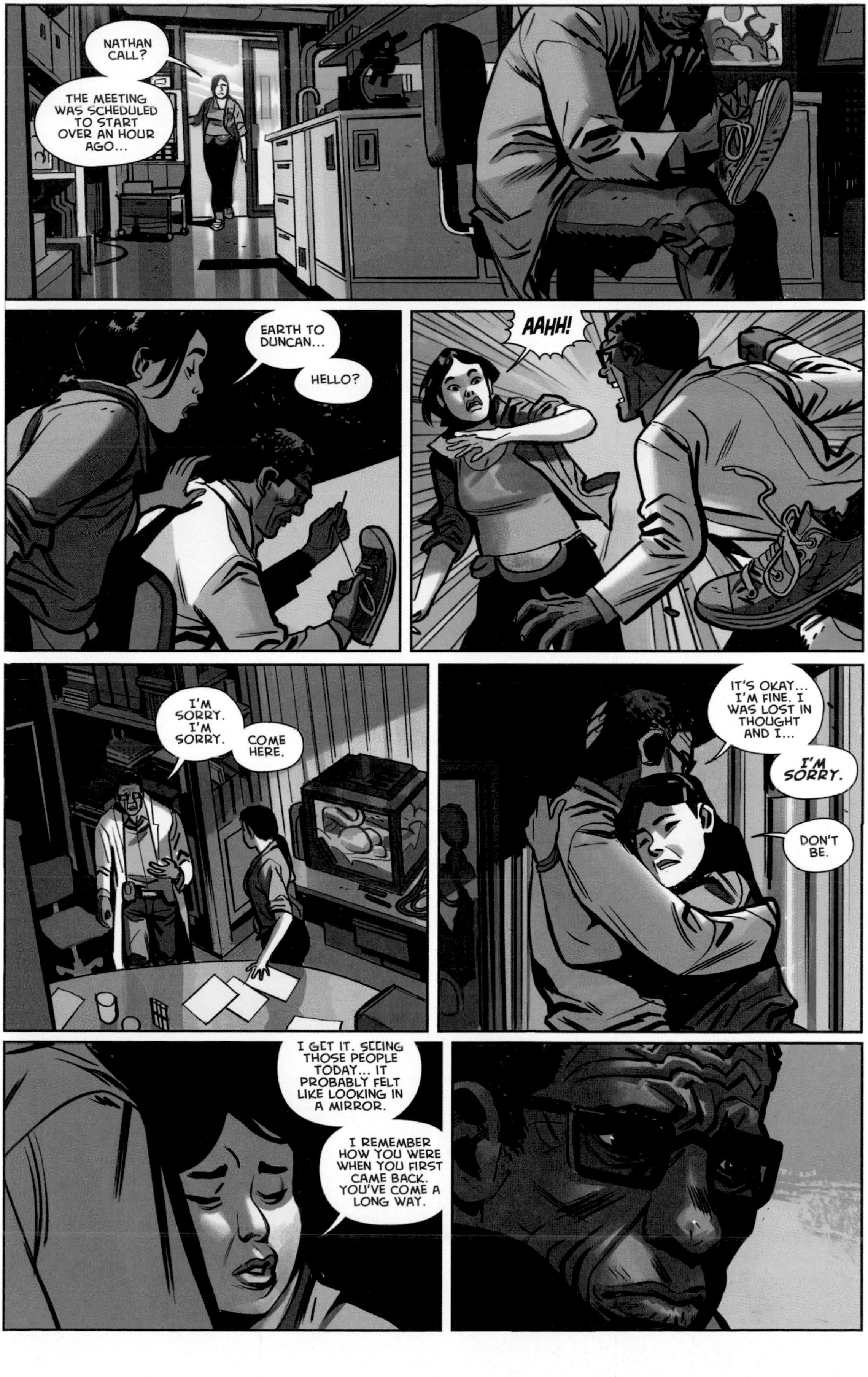
NATHAN CALL?
THE MEETING WAS SCHEDULED TO START OVER AN HOUR AGO...
EARTH TO DUNCAN...
HELLO?
AAHH!
I'M SORRY. I'M SORRY.
COME HERE.
IT'S OKAY... I'M FINE. I WAS LOST IN THOUGHT AND I...
I'M SORRY.
DON'T BE.
I GET IT. SEEING THOSE PEOPLE TODAY... IT PROBABLY FELT LIKE LOOKING IN A MIRROR.
I REMEMBER HOW YOU WERE WHEN YOU FIRST CAME BACK. YOU'VE COME A LONG WAY.

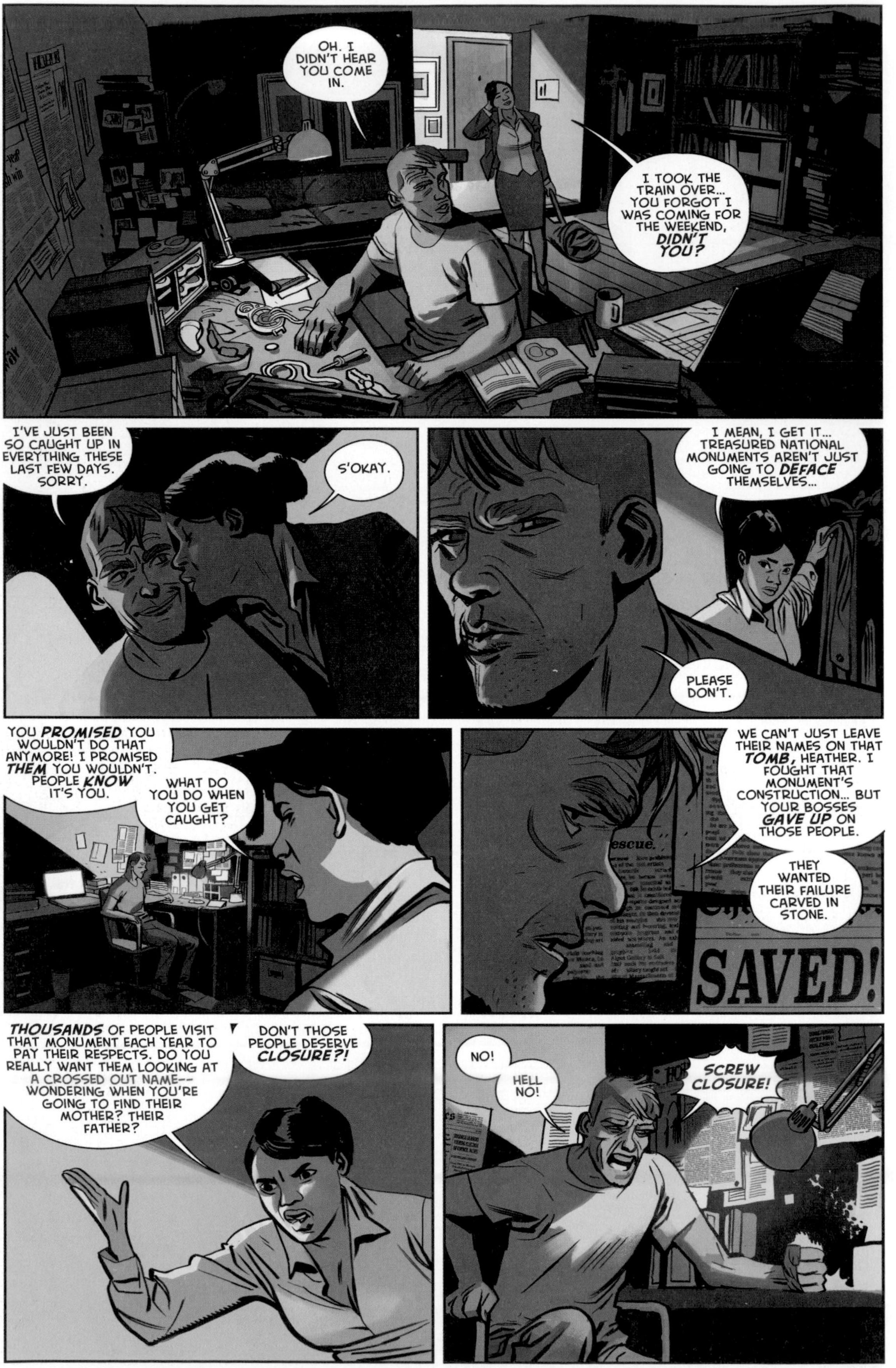
OH. I DIDN'T HEAR YOU COME IN.
I TOOK THE TRAIN OVER... YOU FORGOT I WAS COMING FOR THE WEEKEND, DIDN'T YOU?
I'VE JUST BEEN SO CAUGHT UP IN EVERYTHING THESE LAST FEW DAYS. SORRY.
S'OKAY.
I MEAN, I GET IT... TREASURED NATIONAL MONUMENTS AREN'T JUST GOING TO DEFACE THEMSELVES...
PLEASE DON'T.
YOU PROMISED YOU WOULDN'T DO THAT ANYMORE! I PROMISED THEM YOU WOULDN'T. PEOPLE KNOW IT'S YOU.
WHAT DO YOU DO WHEN YOU GET CAUGHT?
WE CAN'T JUST LEAVE THEIR NAMES ON THAT TOMB, HEATHER. I FOUGHT THAT MONUMENT'S CONSTRUCTION... BUT YOUR BOSSES GAVE UP ON THOSE PEOPLE.
THEY WANTED THEIR FAILURE CARVED IN STONE.
SAVED!
THOUSANDS OF PEOPLE VISIT THAT MONUMENT EACH YEAR TO PAY THEIR RESPECTS. DO YOU REALLY WANT THEM LOOKING AT A CROSSED OUT NAME-- WONDERING WHEN YOU'RE GOING TO FIND THEIR MOTHER? THEIR FATHER?
DON'T THOSE PEOPLE DESERVE CLOSURE?!
NO!
HELL NO!
SCREW CLOSURE!

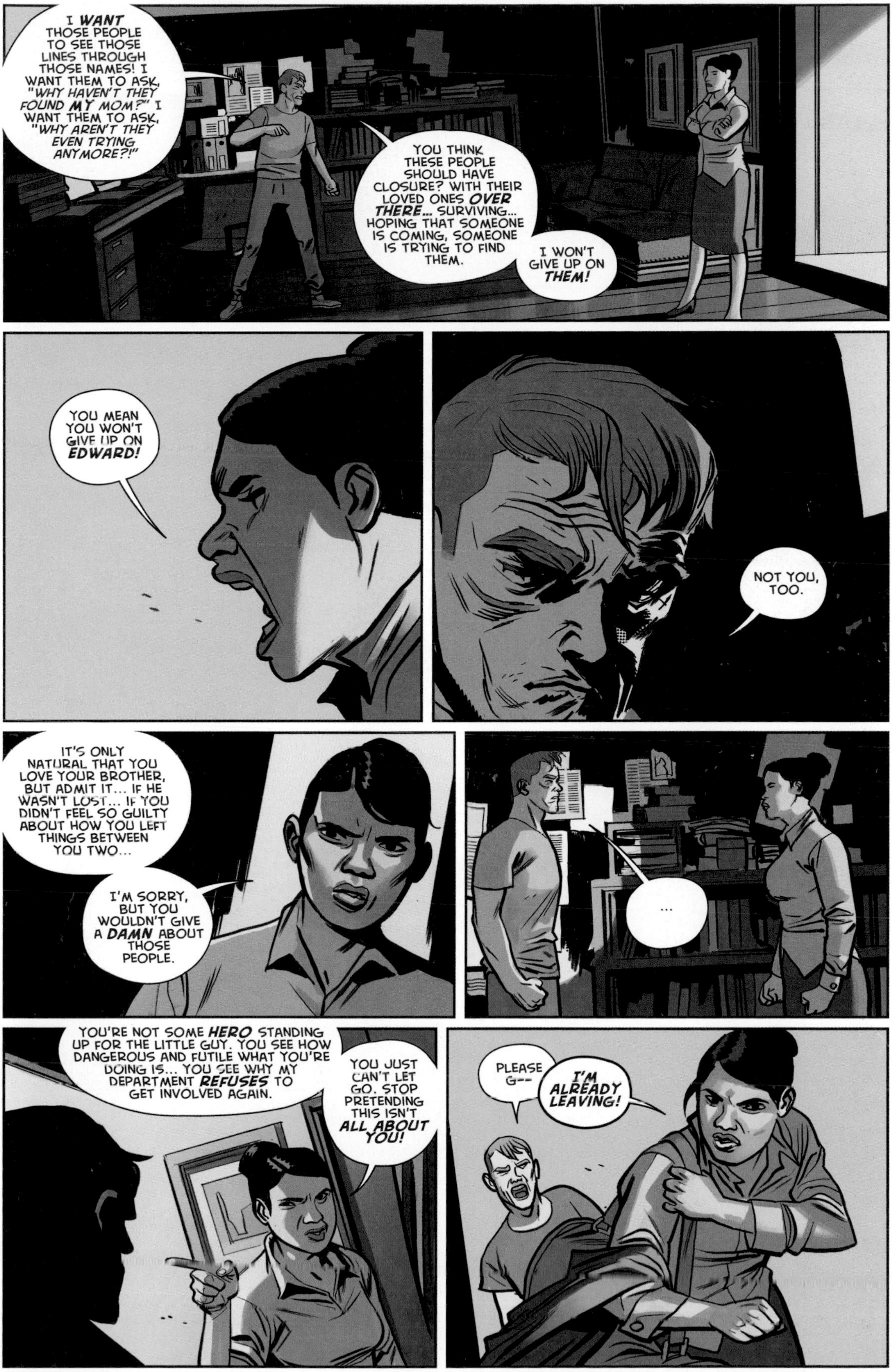

I WANT THOSE PEOPLE TO SEE THOSE LINES THROUGH THOSE NAMES! I WANT THEM TO ASK, "WHY HAVEN'T THEY FOUND MY MOM?" I WANT THEM TO ASK, "WHY AREN'T THEY EVEN TRYING ANYMORE?!"
YOU THINK THESE PEOPLE SHOULD HAVE CLOSURE? WITH THEIR LOVED ONES OVER THERE... SURVIVING... HOPING THAT SOMEONE IS COMING, SOMEONE IS TRYING TO FIND THEM.
I WON'T GIVE UP ON THEM!
YOU MEAN YOU WON'T GIVE UP ON EDWARD!
NOT YOU, TOO.
IT'S ONLY NATURAL THAT YOU LOVE YOUR BROTHER, BUT ADMIT IT... IF HE WASN'T LOST... IF YOU DIDN'T FEEL SO GUILTY ABOUT HOW YOU LEFT THINGS BETWEEN YOU TWO...
I'M SORRY, BUT YOU WOULDN'T GIVE A DAMN ABOUT THOSE PEOPLE.
...
YOU'RE NOT SOME HERO STANDING UP FOR THE LITTLE GUY. YOU SEE HOW DANGEROUS AND FUTILE WHAT YOU'RE DOING IS... YOU SEE WHY MY DEPARTMENT REFUSES TO GET INVOLVED AGAIN.
YOU JUST CAN'T LET GO. STOP PRETENDING THIS ISN'T ALL ABOUT YOU!
PLEASE G--
I'M ALREADY LEAVING!

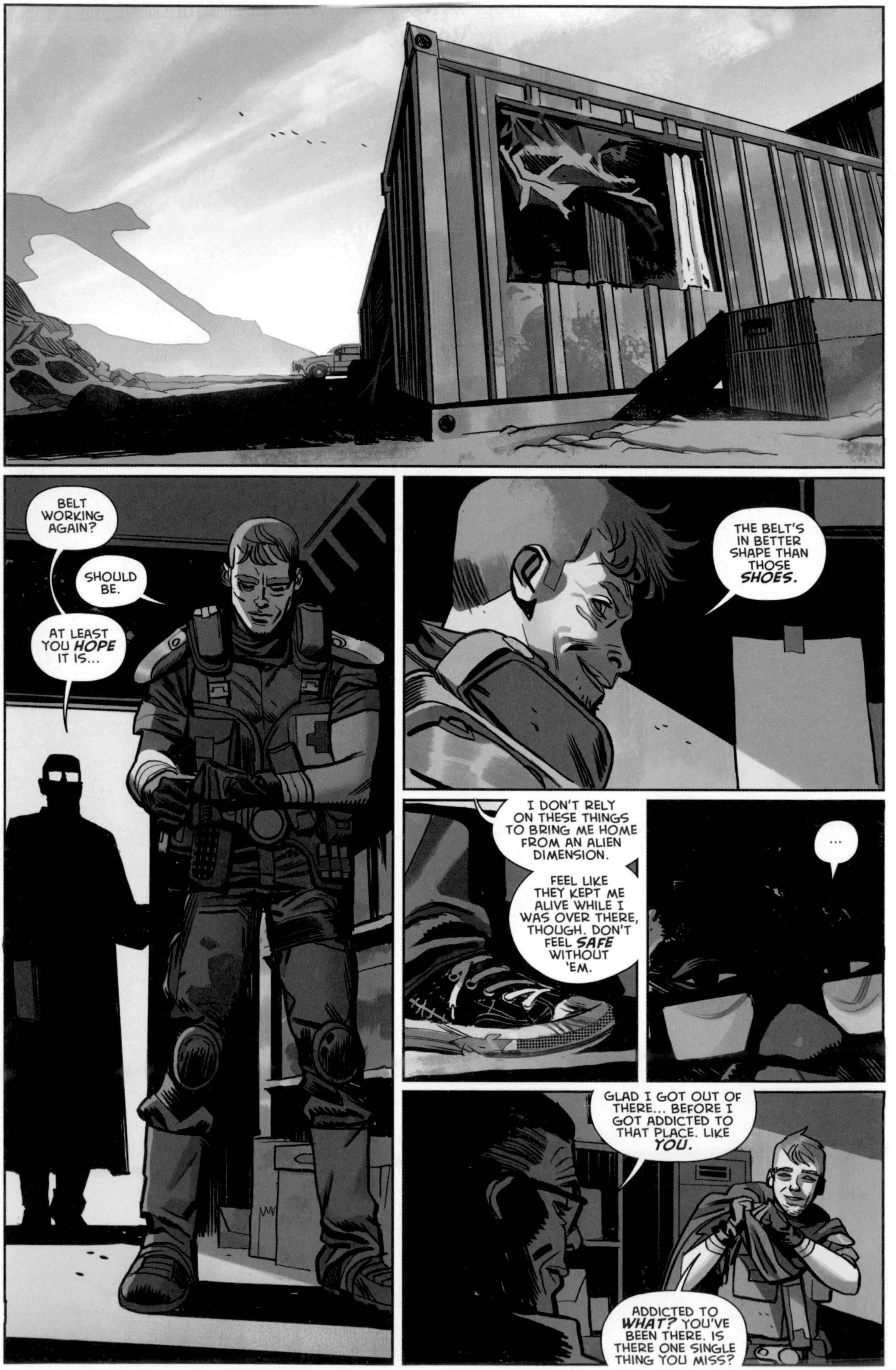
BELT WORKING AGAIN?
SHOULD BE.
AT LEAST YOU HOPE IT IS...
THE BELT'S IN BETTER SHAPE THAN THOSE SHOES.
I DON'T RELY ON THESE THINGS TO BRING ME HOME FROM AN ALIEN DIMENSION.
FEEL LIKE THEY KEPT ME ALIVE WHILE I WAS OVER THERE, THOUGH. DON'T FEEL SAFE WITHOUT 'EM.
...
GLAD I GOT OUT OF THERE... BEFORE I GOT ADDICTED TO THAT PLACE. LIKE YOU.
ADDICTED TO WHAT? YOU'VE BEEN THERE. IS THERE ONE SINGLE THING YOU MISS?

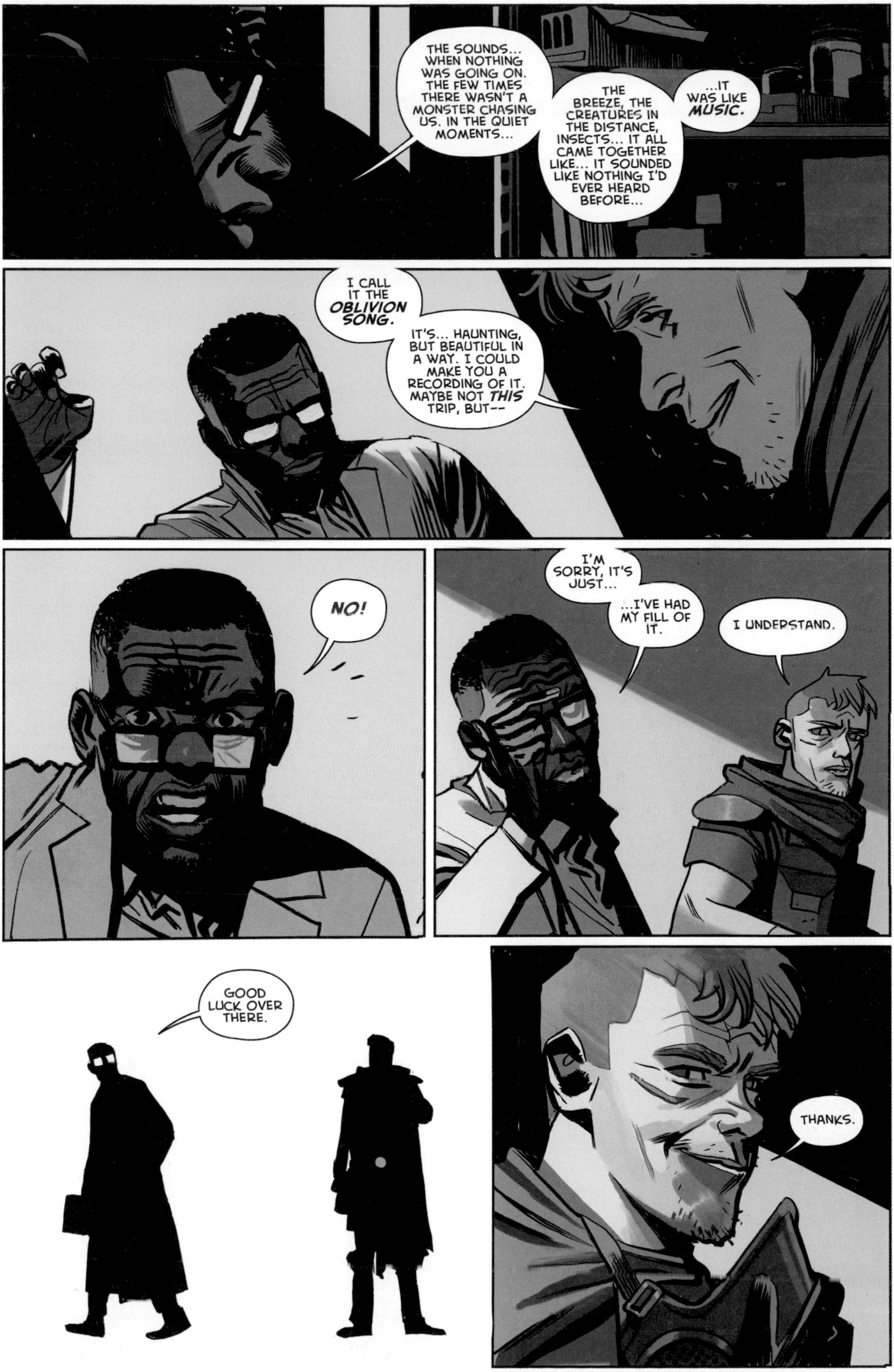
THE SOUNDS... WHEN NOTHING WAS GOING ON. THE FEW TIMES THERE WASN'T A MONSTER CHASING US. IN THE QUIET MOMENTS...
THE BREEZE, THE CREATURES IN THE DISTANCE, INSECTS... IT ALL CAME TOGETHER LIKE... IT SOUNDED LIKE NOTHING I'D EVER HEARD BEFORE...
...IT WAS LIKE MUSIC.
I CALL IT THE OBLIVION SONG.
IT'S... HAUNTING, BUT BEAUTIFUL IN A WAY. I COULD MAKE YOU A RECORDING OF IT. MAYBE NOT THIS TRIP, BUT--
NO!
I'M SORRY, IT'S JUST...
...I'VE HAD MY FILL OF IT.
I UNDERSTAND.
GOOD LUCK OVER THERE.
THANKS.

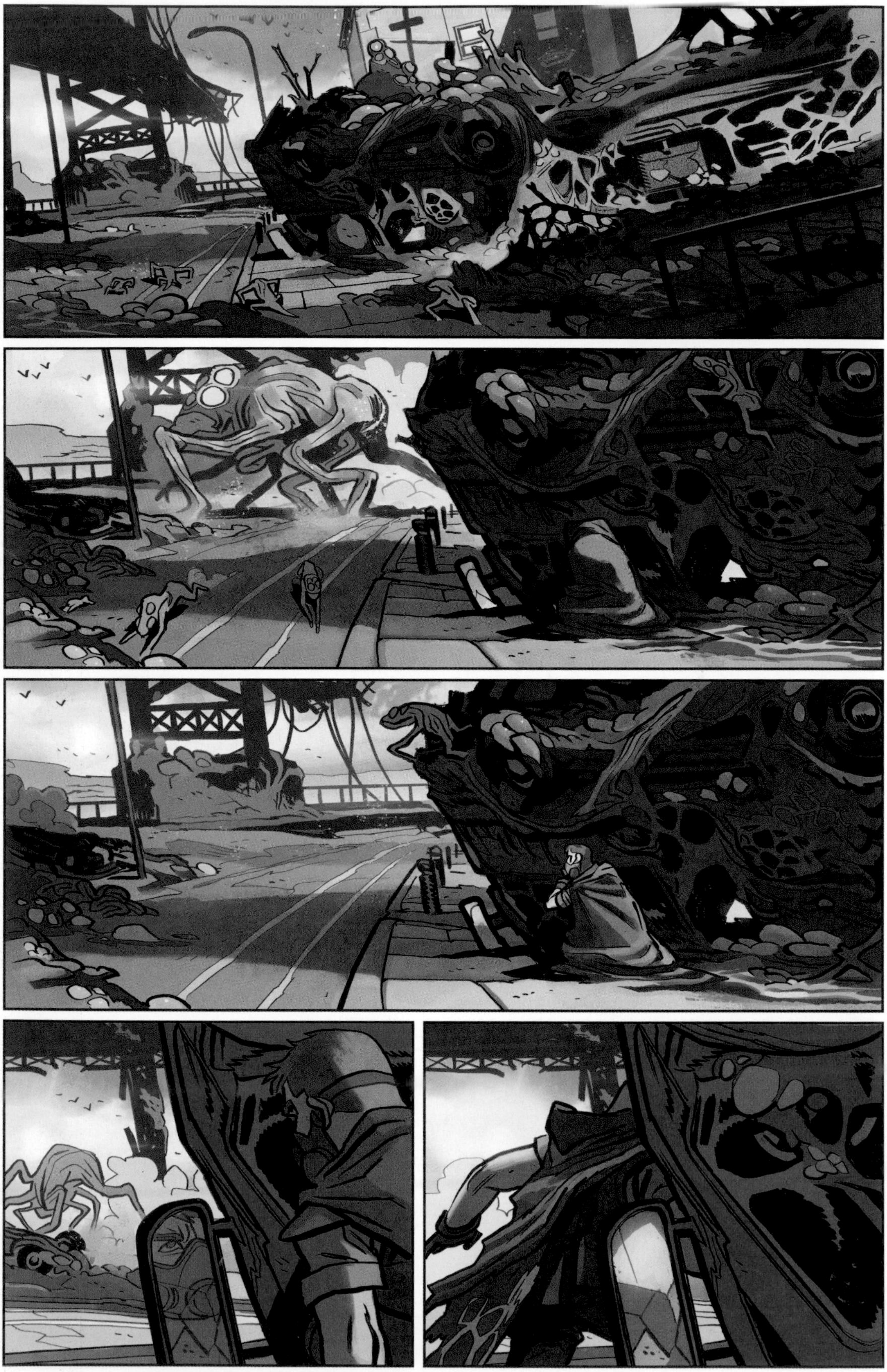

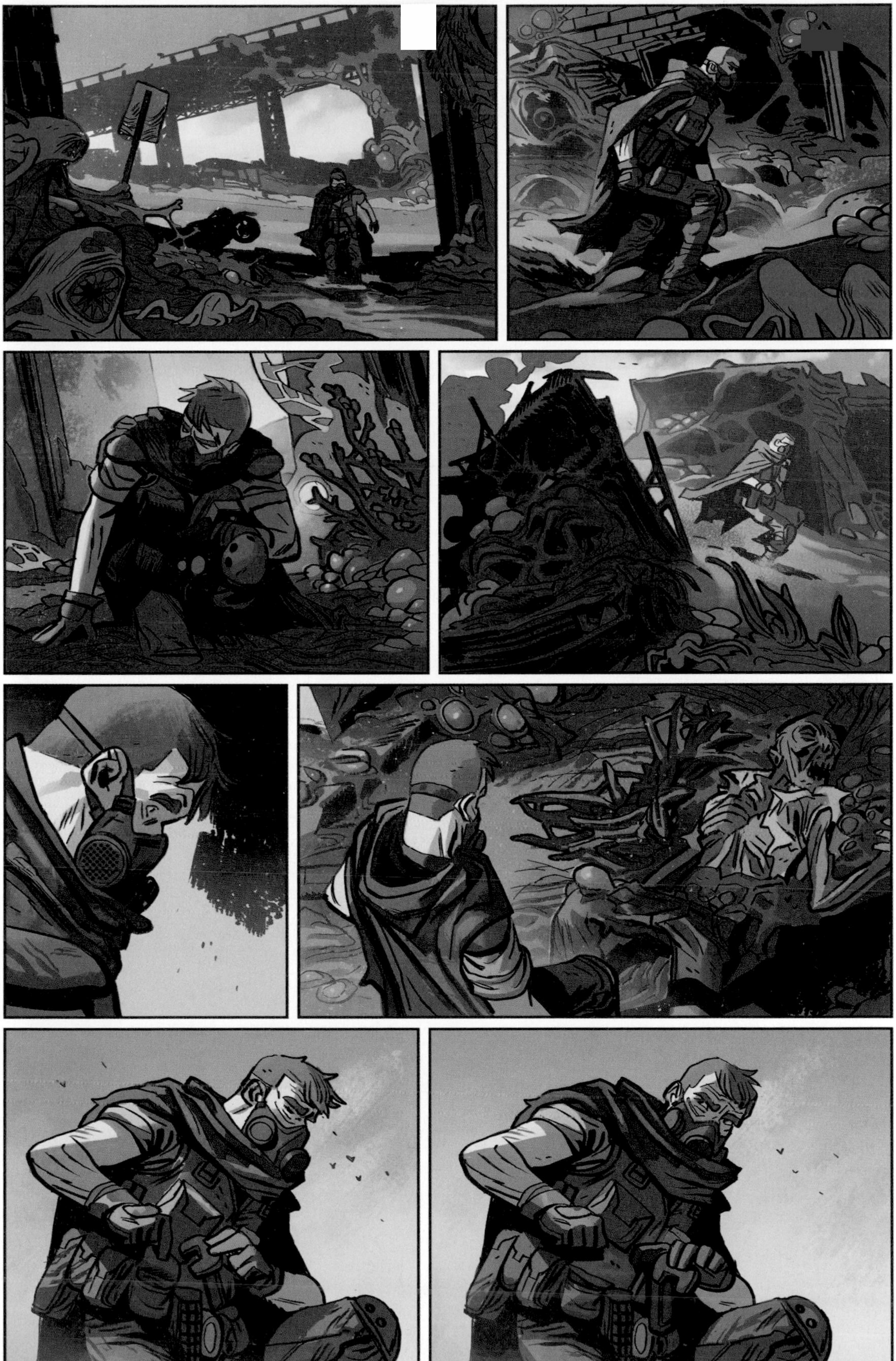

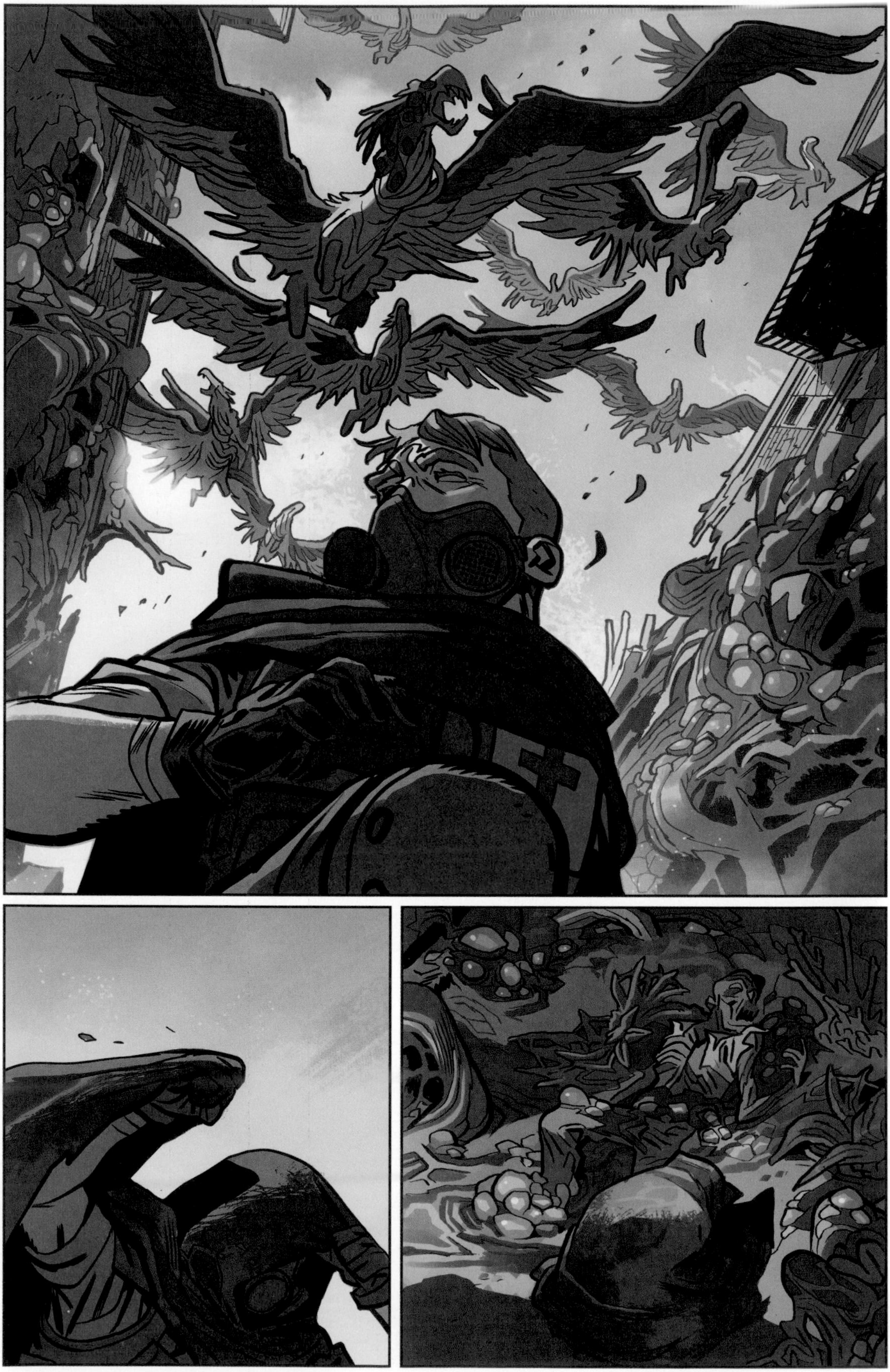

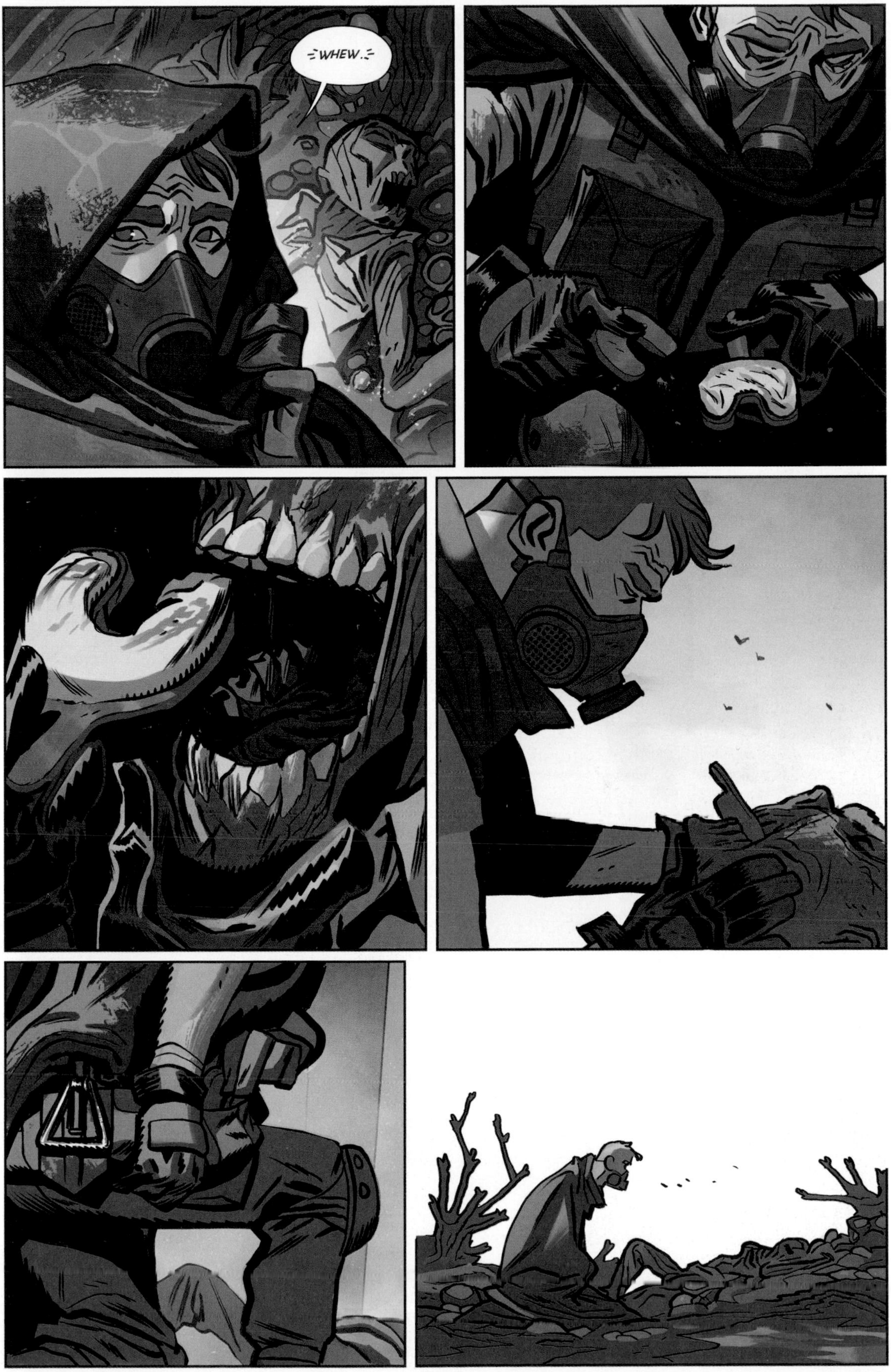
WHEW.

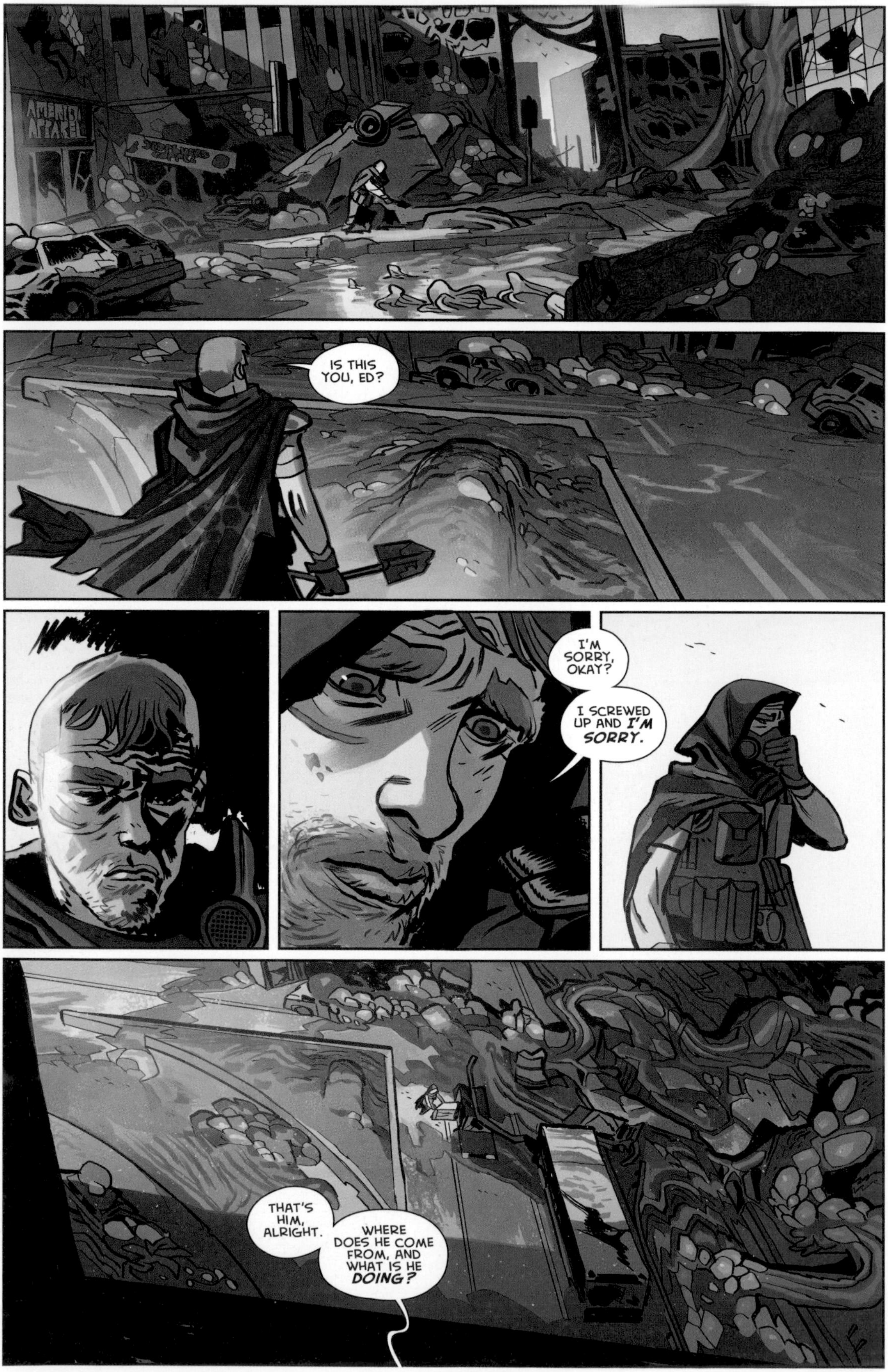
IS THIS YOU, ED?
I'M SORRY, OKAY?
I SCREWED UP AND *I'M SORRY.*
THAT'S HIM, ALRIGHT.
WHERE DOES HE COME FROM, AND WHAT IS HE *DOING?*

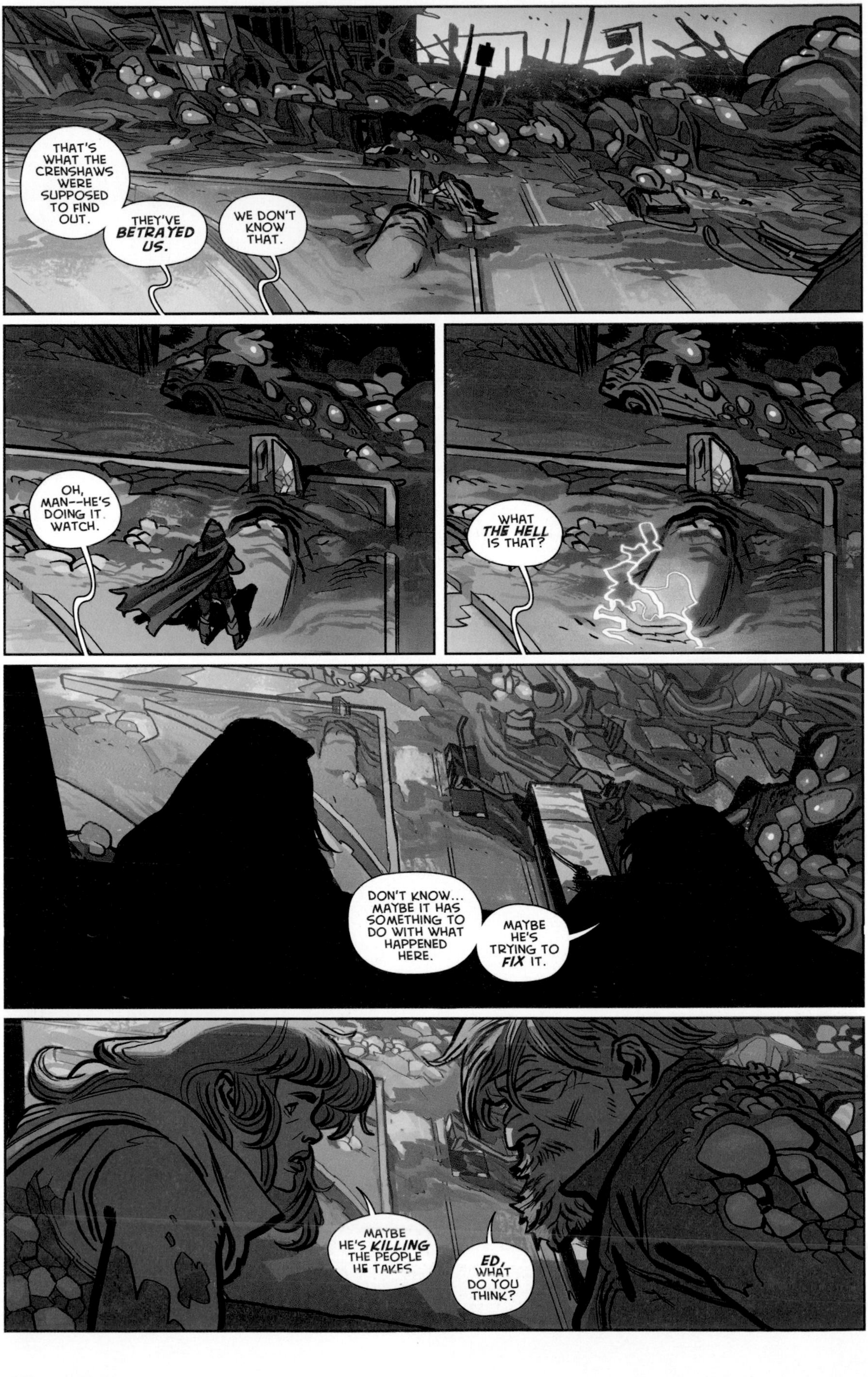

THAT'S WHAT THE CRENSHAWS WERE SUPPOSED TO FIND OUT.
THEY'VE BETRAYED US.
WE DON'T KNOW THAT.
OH, MAN--HE'S DOING IT. WATCH.
WHAT THE HELL IS THAT?
DON'T KNOW... MAYBE IT HAS SOMETHING TO DO WITH WHAT HAPPENED HERE.
MAYBE HE'S TRYING TO FIX IT.
MAYBE HE'S KILLING THE PEOPLE HE TAKES
ED, WHAT DO YOU THINK?

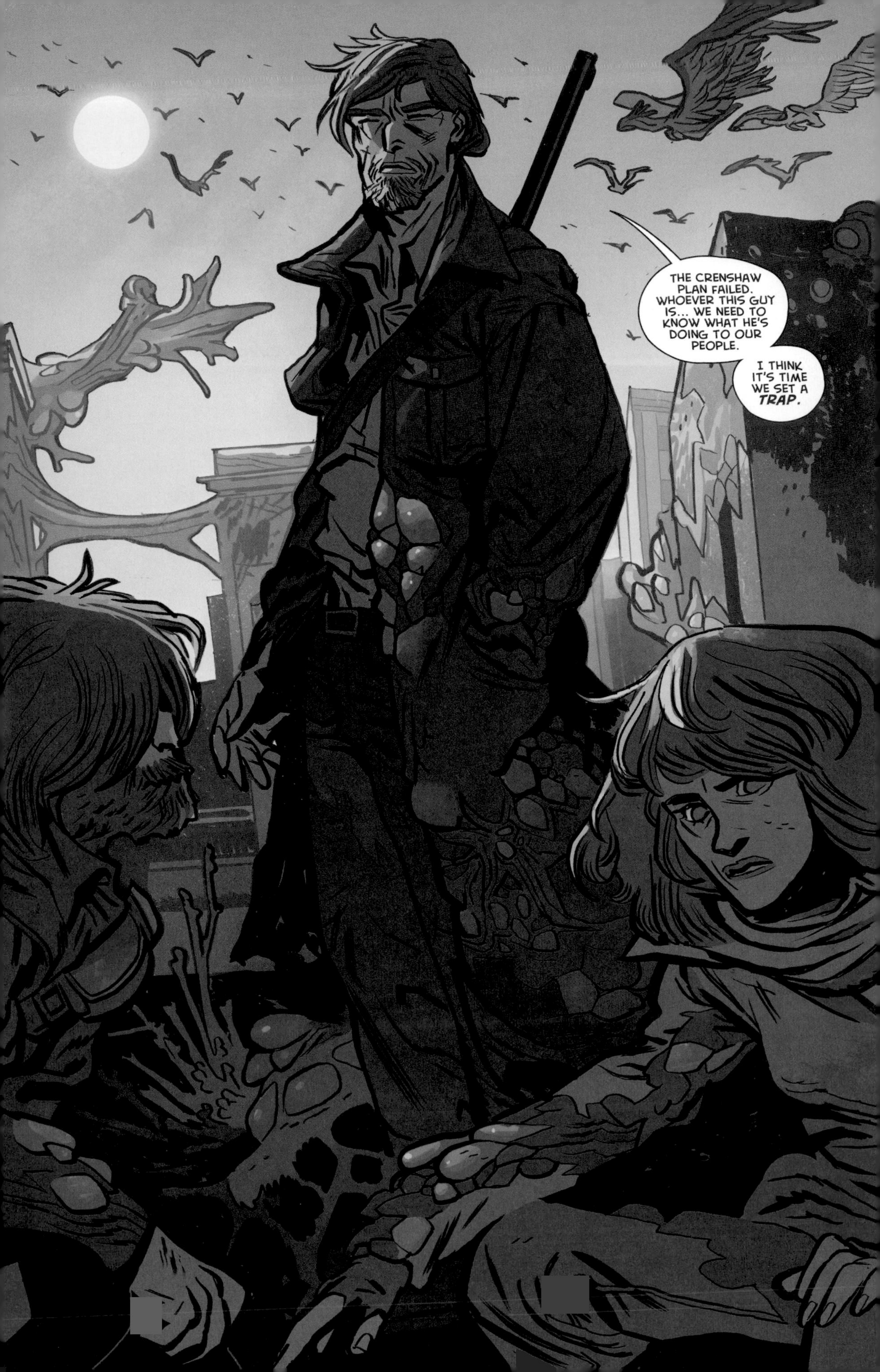
THE CRENSHAW PLAN FAILED. WHOEVER THIS GUY IS... WE NEED TO KNOW WHAT HE'S DOING TO OUR PEOPLE.
I THINK IT'S TIME WE SET A ***TRAP.***

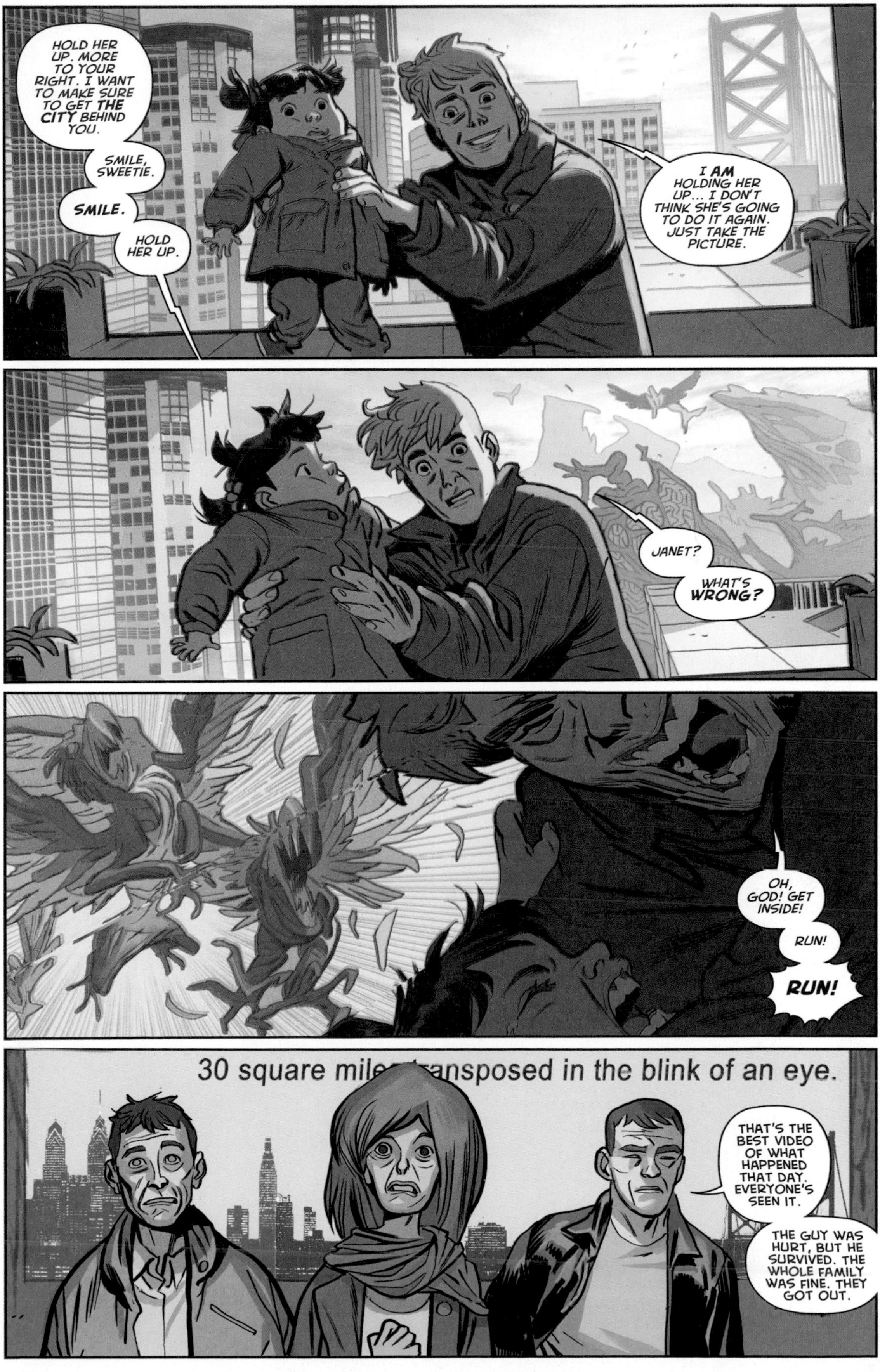
HOLD HER UP. MORE TO YOUR RIGHT. I WANT TO MAKE SURE TO GET THE CITY BEHIND YOU.
SMILE, SWEETIE.
SMILE.
HOLD HER UP.
I AM HOLDING HER UP... I DON'T THINK SHE'S GOING TO DO IT AGAIN. JUST TAKE THE PICTURE.
JANET?
WHAT'S WRONG?
OH, GOD! GET INSIDE!
RUN!
RUN!
30 square mile ransposed in the blink of an eye.
THAT'S THE BEST VIDEO OF WHAT HAPPENED THAT DAY. EVERYONE'S SEEN IT.
THE GUY WAS HURT, BUT HE SURVIVED. THE WHOLE FAMILY WAS FINE. THEY GOT OUT.

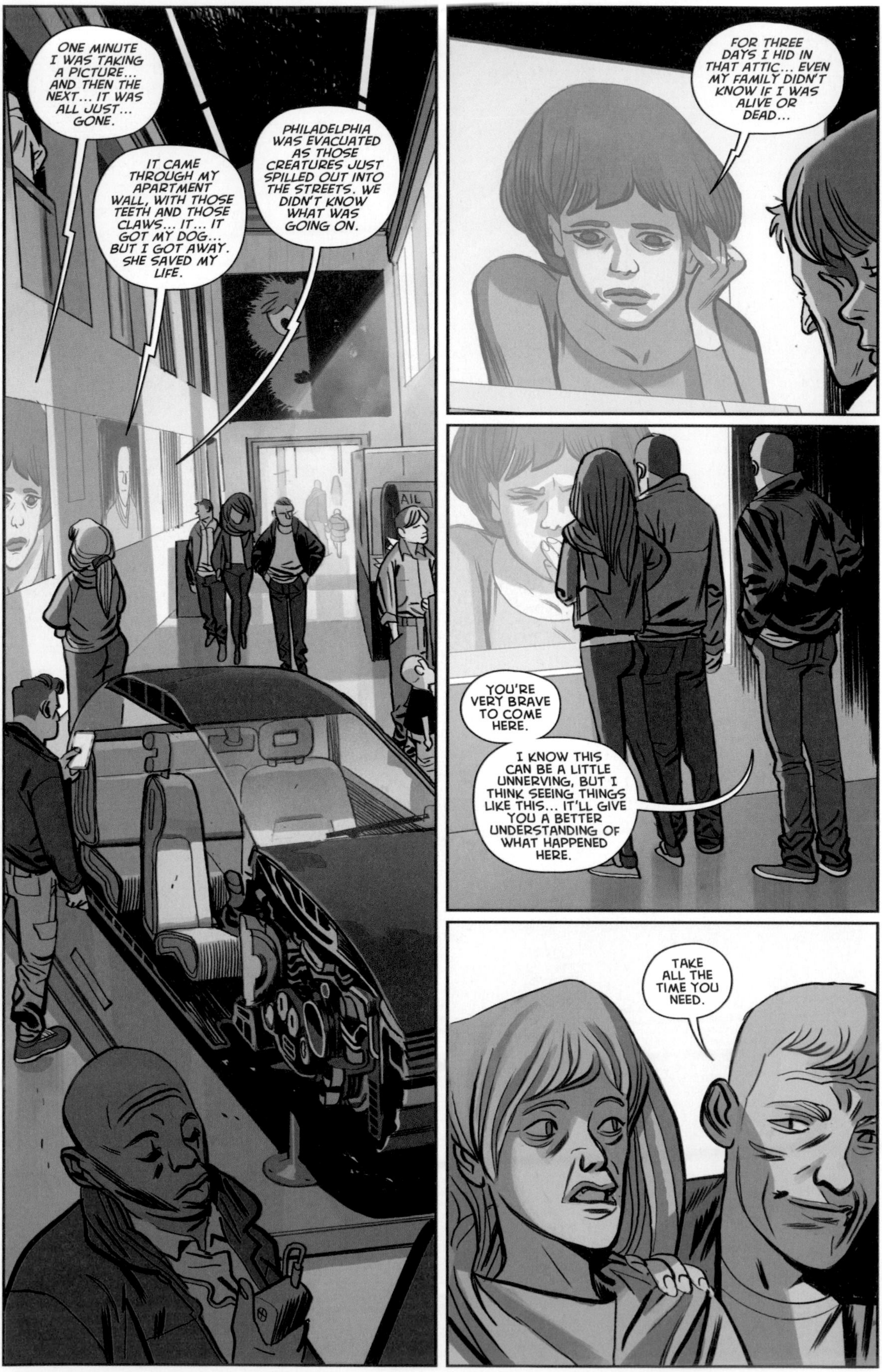
ONE MINUTE I WAS TAKING A PICTURE... AND THEN THE NEXT... IT WAS ALL JUST... GONE.
IT CAME THROUGH MY APARTMENT WALL, WITH THOSE TEETH AND THOSE CLAWS... IT... IT GOT MY DOG... BUT I GOT AWAY. SHE SAVED MY LIFE.
PHILADELPHIA WAS EVACUATED AS THOSE CREATURES JUST SPILLED OUT INTO THE STREETS. WE DIDN'T KNOW WHAT WAS GOING ON.
FOR THREE DAYS I HID IN THAT ATTIC... EVEN MY FAMILY DIDN'T KNOW IF I WAS ALIVE OR DEAD...
YOU'RE VERY BRAVE TO COME HERE.
I KNOW THIS CAN BE A LITTLE UNNERVING, BUT I THINK SEEING THINGS LIKE THIS... IT'LL GIVE YOU A BETTER UNDERSTANDING OF WHAT HAPPENED HERE.
TAKE ALL THE TIME YOU NEED.

PEOPLE HERE... IT WAS *YEARS* BEFORE WE KNEW WHAT HAD ACTUALLY HAPPENED. TO US... MAYBE THESE MONSTERS *WERE* THE PEOPLE MISSING.

MAYBE THIS NEW TERRAIN HAD SOMEHOW *CRUSHED* WHAT WAS HERE BEFORE.

ANOTHER DIMENSION? THE POSSIBILITY THOSE PEOPLE WERE STILL OUT THERE... IT WAS AN *INSANE* IDEA.

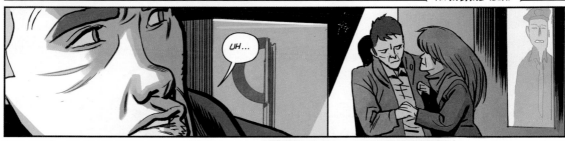

UH...

I'M SORRY, I KNOW THIS IS A LOT TO TAKE IN ALL AT ONCE.

WE'LL BE FINE.

DON'T WORRY ABOUT--

--US.

THAT THING'S STUFFED... IT'S NOT GOING ANYWHERE. DON'T WORRY.

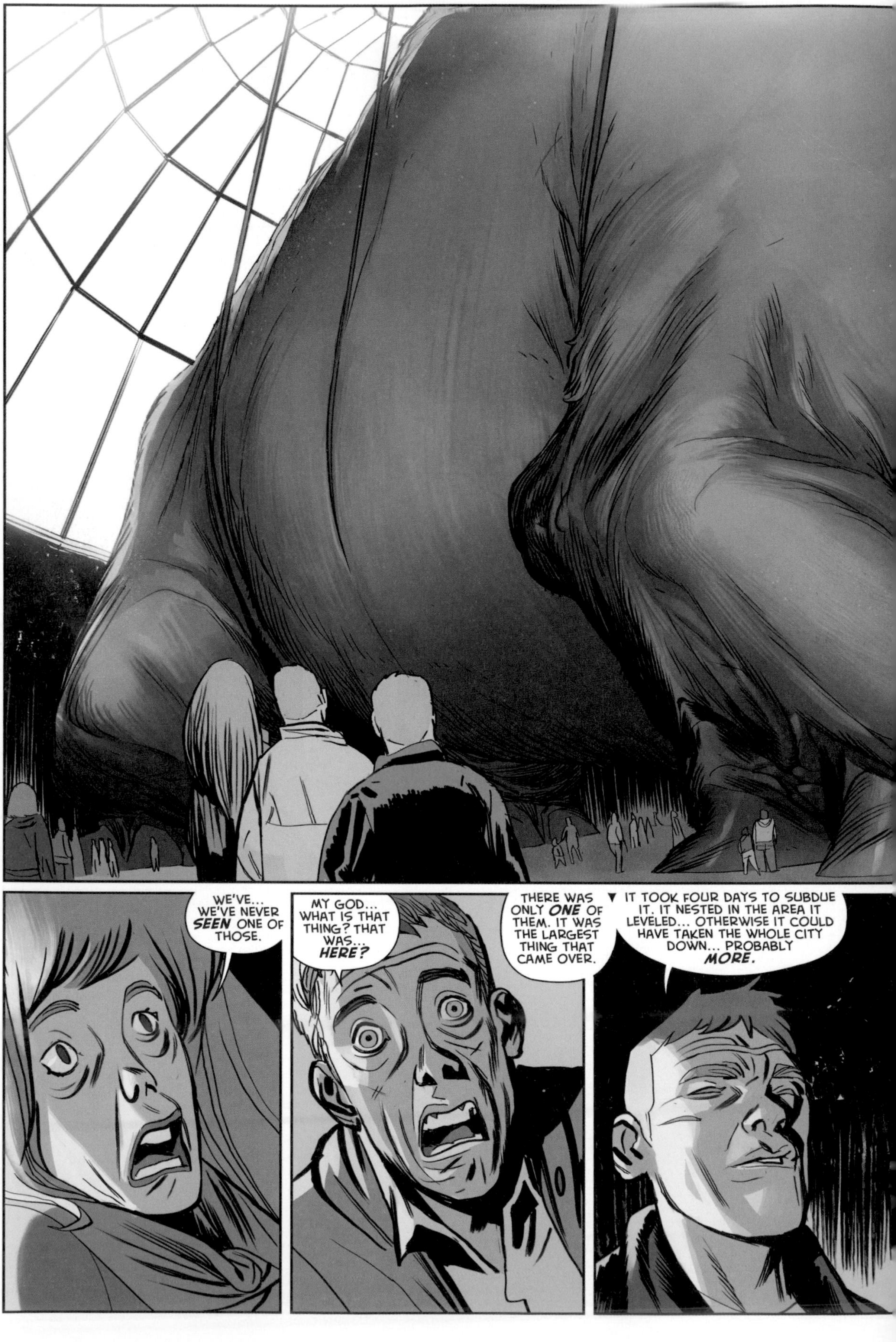
WE'VE... WE'VE NEVER SEEN ONE OF THOSE.
MY GOD... WHAT IS THAT THING? THAT WAS... HERE?
THERE WAS ONLY ONE OF THEM. IT WAS THE LARGEST THING THAT CAME OVER.
IT TOOK FOUR DAYS TO SUBDUE IT. IT NESTED IN THE AREA IT LEVELED... OTHERWISE IT COULD HAVE TAKEN THE WHOLE CITY DOWN... PROBABLY MORE.

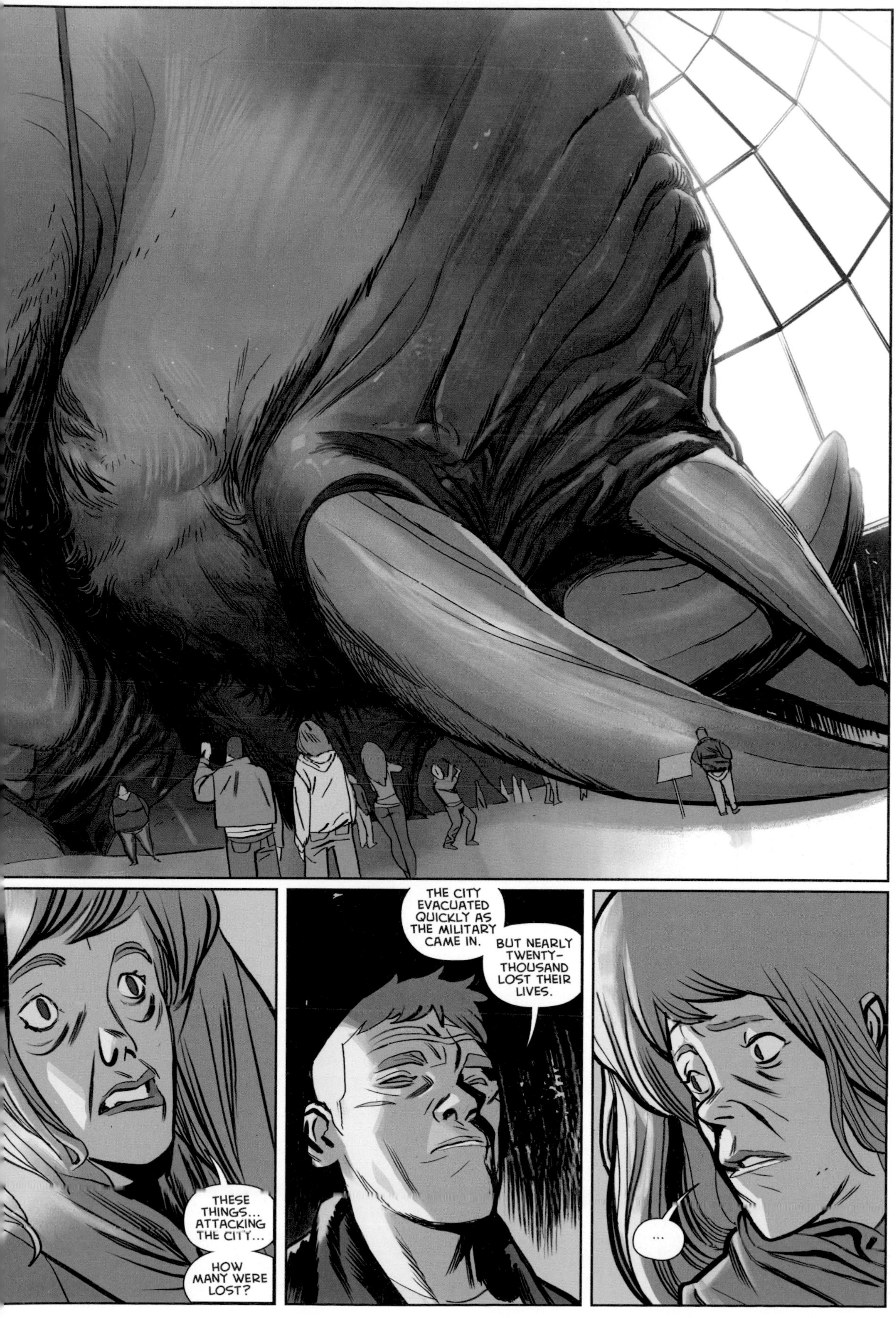
THESE THINGS... ATTACKING THE CITY...
HOW MANY WERE LOST?
THE CITY EVACUATED QUICKLY AS THE MILITARY CAME IN.
BUT NEARLY TWENTY-THOUSAND LOST THEIR LIVES.
...

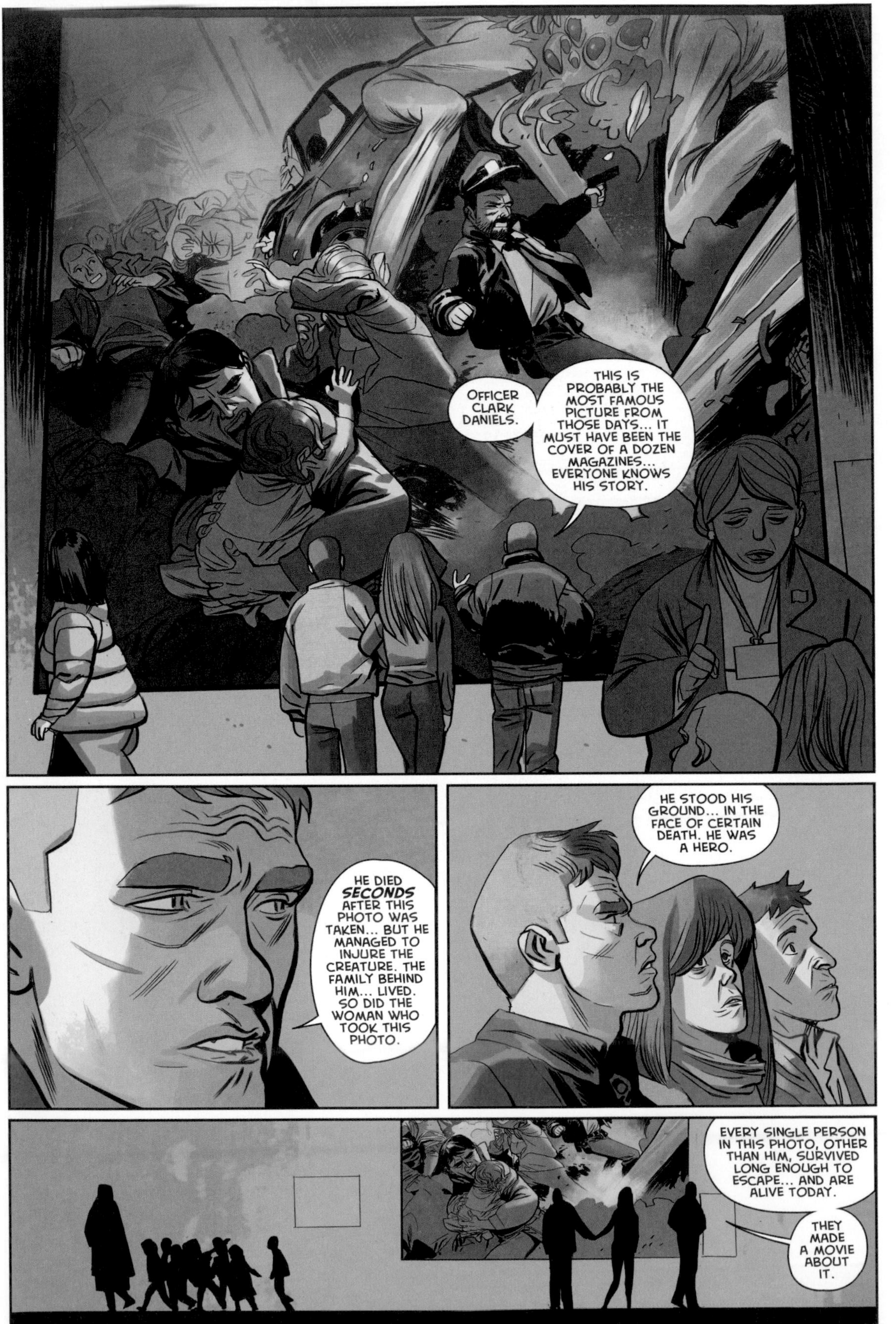
OFFICER CLARK DANIELS.
THIS IS PROBABLY THE MOST FAMOUS PICTURE FROM THOSE DAYS... IT MUST HAVE BEEN THE COVER OF A DOZEN MAGAZINES... EVERYONE KNOWS HIS STORY.
HE DIED *SECONDS* AFTER THIS PHOTO WAS TAKEN... BUT HE MANAGED TO INJURE THE CREATURE. THE FAMILY BEHIND HIM... LIVED. SO DID THE WOMAN WHO TOOK THIS PHOTO.
HE STOOD HIS GROUND... IN THE FACE OF CERTAIN DEATH. HE WAS A HERO.
EVERY SINGLE PERSON IN THIS PHOTO, OTHER THAN HIM, SURVIVED LONG ENOUGH TO ESCAPE... AND ARE ALIVE TODAY.
THEY MADE A MOVIE ABOUT IT.

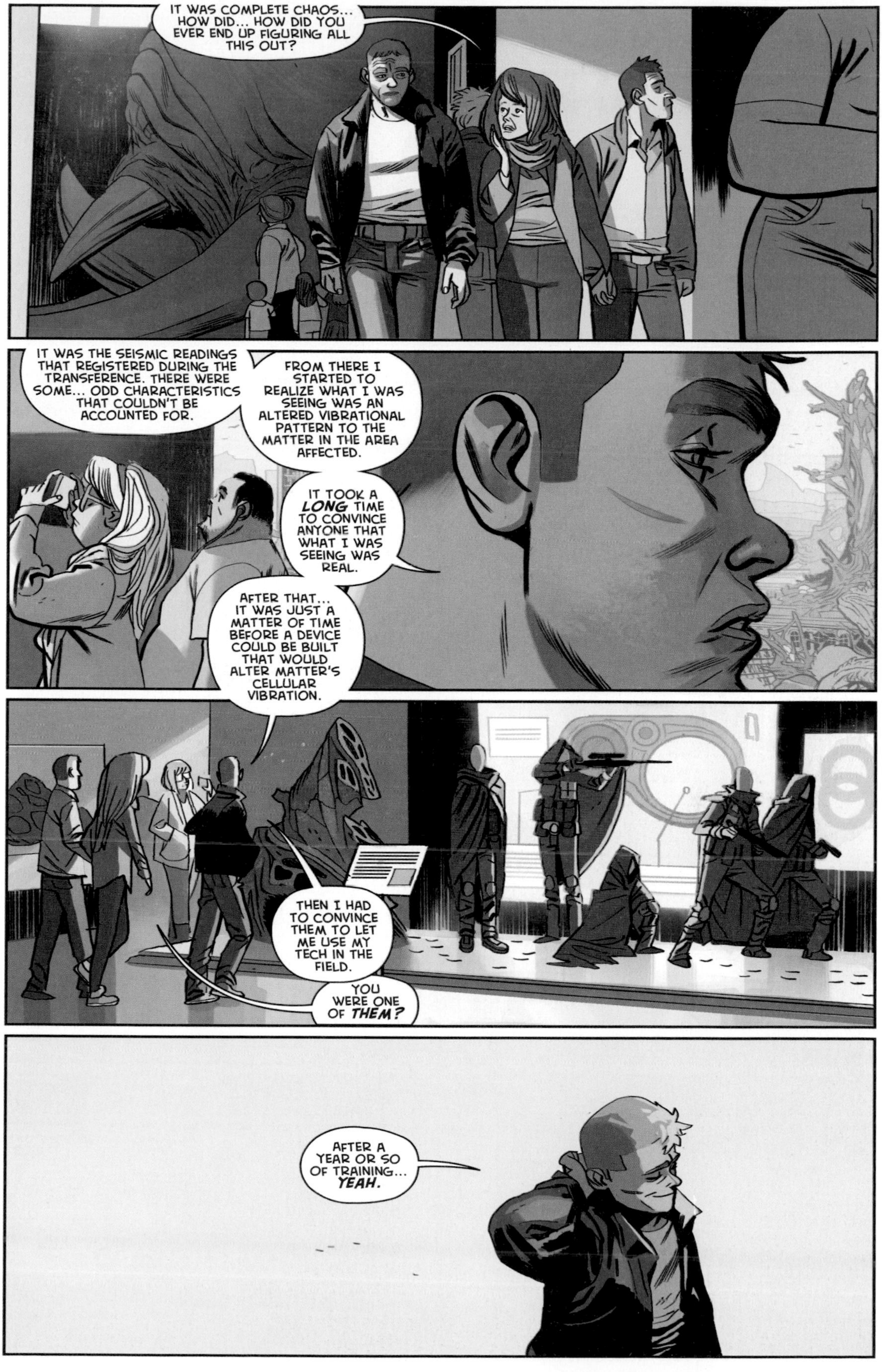
IT WAS COMPLETE CHAOS... HOW DID... HOW DID YOU EVER END UP FIGURING ALL THIS OUT?
IT WAS THE SEISMIC READINGS THAT REGISTERED DURING THE TRANSFERENCE. THERE WERE SOME... ODD CHARACTERISTICS THAT COULDN'T BE ACCOUNTED FOR.
FROM THERE I STARTED TO REALIZE WHAT I WAS SEEING WAS AN ALTERED VIBRATIONAL PATTERN TO THE MATTER IN THE AREA AFFECTED.
IT TOOK A ***LONG*** TIME TO CONVINCE ANYONE THAT WHAT I WAS SEEING WAS REAL.
AFTER THAT... IT WAS JUST A MATTER OF TIME BEFORE A DEVICE COULD BE BUILT THAT WOULD ALTER MATTER'S CELLULAR VIBRATION.
THEN I HAD TO CONVINCE THEM TO LET ME USE MY TECH IN THE FIELD.
YOU WERE ONE OF ***THEM?***
AFTER A YEAR OR SO OF TRAINING... ***YEAH.***

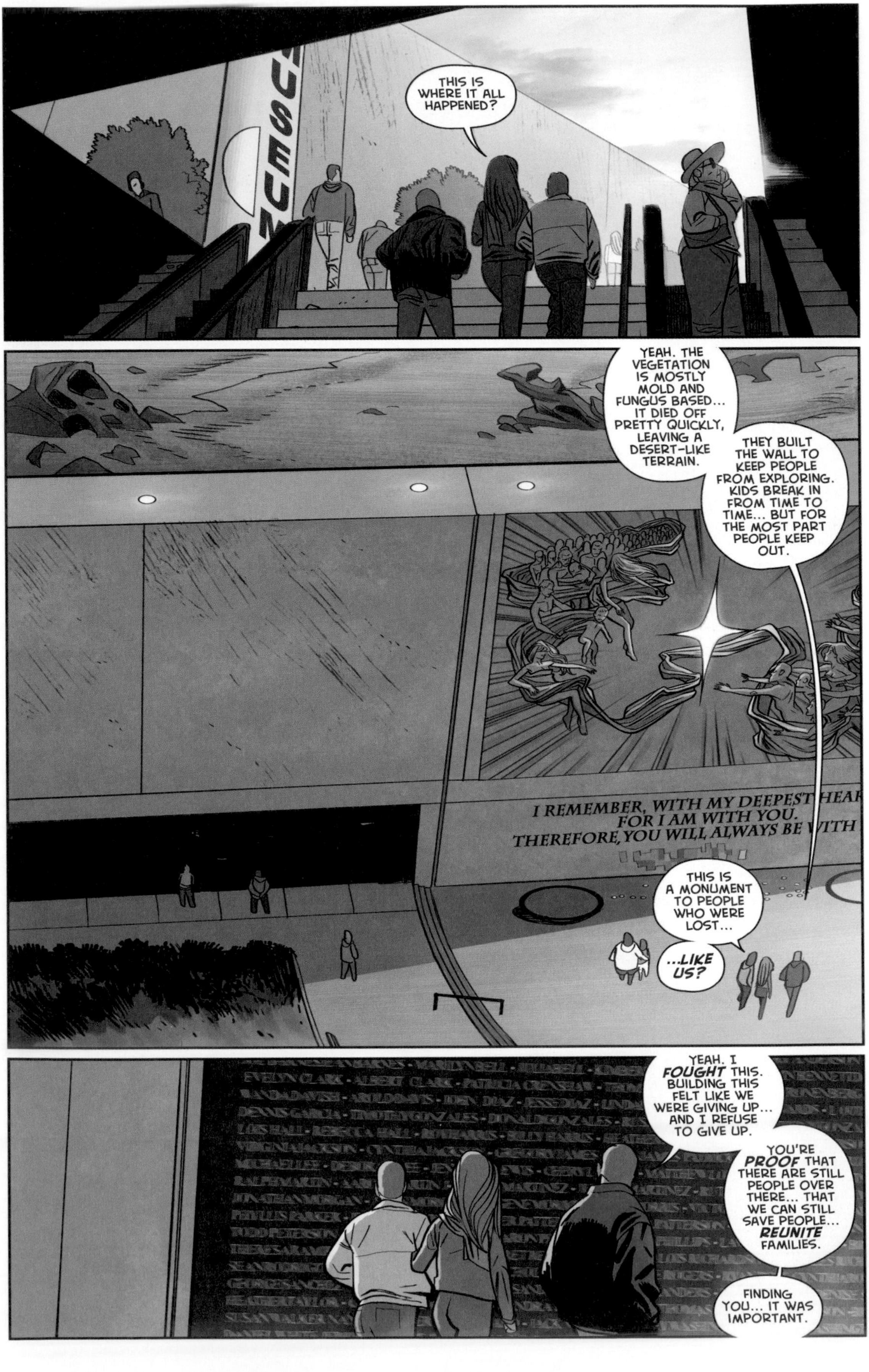

THIS IS WHERE IT ALL HAPPENED?
YEAH. THE VEGETATION IS MOSTLY MOLD AND FUNGUS BASED... IT DIED OFF PRETTY QUICKLY, LEAVING A DESERT-LIKE TERRAIN.
THEY BUILT THE WALL TO KEEP PEOPLE FROM EXPLORING. KIDS BREAK IN FROM TIME TO TIME... BUT FOR THE MOST PART PEOPLE KEEP OUT.
I REMEMBER, WITH MY DEEPEST HEAR
FOR I AM WITH YOU.
THEREFORE, YOU WILL ALWAYS BE WITH
THIS IS A MONUMENT TO PEOPLE WHO WERE LOST...
...LIKE US?
YEAH. I **FOUGHT** THIS. BUILDING THIS FELT LIKE WE WERE GIVING UP... AND I REFUSE TO GIVE UP.
YOU'RE **PROOF** THAT THERE ARE STILL PEOPLE OVER THERE... THAT WE CAN STILL SAVE PEOPLE... **REUNITE** FAMILIES.
FINDING YOU... IT WAS IMPORTANT.

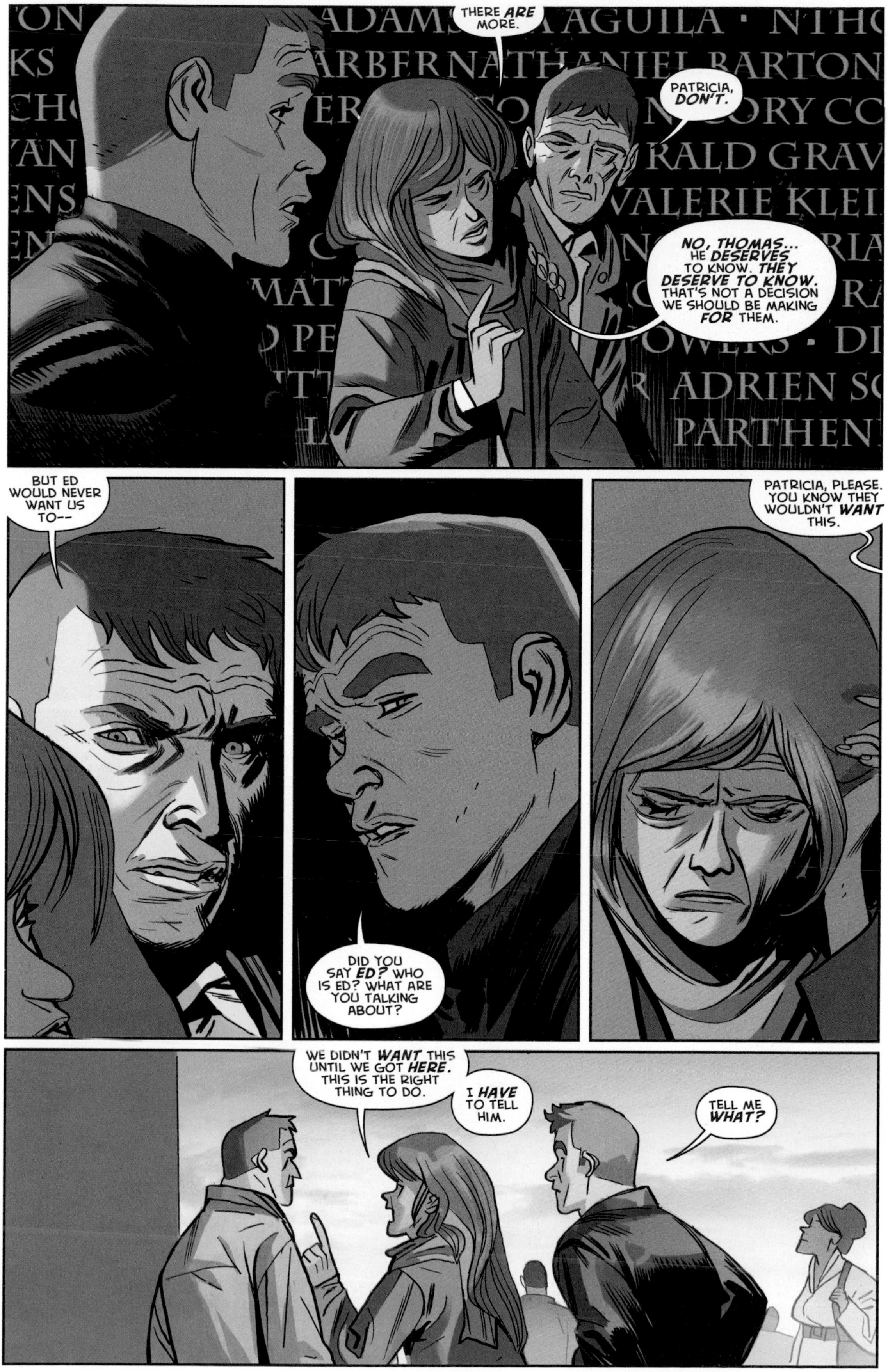
THERE ARE MORE.
PATRICIA, DON'T.
NO, THOMAS... HE DESERVES TO KNOW. THEY DESERVE TO KNOW. THAT'S NOT A DECISION WE SHOULD BE MAKING FOR THEM.
BUT ED WOULD NEVER WANT US TO--
DID YOU SAY ED? WHO IS ED? WHAT ARE YOU TALKING ABOUT?
PATRICIA, PLEASE. YOU KNOW THEY WOULDN'T WANT THIS.
WE DIDN'T WANT THIS UNTIL WE GOT HERE. THIS IS THE RIGHT THING TO DO.
I HAVE TO TELL HIM.
TELL ME WHAT?

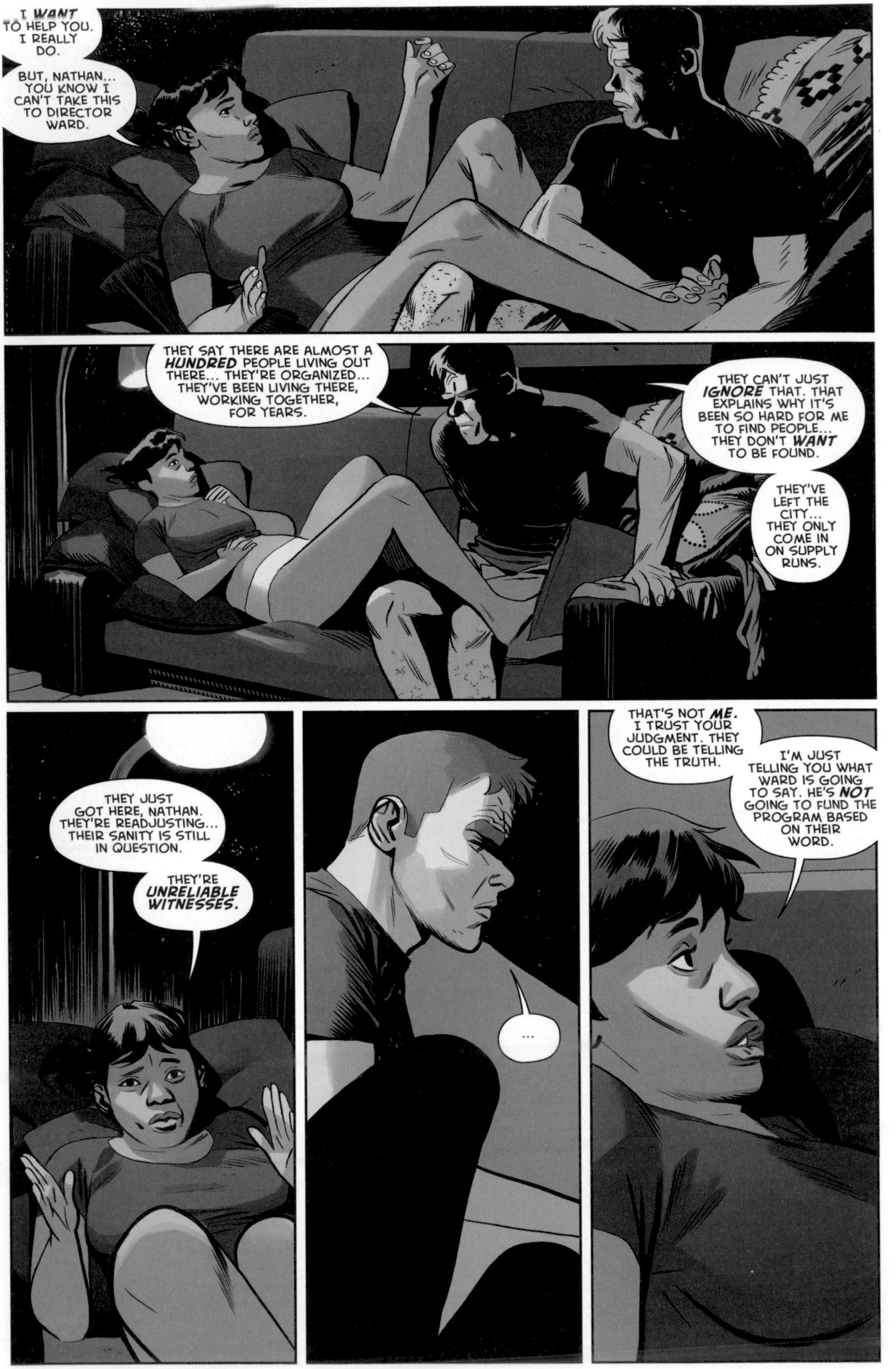
I WANT TO HELP YOU. I REALLY DO.
BUT, NATHAN... YOU KNOW I CAN'T TAKE THIS TO DIRECTOR WARD.
THEY SAY THERE ARE ALMOST A HUNDRED PEOPLE LIVING OUT THERE... THEY'RE ORGANIZED... THEY'VE BEEN LIVING THERE, WORKING TOGETHER, FOR YEARS.
THEY CAN'T JUST IGNORE THAT. THAT EXPLAINS WHY IT'S BEEN SO HARD FOR ME TO FIND PEOPLE... THEY DON'T WANT TO BE FOUND.
THEY'VE LEFT THE CITY... THEY ONLY COME IN ON SUPPLY RUNS.
THEY JUST GOT HERE, NATHAN. THEY'RE READJUSTING... THEIR SANITY IS STILL IN QUESTION.
THEY'RE UNRELIABLE WITNESSES.
...
THAT'S NOT ME. I TRUST YOUR JUDGMENT. THEY COULD BE TELLING THE TRUTH.
I'M JUST TELLING YOU WHAT WARD IS GOING TO SAY. HE'S NOT GOING TO FUND THE PROGRAM BASED ON THEIR WORD.

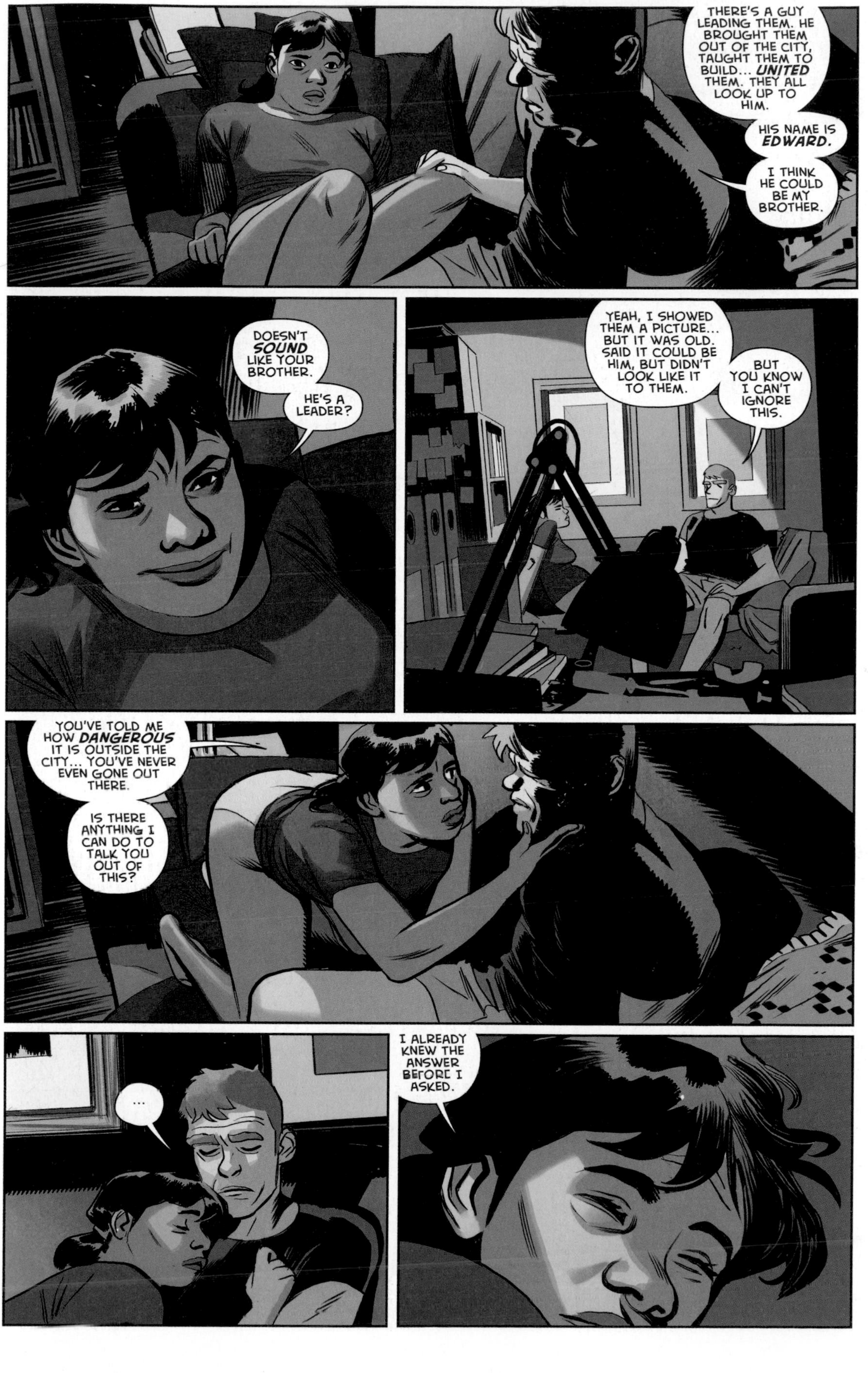
THERE'S A GUY LEADING THEM. HE BROUGHT THEM OUT OF THE CITY, TAUGHT THEM TO BUILD... *UNITED* THEM. THEY ALL LOOK UP TO HIM.
HIS NAME IS *EDWARD.*
I THINK HE COULD BE MY BROTHER.
DOESN'T *SOUND* LIKE YOUR BROTHER.
HE'S A LEADER?
YEAH, I SHOWED THEM A PICTURE... BUT IT WAS OLD. SAID IT COULD BE HIM, BUT DIDN'T LOOK LIKE IT TO THEM.
BUT YOU KNOW I CAN'T IGNORE THIS.
YOU'VE TOLD ME HOW *DANGEROUS* IT IS OUTSIDE THE CITY... YOU'VE NEVER EVEN GONE OUT THERE.
IS THERE ANYTHING I CAN DO TO TALK YOU OUT OF THIS?
...
I ALREADY KNEW THE ANSWER BEFORE I ASKED.

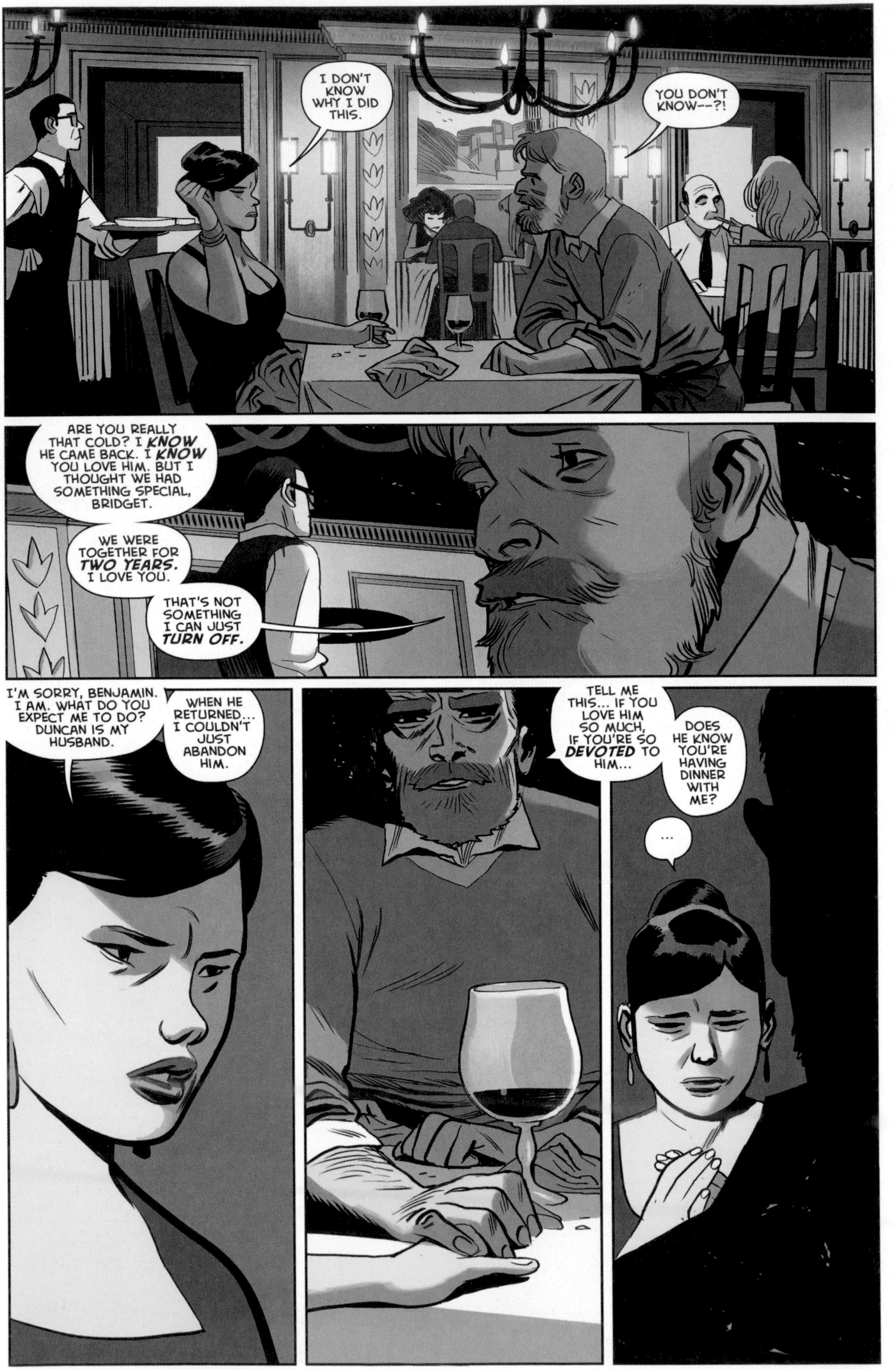
I DON'T KNOW WHY I DID THIS.
YOU DON'T KNOW--?!
ARE YOU REALLY THAT COLD? I KNOW HE CAME BACK. I KNOW YOU LOVE HIM. BUT I THOUGHT WE HAD SOMETHING SPECIAL, BRIDGET.
WE WERE TOGETHER FOR TWO YEARS. I LOVE YOU.
THAT'S NOT SOMETHING I CAN JUST TURN OFF.
I'M SORRY, BENJAMIN. I AM. WHAT DO YOU EXPECT ME TO DO? DUNCAN IS MY HUSBAND.
WHEN HE RETURNED... I COULDN'T JUST ABANDON HIM.
TELL ME THIS... IF YOU LOVE HIM SO MUCH, IF YOU'RE SO DEVOTED TO HIM...
DOES HE KNOW YOU'RE HAVING DINNER WITH ME?
...

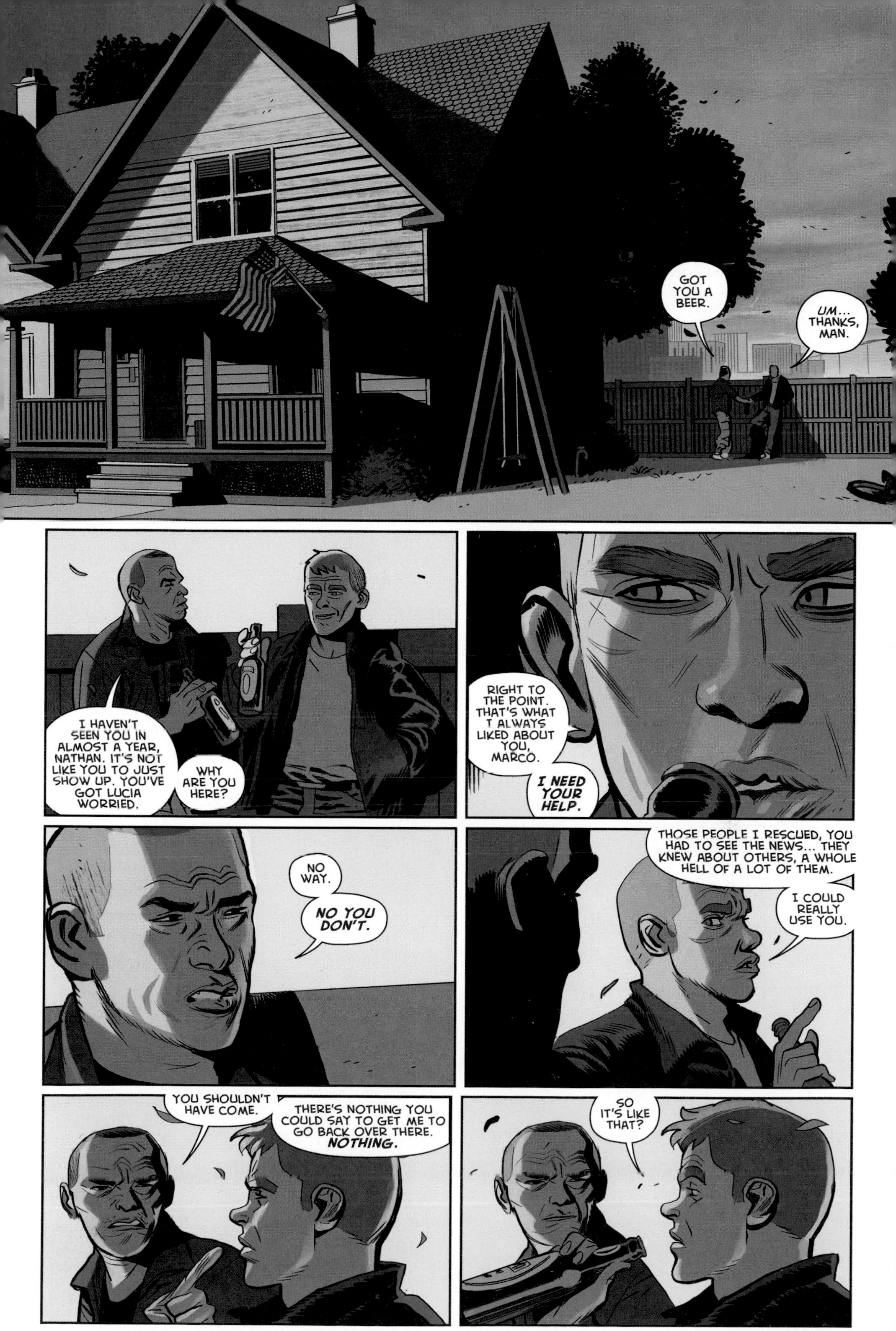
GOT YOU A BEER.
UM... THANKS, MAN.
I HAVEN'T SEEN YOU IN ALMOST A YEAR, NATHAN. IT'S NOT LIKE YOU TO JUST SHOW UP. YOU'VE GOT LUCIA WORRIED.
WHY ARE YOU HERE?
RIGHT TO THE POINT. THAT'S WHAT I ALWAYS LIKED ABOUT YOU, MARCO.
I NEED YOUR HELP.
NO WAY.
NO YOU DON'T.
THOSE PEOPLE I RESCUED, YOU HAD TO SEE THE NEWS... THEY KNEW ABOUT OTHERS, A WHOLE HELL OF A LOT OF THEM.
I COULD REALLY USE YOU.
YOU SHOULDN'T HAVE COME.
THERE'S NOTHING YOU COULD SAY TO GET ME TO GO BACK OVER THERE. NOTHING.
SO IT'S LIKE THAT?

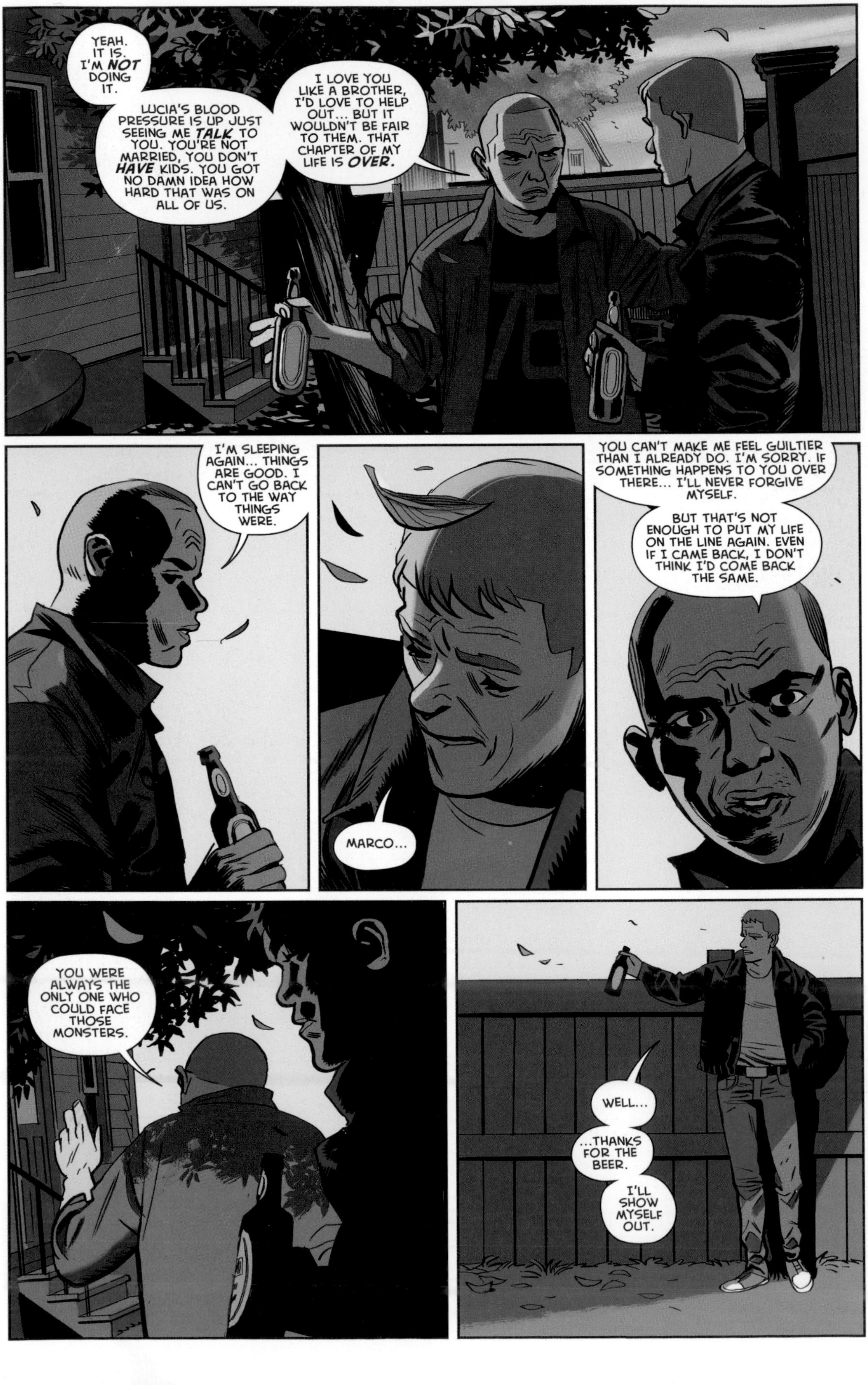
YEAH. IT IS. I'M NOT DOING IT.
LUCIA'S BLOOD PRESSURE IS UP JUST SEEING ME TALK TO YOU. YOU'RE NOT MARRIED, YOU DON'T HAVE KIDS. YOU GOT NO DAMN IDEA HOW HARD THAT WAS ON ALL OF US.
I LOVE YOU LIKE A BROTHER, I'D LOVE TO HELP OUT... BUT IT WOULDN'T BE FAIR TO THEM. THAT CHAPTER OF MY LIFE IS OVER.
I'M SLEEPING AGAIN... THINGS ARE GOOD. I CAN'T GO BACK TO THE WAY THINGS WERE.
MARCO...
YOU CAN'T MAKE ME FEEL GUILTIER THAN I ALREADY DO. I'M SORRY. IF SOMETHING HAPPENS TO YOU OVER THERE... I'LL NEVER FORGIVE MYSELF.
BUT THAT'S NOT ENOUGH TO PUT MY LIFE ON THE LINE AGAIN. EVEN IF I CAME BACK, I DON'T THINK I'D COME BACK THE SAME.
YOU WERE ALWAYS THE ONLY ONE WHO COULD FACE THOSE MONSTERS.
WELL...
...THANKS FOR THE BEER.
I'LL SHOW MYSELF OUT.

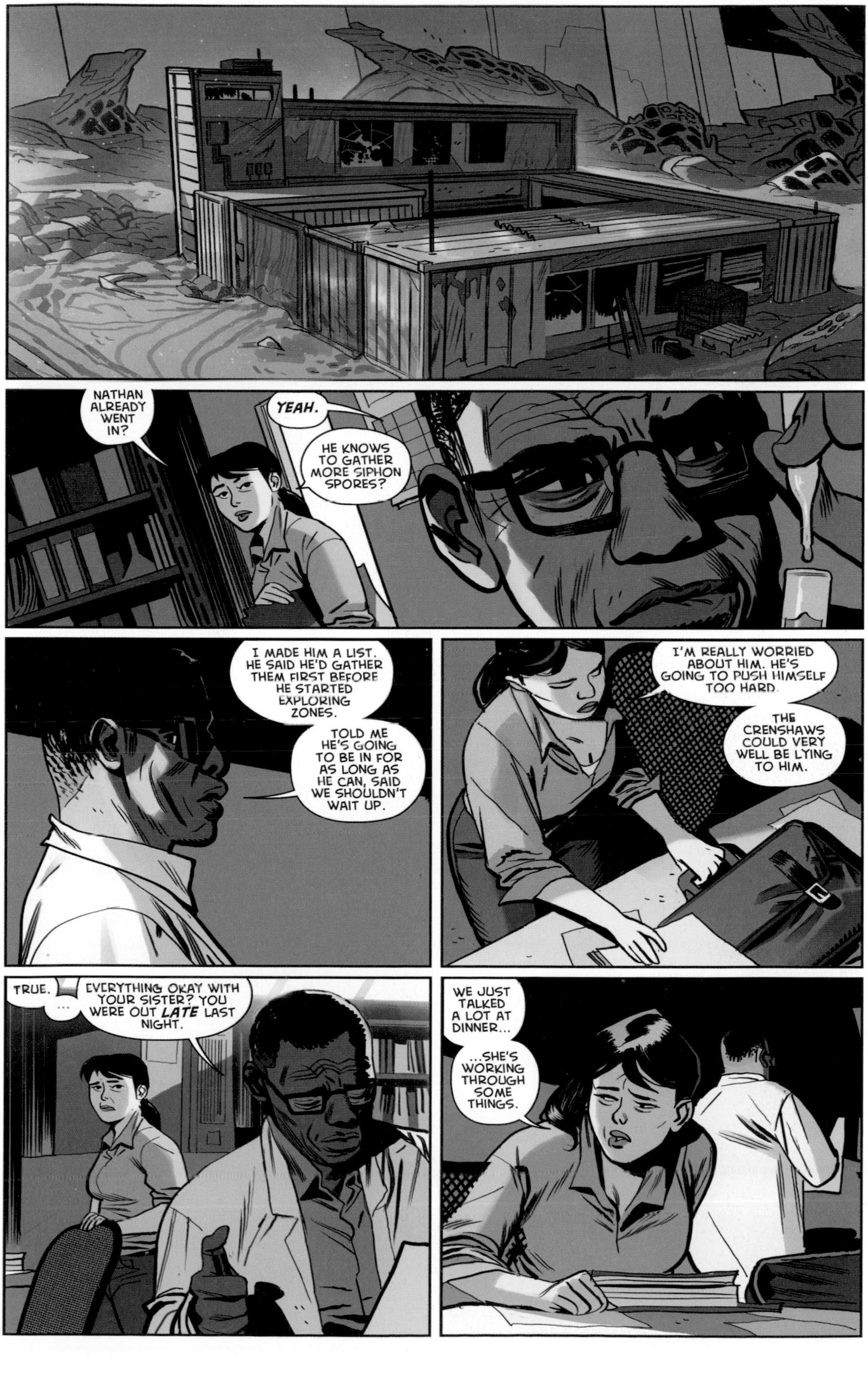

NATHAN ALREADY WENT IN?
YEAH.
HE KNOWS TO GATHER MORE SIPHON SPORES?
I MADE HIM A LIST. HE SAID HE'D GATHER THEM FIRST BEFORE HE STARTED EXPLORING ZONES.
TOLD ME HE'S GOING TO BE IN FOR AS LONG AS HE CAN, SAID WE SHOULDN'T WAIT UP.
I'M REALLY WORRIED ABOUT HIM. HE'S GOING TO PUSH HIMSELF TOO HARD.
THE CRENSHAWS COULD VERY WELL BE LYING TO HIM.
TRUE.
...
EVERYTHING OKAY WITH YOUR SISTER? YOU WERE OUT LATE LAST NIGHT.
WE JUST TALKED A LOT AT DINNER...
...SHE'S WORKING THROUGH SOME THINGS.

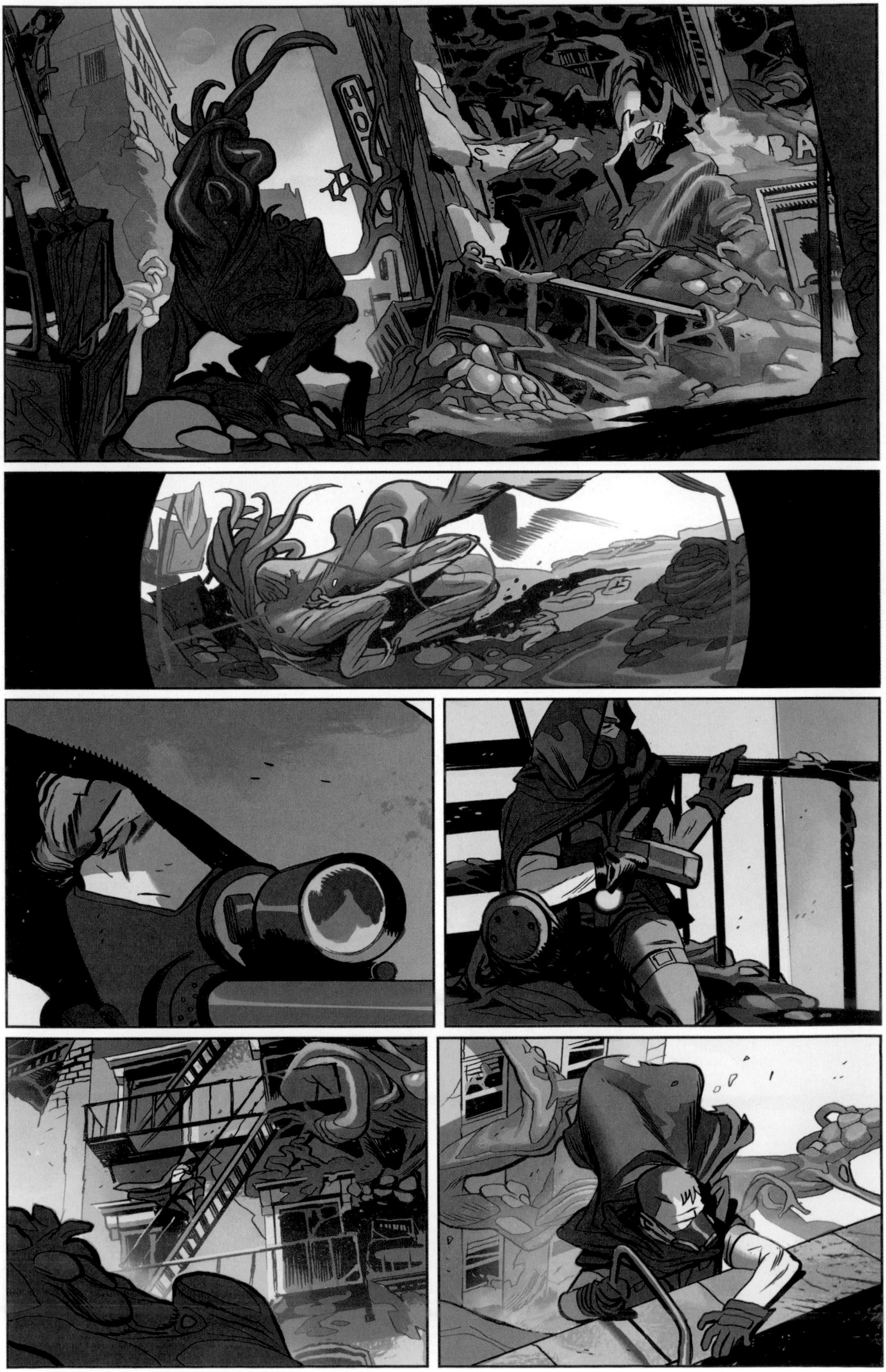
HO
BA

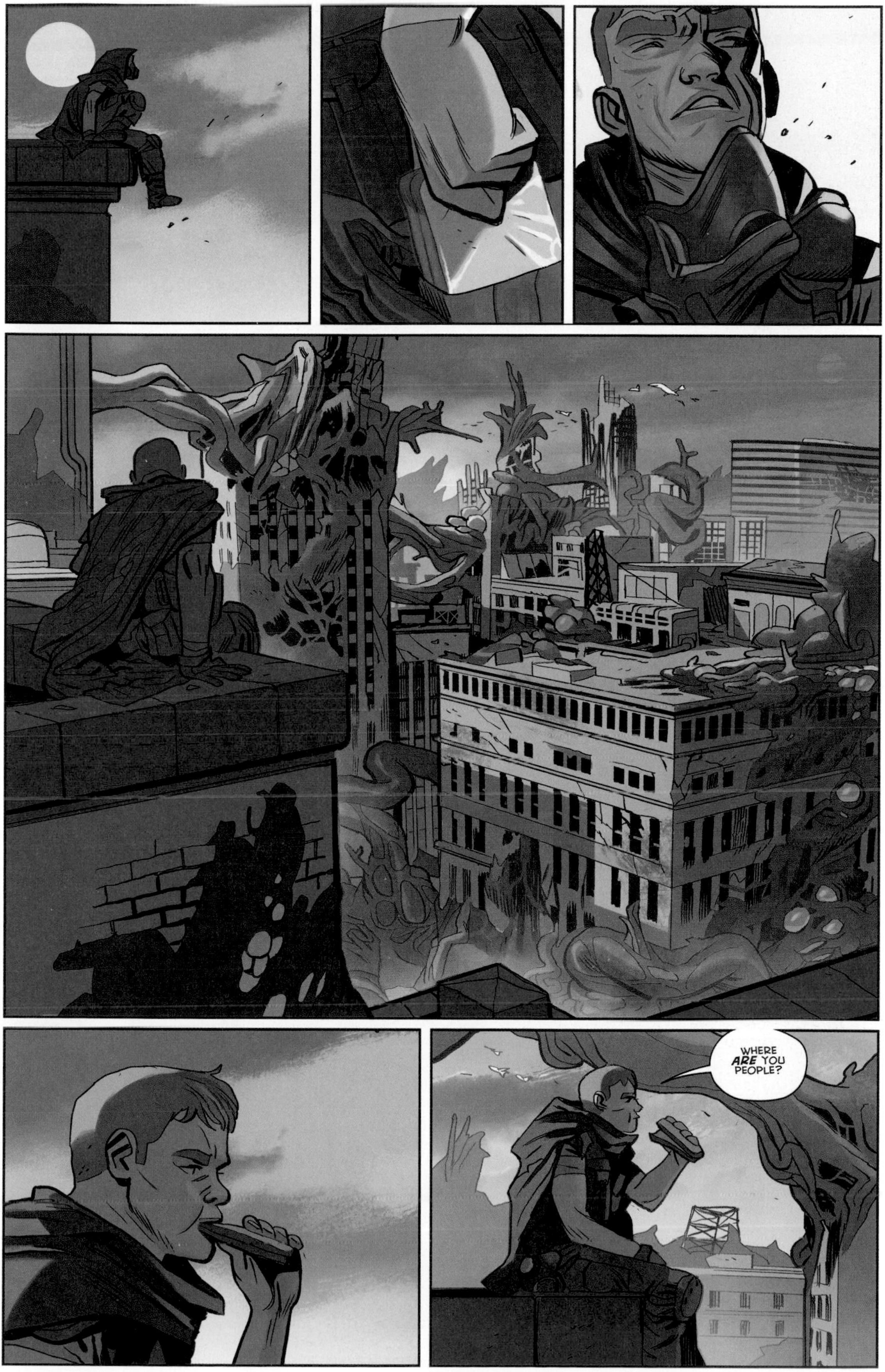
WHERE ARE YOU PEOPLE?

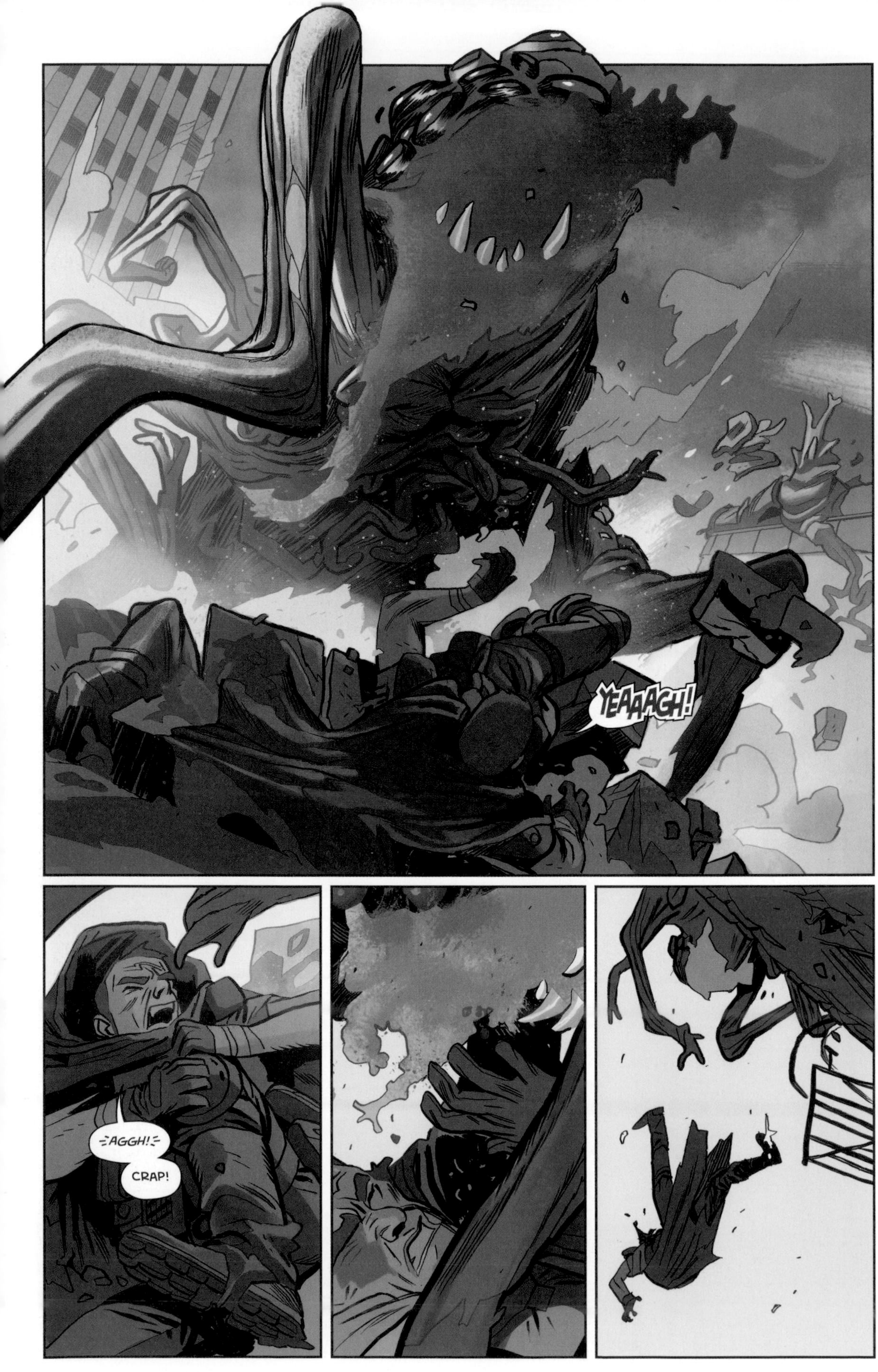

YEAAAAGH!
AGGH!
CRAP!

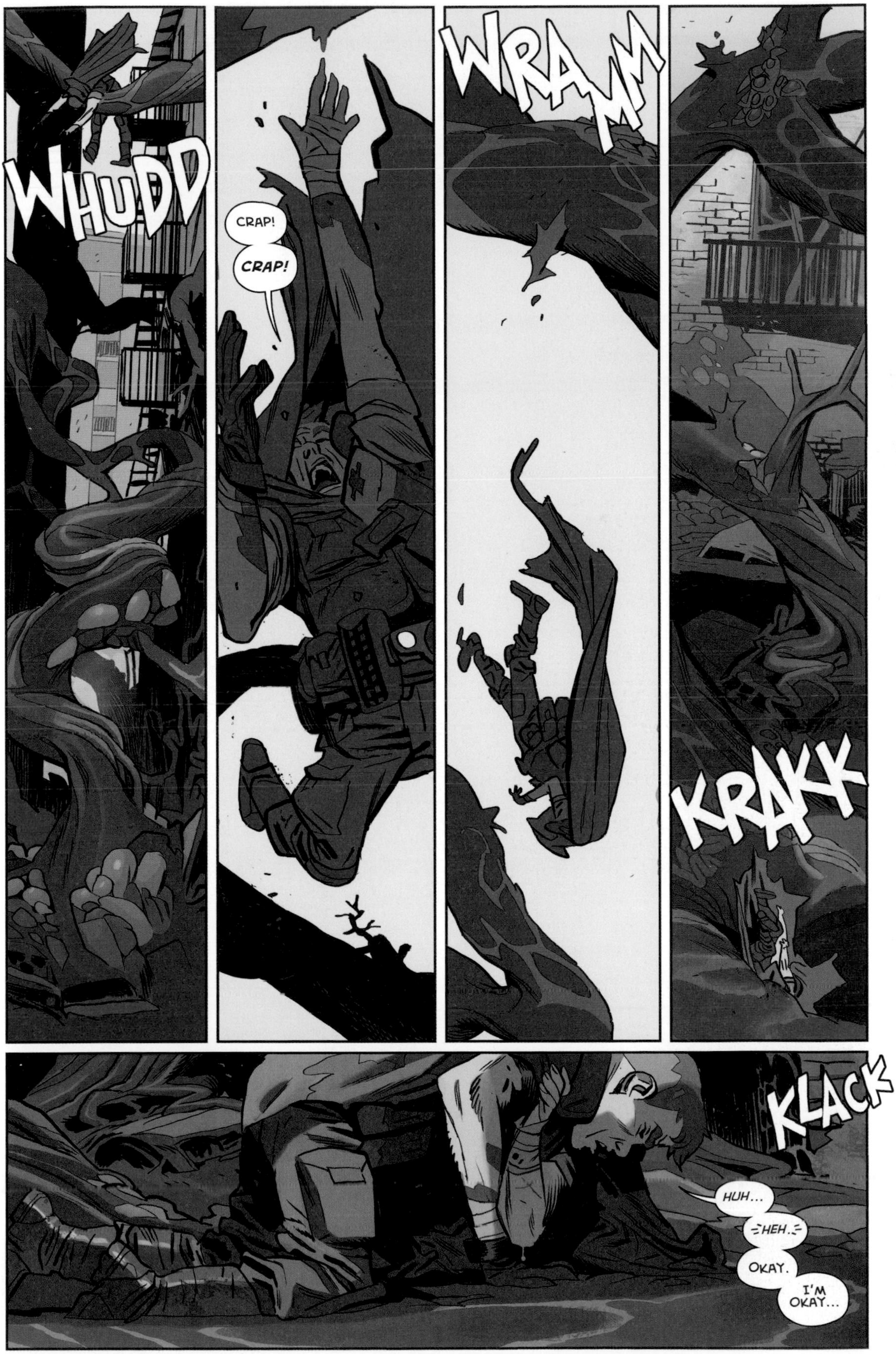
WHUDD
CRAP!
CRAP!
WRAMM
KRAKK
KLACK
HUH...
HEH.
OKAY.
I'M OKAY...

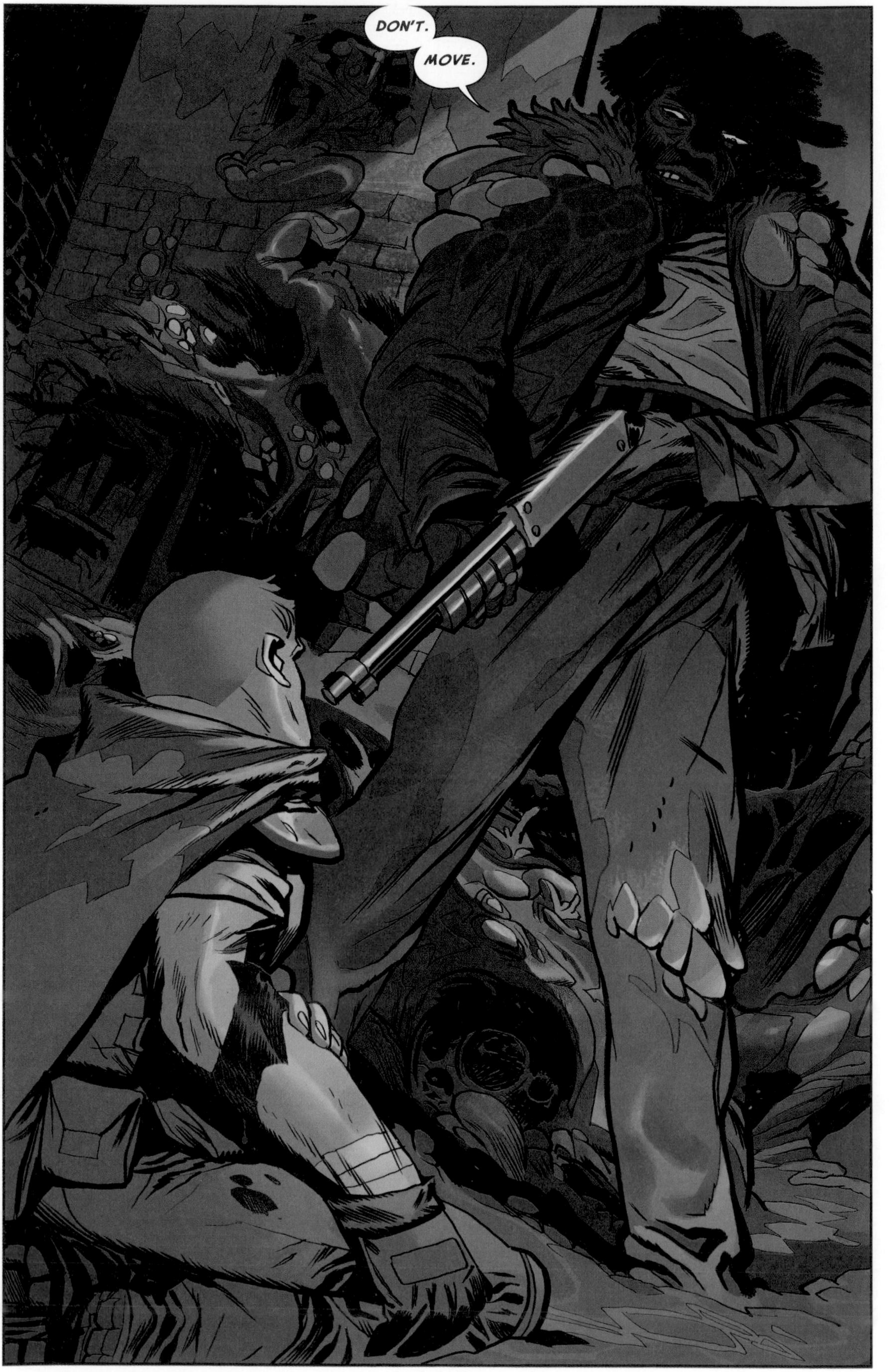
DON'T.
MOVE.

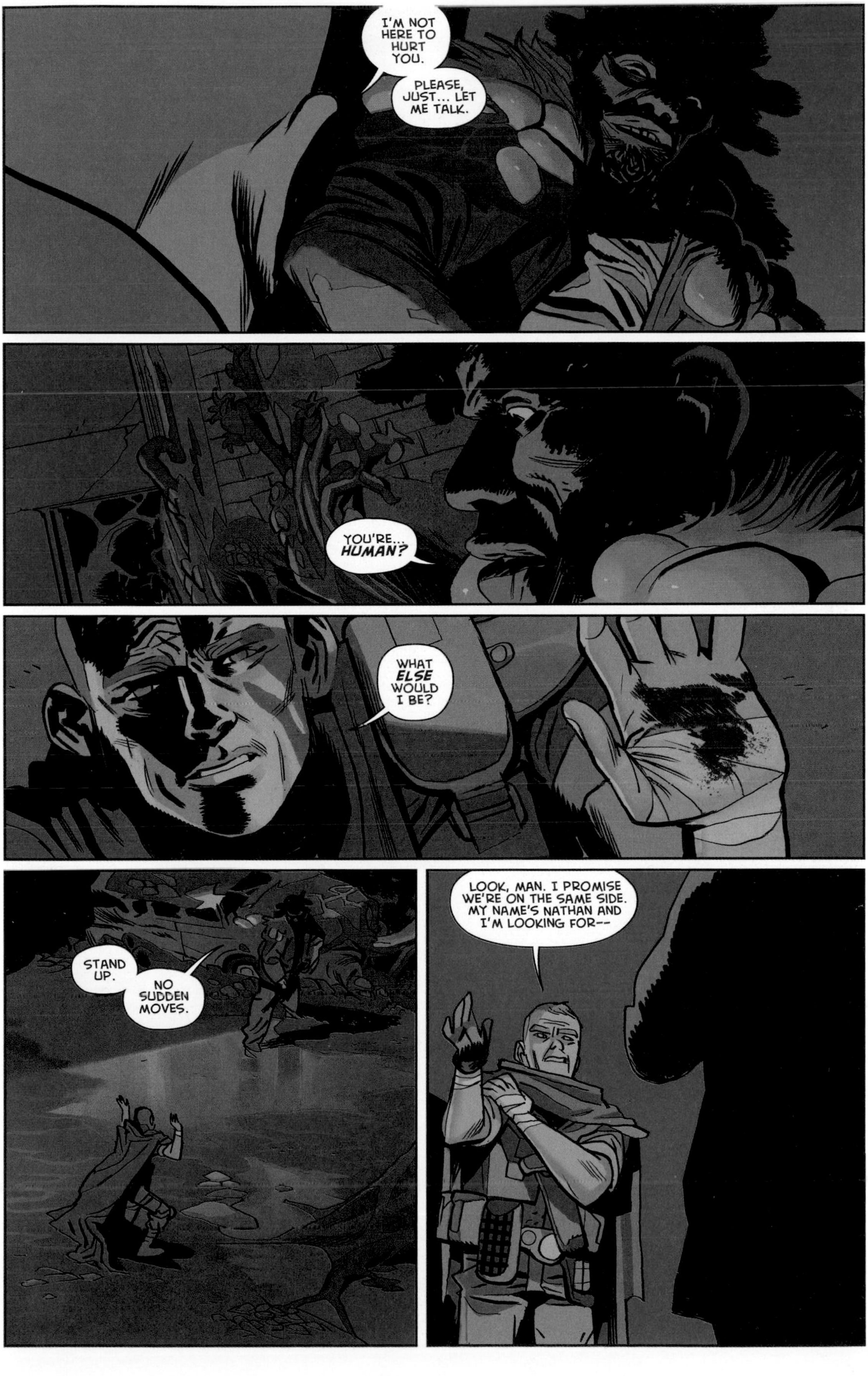
I'M NOT HERE TO HURT YOU.
PLEASE, JUST... LET ME TALK.
YOU'RE... HUMAN?
WHAT ELSE WOULD I BE?
STAND UP.
NO SUDDEN MOVES.
LOOK, MAN. I PROMISE WE'RE ON THE SAME SIDE. MY NAME'S NATHAN AND I'M LOOKING FOR--

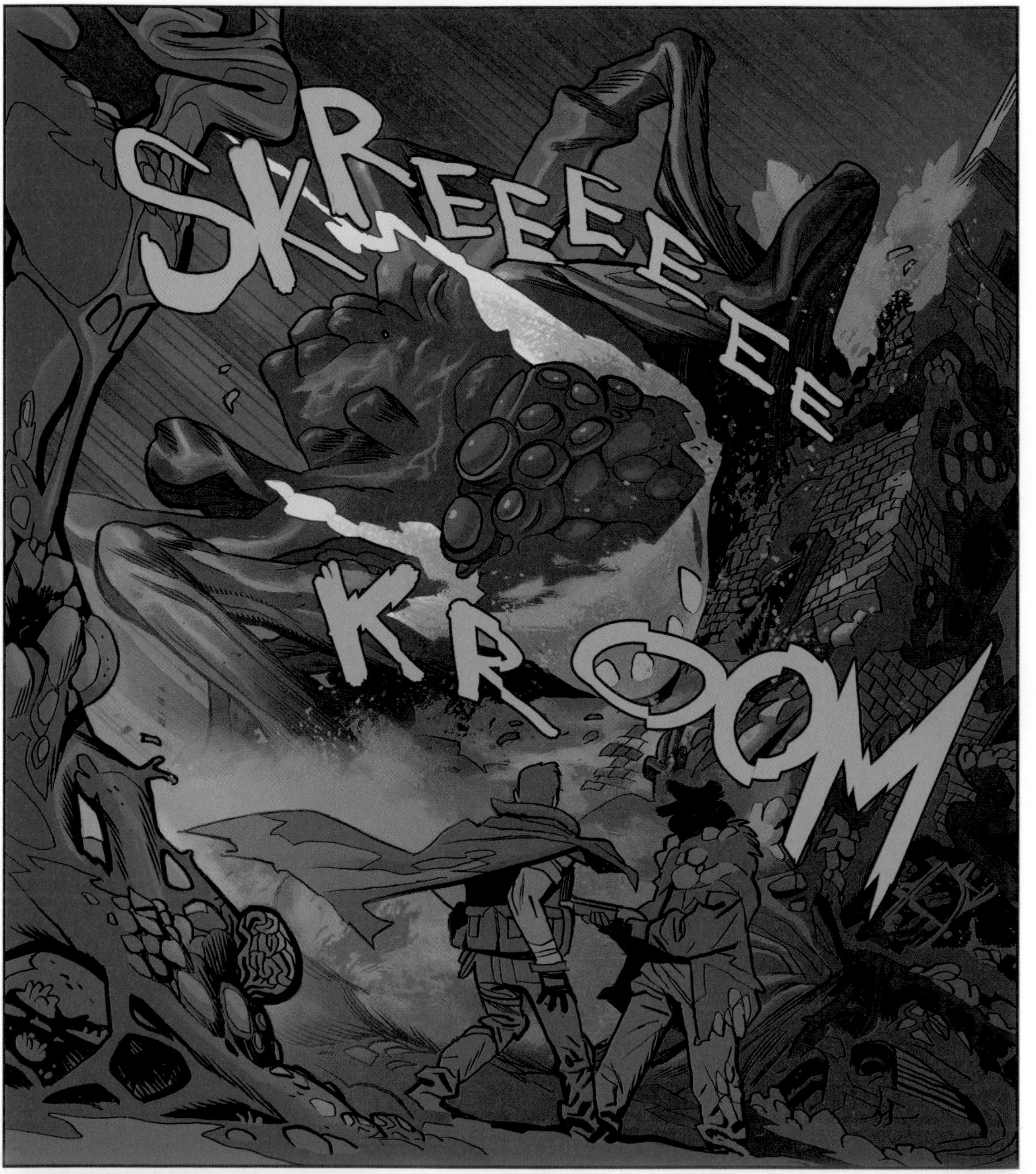
SKREEEEEE
KROOOM
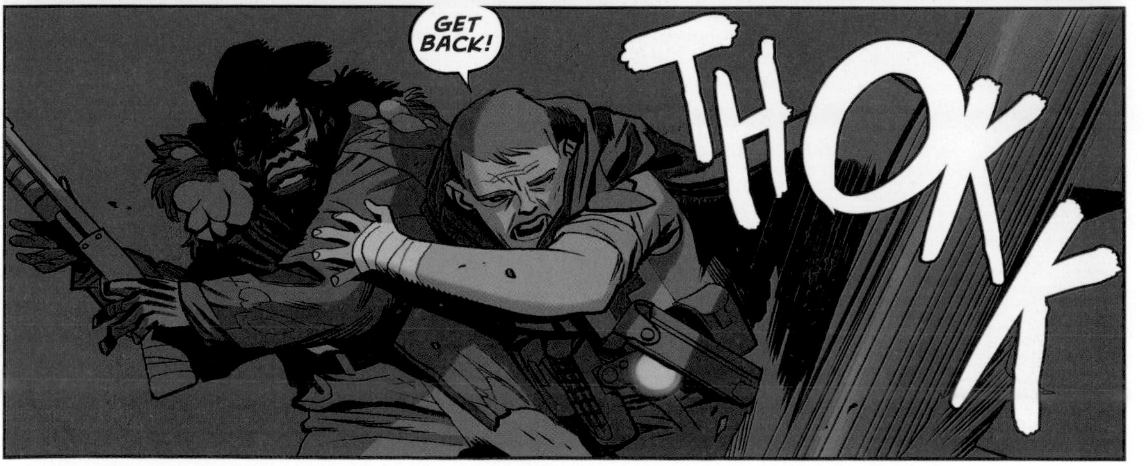
GET BACK!
THOKK

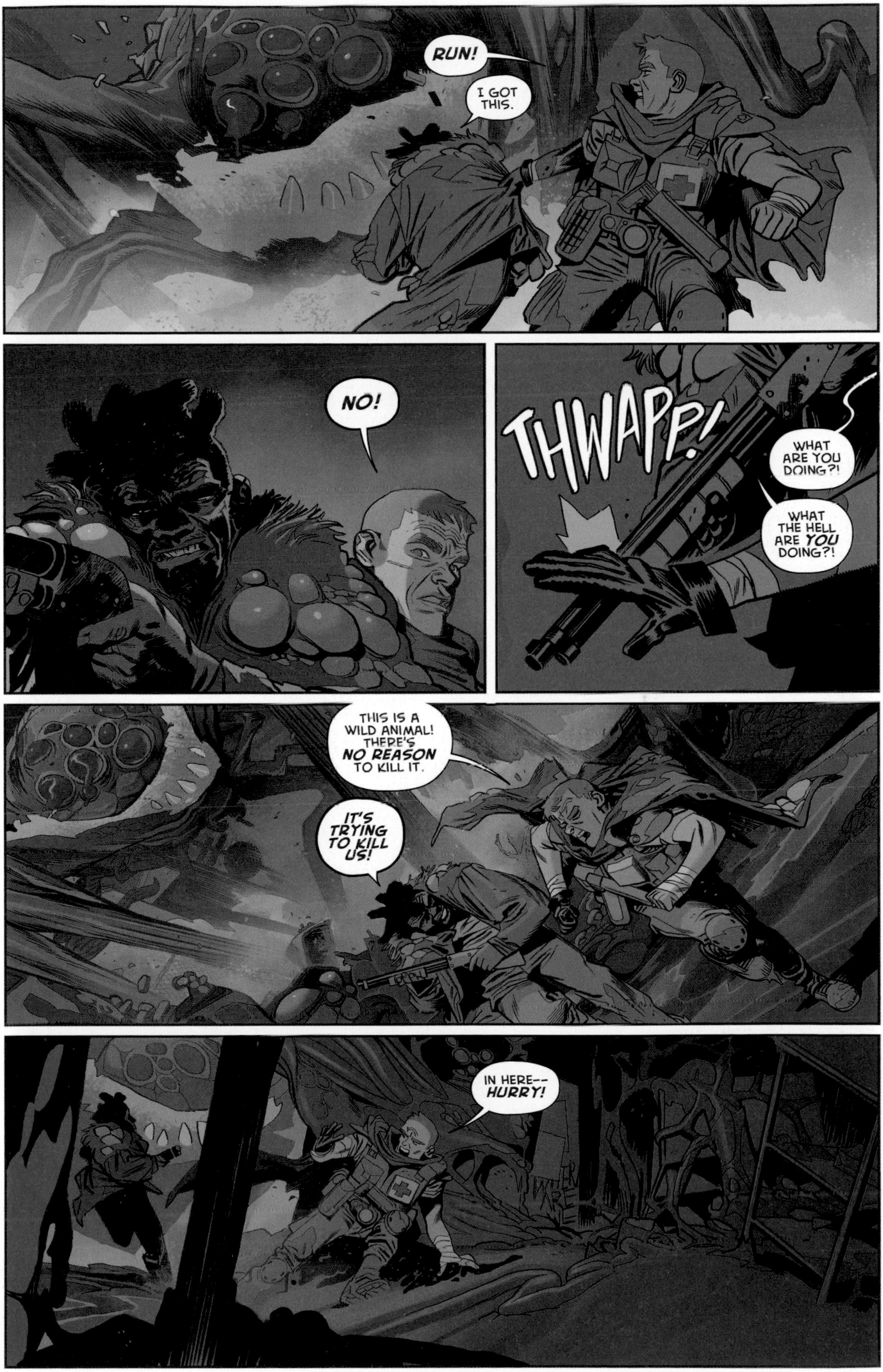
RUN!
I GOT THIS.
NO!
THWAPP!
WHAT ARE YOU DOING?!
WHAT THE HELL ARE YOU DOING?!
THIS IS A WILD ANIMAL! THERE'S NO REASON TO KILL IT.
IT'S TRYING TO KILL US!
IN HERE-- HURRY!

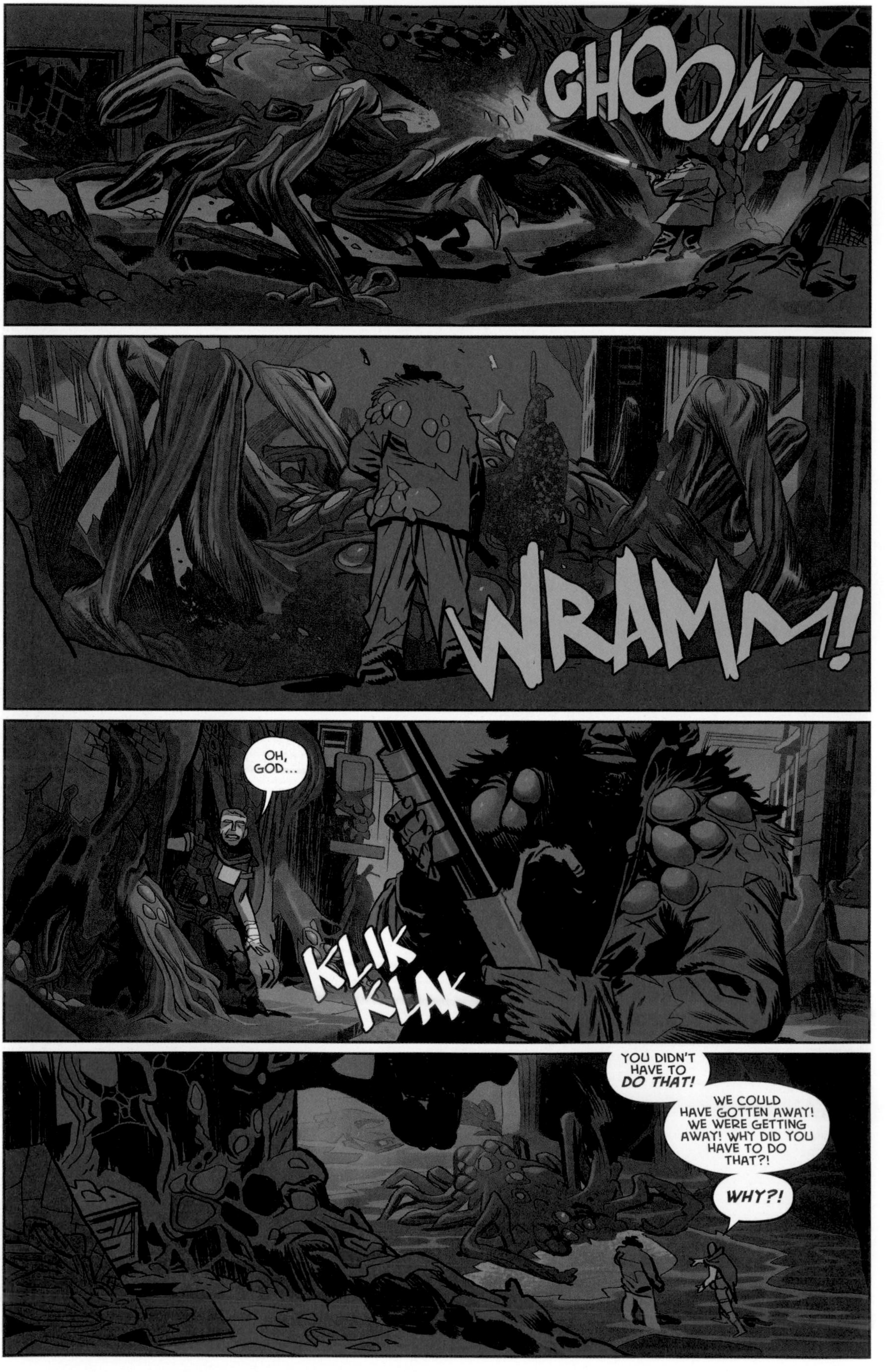
GHOOM!
WRAMM!
OH, GOD...
KLIK KLAK
YOU DIDN'T HAVE TO DO THAT!
WE COULD HAVE GOTTEN AWAY! WE WERE GETTING AWAY! WHY DID YOU HAVE TO DO THAT?!
WHY?!

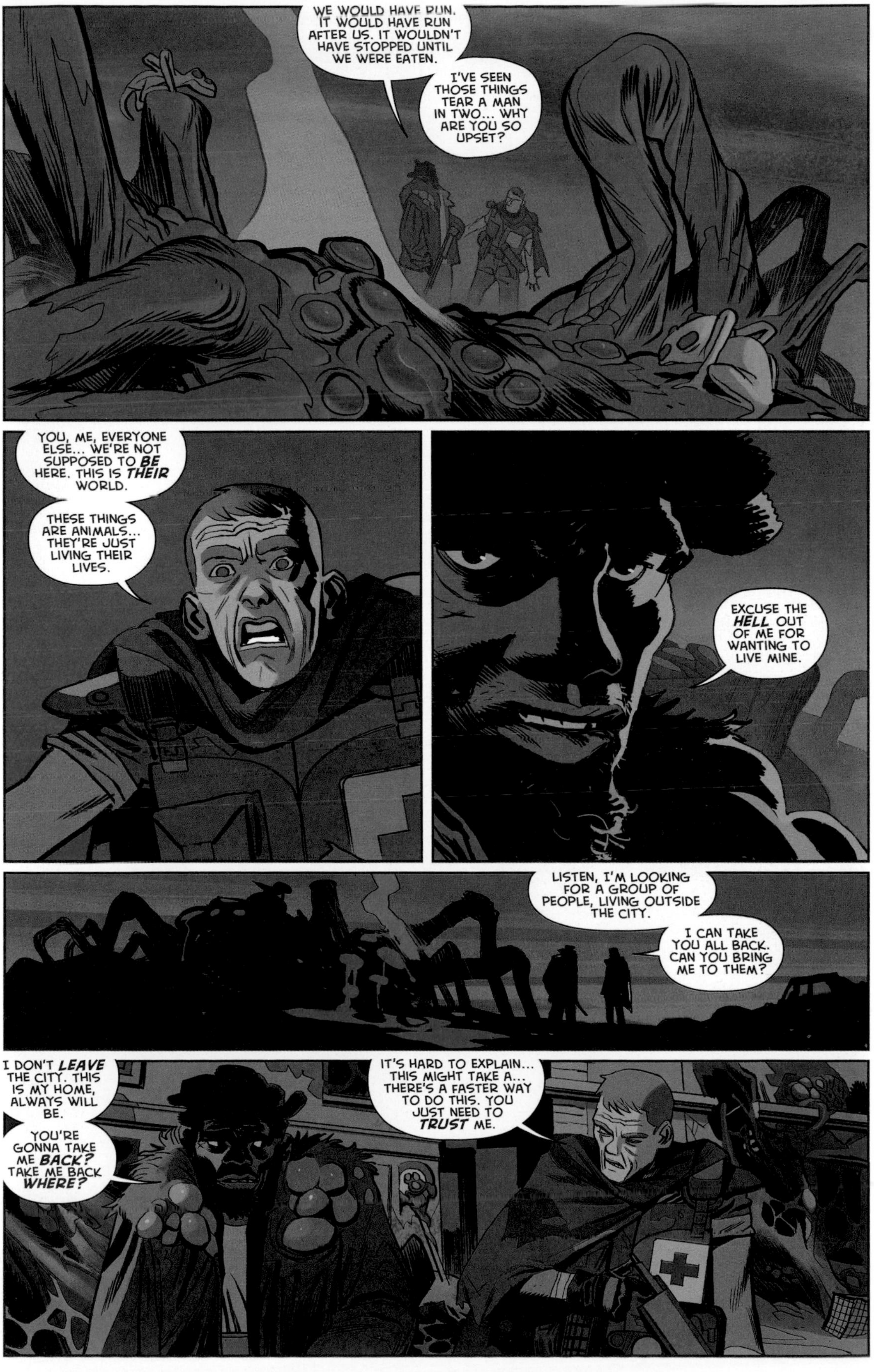

WE WOULD HAVE RUN. IT WOULD HAVE RUN AFTER US. IT WOULDN'T HAVE STOPPED UNTIL WE WERE EATEN.
I'VE SEEN THOSE THINGS TEAR A MAN IN TWO... WHY ARE YOU SO UPSET?
YOU, ME, EVERYONE ELSE... WE'RE NOT SUPPOSED TO BE HERE. THIS IS THEIR WORLD.
THESE THINGS ARE ANIMALS... THEY'RE JUST LIVING THEIR LIVES.
EXCUSE THE HELL OUT OF ME FOR WANTING TO LIVE MINE.
LISTEN, I'M LOOKING FOR A GROUP OF PEOPLE, LIVING OUTSIDE THE CITY.
I CAN TAKE YOU ALL BACK. CAN YOU BRING ME TO THEM?
I DON'T LEAVE THE CITY. THIS IS MY HOME, ALWAYS WILL BE.
YOU'RE GONNA TAKE ME BACK? TAKE ME BACK WHERE?
IT'S HARD TO EXPLAIN... THIS MIGHT TAKE A... THERE'S A FASTER WAY TO DO THIS. YOU JUST NEED TO TRUST ME.

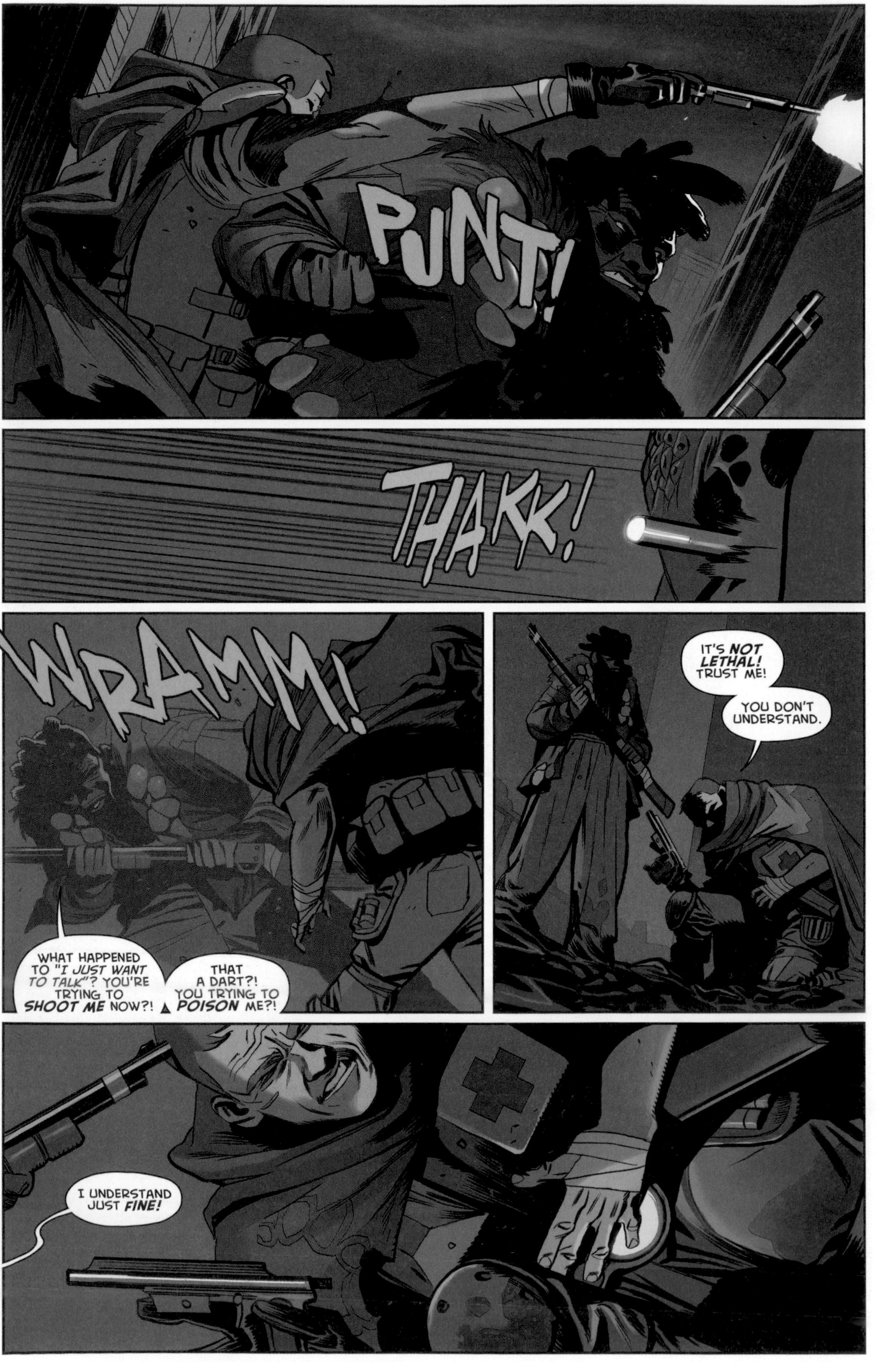

PUNT!
THAKK!
WRAMM!
WHAT HAPPENED TO "*I JUST WANT TO TALK*"? YOU'RE TRYING TO ***SHOOT ME*** NOW?!
THAT A DART?! YOU TRYING TO ***POISON*** ME?!
IT'S ***NOT LETHAL!*** TRUST ME!
YOU DON'T UNDERSTAND.
I UNDERSTAND JUST ***FINE!***

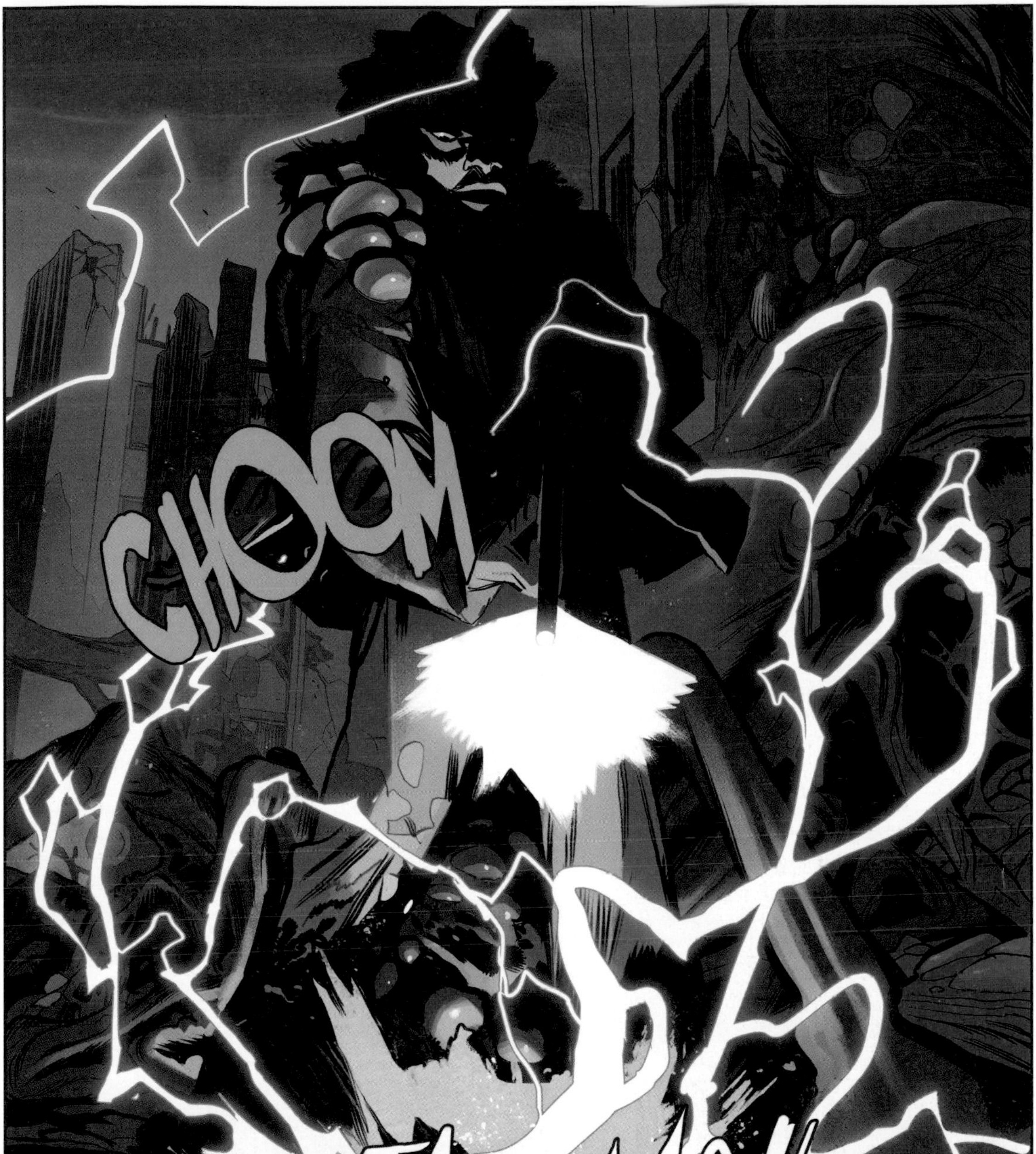
CHOOM
FA-FAASH

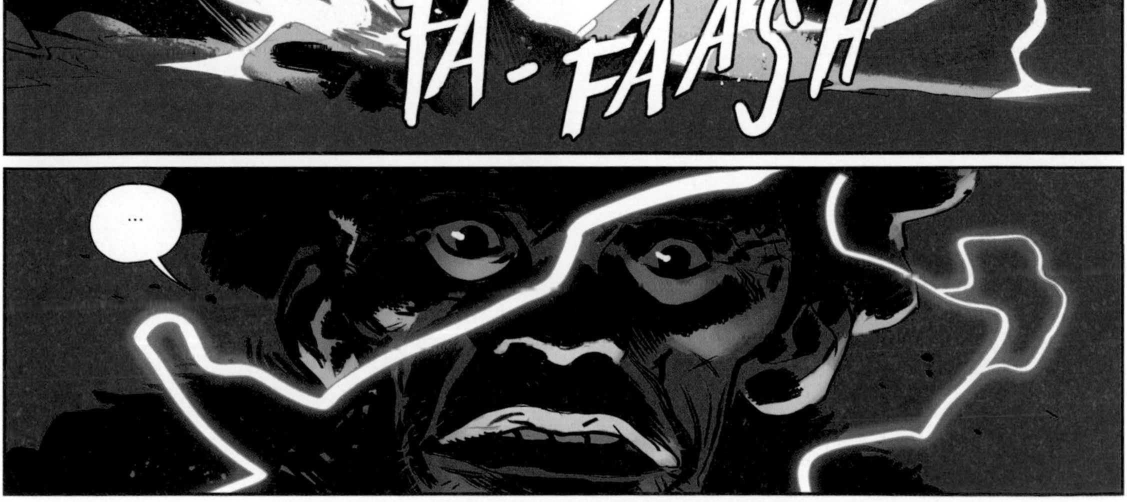
...

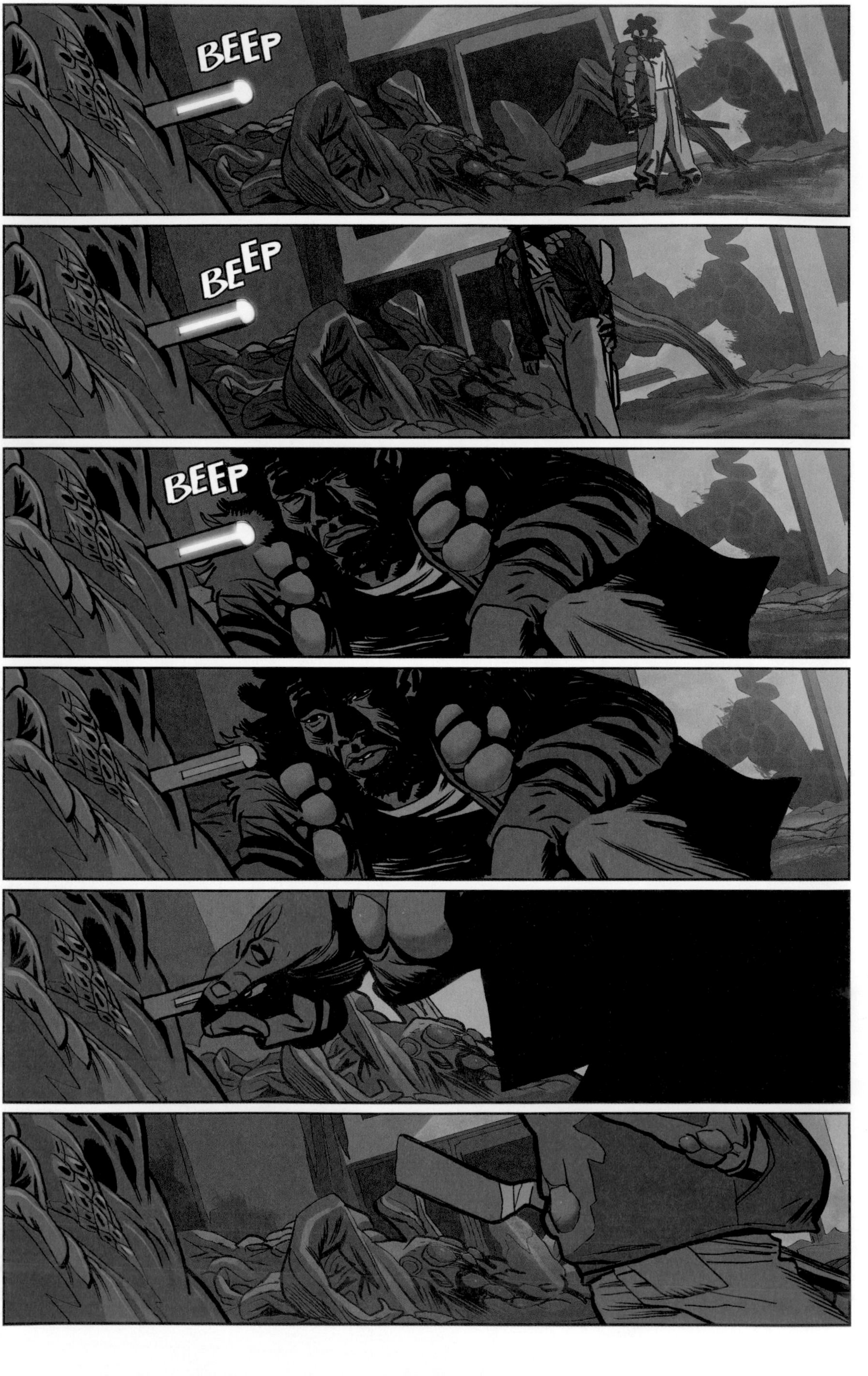
BEEP
BEEP
BEEP

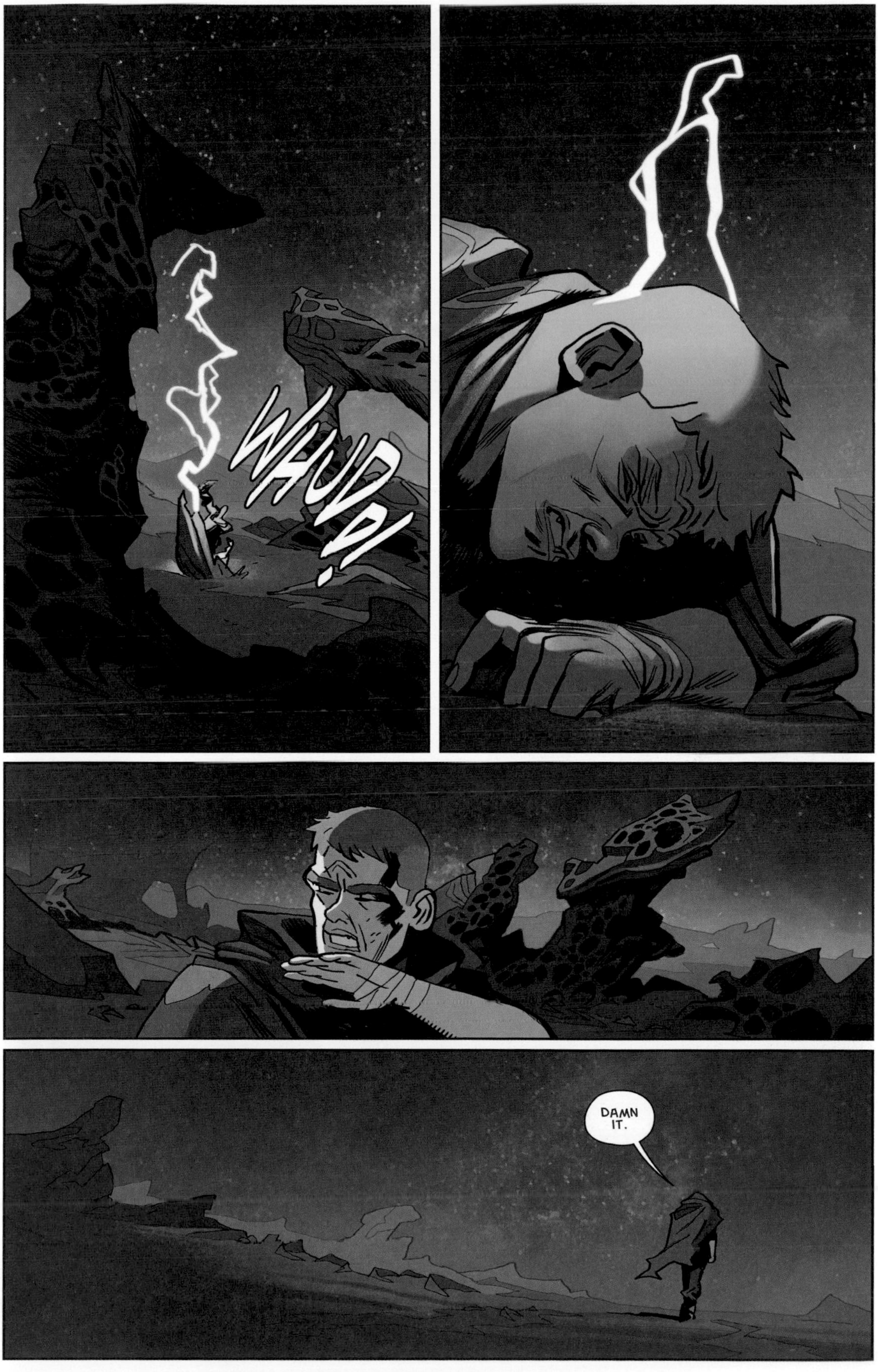
WHUDD!
DAMN IT.

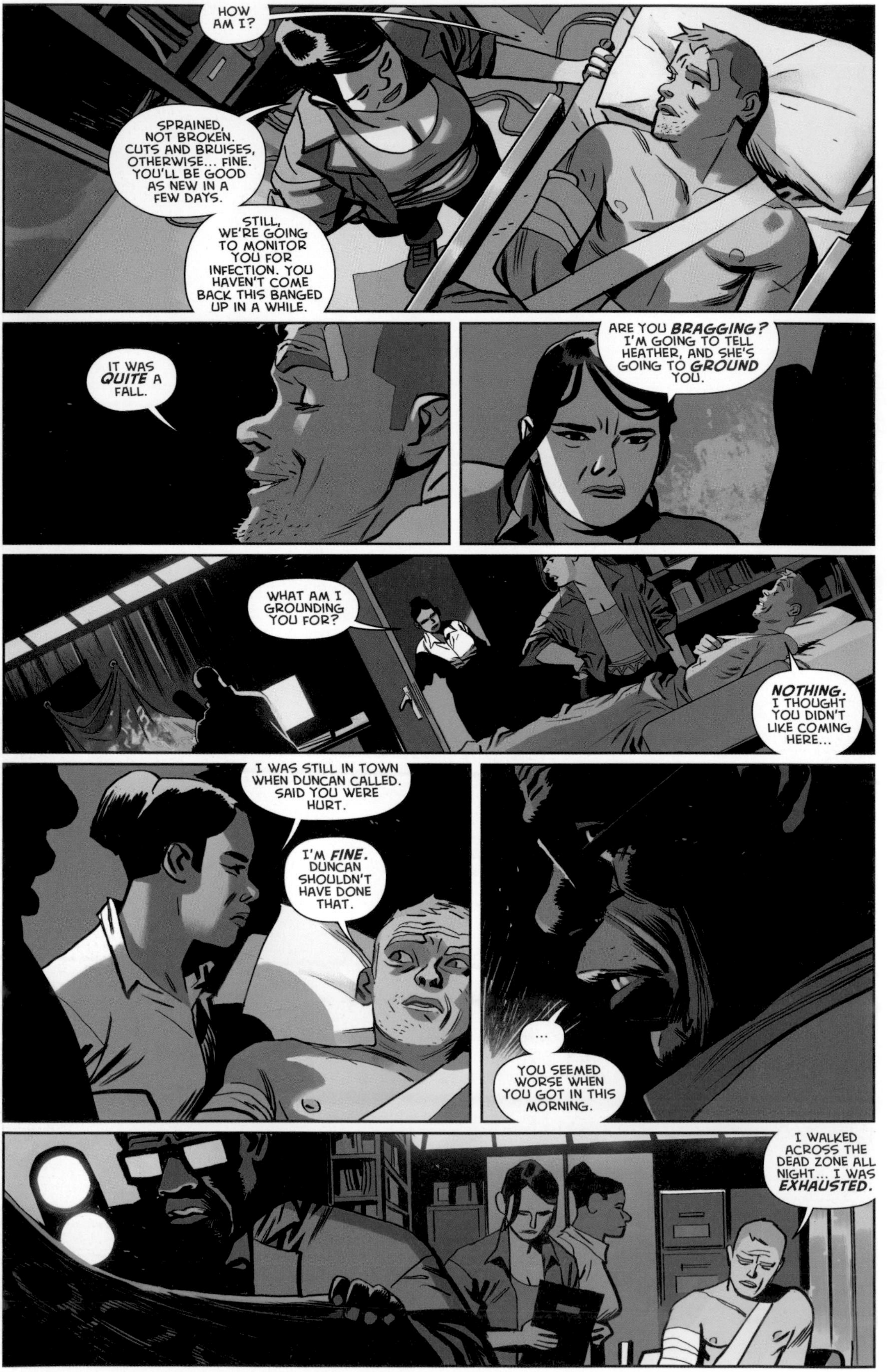
HOW AM I?
SPRAINED, NOT BROKEN. CUTS AND BRUISES, OTHERWISE... FINE. YOU'LL BE GOOD AS NEW IN A FEW DAYS.
STILL, WE'RE GOING TO MONITOR YOU FOR INFECTION. YOU HAVEN'T COME BACK THIS BANGED UP IN A WHILE.
IT WAS QUITE A FALL.
ARE YOU BRAGGING? I'M GOING TO TELL HEATHER, AND SHE'S GOING TO GROUND YOU.
WHAT AM I GROUNDING YOU FOR?
NOTHING. I THOUGHT YOU DIDN'T LIKE COMING HERE...
I WAS STILL IN TOWN WHEN DUNCAN CALLED. SAID YOU WERE HURT.
I'M FINE. DUNCAN SHOULDN'T HAVE DONE THAT.
...
YOU SEEMED WORSE WHEN YOU GOT IN THIS MORNING.
I WALKED ACROSS THE DEAD ZONE ALL NIGHT... I WAS EXHAUSTED.

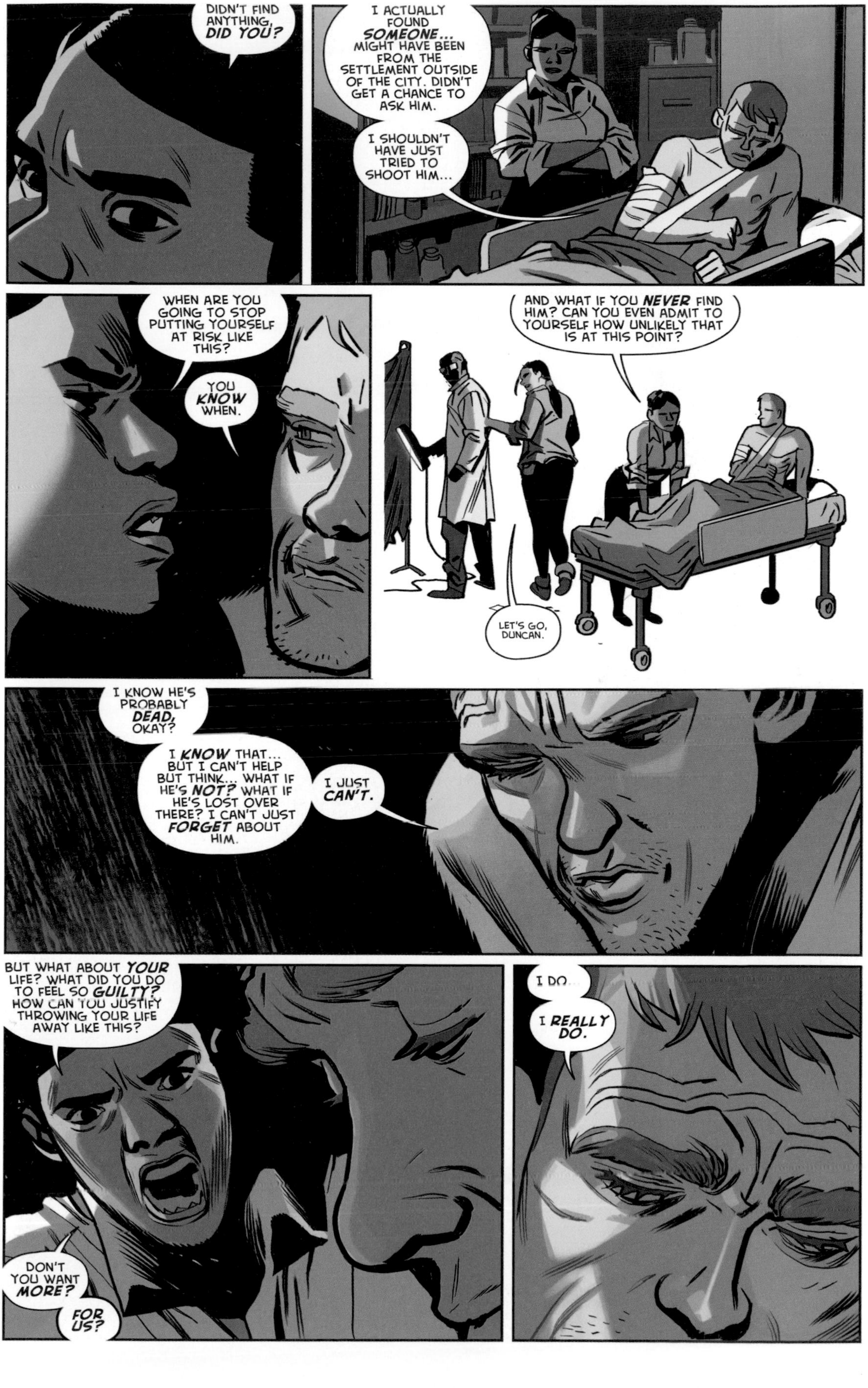
DIDN'T FIND ANYTHING, DID YOU?
I ACTUALLY FOUND SOMEONE... MIGHT HAVE BEEN FROM THE SETTLEMENT OUTSIDE OF THE CITY. DIDN'T GET A CHANCE TO ASK HIM.
I SHOULDN'T HAVE JUST TRIED TO SHOOT HIM...
WHEN ARE YOU GOING TO STOP PUTTING YOURSELF AT RISK LIKE THIS?
YOU KNOW WHEN.
AND WHAT IF YOU NEVER FIND HIM? CAN YOU EVEN ADMIT TO YOURSELF HOW UNLIKELY THAT IS AT THIS POINT?
LET'S GO, DUNCAN.
I KNOW HE'S PROBABLY DEAD, OKAY?
I KNOW THAT... BUT I CAN'T HELP BUT THINK... WHAT IF HE'S NOT? WHAT IF HE'S LOST OVER THERE? I CAN'T JUST FORGET ABOUT HIM.
I JUST CAN'T.
BUT WHAT ABOUT YOUR LIFE? WHAT DID YOU DO TO FEEL SO GUILTY? HOW CAN YOU JUSTIFY THROWING YOUR LIFE AWAY LIKE THIS?
DON'T YOU WANT MORE?
FOR US?
I DO...
I REALLY DO.

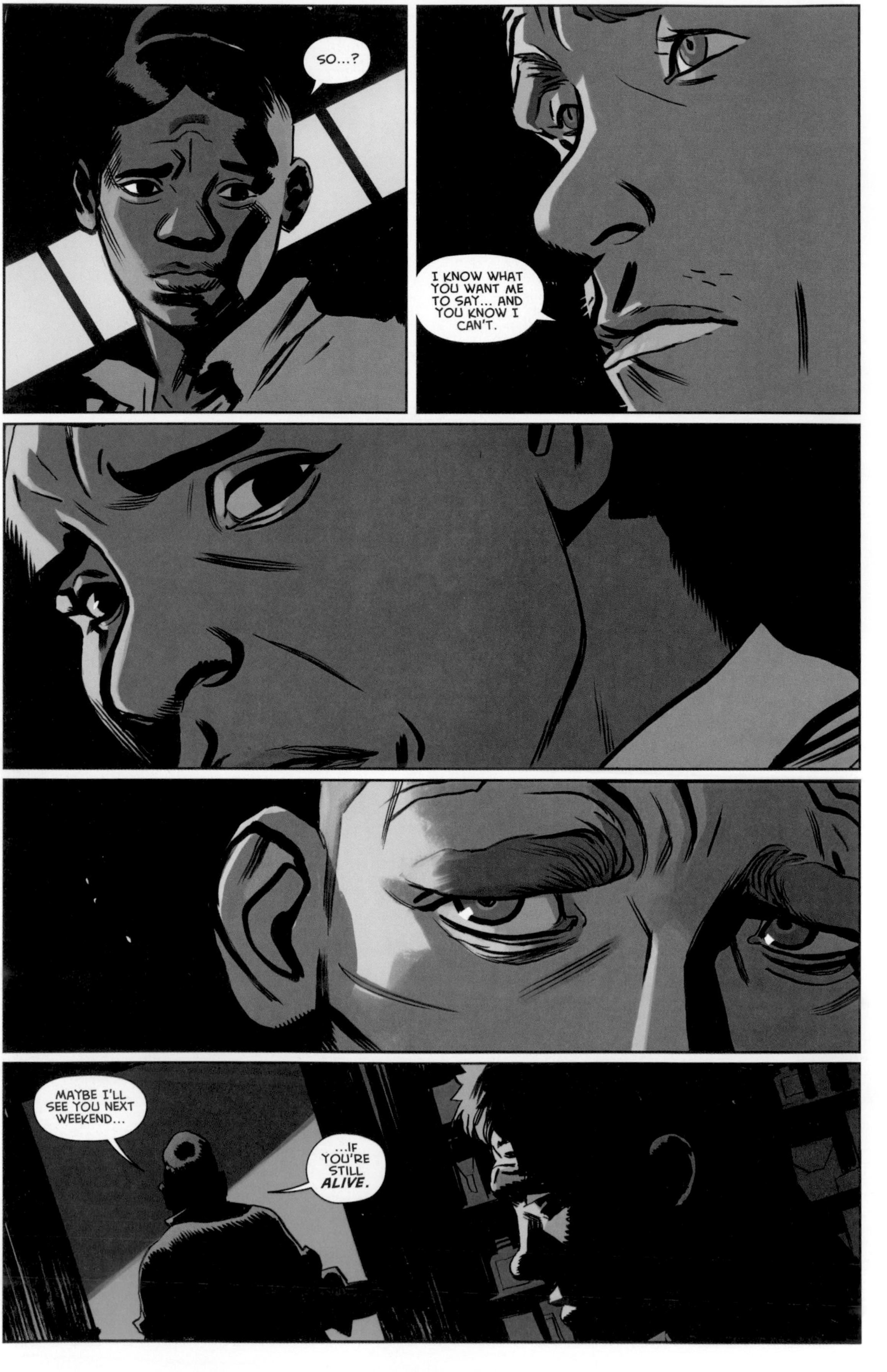
SO...?
I KNOW WHAT YOU WANT ME TO SAY... AND YOU KNOW I CAN'T.
MAYBE I'LL SEE YOU NEXT WEEKEND...
...IF YOU'RE STILL ***ALIVE***.

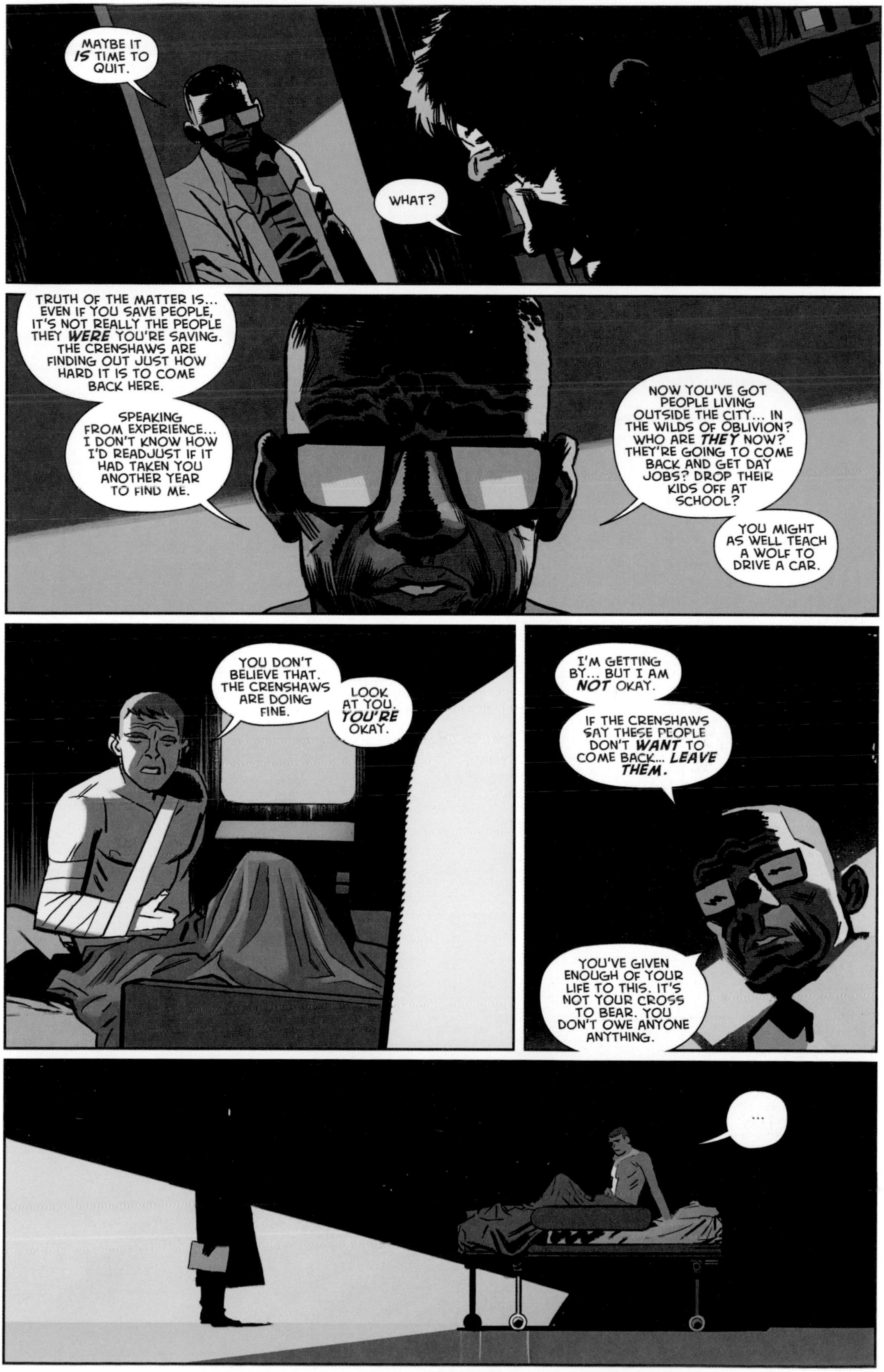
MAYBE IT *IS* TIME TO QUIT.
WHAT?
TRUTH OF THE MATTER IS... EVEN IF YOU SAVE PEOPLE, IT'S NOT REALLY THE PEOPLE THEY *WERE* YOU'RE SAVING. THE CRENSHAWS ARE FINDING OUT JUST HOW HARD IT IS TO COME BACK HERE.
SPEAKING FROM EXPERIENCE... I DON'T KNOW HOW I'D READJUST IF IT HAD TAKEN YOU ANOTHER YEAR TO FIND ME.
NOW YOU'VE GOT PEOPLE LIVING OUTSIDE THE CITY... IN THE WILDS OF OBLIVION? WHO ARE *THEY* NOW? THEY'RE GOING TO COME BACK AND GET DAY JOBS? DROP THEIR KIDS OFF AT SCHOOL?
YOU MIGHT AS WELL TEACH A WOLF TO DRIVE A CAR.
YOU DON'T BELIEVE THAT. THE CRENSHAWS ARE DOING FINE.
LOOK AT YOU. *YOU'RE* OKAY.
I'M GETTING BY... BUT I AM *NOT* OKAY.
IF THE CRENSHAWS SAY THESE PEOPLE DON'T *WANT* TO COME BACK... *LEAVE THEM.*
YOU'VE GIVEN ENOUGH OF YOUR LIFE TO THIS. IT'S NOT YOUR CROSS TO BEAR. YOU DON'T OWE ANYONE ANYTHING.
...

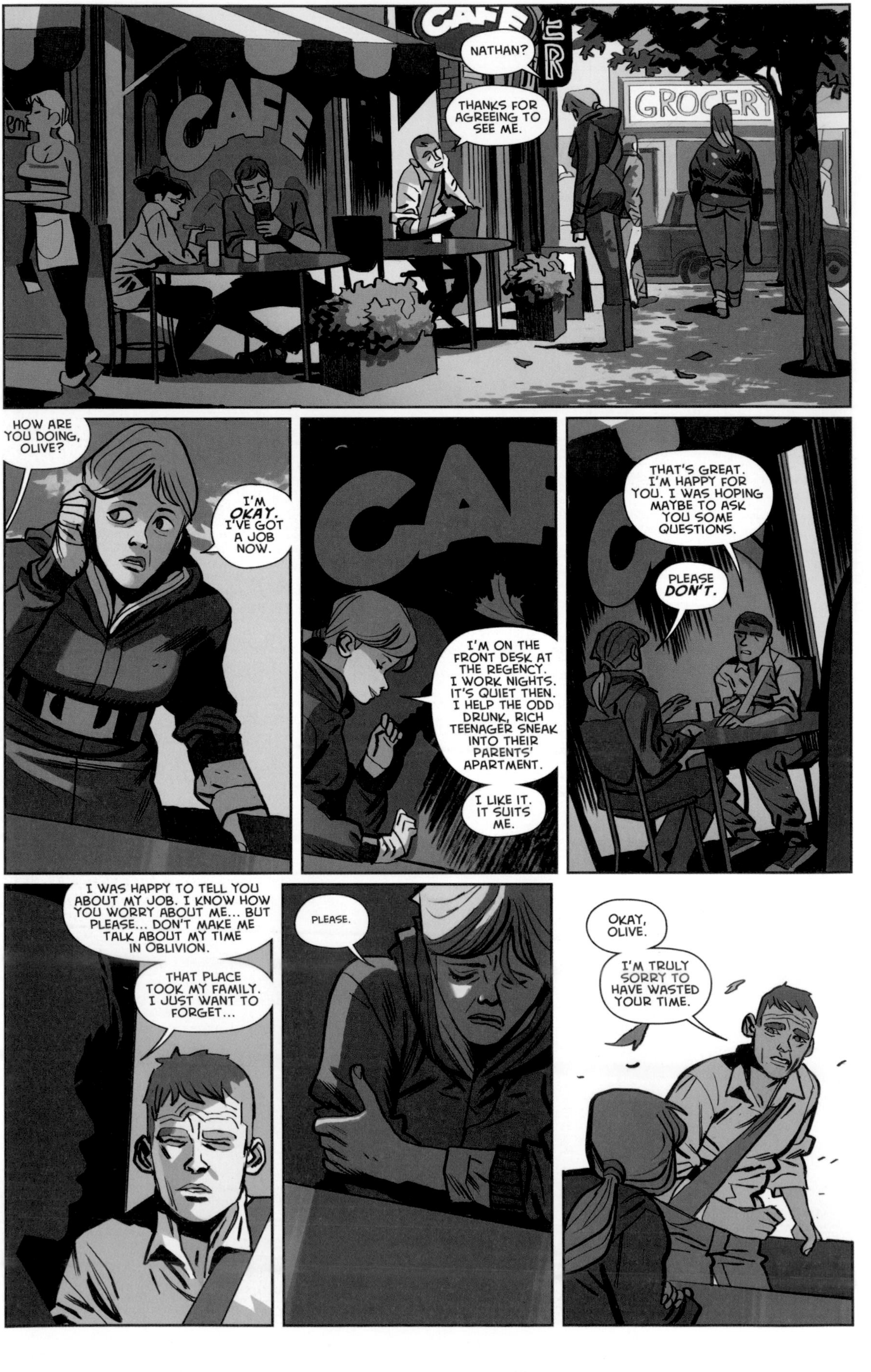
CAFE
NATHAN?
THANKS FOR AGREEING TO SEE ME.
CAFE
GROCERY
HOW ARE YOU DOING, OLIVE?
I'M *OKAY*. I'VE GOT A JOB NOW.
I'M ON THE FRONT DESK AT THE REGENCY. I WORK NIGHTS. IT'S QUIET THEN. I HELP THE ODD DRUNK, RICH TEENAGER SNEAK INTO THEIR PARENTS' APARTMENT.
I LIKE IT. IT SUITS ME.
THAT'S GREAT. I'M HAPPY FOR YOU. I WAS HOPING MAYBE TO ASK YOU SOME QUESTIONS.
PLEASE *DON'T*.
I WAS HAPPY TO TELL YOU ABOUT MY JOB. I KNOW HOW YOU WORRY ABOUT ME... BUT PLEASE... DON'T MAKE ME TALK ABOUT MY TIME IN OBLIVION.
THAT PLACE TOOK MY FAMILY. I JUST WANT TO FORGET...
PLEASE.
OKAY, OLIVE.
I'M TRULY SORRY TO HAVE WASTED YOUR TIME.

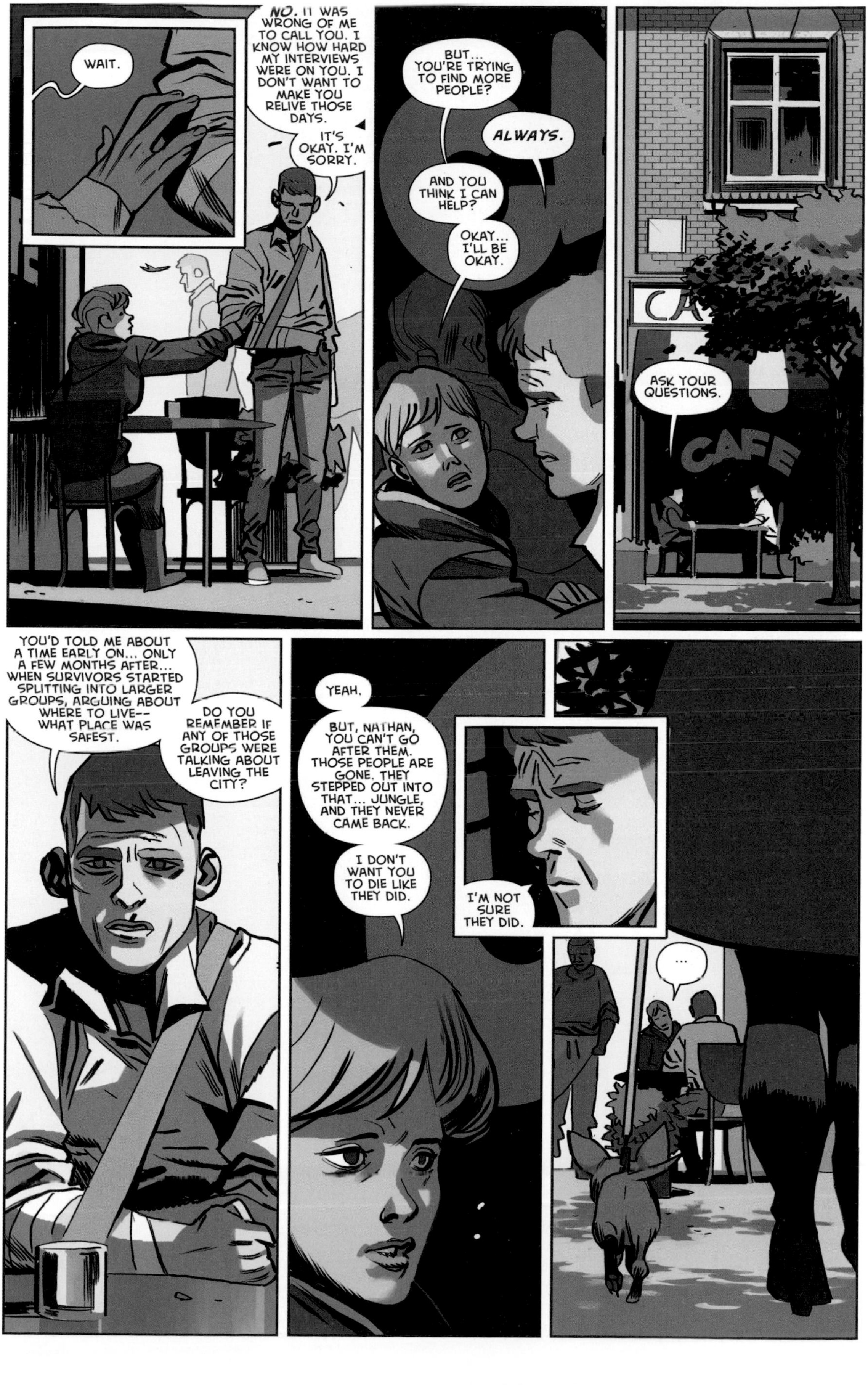
WAIT.
NO. IT WAS WRONG OF ME TO CALL YOU. I KNOW HOW HARD MY INTERVIEWS WERE ON YOU. I DON'T WANT TO MAKE YOU RELIVE THOSE DAYS.
IT'S OKAY. I'M SORRY.
BUT... YOU'RE TRYING TO FIND MORE PEOPLE?
ALWAYS.
AND YOU THINK I CAN HELP?
OKAY... I'LL BE OKAY.
CA
ASK YOUR QUESTIONS.
CAFE
YOU'D TOLD ME ABOUT A TIME EARLY ON... ONLY A FEW MONTHS AFTER... WHEN SURVIVORS STARTED SPLITTING INTO LARGER GROUPS, ARGUING ABOUT WHERE TO LIVE-- WHAT PLACE WAS SAFEST.
DO YOU REMEMBER IF ANY OF THOSE GROUPS WERE TALKING ABOUT LEAVING THE CITY?
YEAH.
BUT, NATHAN, YOU CAN'T GO AFTER THEM. THOSE PEOPLE ARE GONE. THEY STEPPED OUT INTO THAT... JUNGLE, AND THEY NEVER CAME BACK.
I DON'T WANT YOU TO DIE LIKE THEY DID.
I'M NOT SURE THEY DID.
...

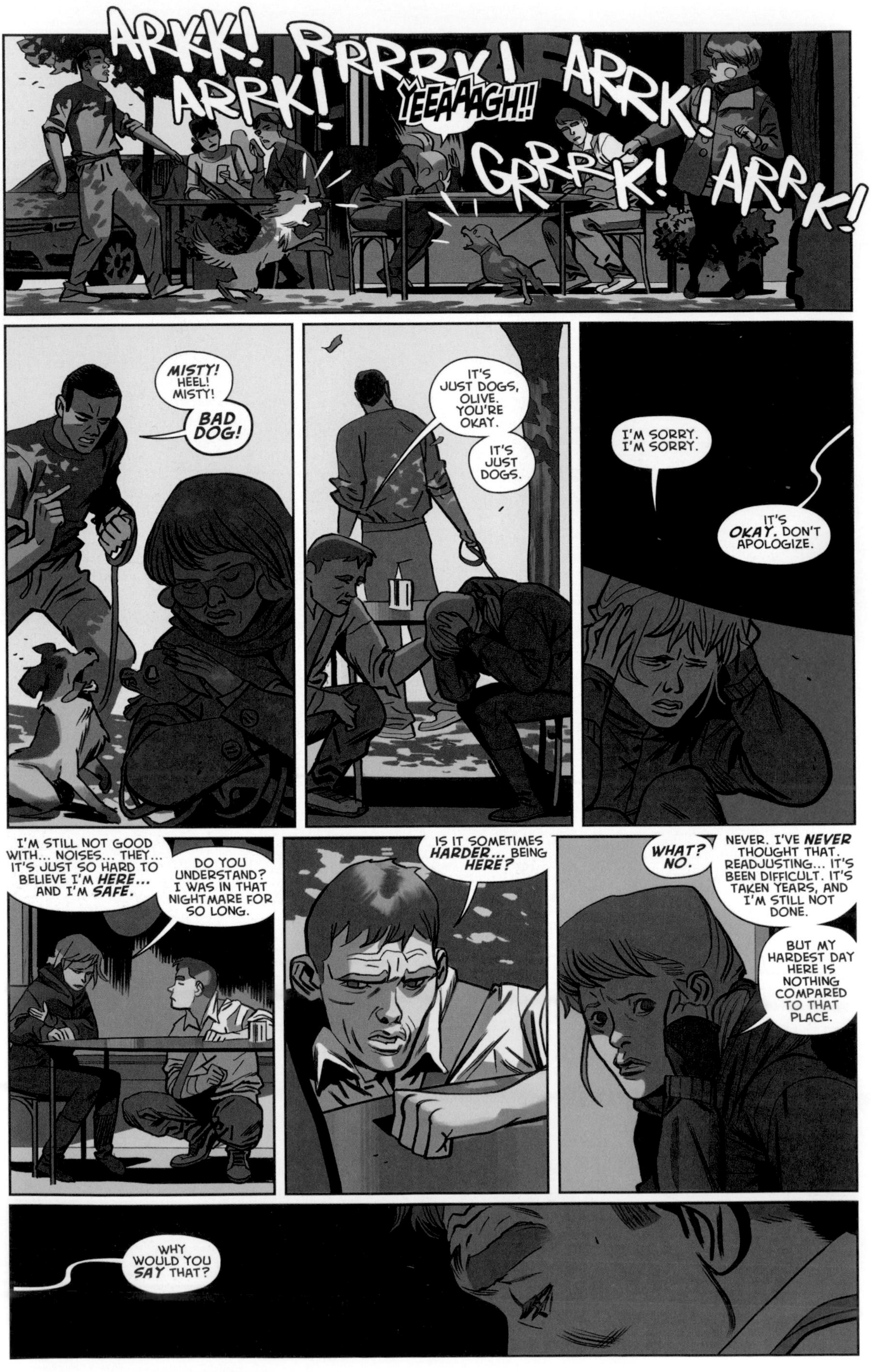

ARKK! RRRRRK! ARRK! ARRK!
YEEAAAGH!!
GRRRK! ARRK!
MISTY! HEEL! MISTY!
BAD DOG!
IT'S JUST DOGS, OLIVE. YOU'RE OKAY.
IT'S JUST DOGS.
I'M SORRY. I'M SORRY.
IT'S OKAY. DON'T APOLOGIZE.
I'M STILL NOT GOOD WITH... NOISES... THEY... IT'S JUST SO HARD TO BELIEVE I'M HERE... AND I'M SAFE.
DO YOU UNDERSTAND? I WAS IN THAT NIGHTMARE FOR SO LONG.
IS IT SOMETIMES HARDER... BEING HERE?
WHAT? NO.
NEVER. I'VE NEVER THOUGHT THAT. READJUSTING... IT'S BEEN DIFFICULT. IT'S TAKEN YEARS, AND I'M STILL NOT DONE.
BUT MY HARDEST DAY HERE IS NOTHING COMPARED TO THAT PLACE.
WHY WOULD YOU SAY THAT?

-ːSIGH.ː-

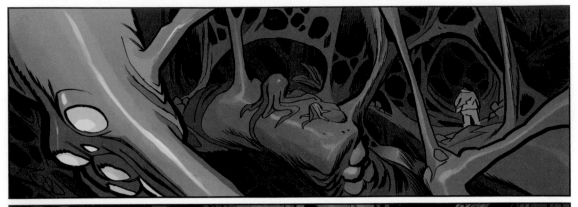

SNERRRRRLLLL

REARRRRRRR!

WRAKK

GRRWGLLL

=NNGH!=

PKROW PKROW PKROW

SKREEEEEE

WHUMP

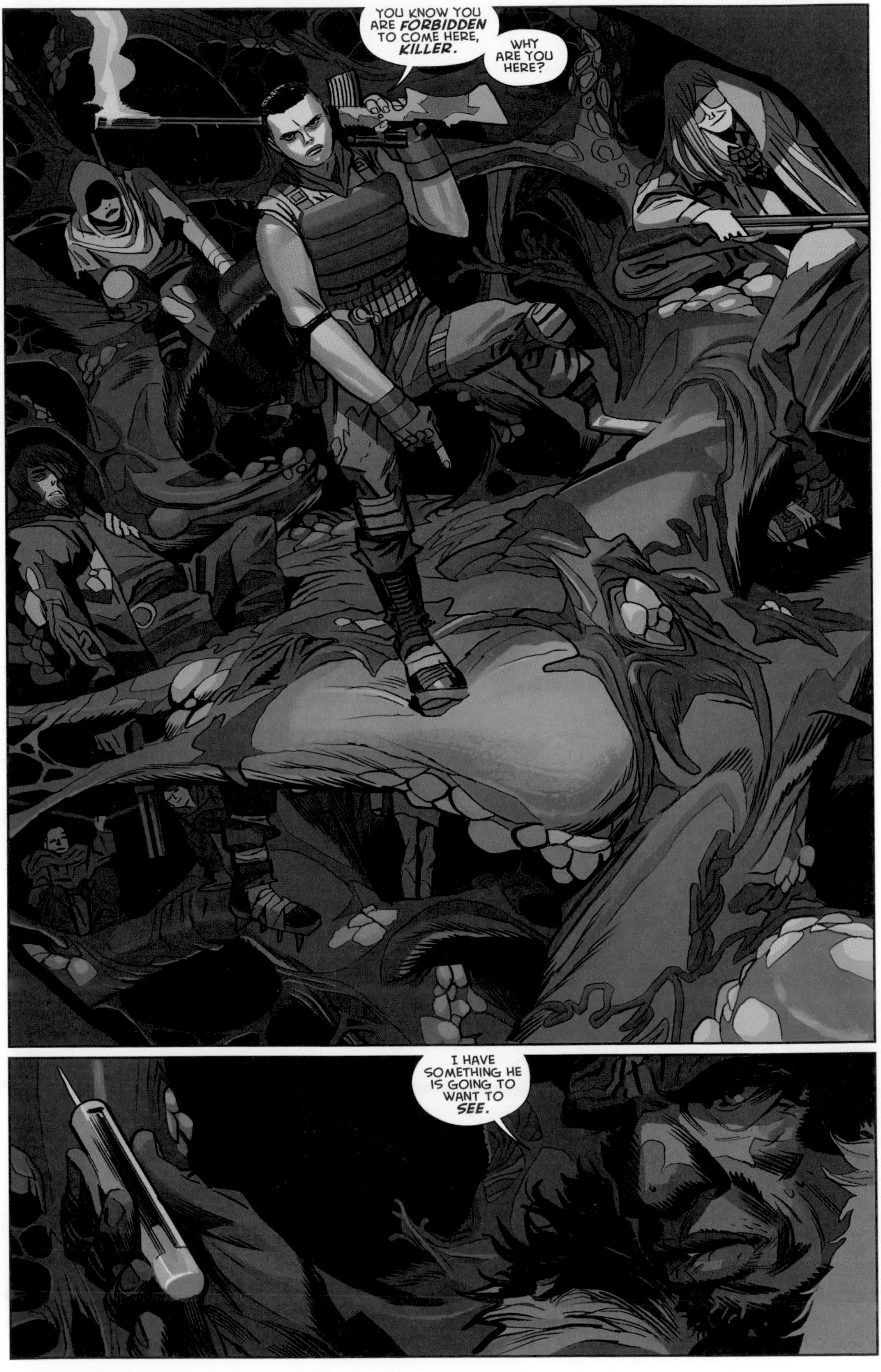
YOU KNOW YOU ARE FORBIDDEN TO COME HERE, KILLER.
WHY ARE YOU HERE?
I HAVE SOMETHING HE IS GOING TO WANT TO SEE.

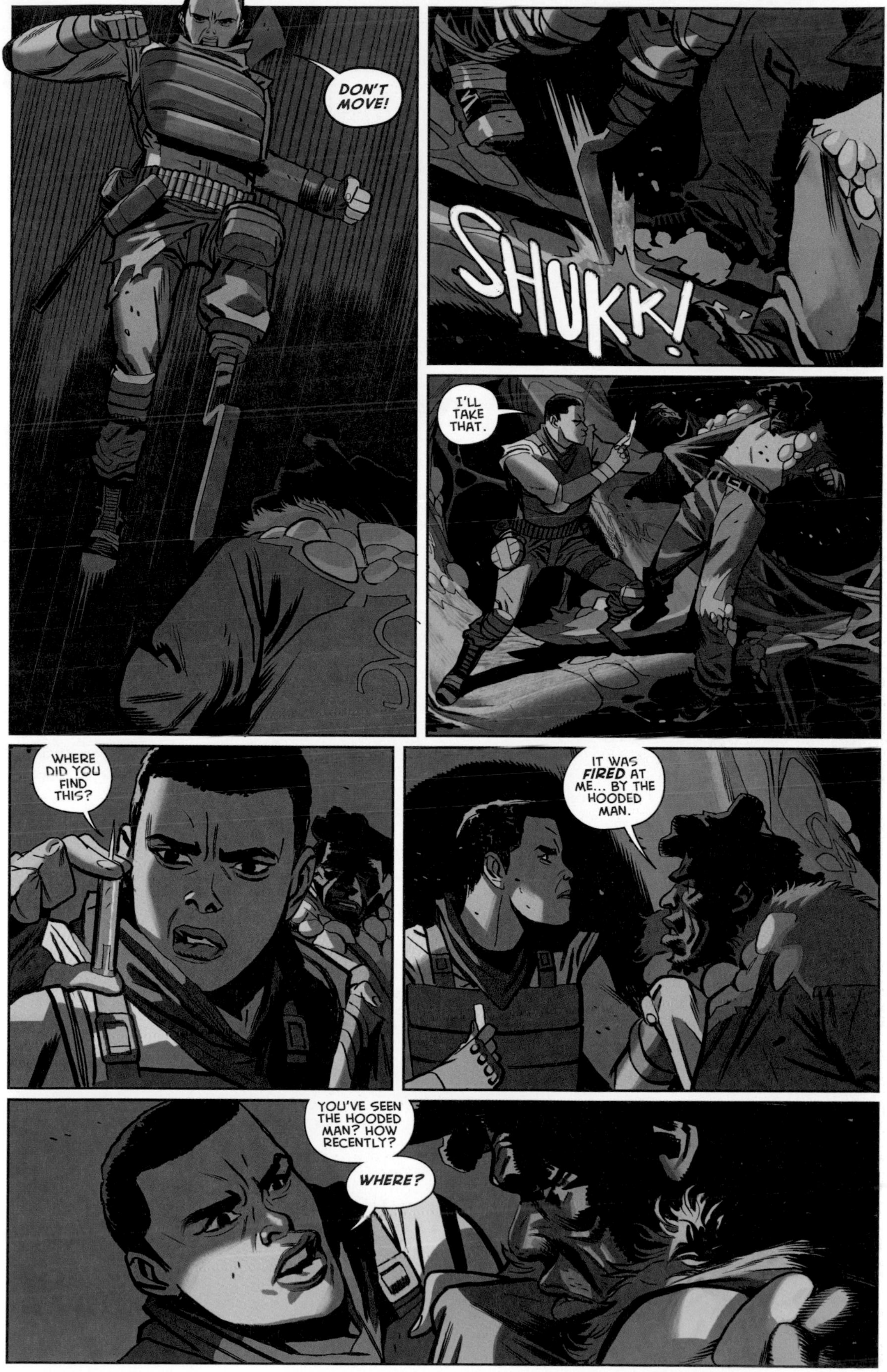
DON'T MOVE!
SHUKK!
I'LL TAKE THAT.
WHERE DID YOU FIND THIS?
IT WAS FIRED AT ME... BY THE HOODED MAN.
YOU'VE SEEN THE HOODED MAN? HOW RECENTLY?
WHERE?

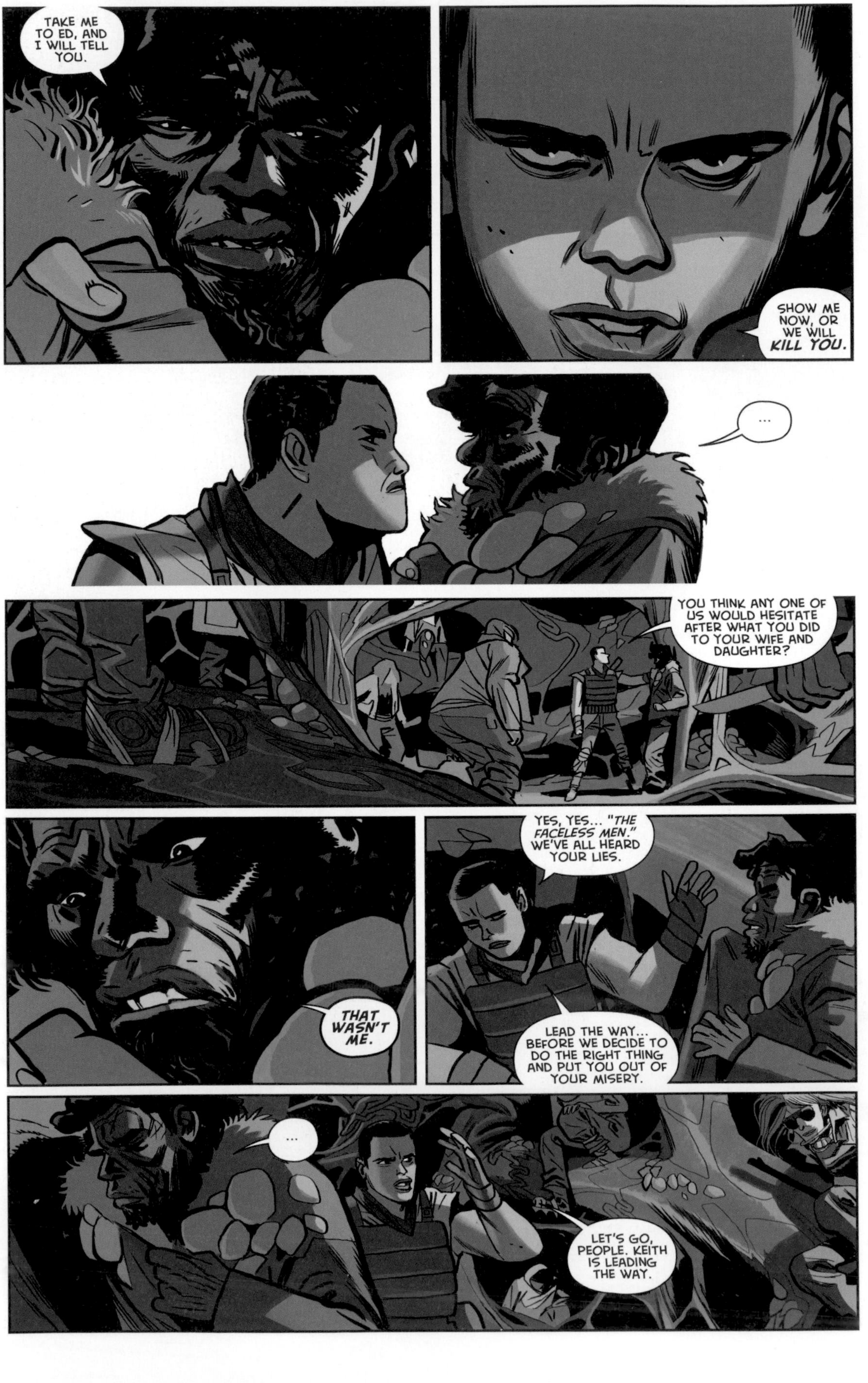
TAKE ME TO ED, AND I WILL TELL YOU.
SHOW ME NOW, OR WE WILL KILL YOU.
...
YOU THINK ANY ONE OF US WOULD HESITATE AFTER WHAT YOU DID TO YOUR WIFE AND DAUGHTER?
THAT WASN'T ME.
YES, YES... "THE FACELESS MEN." WE'VE ALL HEARD YOUR LIES.
LEAD THE WAY... BEFORE WE DECIDE TO DO THE RIGHT THING AND PUT YOU OUT OF YOUR MISERY.
...
LET'S GO, PEOPLE. KEITH IS LEADING THE WAY.

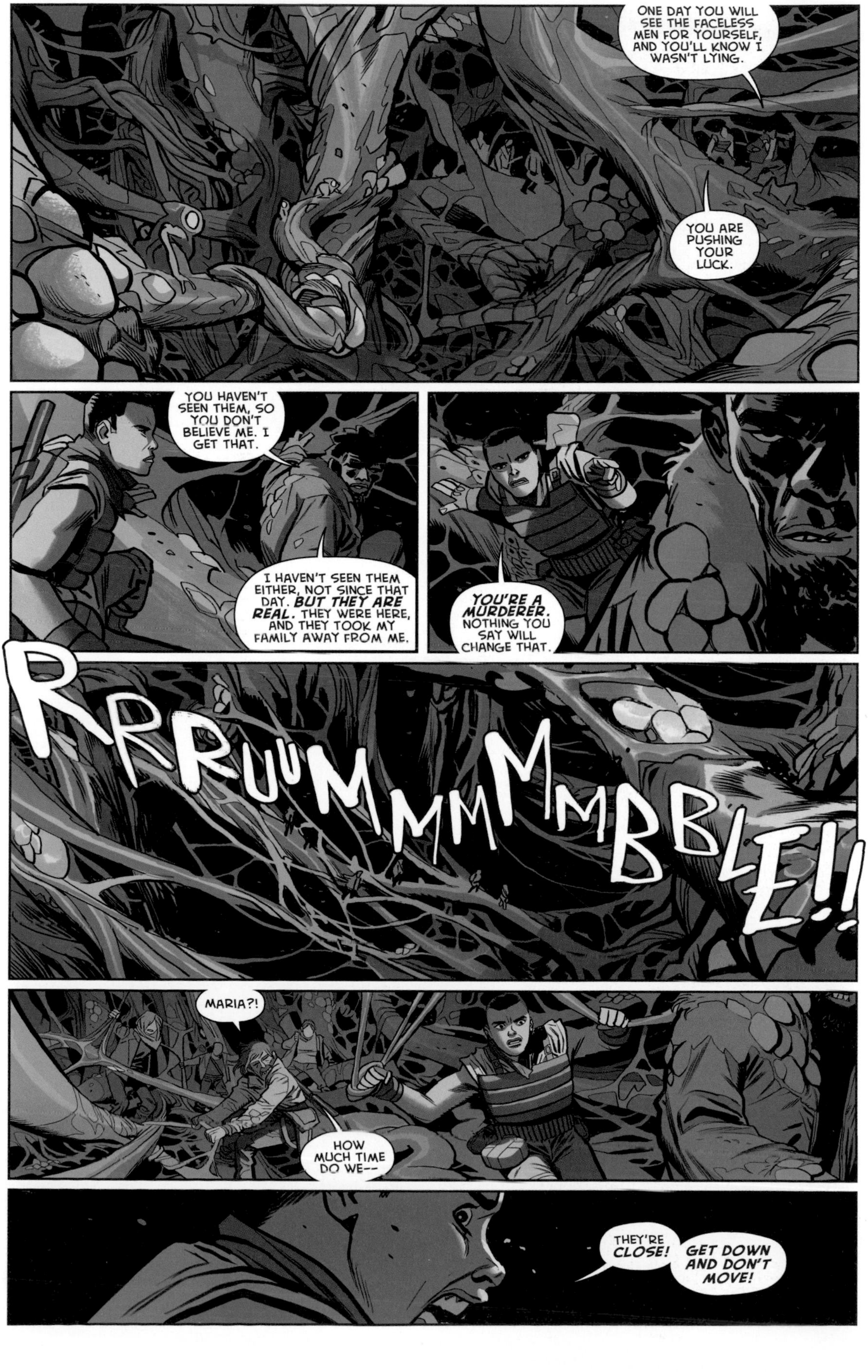
ONE DAY YOU WILL SEE THE FACELESS MEN FOR YOURSELF, AND YOU'LL KNOW I WASN'T LYING.
YOU ARE PUSHING YOUR LUCK.
YOU HAVEN'T SEEN THEM, SO YOU DON'T BELIEVE ME. I GET THAT.
I HAVEN'T SEEN THEM EITHER, NOT SINCE THAT DAY. **BUT THEY ARE REAL.** THEY WERE HERE, AND THEY TOOK MY FAMILY AWAY FROM ME.
YOU'RE A MURDERER. NOTHING YOU SAY WILL CHANGE THAT.
RRRUUMMMMMBBLE!!
MARIA?!
HOW MUCH TIME DO WE--
THEY'RE *CLOSE!*
GET DOWN AND DON'T MOVE!

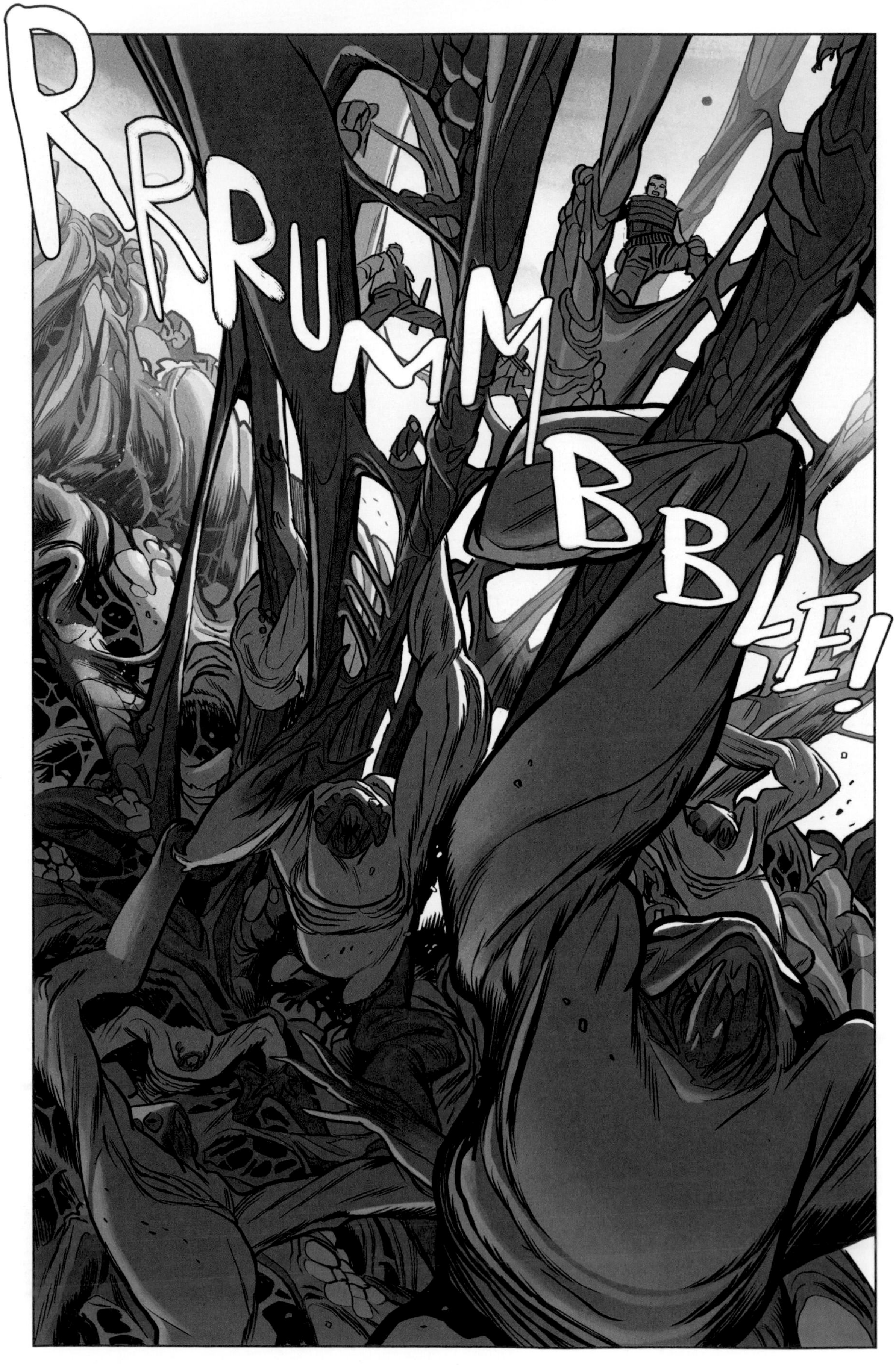
RRRUMMBBLE!

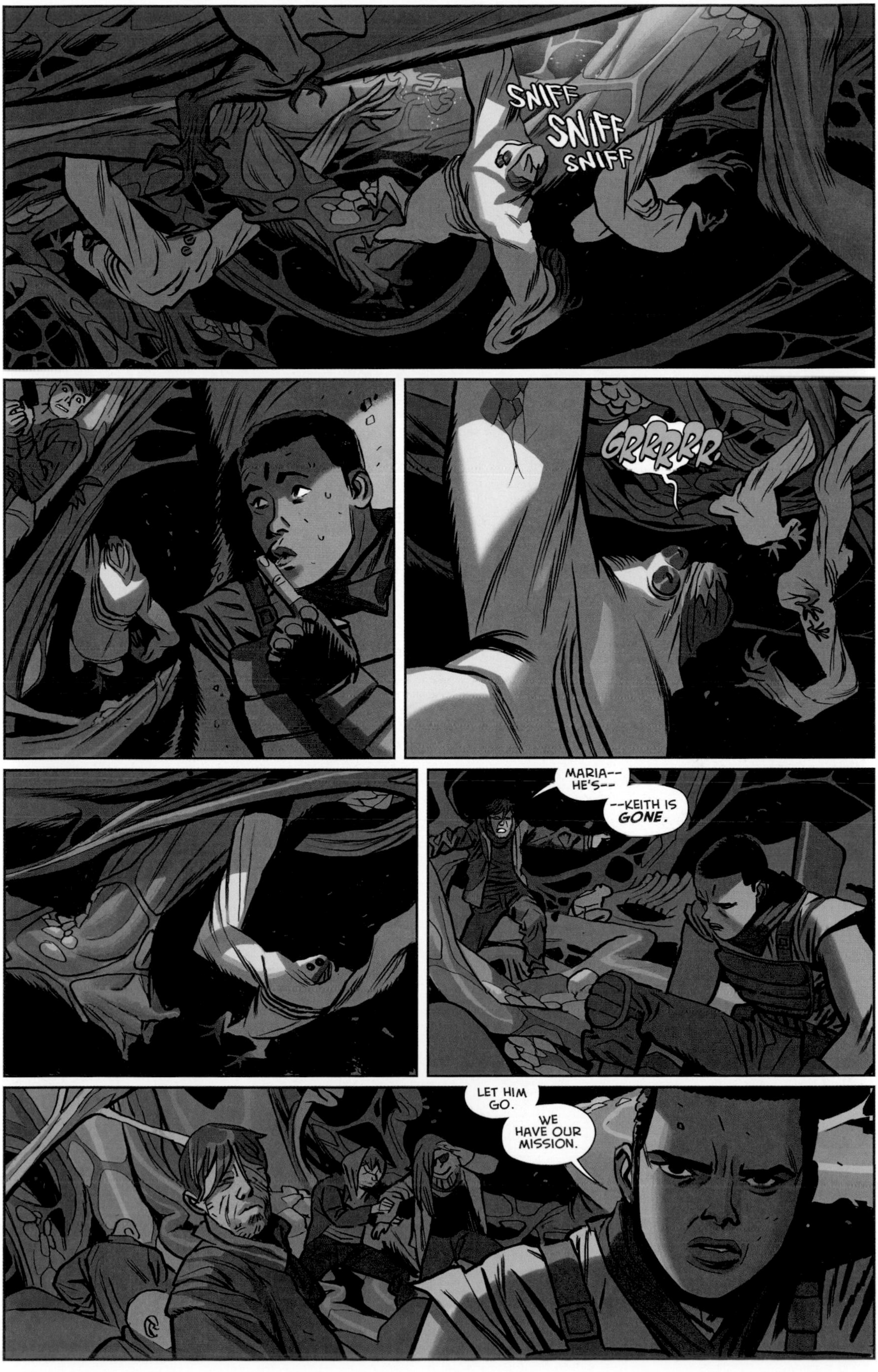
SNIFF
SNIFF
SNIFF
GRRRRR.
MARIA-- HE'S--
--KEITH IS GONE.
LET HIM GO.
WE HAVE OUR MISSION.

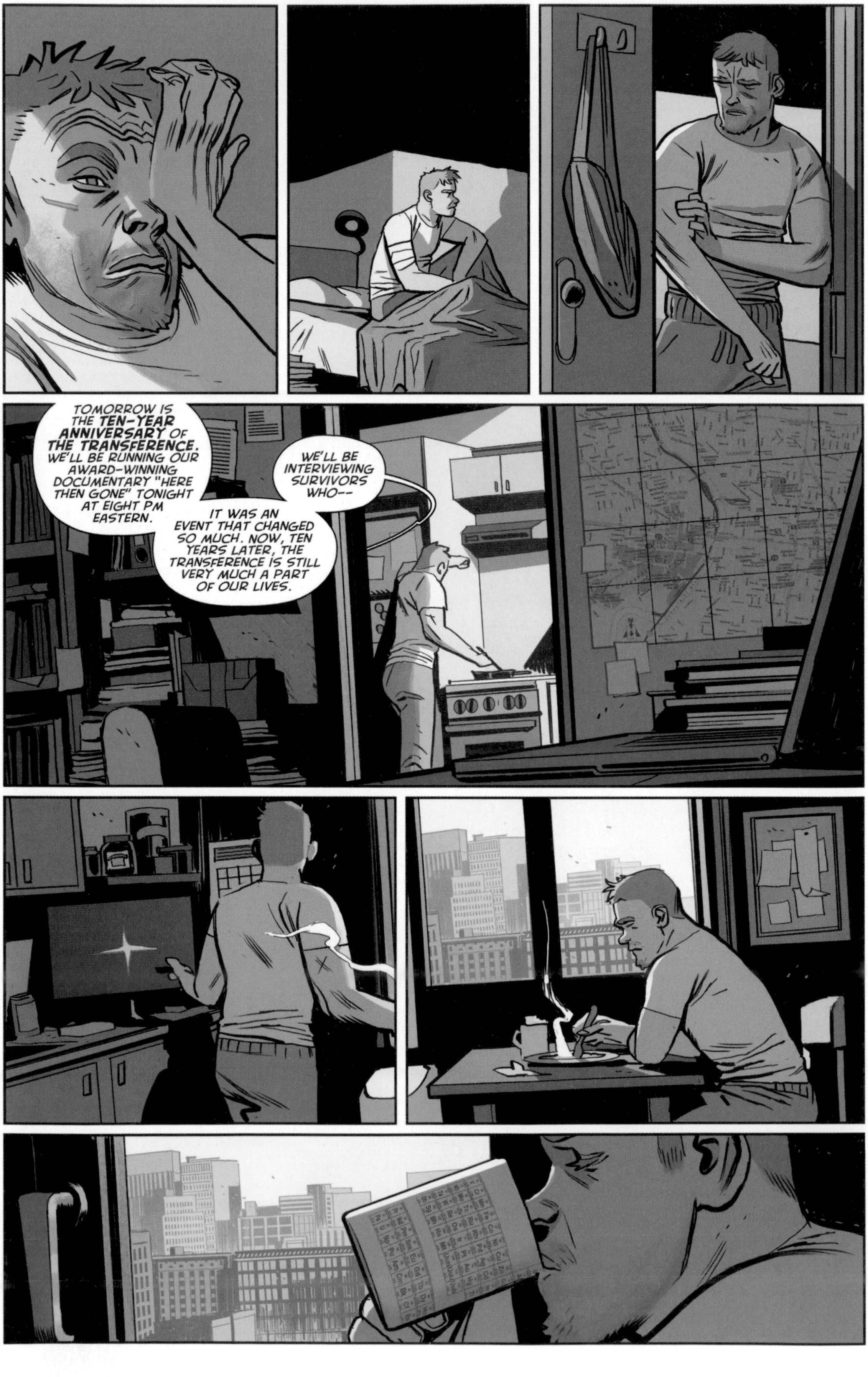
TOMORROW IS THE TEN-YEAR ANNIVERSARY OF THE TRANSFERENCE. WE'LL BE RUNNING OUR AWARD-WINNING DOCUMENTARY "HERE THEN GONE" TONIGHT AT EIGHT PM EASTERN.
WE'LL BE INTERVIEWING SURVIVORS WHO--
IT WAS AN EVENT THAT CHANGED SO MUCH. NOW, TEN YEARS LATER, THE TRANSFERENCE IS STILL VERY MUCH A PART OF OUR LIVES.

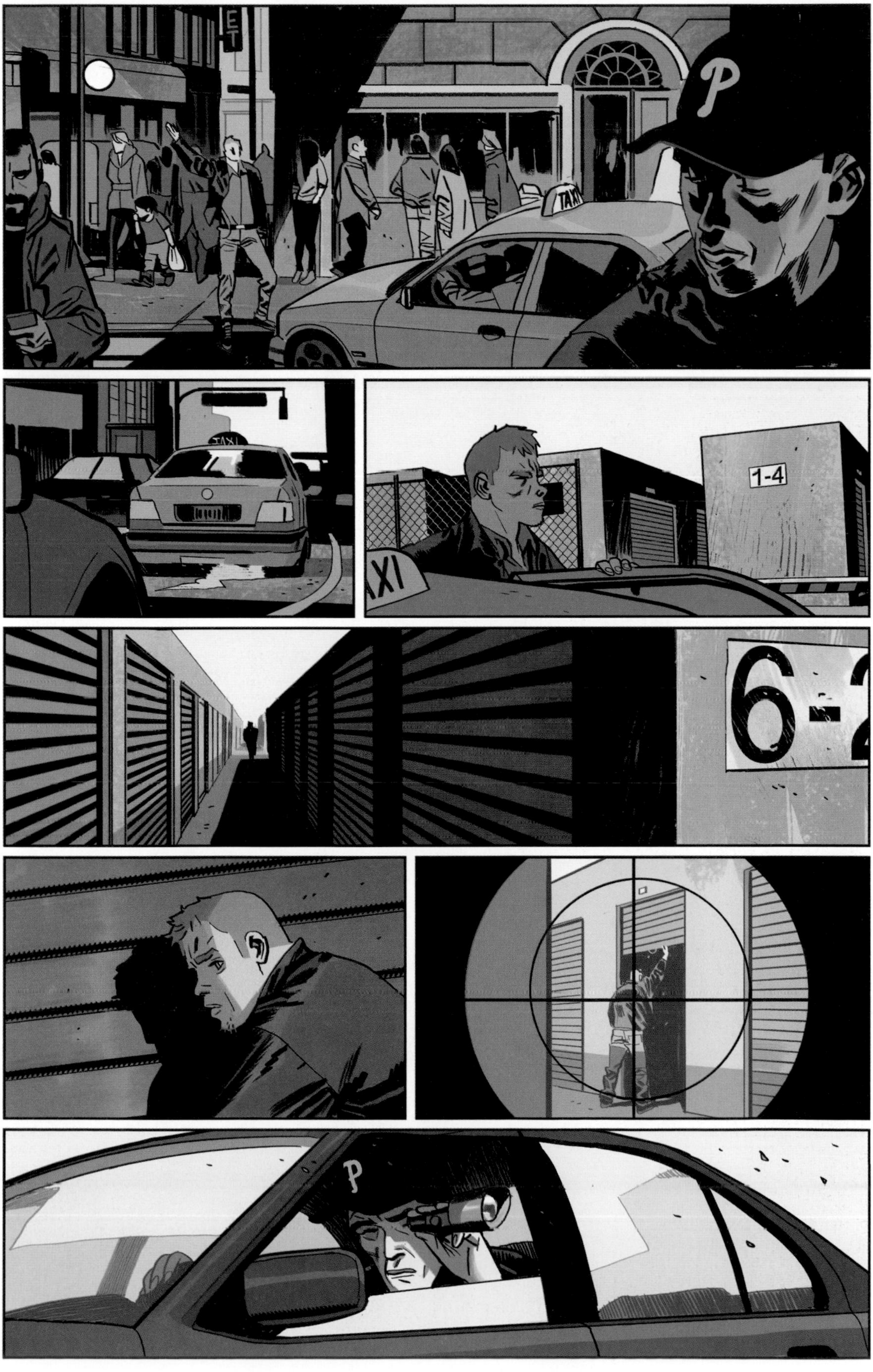
TAXI
TAXI
1-4
TAXI
6-2

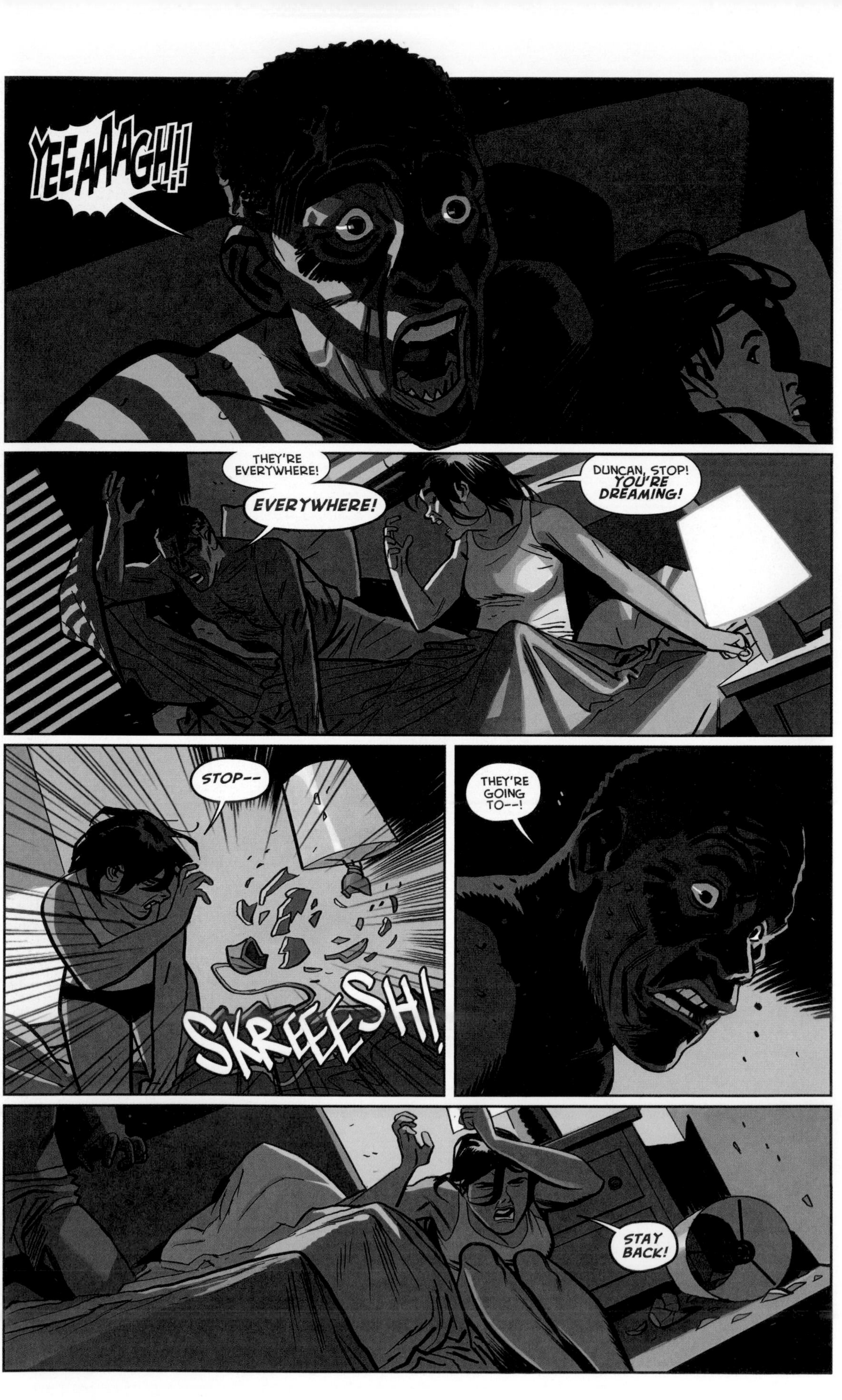
YEEAAAGH!!
THEY'RE EVERYWHERE!
EVERYWHERE!
DUNCAN, STOP! YOU'RE DREAMING!
STOP--
SKREEESH!
THEY'RE GOING TO--!
STAY BACK!

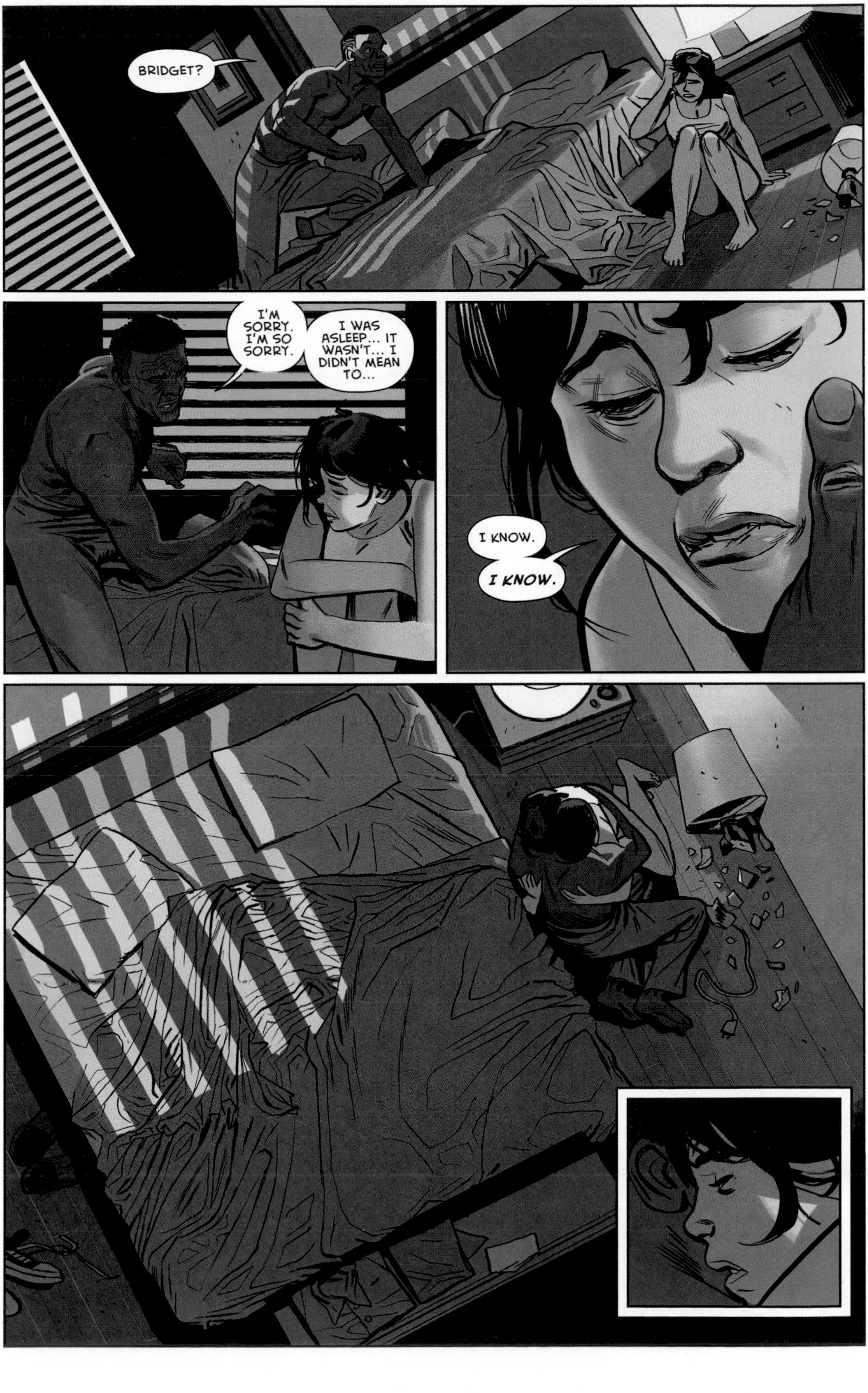
BRIDGET?
I'M SORRY. I'M SO SORRY.
I WAS ASLEEP... IT WASN'T... I DIDN'T MEAN TO...
I KNOW.
I KNOW.

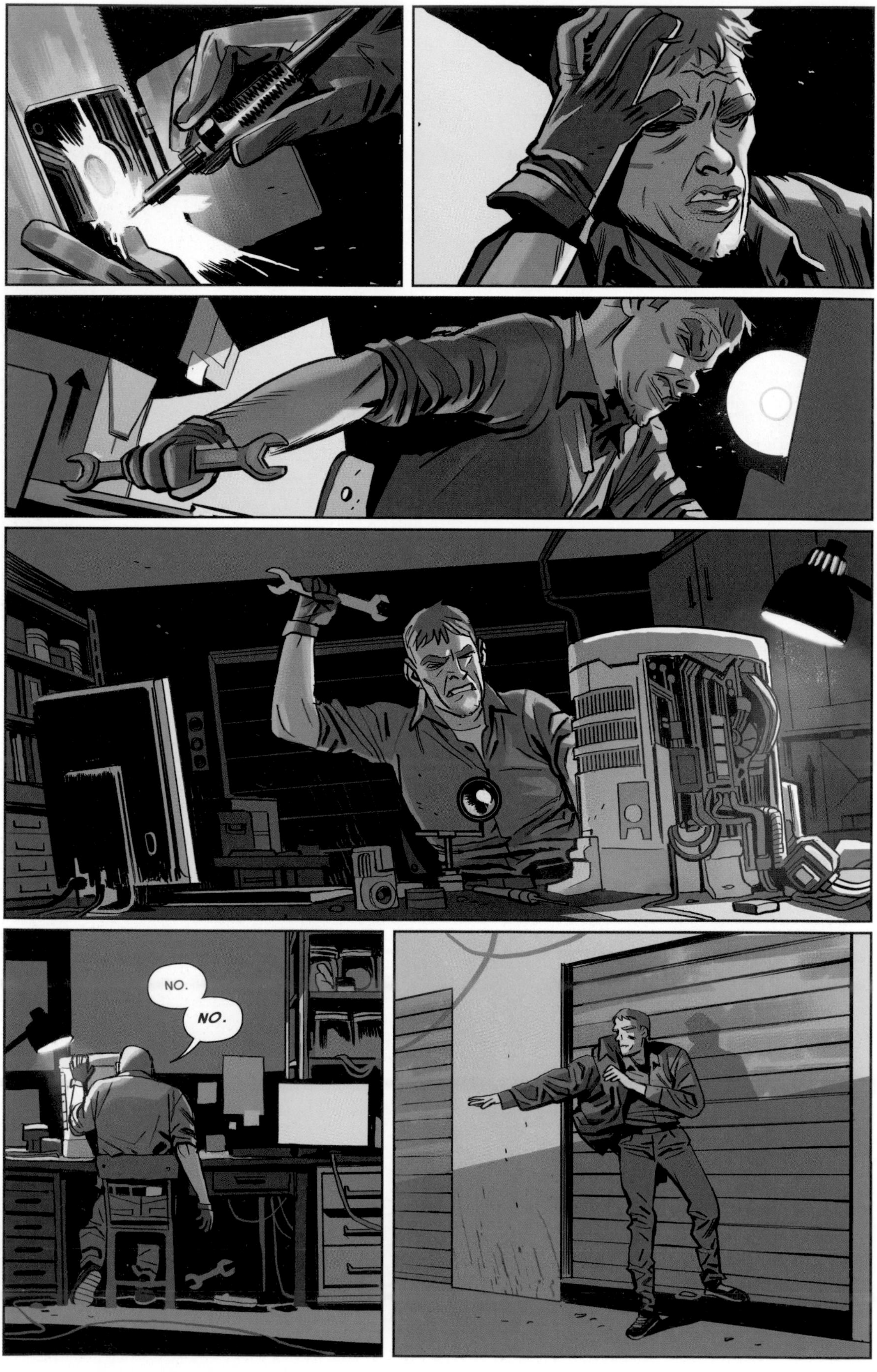
NO.
NO.

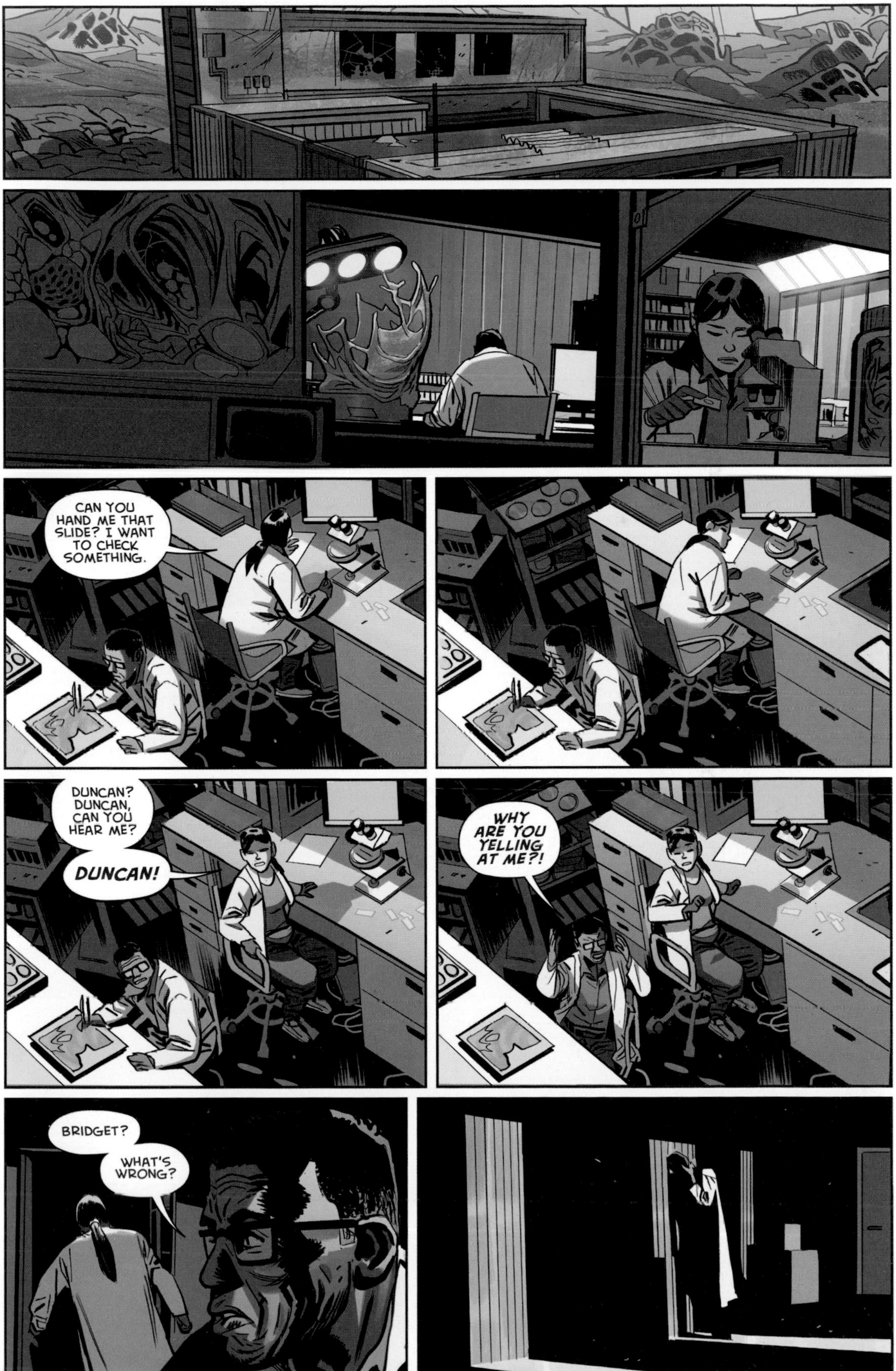
CAN YOU HAND ME THAT SLIDE? I WANT TO CHECK SOMETHING.
DUNCAN? DUNCAN, CAN YOU HEAR ME?
DUNCAN!
WHY ARE YOU YELLING AT ME?!
BRIDGET?
WHAT'S WRONG?

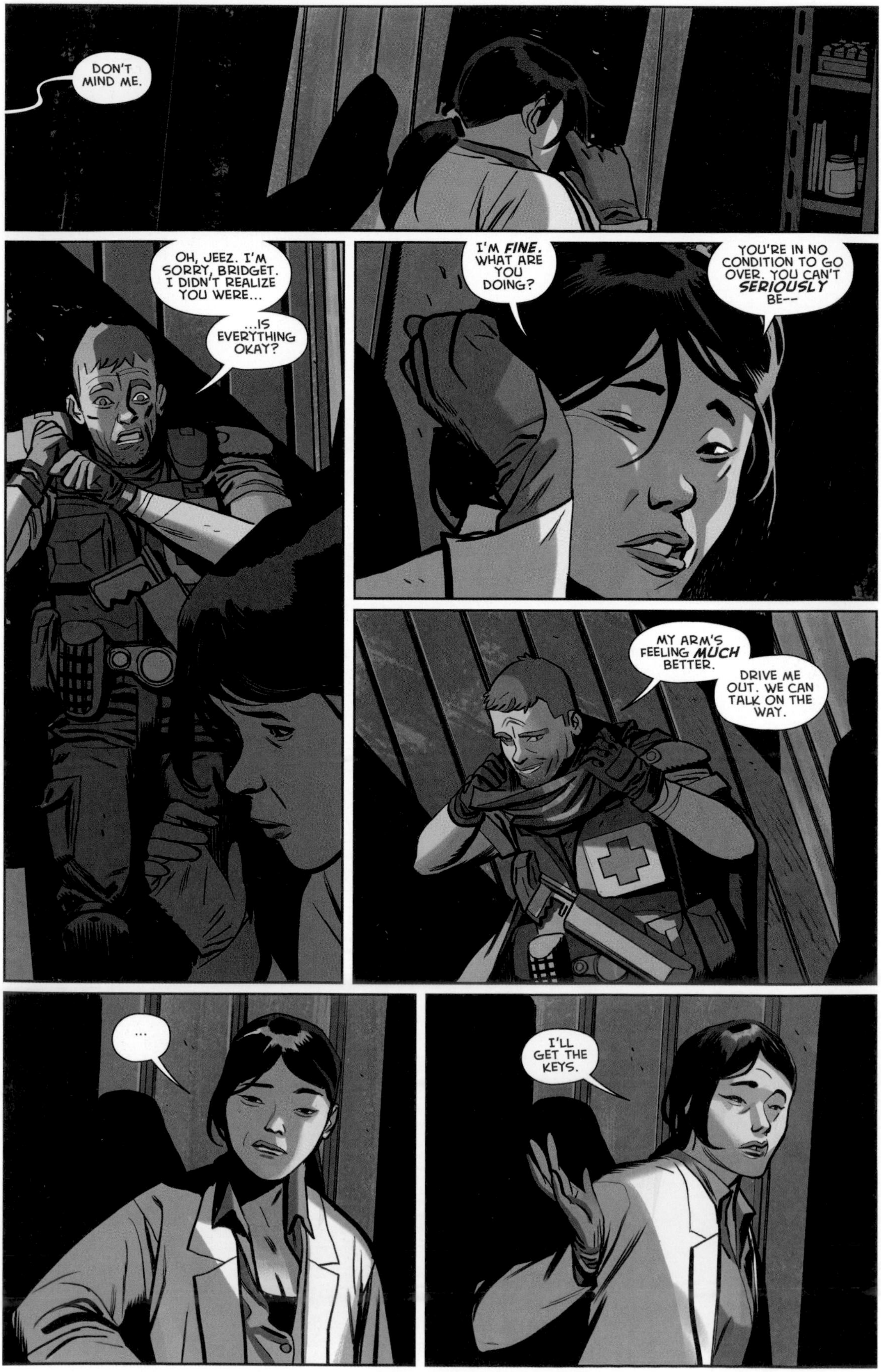
DON'T MIND ME.
OH, JEEZ. I'M SORRY, BRIDGET. I DIDN'T REALIZE YOU WERE...
...IS EVERYTHING OKAY?
I'M FINE. WHAT ARE YOU DOING?
YOU'RE IN NO CONDITION TO GO OVER. YOU CAN'T SERIOUSLY BE--
MY ARM'S FEELING MUCH BETTER.
DRIVE ME OUT. WE CAN TALK ON THE WAY.
...
I'LL GET THE KEYS.

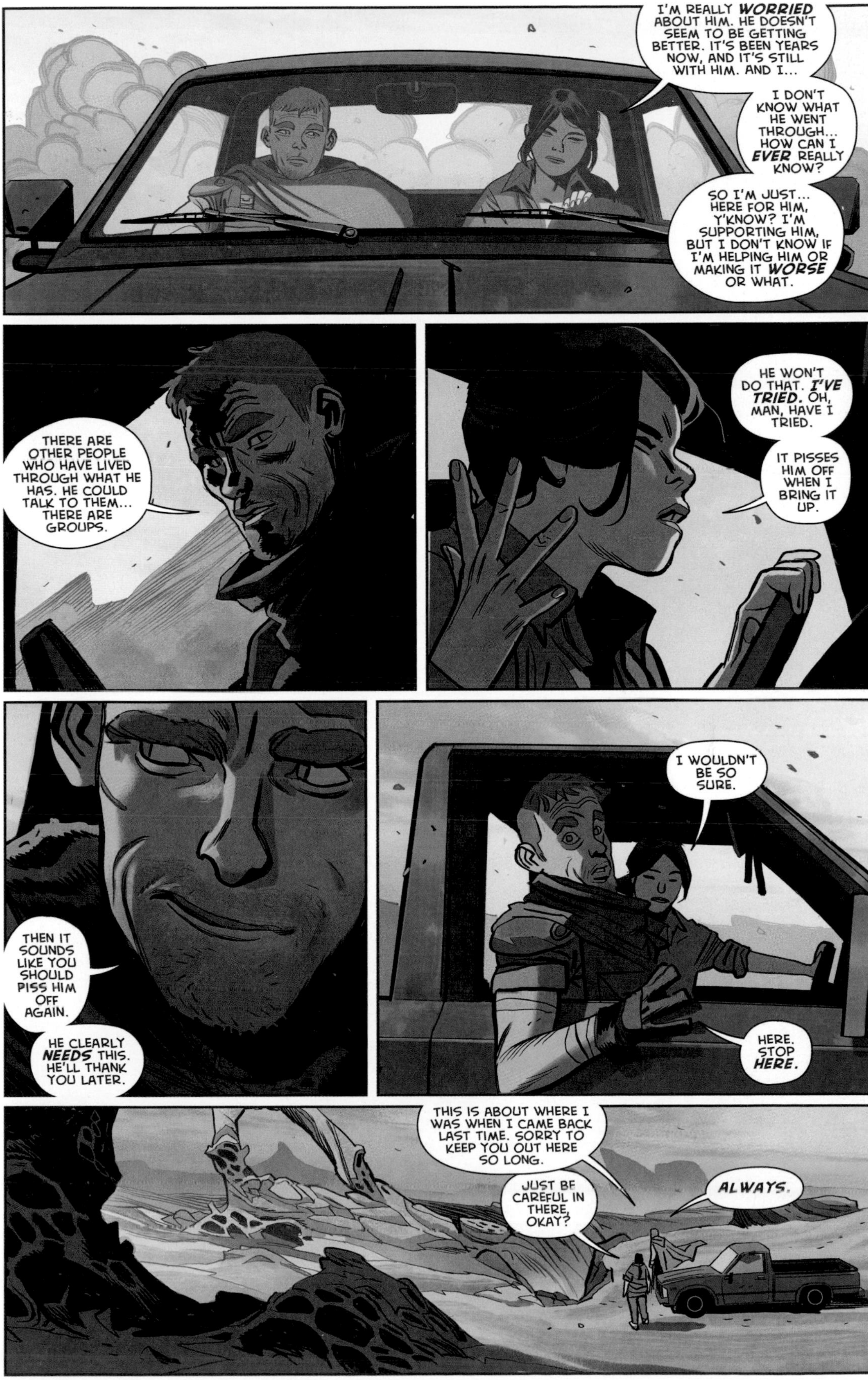
I'M REALLY WORRIED ABOUT HIM. HE DOESN'T SEEM TO BE GETTING BETTER. IT'S BEEN YEARS NOW, AND IT'S STILL WITH HIM. AND I...
I DON'T KNOW WHAT HE WENT THROUGH... HOW CAN I EVER REALLY KNOW?
SO I'M JUST... HERE FOR HIM, Y'KNOW? I'M SUPPORTING HIM, BUT I DON'T KNOW IF I'M HELPING HIM OR MAKING IT WORSE OR WHAT.
THERE ARE OTHER PEOPLE WHO HAVE LIVED THROUGH WHAT HE HAS. HE COULD TALK TO THEM... THERE ARE GROUPS.
HE WON'T DO THAT. I'VE TRIED. OH, MAN, HAVE I TRIED.
IT PISSES HIM OFF WHEN I BRING IT UP.
THEN IT SOUNDS LIKE YOU SHOULD PISS HIM OFF AGAIN.
HE CLEARLY NEEDS THIS. HE'LL THANK YOU LATER.
I WOULDN'T BE SO SURE.
HERE. STOP HERE.
THIS IS ABOUT WHERE I WAS WHEN I CAME BACK LAST TIME. SORRY TO KEEP YOU OUT HERE SO LONG.
JUST BE CAREFUL IN THERE, OKAY?
ALWAYS.

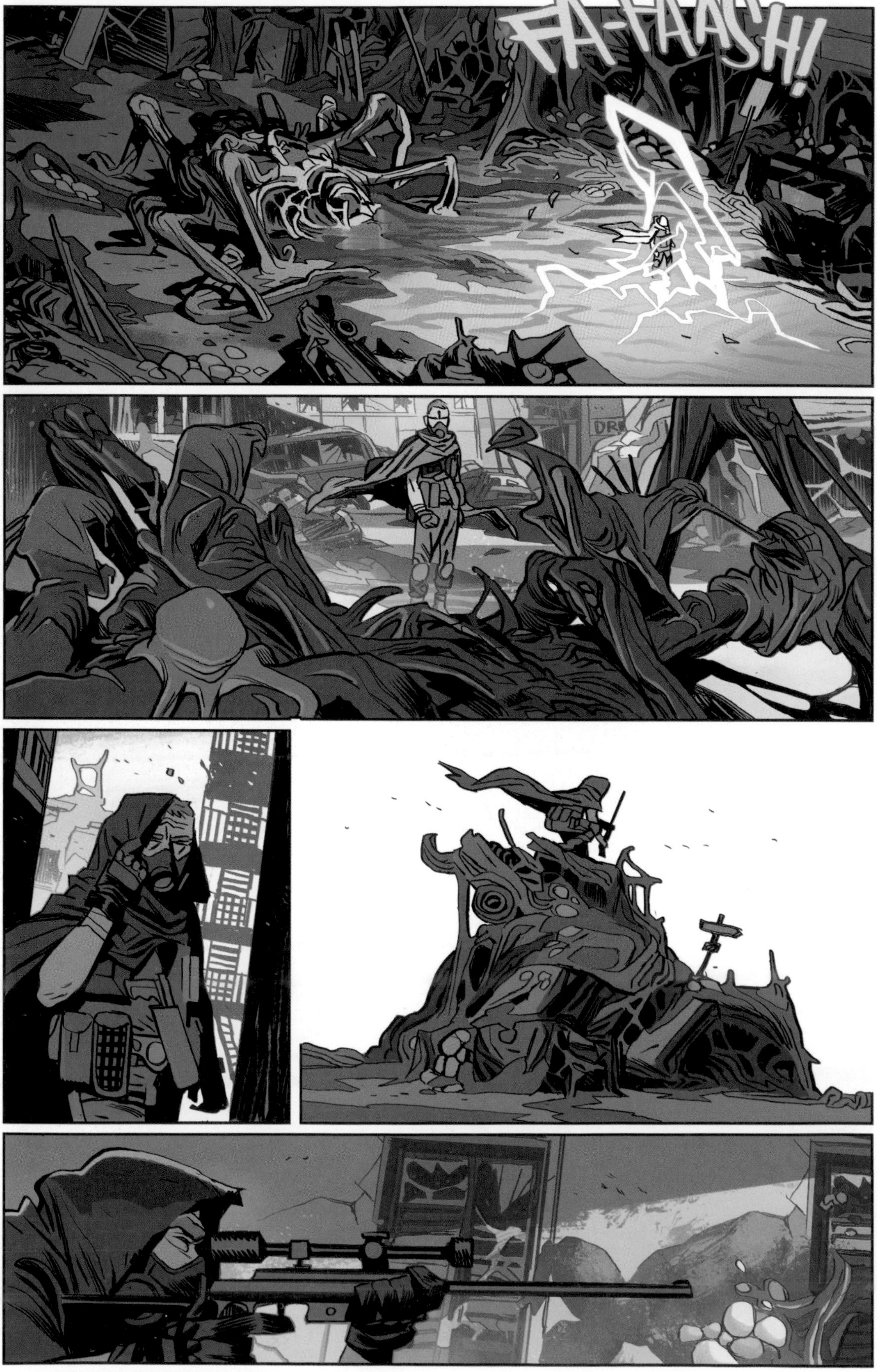
FA-FAASH!

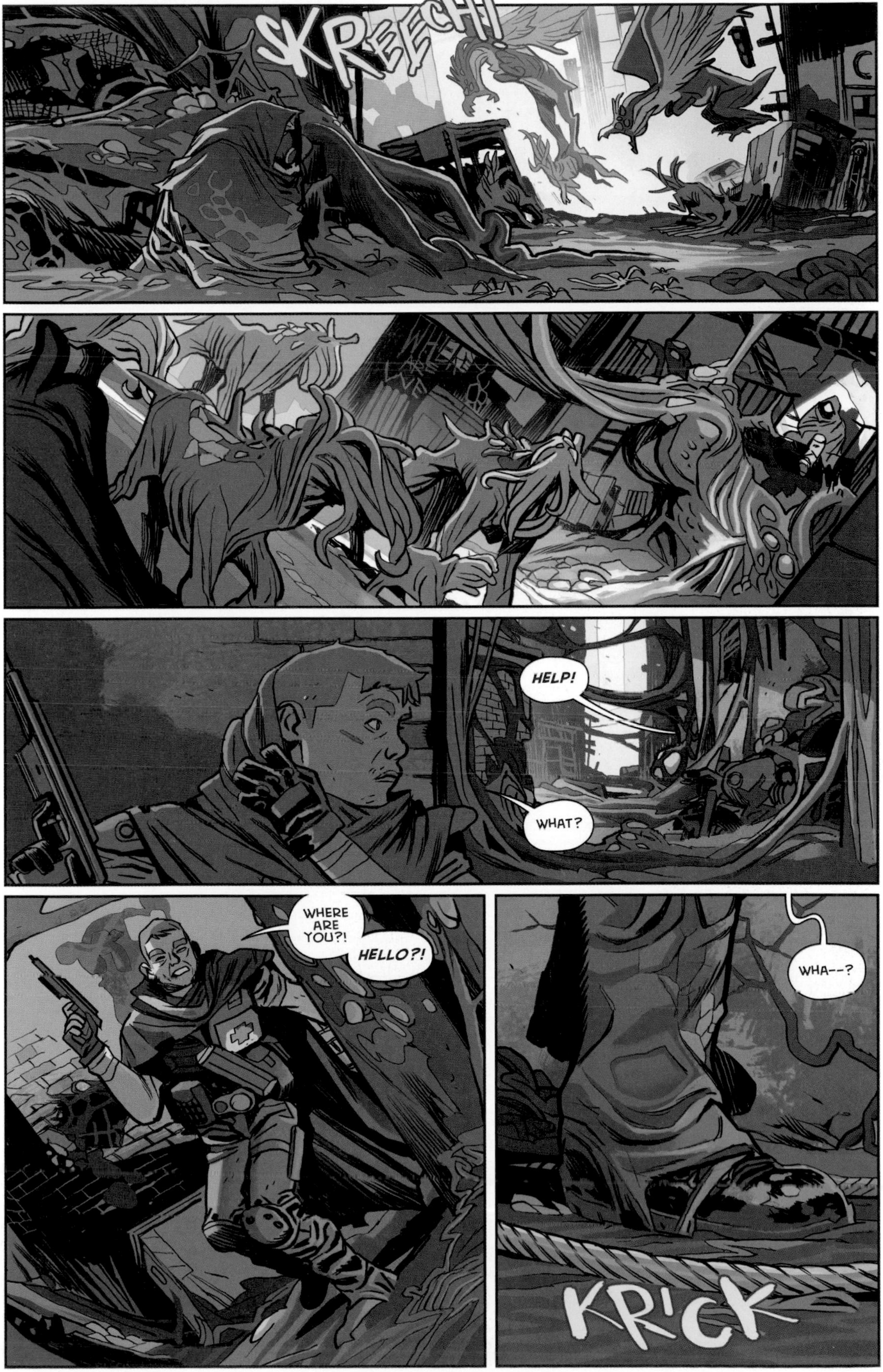
SKREECH!
HELP!
WHAT?
WHERE ARE YOU?!
HELLO?!
WHA--?
KR'CK

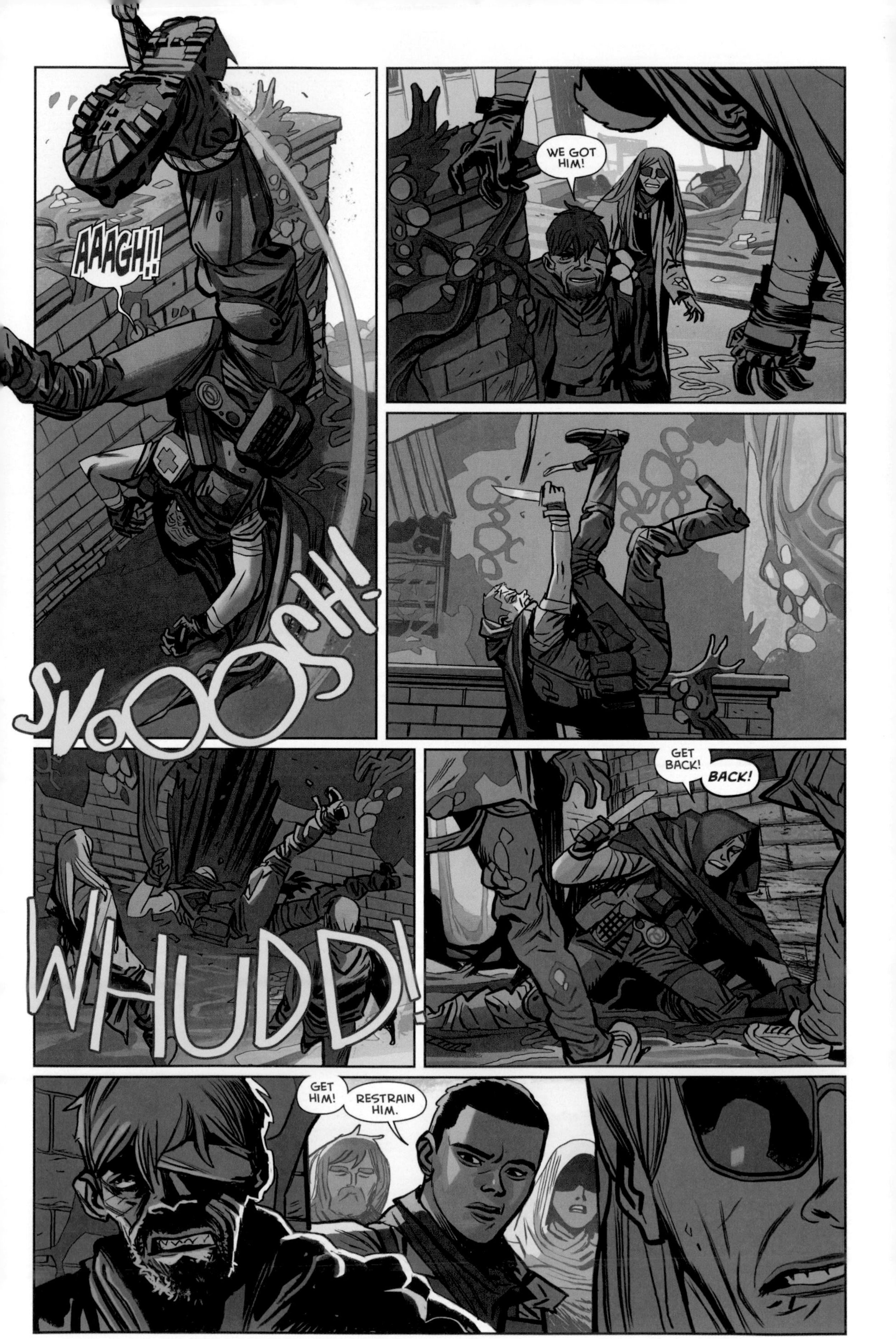
AAAGH!!
WE GOT HIM!
SWOOOSH!
WHUDD!
GET BACK!
BACK!
GET HIM!
RESTRAIN HIM.

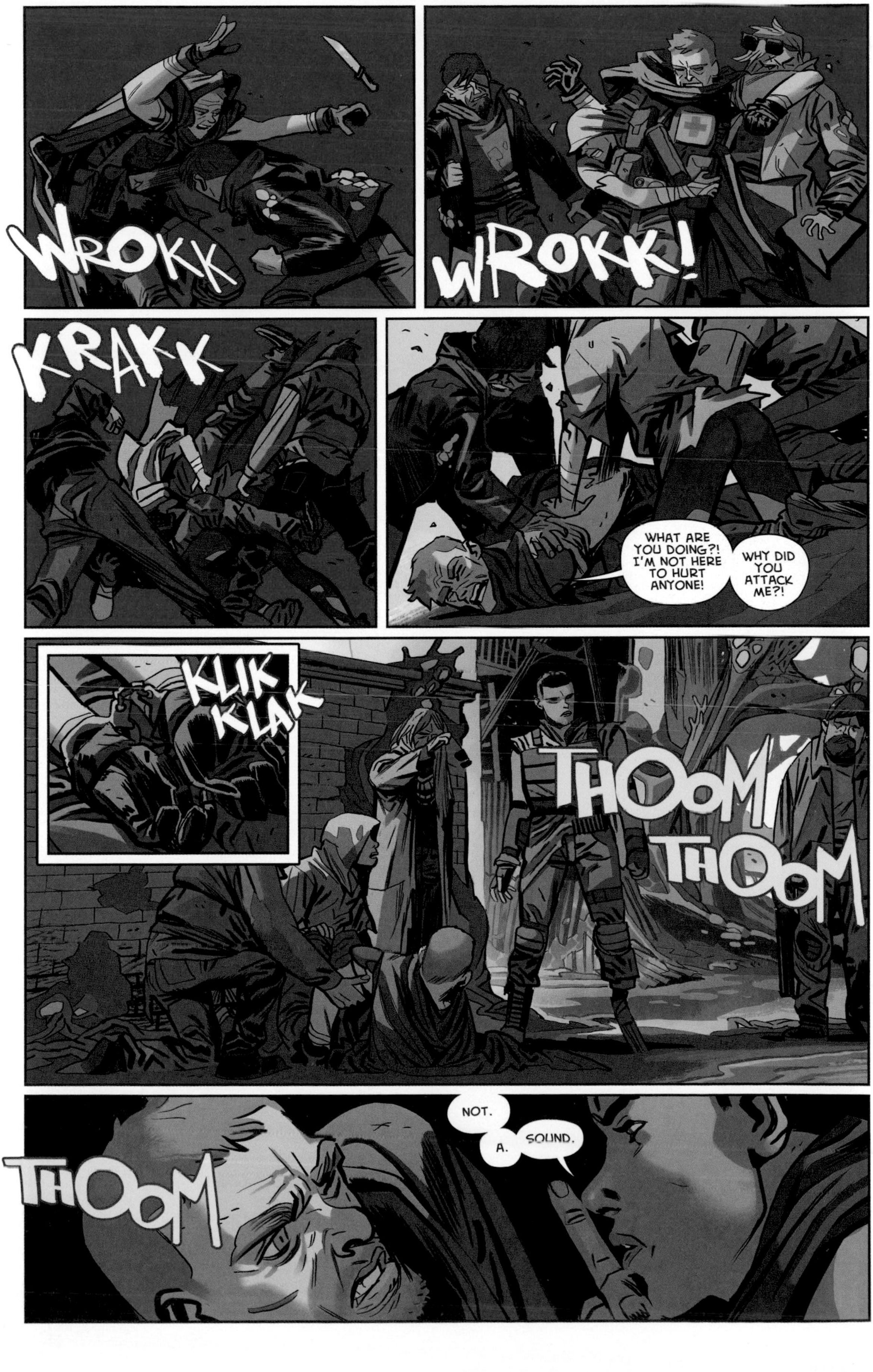
WROKK
WROKK!
KRAKK
WHAT ARE YOU DOING?! I'M NOT HERE TO HURT ANYONE!
WHY DID YOU ATTACK ME?!
KLIK KLAK
THOOM THOOM
THOOM
NOT.
A.
SOUND.

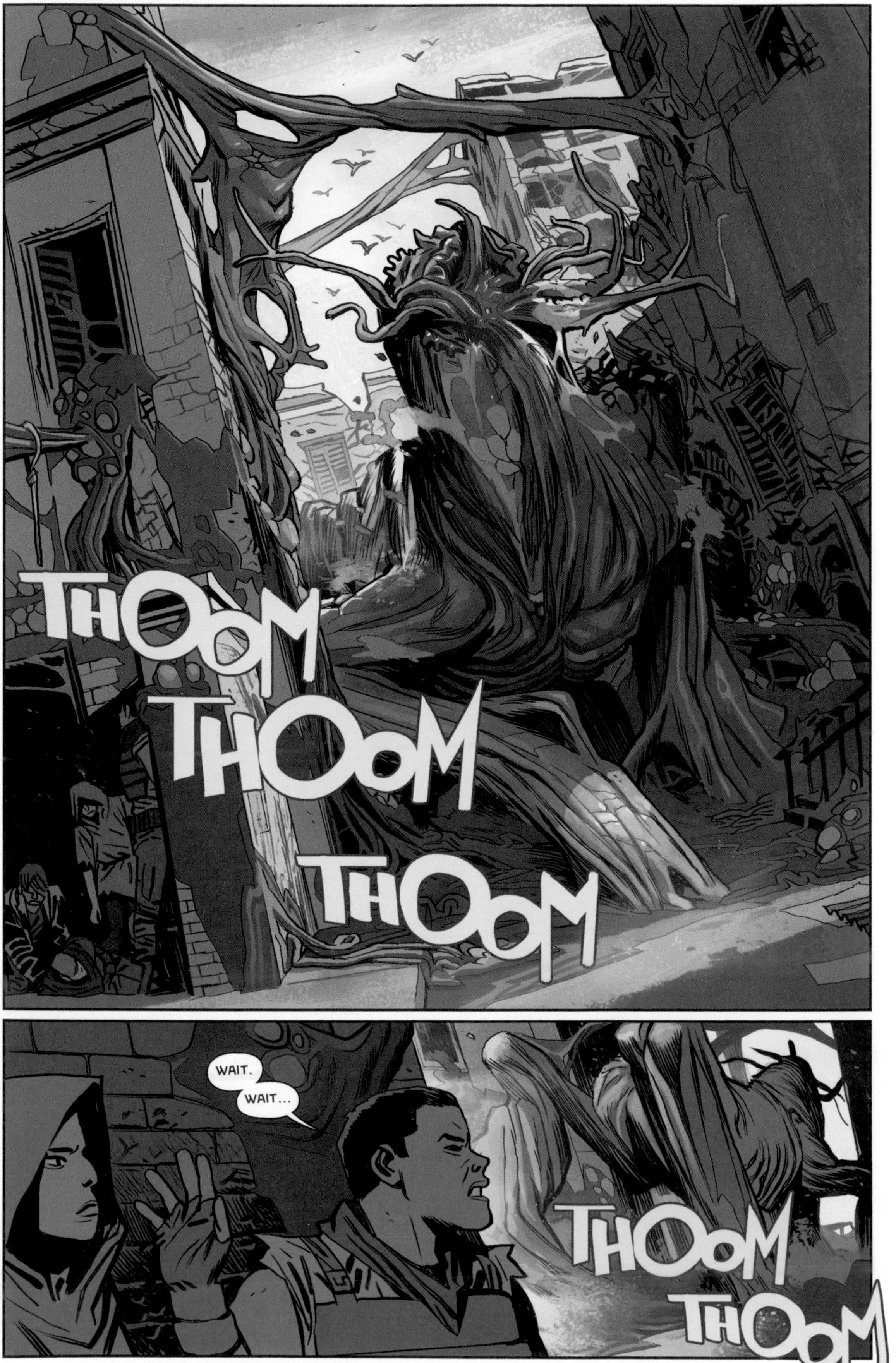
THOOM
THOOM
THOOM
WAIT.
WAIT...
THOOM
THOOM

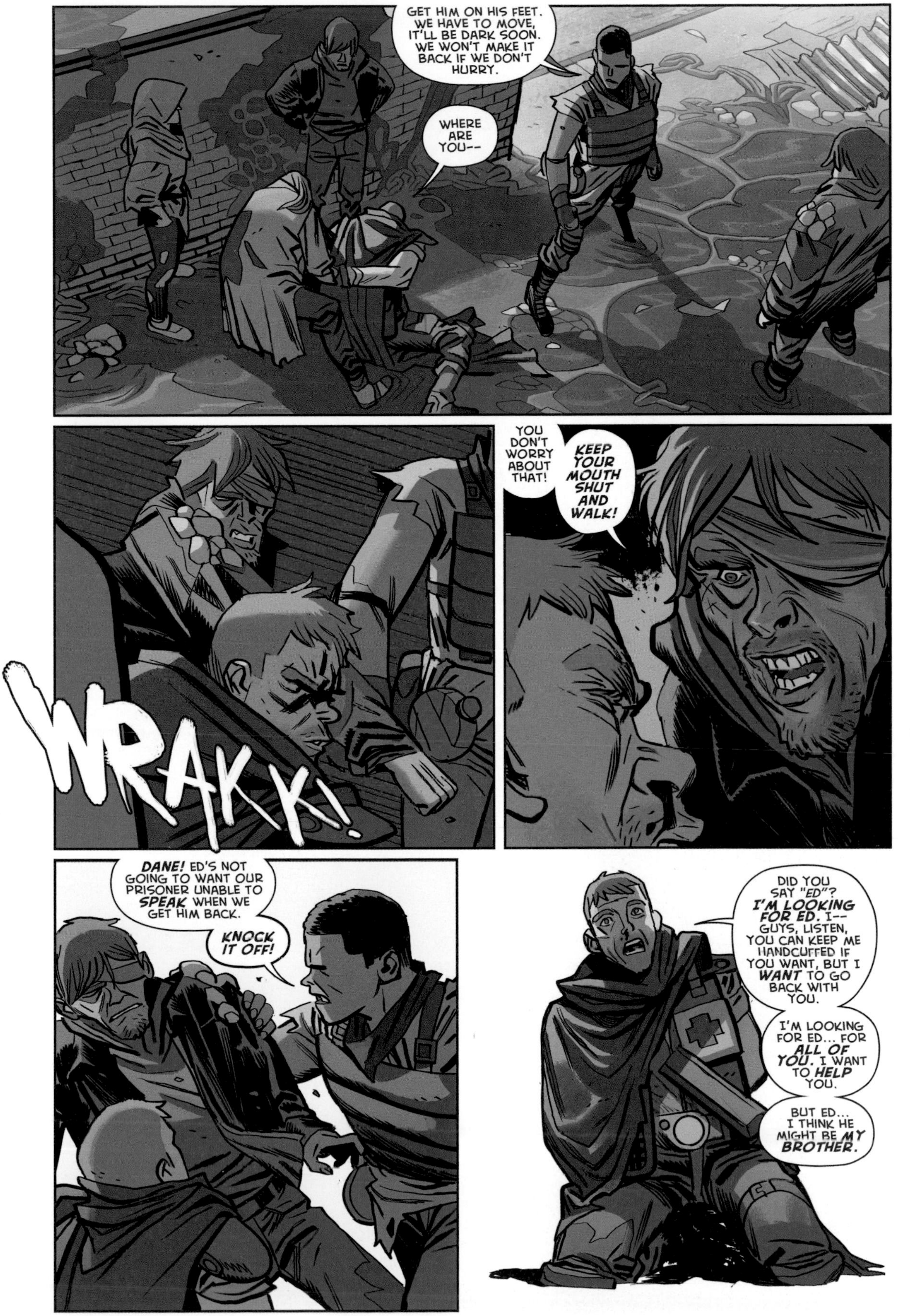
GET HIM ON HIS FEET. WE HAVE TO MOVE, IT'LL BE DARK SOON. WE WON'T MAKE IT BACK IF WE DON'T HURRY.
WHERE ARE YOU--
WRAKK!
YOU DON'T WORRY ABOUT THAT!
KEEP YOUR MOUTH SHUT AND WALK!
DANE! ED'S NOT GOING TO WANT OUR PRISONER UNABLE TO SPEAK WHEN WE GET HIM BACK.
KNOCK IT OFF!
DID YOU SAY "ED"? I'M LOOKING FOR ED. I-- GUYS, LISTEN, YOU CAN KEEP ME HANDCUFFED IF YOU WANT, BUT I WANT TO GO BACK WITH YOU.
I'M LOOKING FOR ED... FOR ALL OF YOU. I WANT TO HELP YOU.
BUT ED... I THINK HE MIGHT BE MY BROTHER.

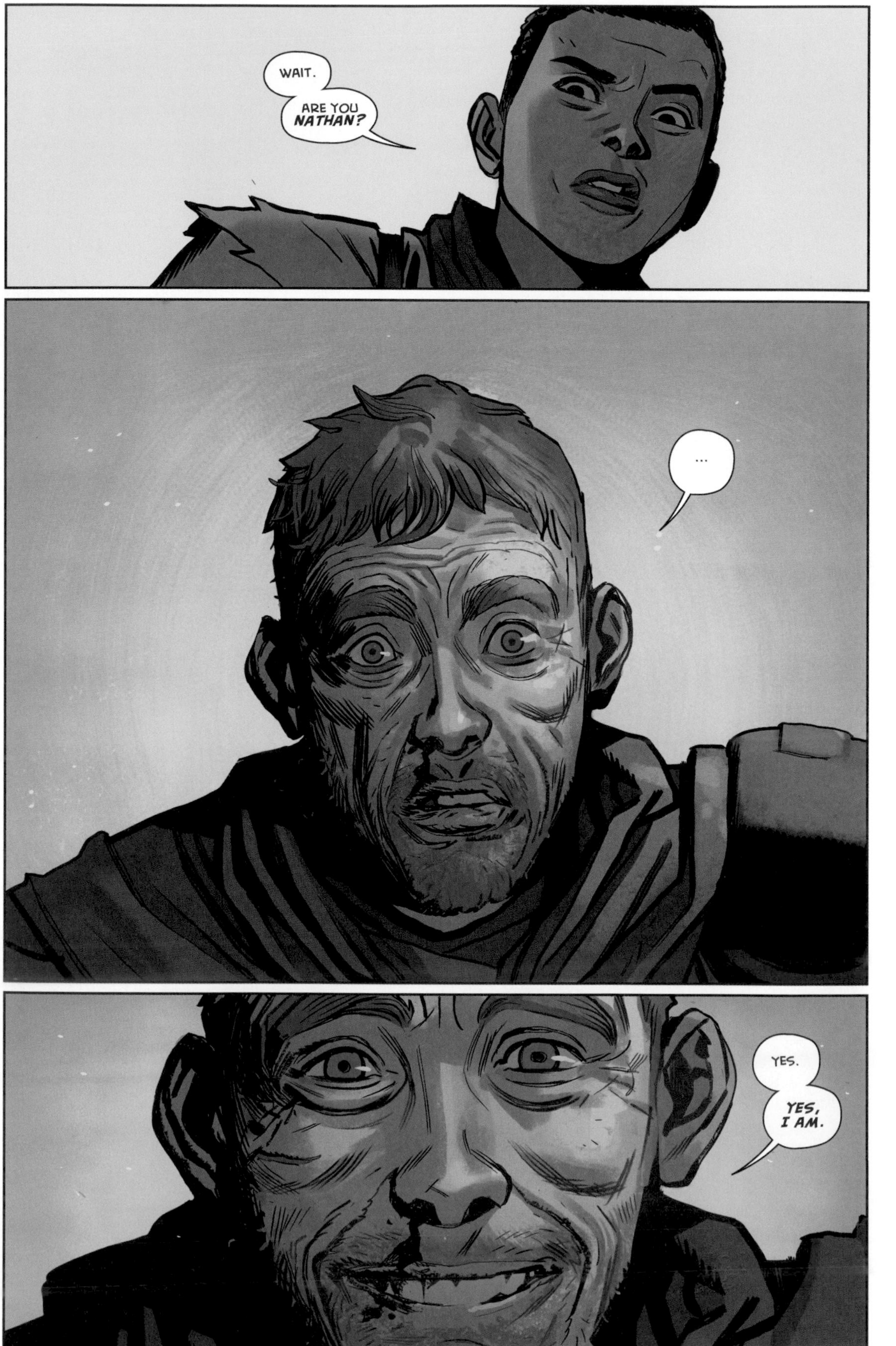
WAIT.
ARE YOU NATHAN?
...
YES.
YES, I AM.

HOLD UP.

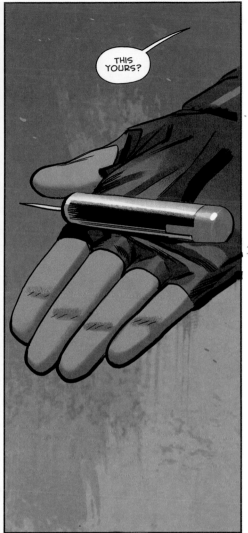

THIS YOURS?

YES. THAT'S AN ALIGNMENT DART. IT REALIGNS THE FREQUENCY OF YOUR MOLECULES TO PLACE YOU BACK IN THE PROPER DIMENSION AND--

JUST TELL IT TO YOUR BROTHER.

YOU'VE GOT A LOT OF EXPLAINING TO DO.

LEAD THE WAY.

EVERYONE... KEEP EYES ON THIS ONE. NO SURPRISES.

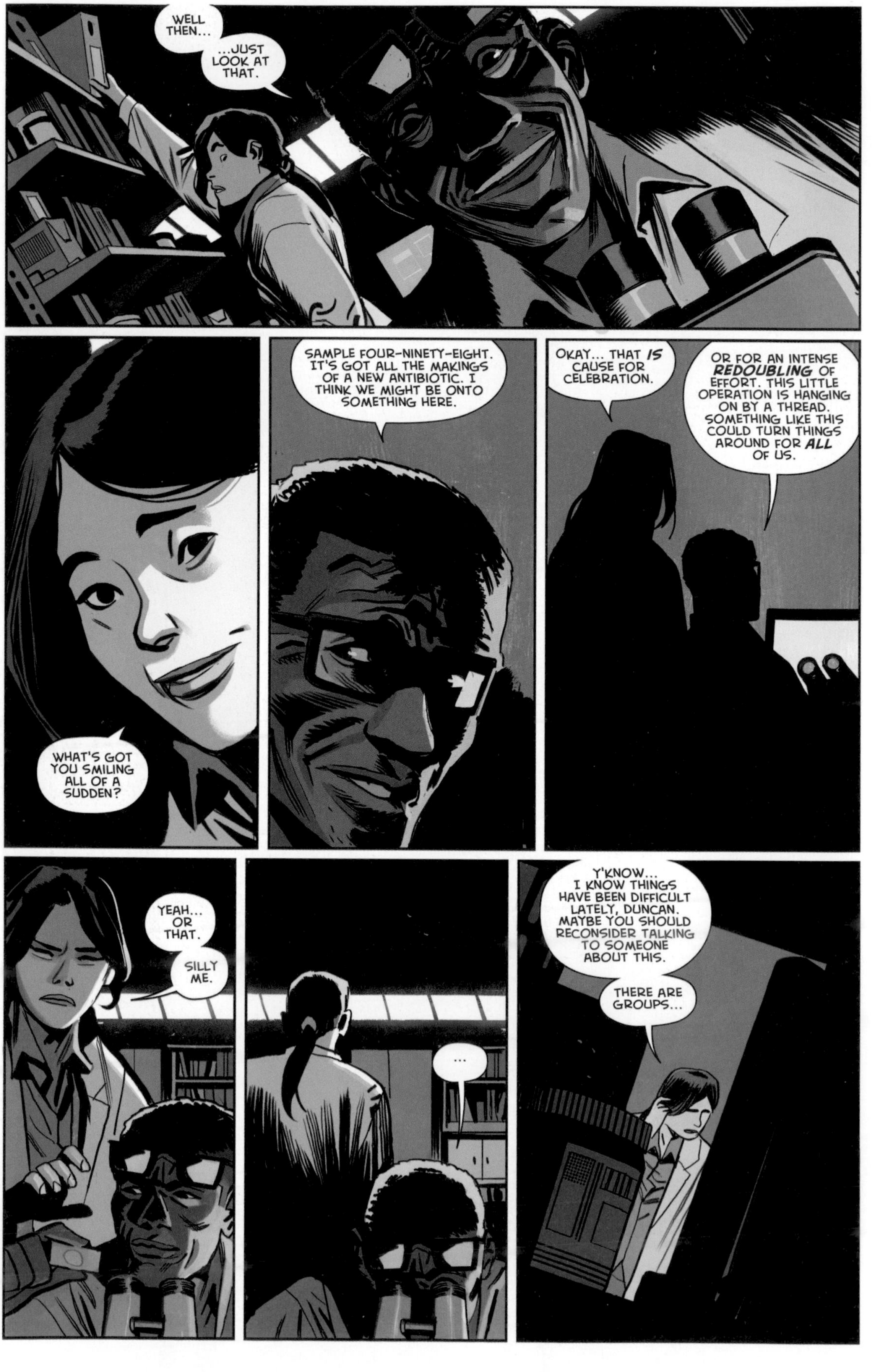
WELL THEN...
...JUST LOOK AT THAT.
SAMPLE FOUR-NINETY-EIGHT. IT'S GOT ALL THE MAKINGS OF A NEW ANTIBIOTIC. I THINK WE MIGHT BE ONTO SOMETHING HERE.
WHAT'S GOT YOU SMILING ALL OF A SUDDEN?
OKAY... THAT IS CAUSE FOR CELEBRATION.
OR FOR AN INTENSE REDOUBLING OF EFFORT. THIS LITTLE OPERATION IS HANGING ON BY A THREAD. SOMETHING LIKE THIS COULD TURN THINGS AROUND FOR ALL OF US.
YEAH... OR THAT.
SILLY ME.
...
Y'KNOW... I KNOW THINGS HAVE BEEN DIFFICULT LATELY, DUNCAN. MAYBE YOU SHOULD RECONSIDER TALKING TO SOMEONE ABOUT THIS.
THERE ARE GROUPS...

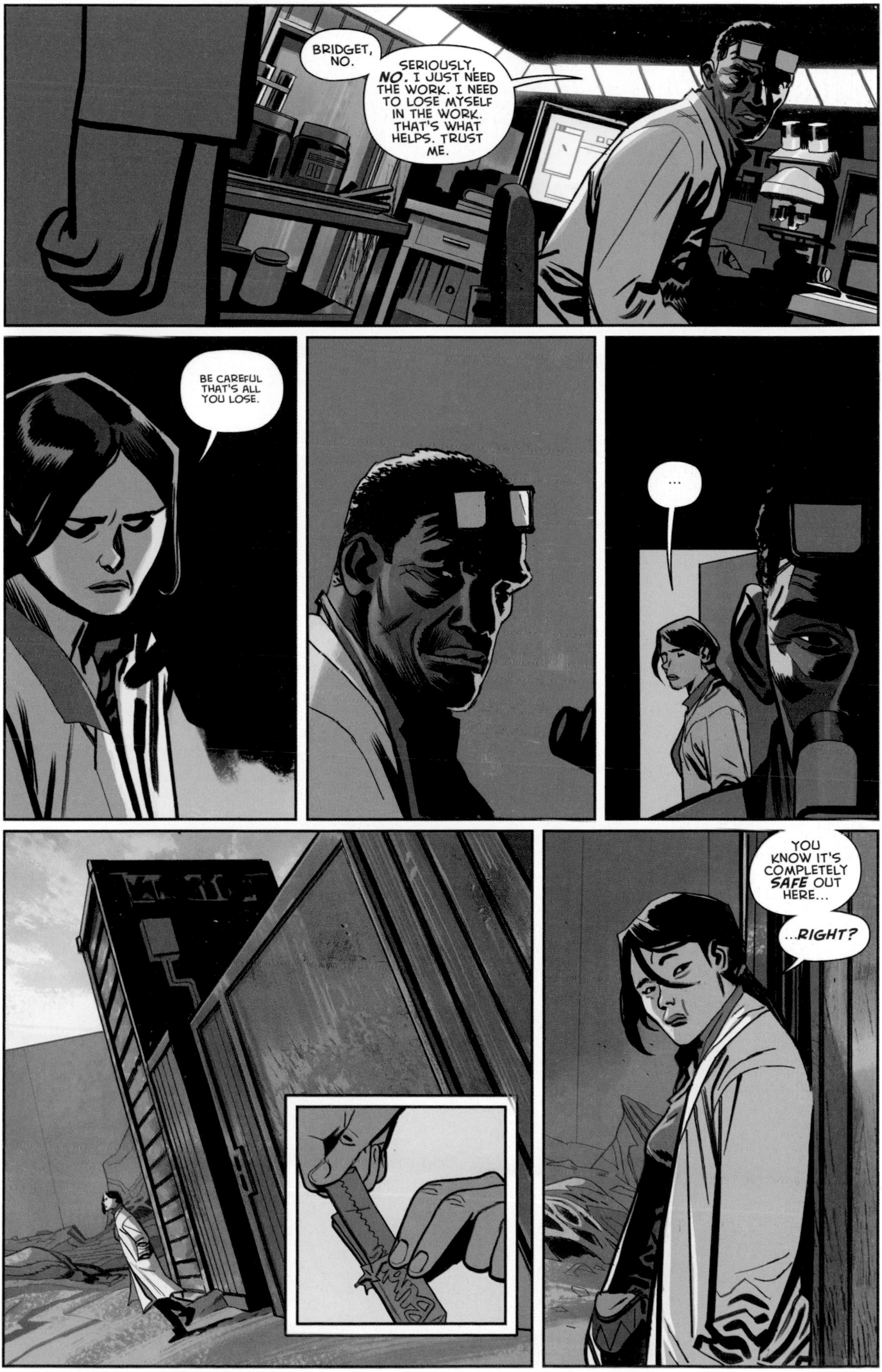

BRIDGET, NO.
SERIOUSLY, NO. I JUST NEED THE WORK. I NEED TO LOSE MYSELF IN THE WORK. THAT'S WHAT HELPS. TRUST ME.
BE CAREFUL THAT'S ALL YOU LOSE.
...
YOU KNOW IT'S COMPLETELY SAFE OUT HERE...
...RIGHT?

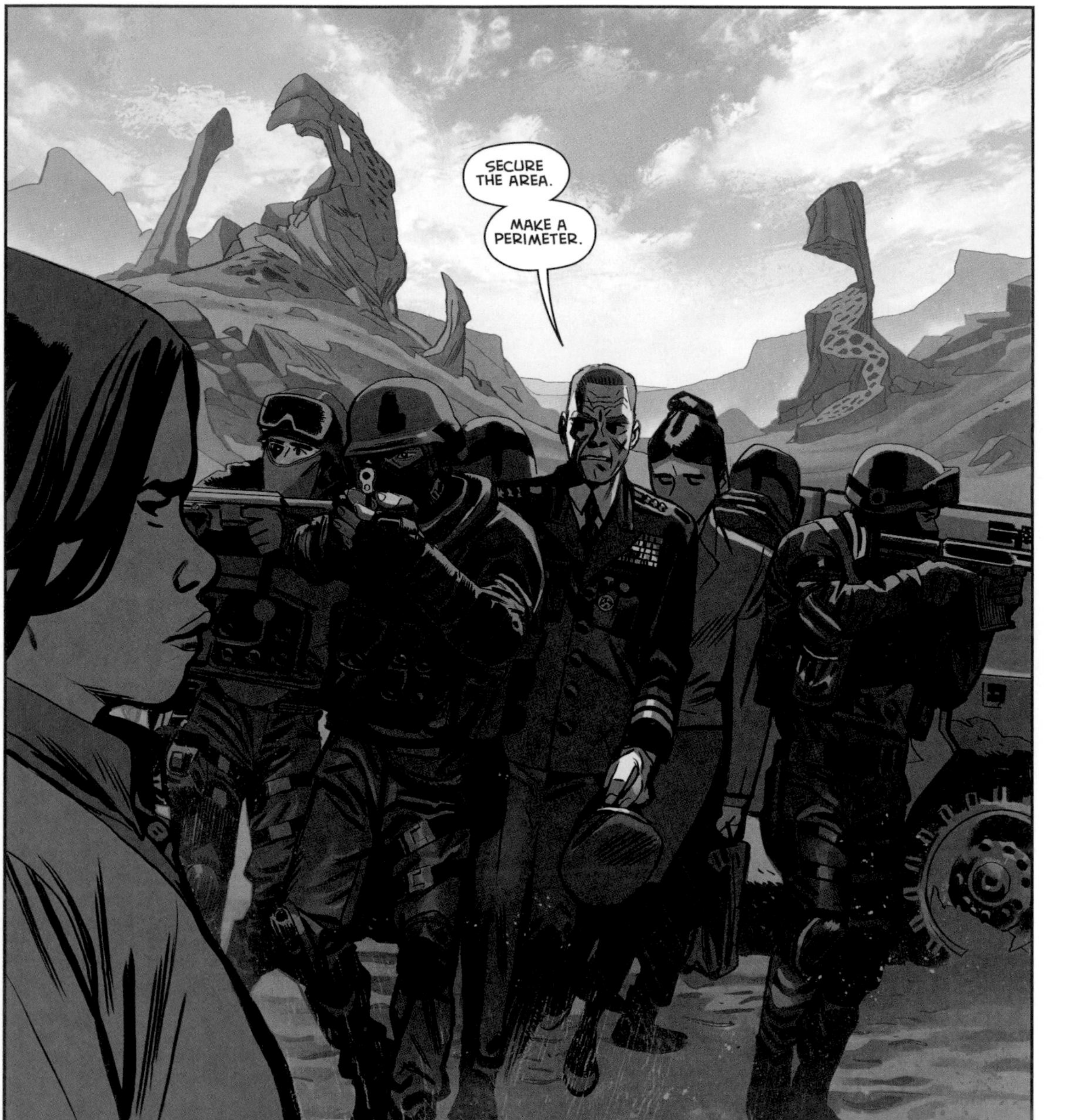
SECURE THE AREA.
MAKE A PERIMETER.

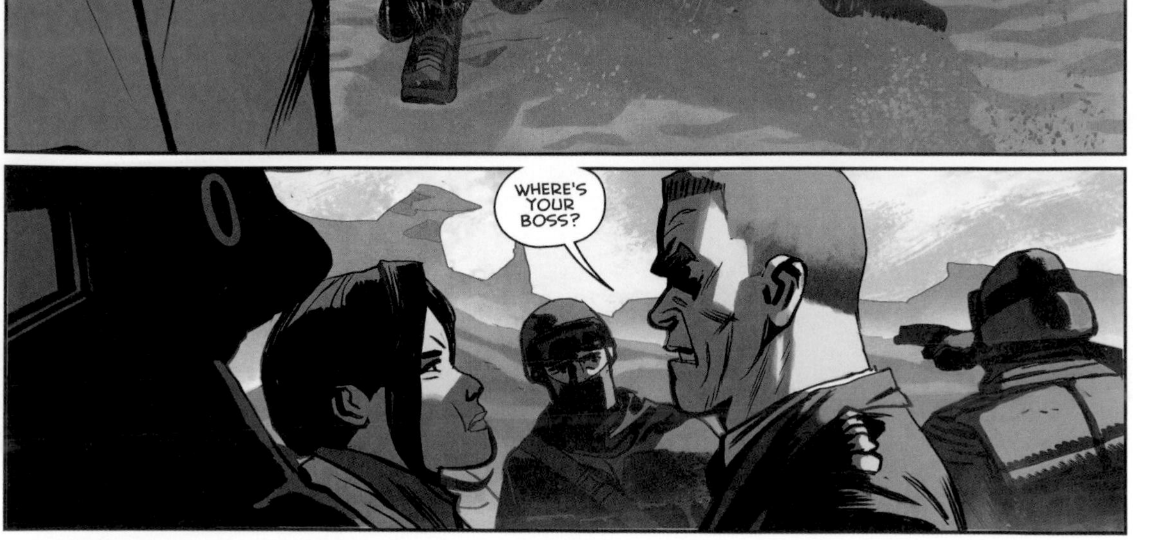
WHERE'S YOUR BOSS?

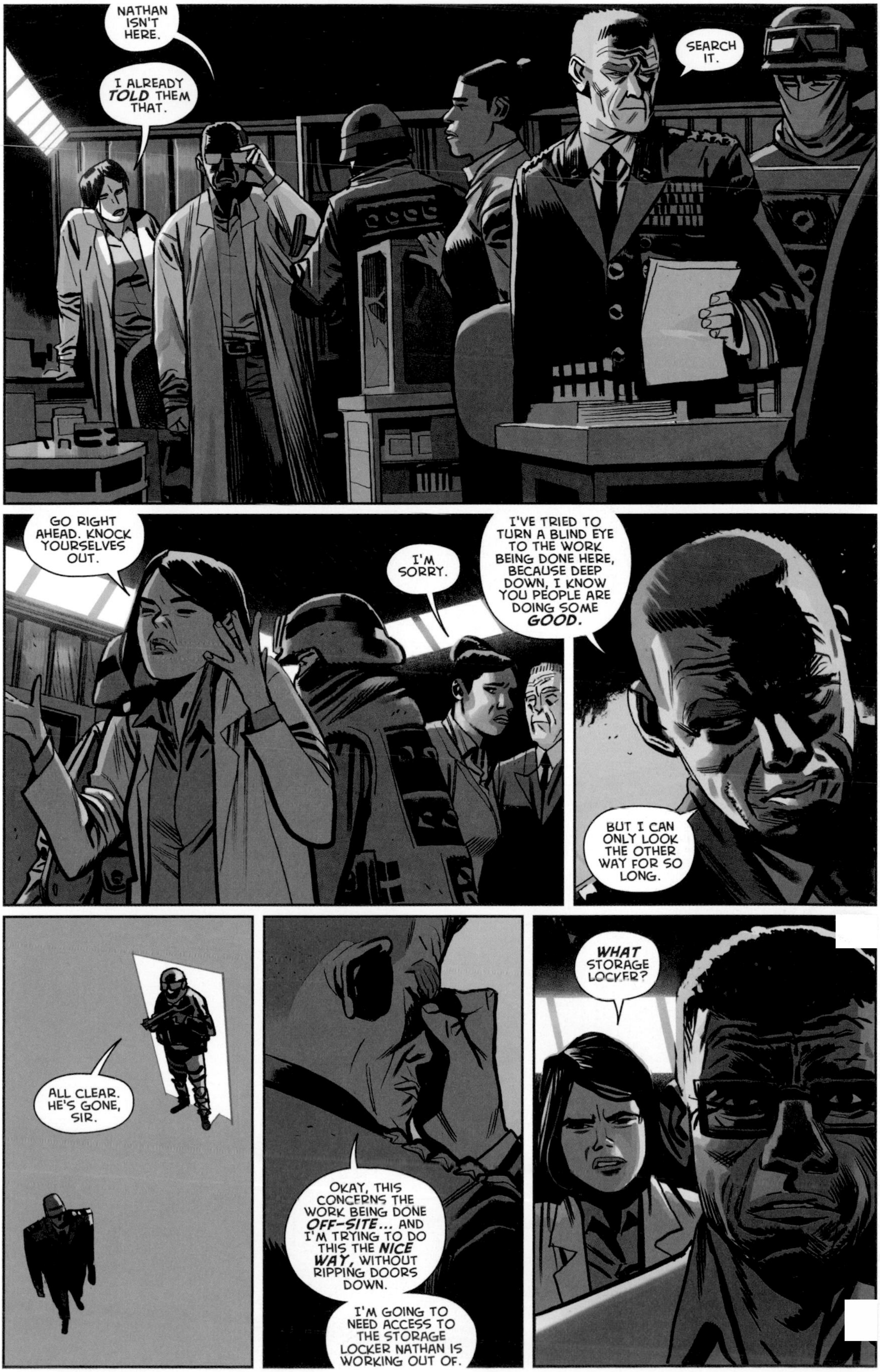
NATHAN ISN'T HERE.
I ALREADY TOLD THEM THAT.
SEARCH IT.
GO RIGHT AHEAD. KNOCK YOURSELVES OUT.
I'M SORRY.
I'VE TRIED TO TURN A BLIND EYE TO THE WORK BEING DONE HERE, BECAUSE DEEP DOWN, I KNOW YOU PEOPLE ARE DOING SOME GOOD.
BUT I CAN ONLY LOOK THE OTHER WAY FOR SO LONG.
ALL CLEAR. HE'S GONE, SIR.
OKAY, THIS CONCERNS THE WORK BEING DONE OFF-SITE... AND I'M TRYING TO DO THIS THE NICE WAY, WITHOUT RIPPING DOORS DOWN.
I'M GOING TO NEED ACCESS TO THE STORAGE LOCKER NATHAN IS WORKING OUT OF.
WHAT STORAGE LOCKER?

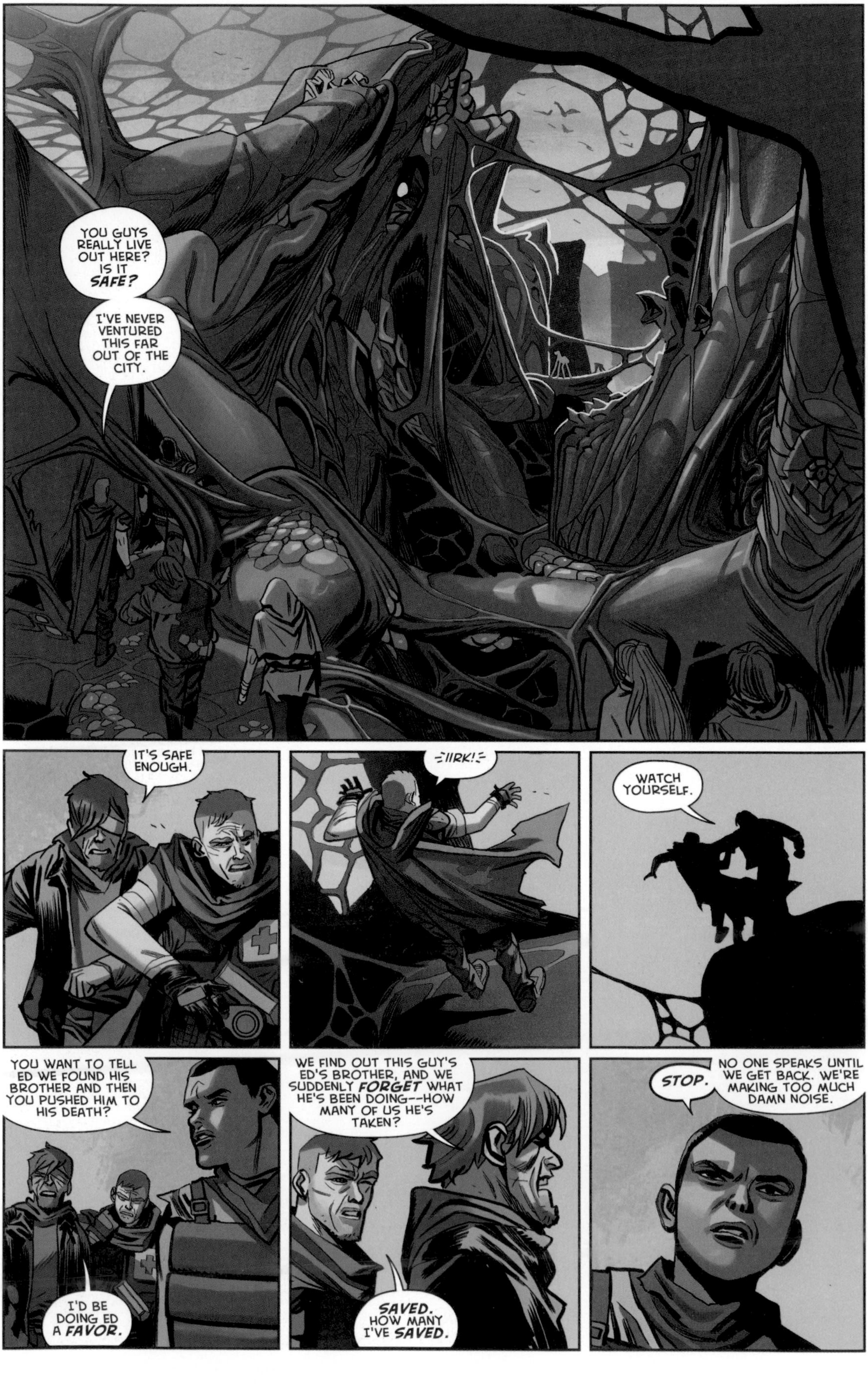
YOU GUYS REALLY LIVE OUT HERE? IS IT SAFE?
I'VE NEVER VENTURED THIS FAR OUT OF THE CITY.
IT'S SAFE ENOUGH.
IIRK!
WATCH YOURSELF.
YOU WANT TO TELL ED WE FOUND HIS BROTHER AND THEN YOU PUSHED HIM TO HIS DEATH?
I'D BE DOING ED A FAVOR.
WE FIND OUT THIS GUY'S ED'S BROTHER, AND WE SUDDENLY FORGET WHAT HE'S BEEN DOING--HOW MANY OF US HE'S TAKEN?
SAVED. HOW MANY I'VE SAVED.
STOP.
NO ONE SPEAKS UNTIL WE GET BACK. WE'RE MAKING TOO MUCH DAMN NOISE.

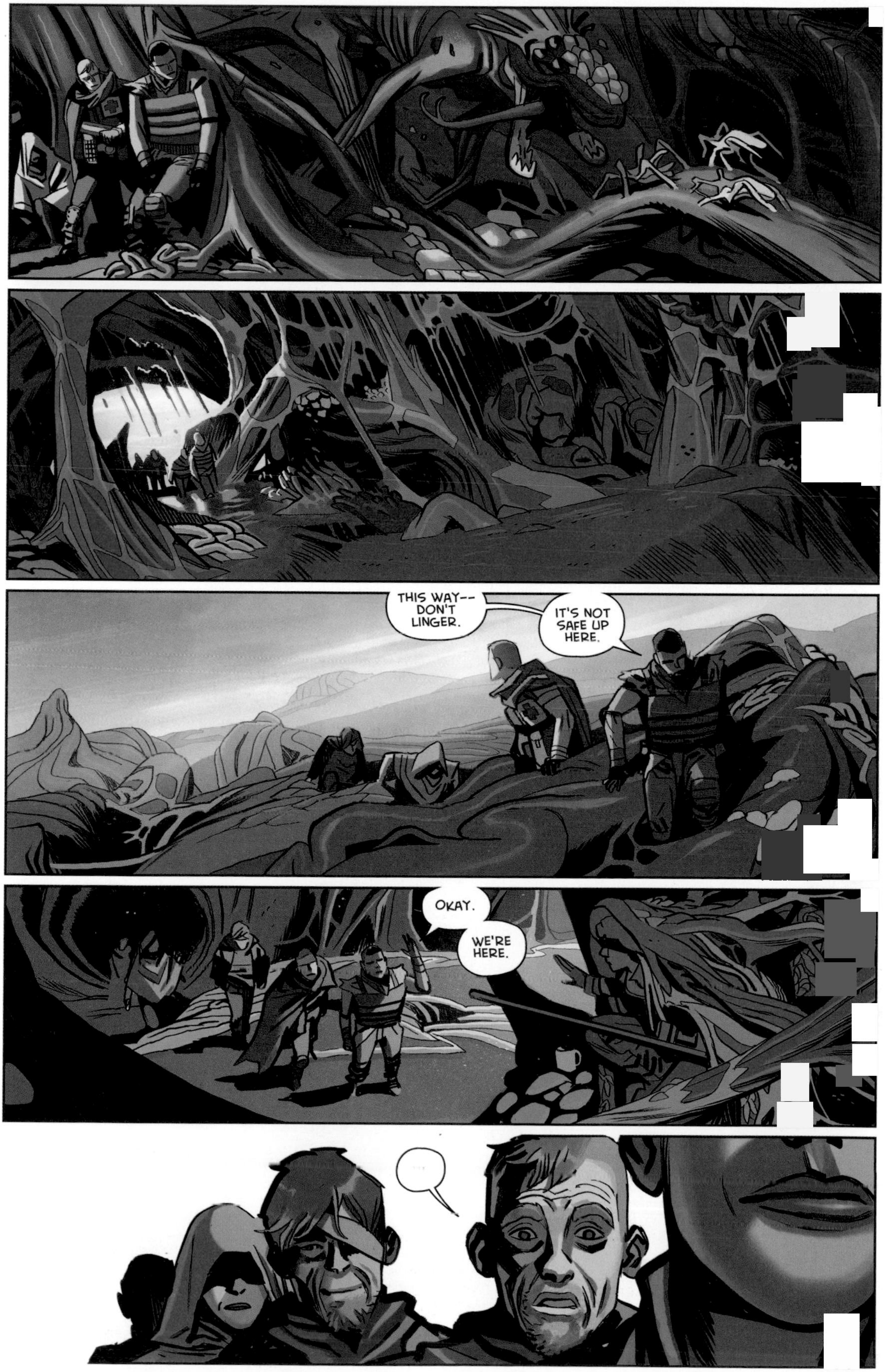
THIS WAY--
DON'T LINGER.
IT'S NOT SAFE UP HERE.
OKAY.
WE'RE HERE.
...

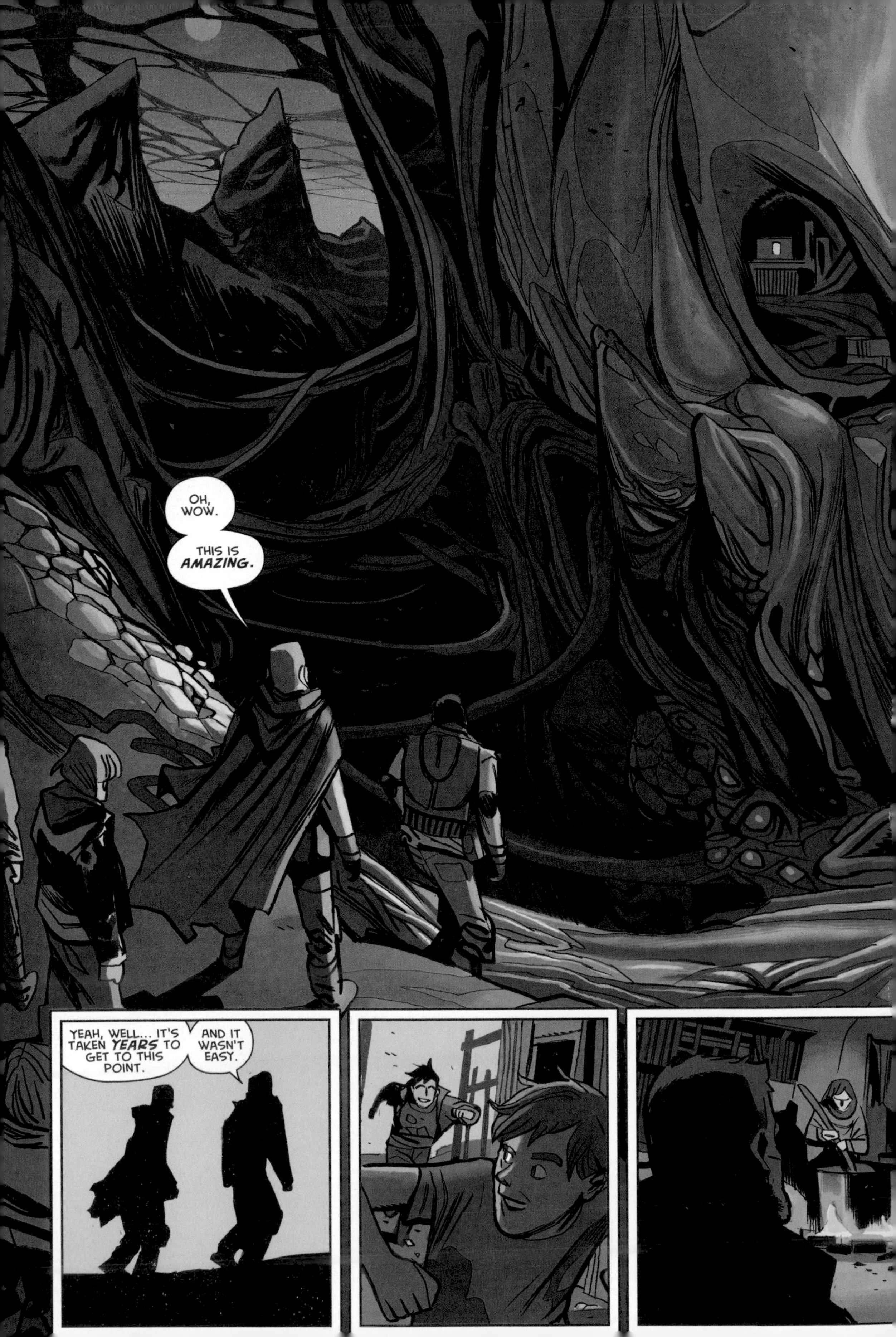
OH, WOW.
THIS IS AMAZING.
YEAH, WELL... IT'S TAKEN YEARS TO GET TO THIS POINT.
AND IT WASN'T EASY.

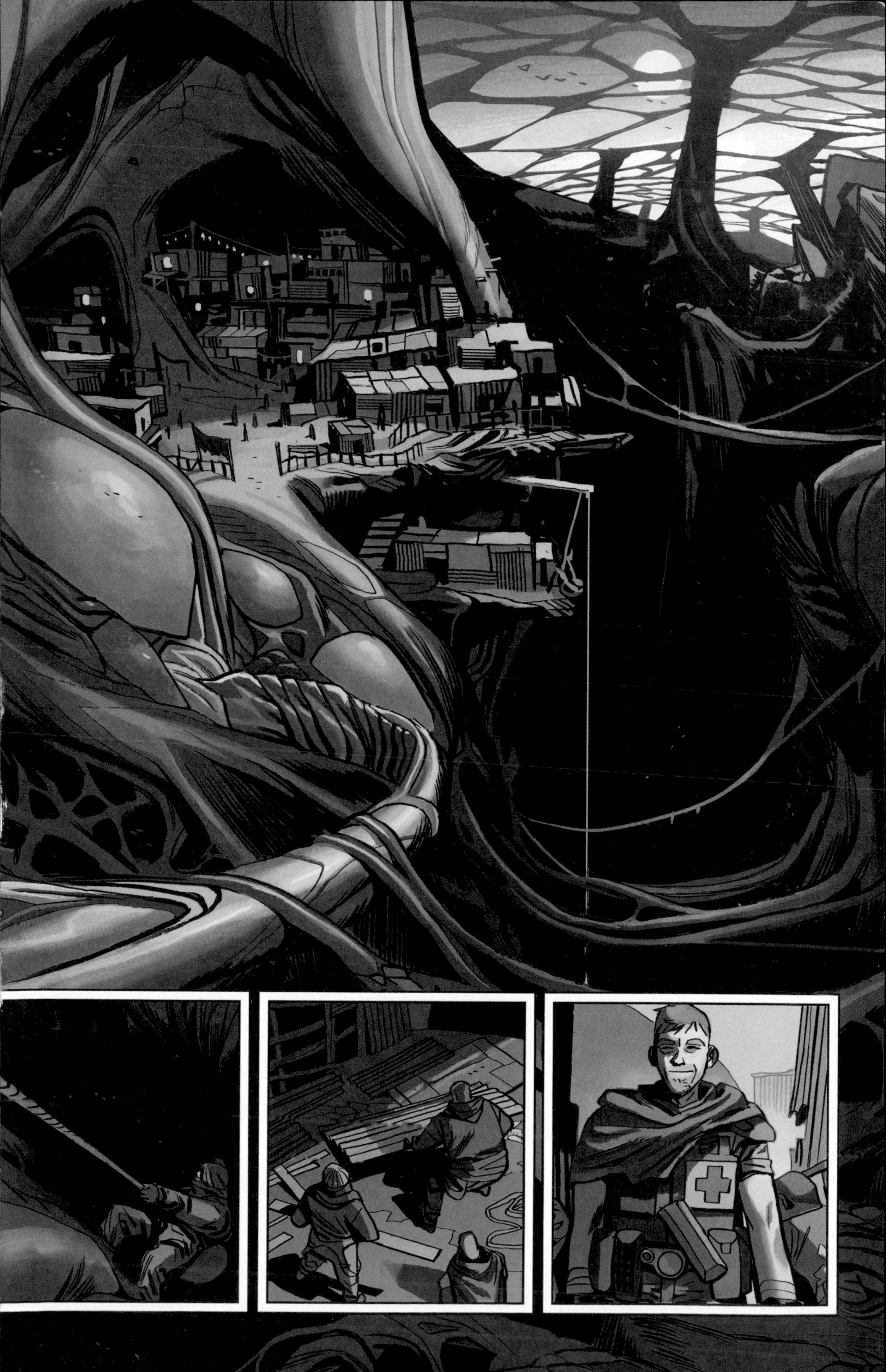

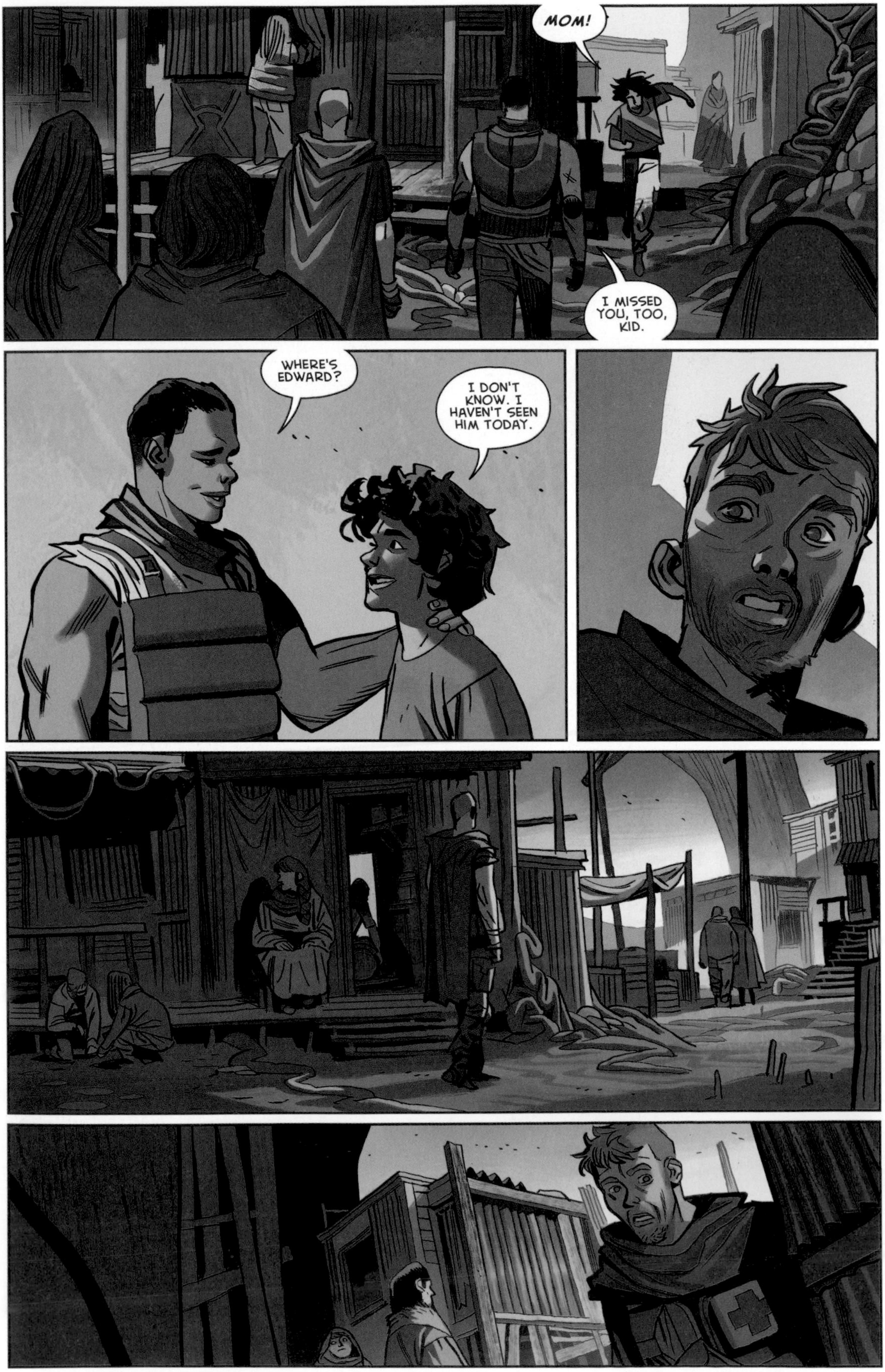
MOM!
I MISSED YOU, TOO, KID.
WHERE'S EDWARD?
I DON'T KNOW. I HAVEN'T SEEN HIM TODAY.

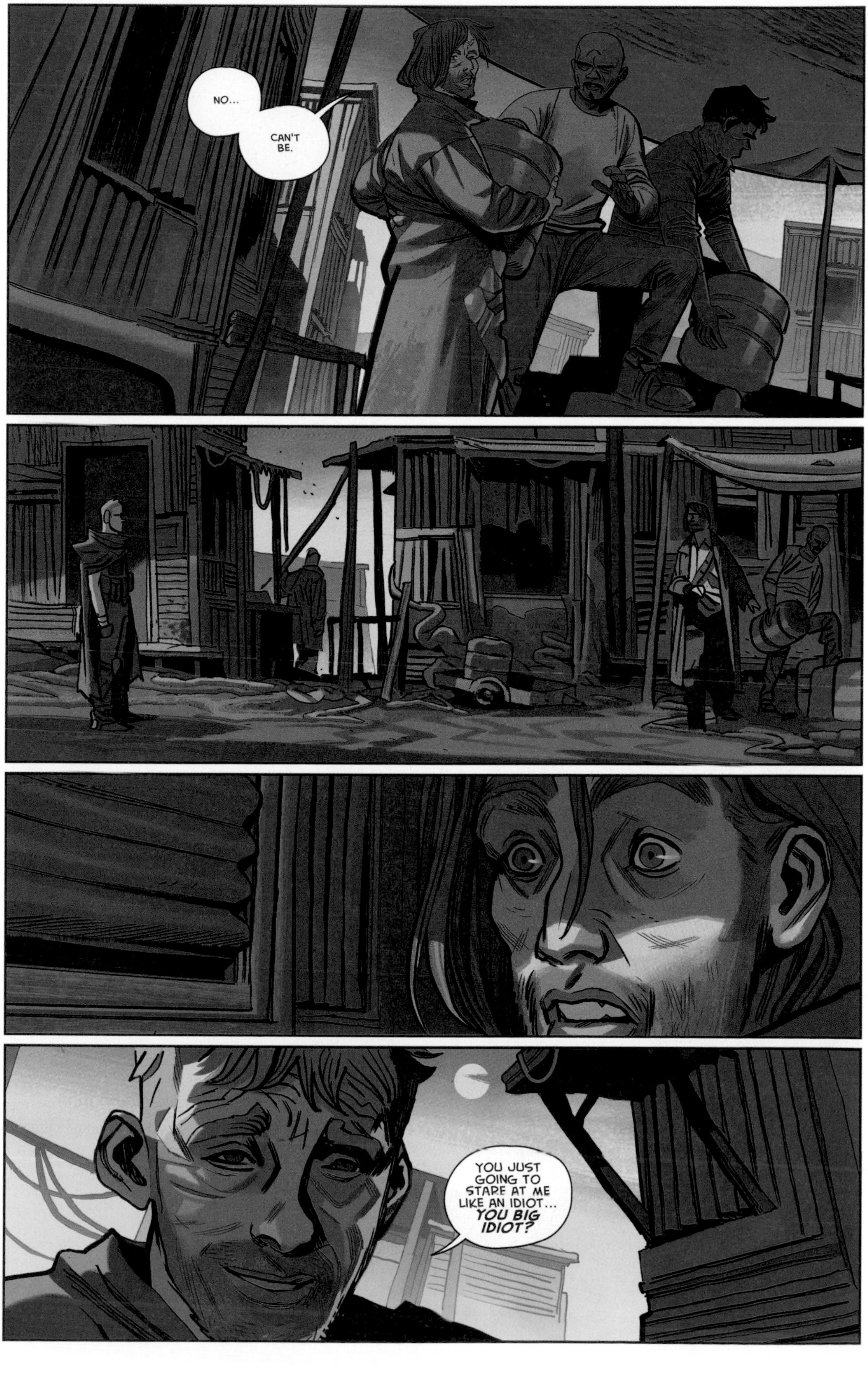
NO...
CAN'T BE.
YOU JUST GOING TO STARE AT ME LIKE AN IDIOT... *YOU BIG IDIOT?*

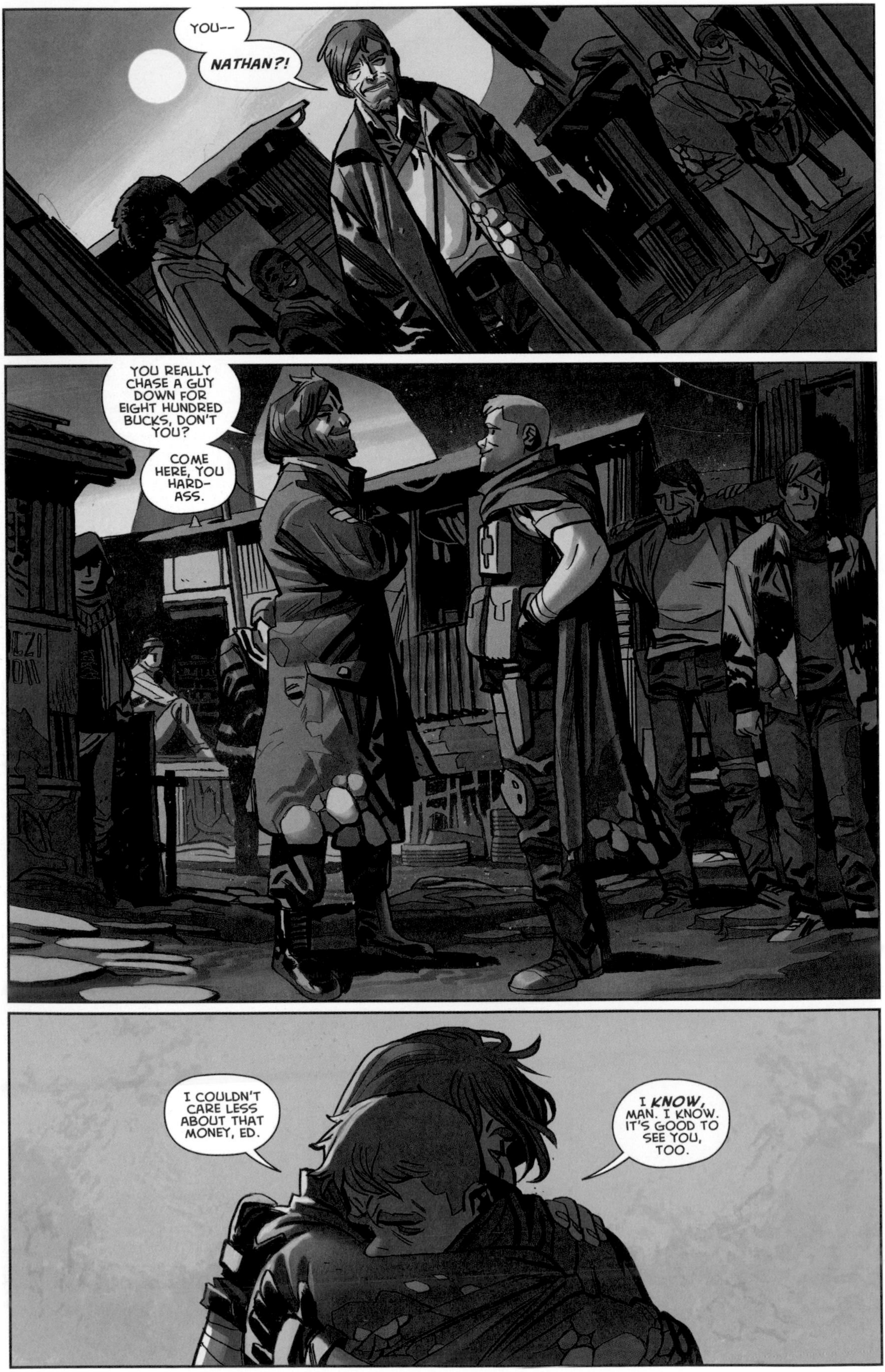
YOU--
NATHAN?!
YOU REALLY CHASE A GUY DOWN FOR EIGHT HUNDRED BUCKS, DON'T YOU?
COME HERE, YOU HARD-ASS.
I COULDN'T CARE LESS ABOUT THAT MONEY, ED.
I KNOW, MAN. I KNOW. IT'S GOOD TO SEE YOU, TOO.

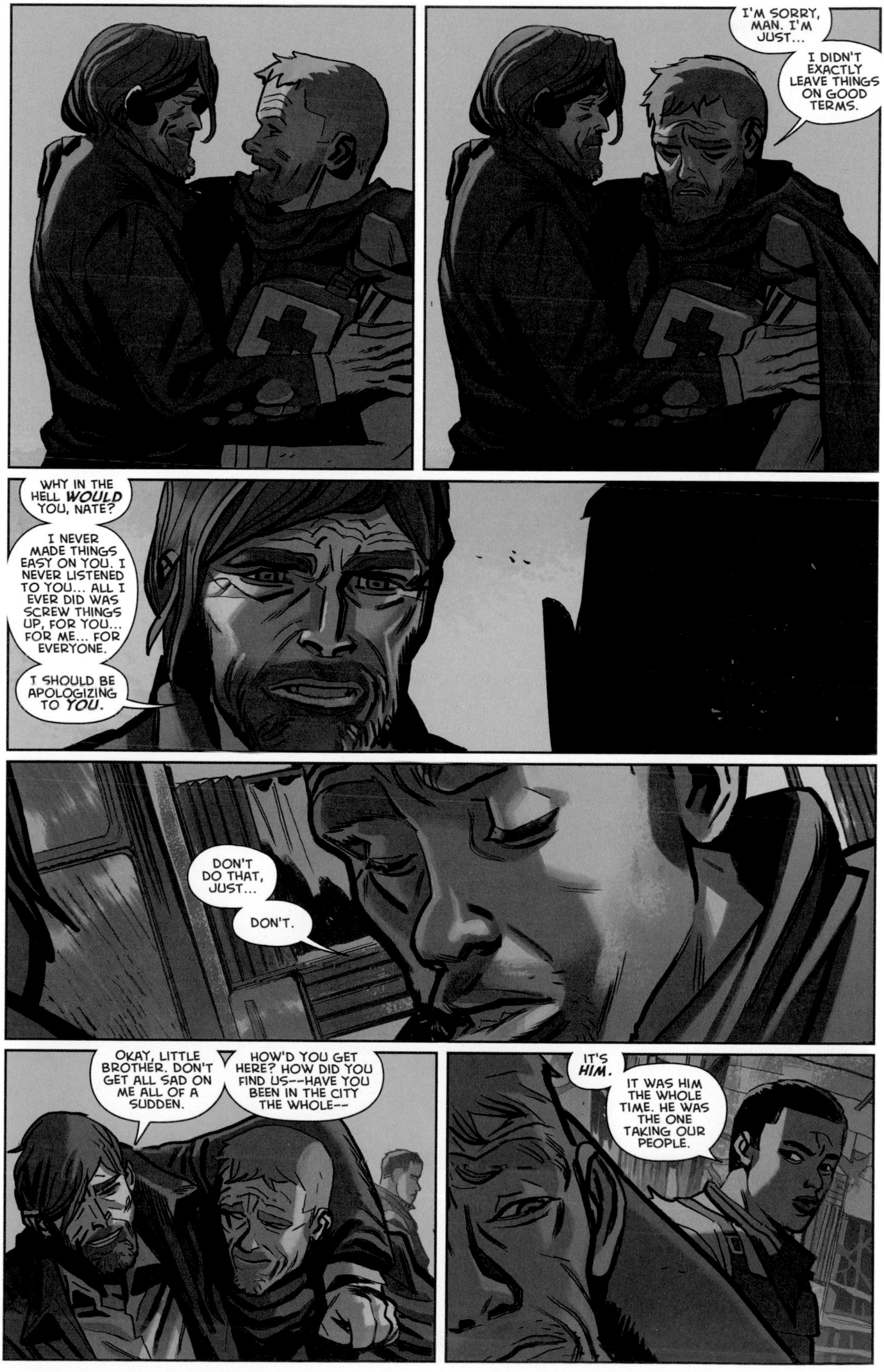
I'M SORRY, MAN. I'M JUST...
I DIDN'T EXACTLY LEAVE THINGS ON GOOD TERMS.
WHY IN THE HELL WOULD YOU, NATE?
I NEVER MADE THINGS EASY ON YOU. I NEVER LISTENED TO YOU... ALL I EVER DID WAS SCREW THINGS UP, FOR YOU... FOR ME... FOR EVERYONE.
I SHOULD BE APOLOGIZING TO YOU.
DON'T DO THAT, JUST...
DON'T.
OKAY, LITTLE BROTHER. DON'T GET ALL SAD ON ME ALL OF A SUDDEN.
HOW'D YOU GET HERE? HOW DID YOU FIND US--HAVE YOU BEEN IN THE CITY THE WHOLE--
IT'S HIM.
IT WAS HIM THE WHOLE TIME. HE WAS THE ONE TAKING OUR PEOPLE.

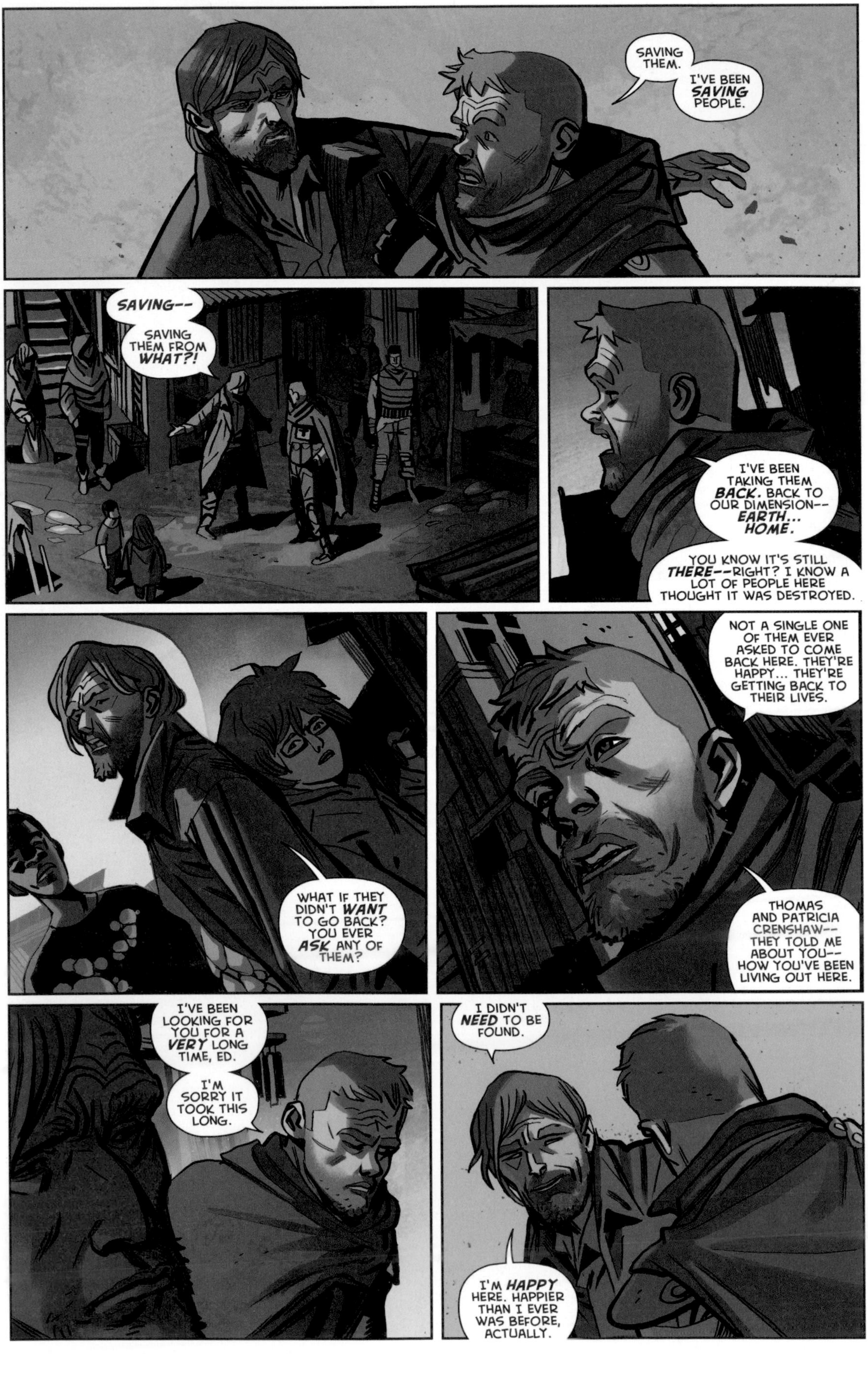
SAVING THEM.
I'VE BEEN SAVING PEOPLE.
SAVING--
SAVING THEM FROM WHAT?!
I'VE BEEN TAKING THEM BACK. BACK TO OUR DIMENSION-- EARTH... HOME.
YOU KNOW IT'S STILL THERE--RIGHT? I KNOW A LOT OF PEOPLE HERE THOUGHT IT WAS DESTROYED.
WHAT IF THEY DIDN'T WANT TO GO BACK? YOU EVER ASK ANY OF THEM?
NOT A SINGLE ONE OF THEM EVER ASKED TO COME BACK HERE. THEY'RE HAPPY... THEY'RE GETTING BACK TO THEIR LIVES.
THOMAS AND PATRICIA CRENSHAW-- THEY TOLD ME ABOUT YOU-- HOW YOU'VE BEEN LIVING OUT HERE.
I'VE BEEN LOOKING FOR YOU FOR A VERY LONG TIME, ED.
I'M SORRY IT TOOK THIS LONG.
I DIDN'T NEED TO BE FOUND.
I'M HAPPY HERE. HAPPIER THAN I EVER WAS BEFORE, ACTUALLY.

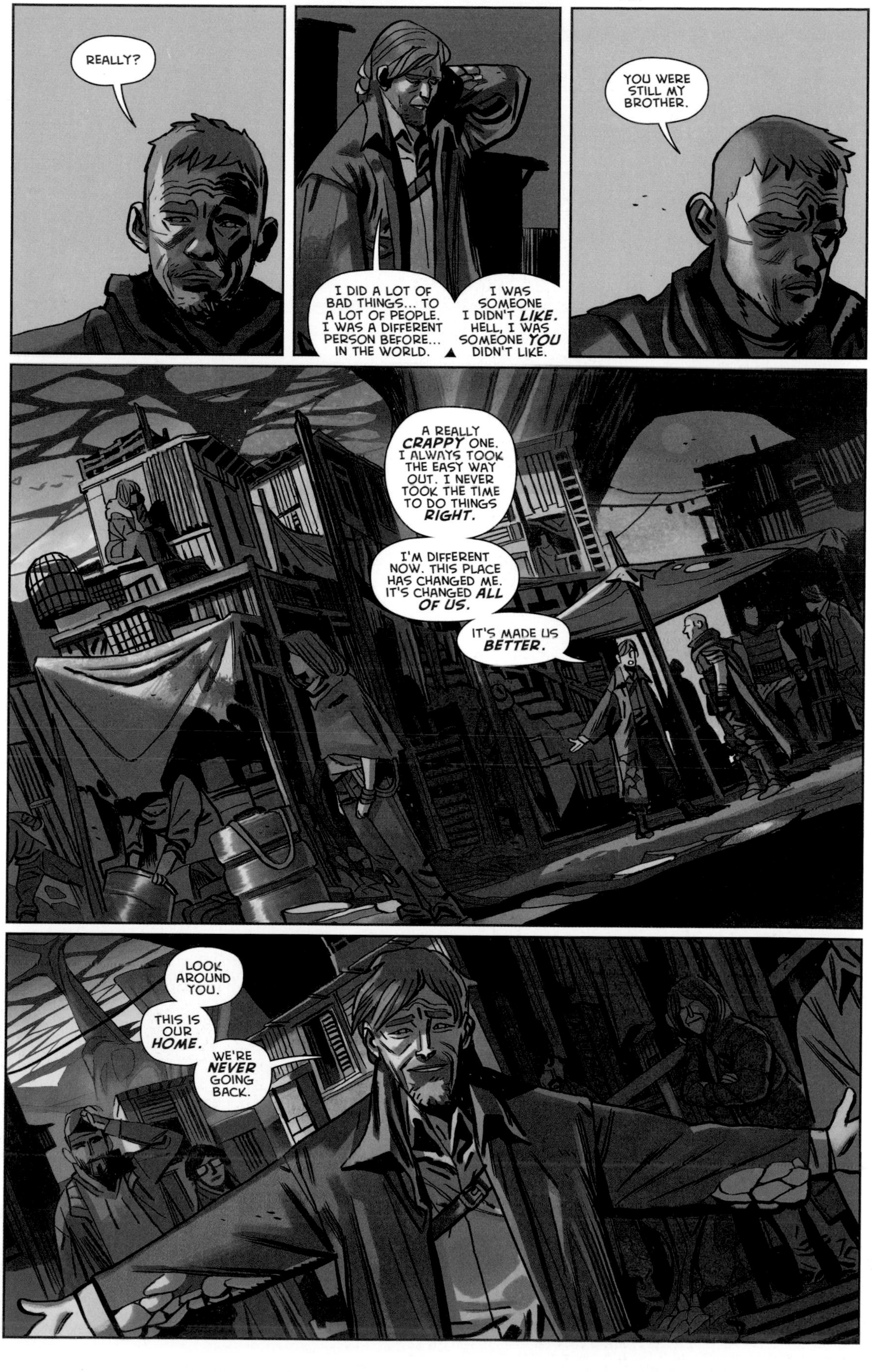
REALLY?
I DID A LOT OF BAD THINGS... TO A LOT OF PEOPLE. I WAS A DIFFERENT PERSON BEFORE... IN THE WORLD.
I WAS SOMEONE I DIDN'T LIKE. HELL, I WAS SOMEONE YOU DIDN'T LIKE.
YOU WERE STILL MY BROTHER.
A REALLY CRAPPY ONE. I ALWAYS TOOK THE EASY WAY OUT. I NEVER TOOK THE TIME TO DO THINGS RIGHT.
I'M DIFFERENT NOW. THIS PLACE HAS CHANGED ME. IT'S CHANGED ALL OF US.
IT'S MADE US BETTER.
LOOK AROUND YOU.
THIS IS OUR HOME.
WE'RE NEVER GOING BACK.

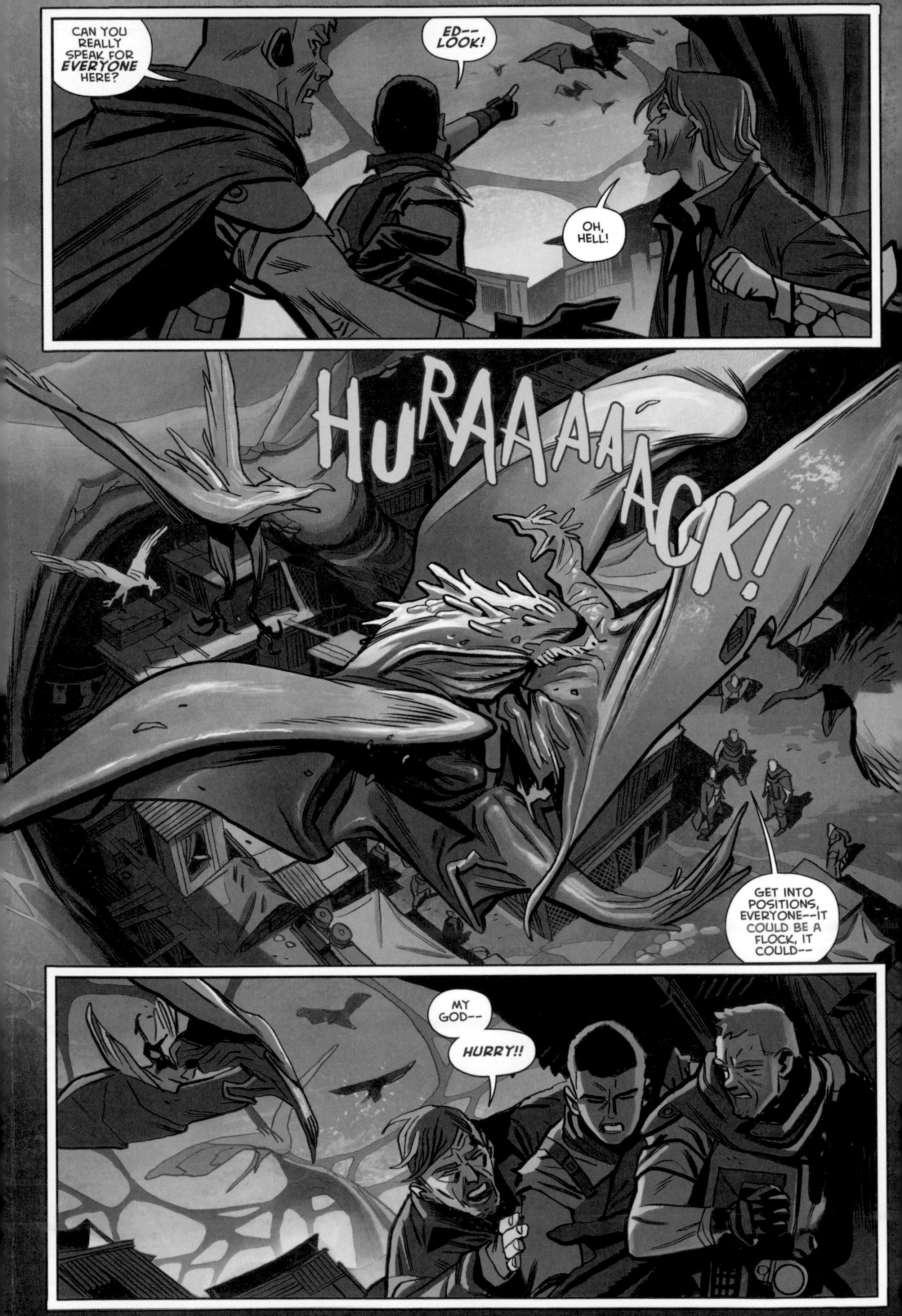
CAN YOU REALLY SPEAK FOR EVERYONE HERE?
ED-- LOOK!
OH, HELL!
HURAAAAACK!
GET INTO POSITIONS, EVERYONE--IT COULD BE A FLOCK, IT COULD--
MY GOD--
HURRY!!

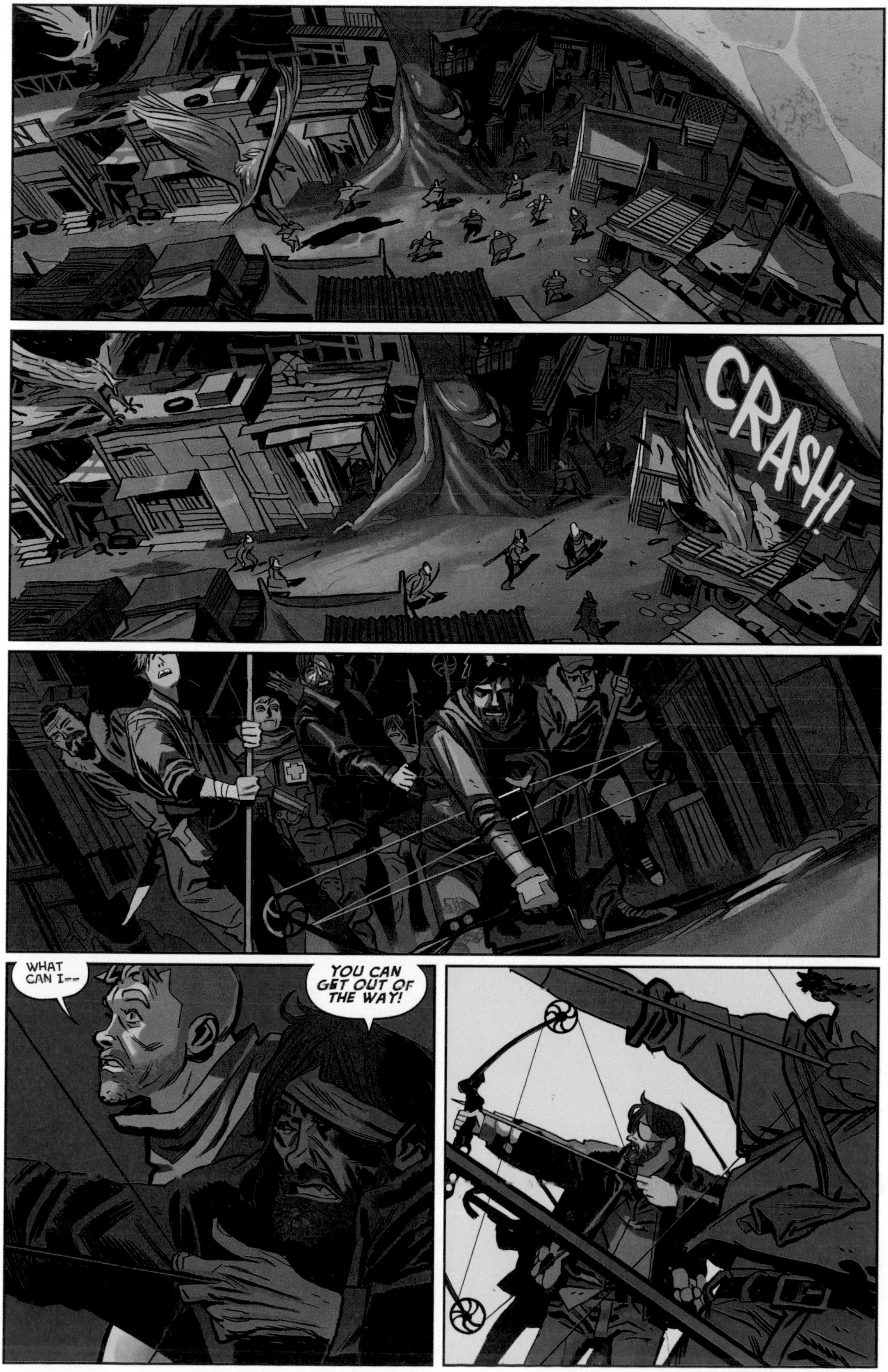
CRASH!
WHAT CAN I--
YOU CAN GET OUT OF THE WAY!

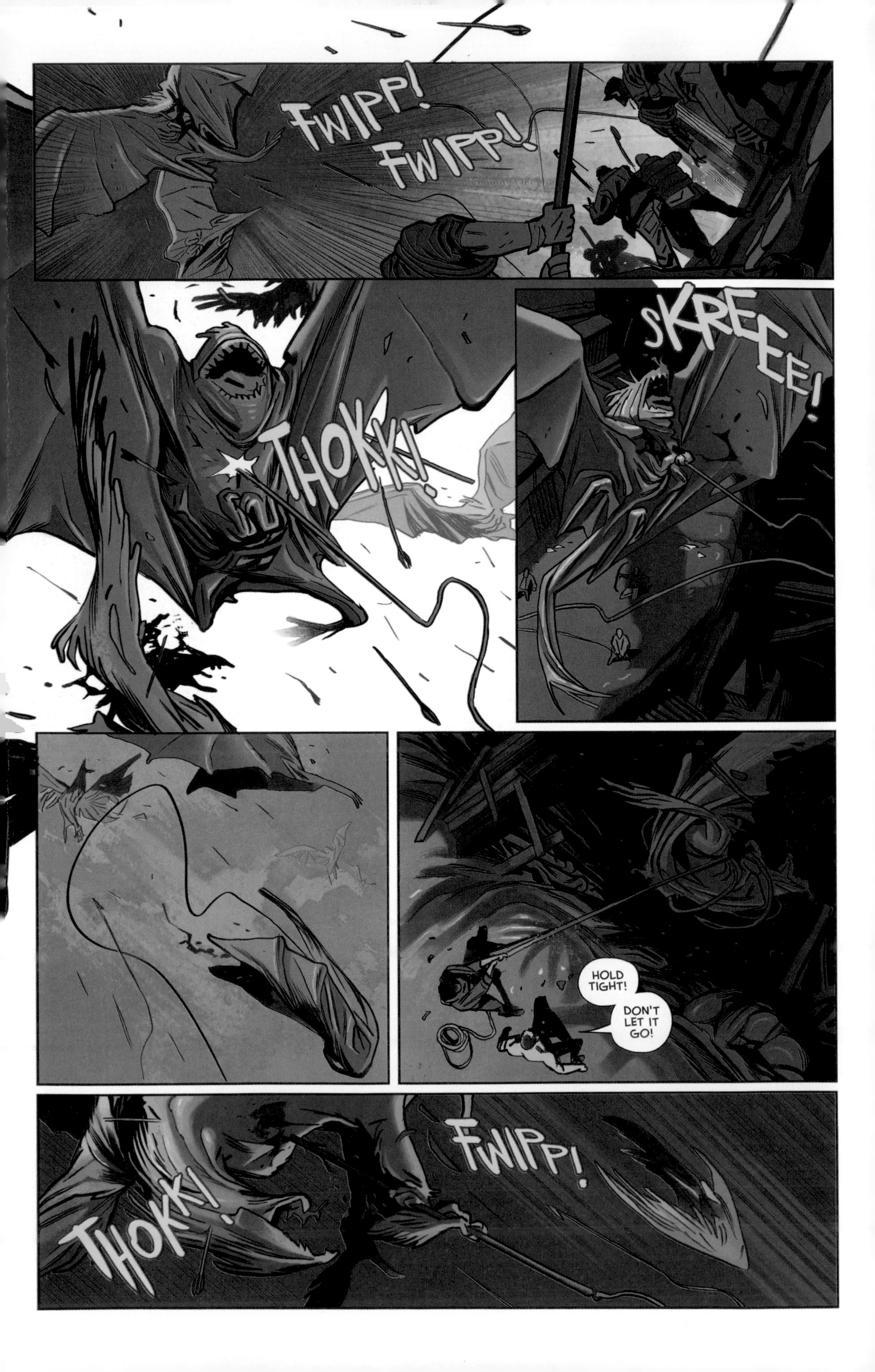
FWIPP! FWIPP!
THOKK!
SKREEEEE!
HOLD TIGHT!
DON'T LET IT GO!
FWIPP!
THOKK!

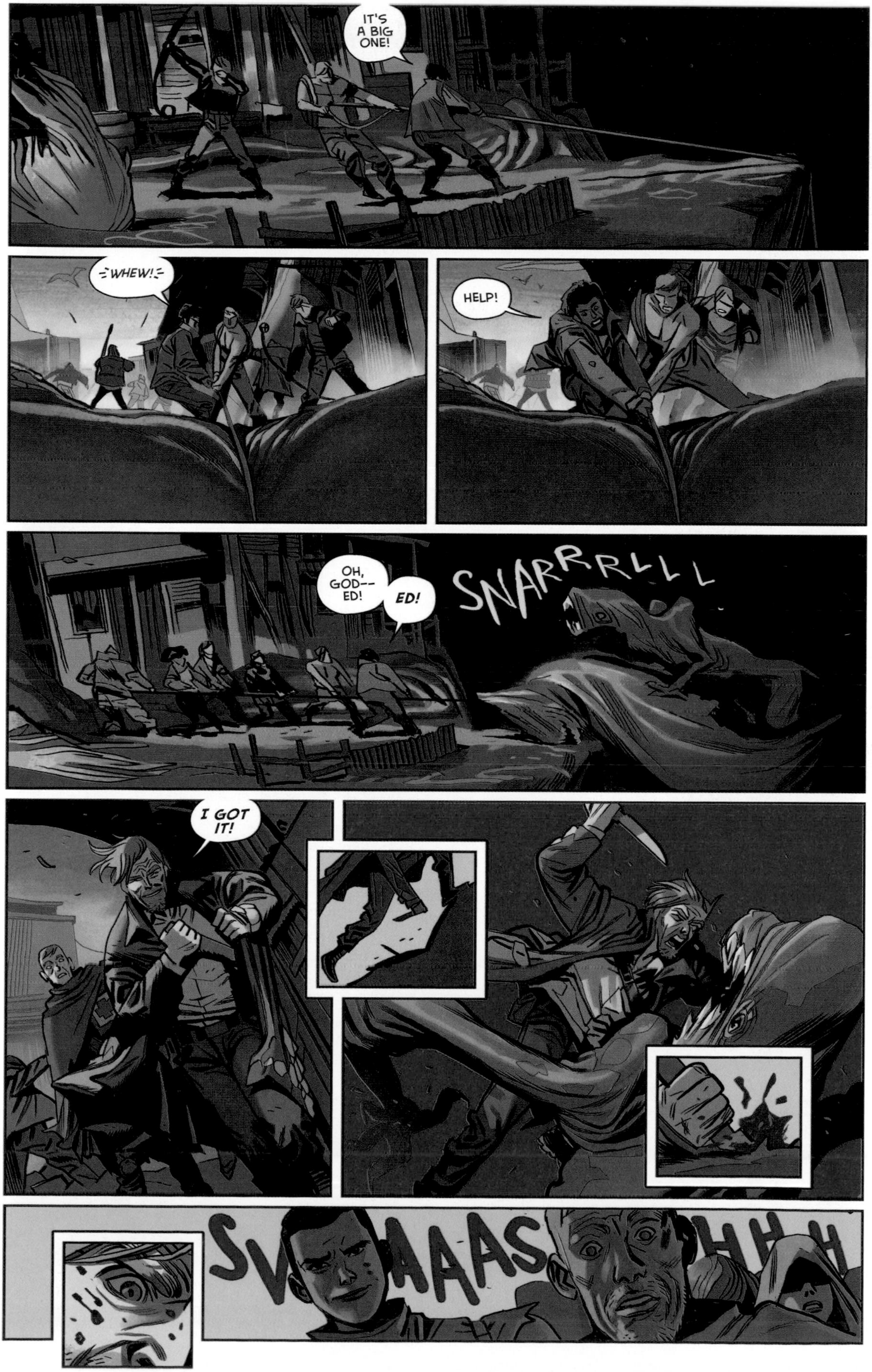
IT'S A BIG ONE!
WHEW!
HELP!
OH, GOD-- ED!
ED!
SNARRRLLLL
I GOT IT!
SVAAAASHHHH

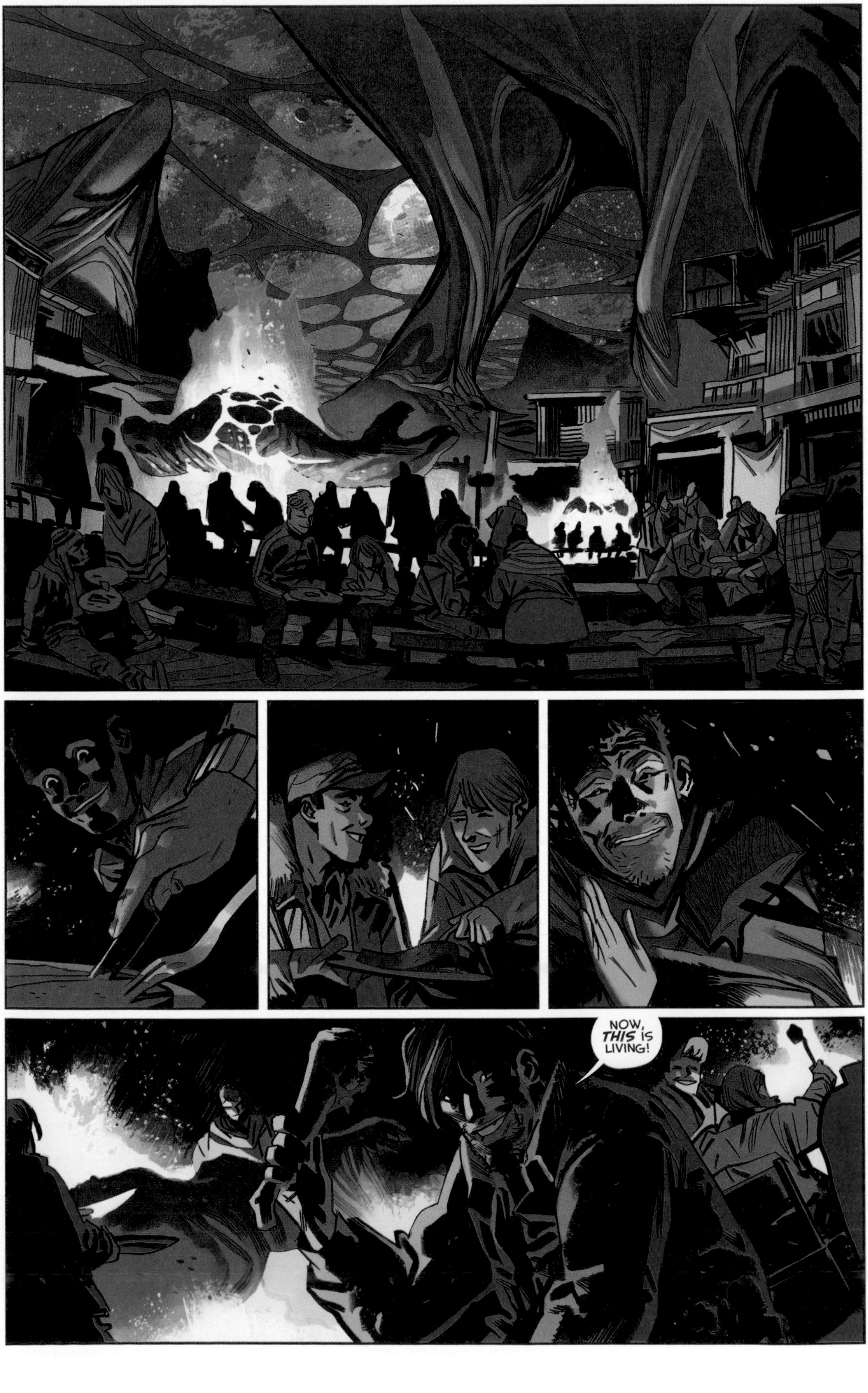
NOW, THIS IS LIVING!

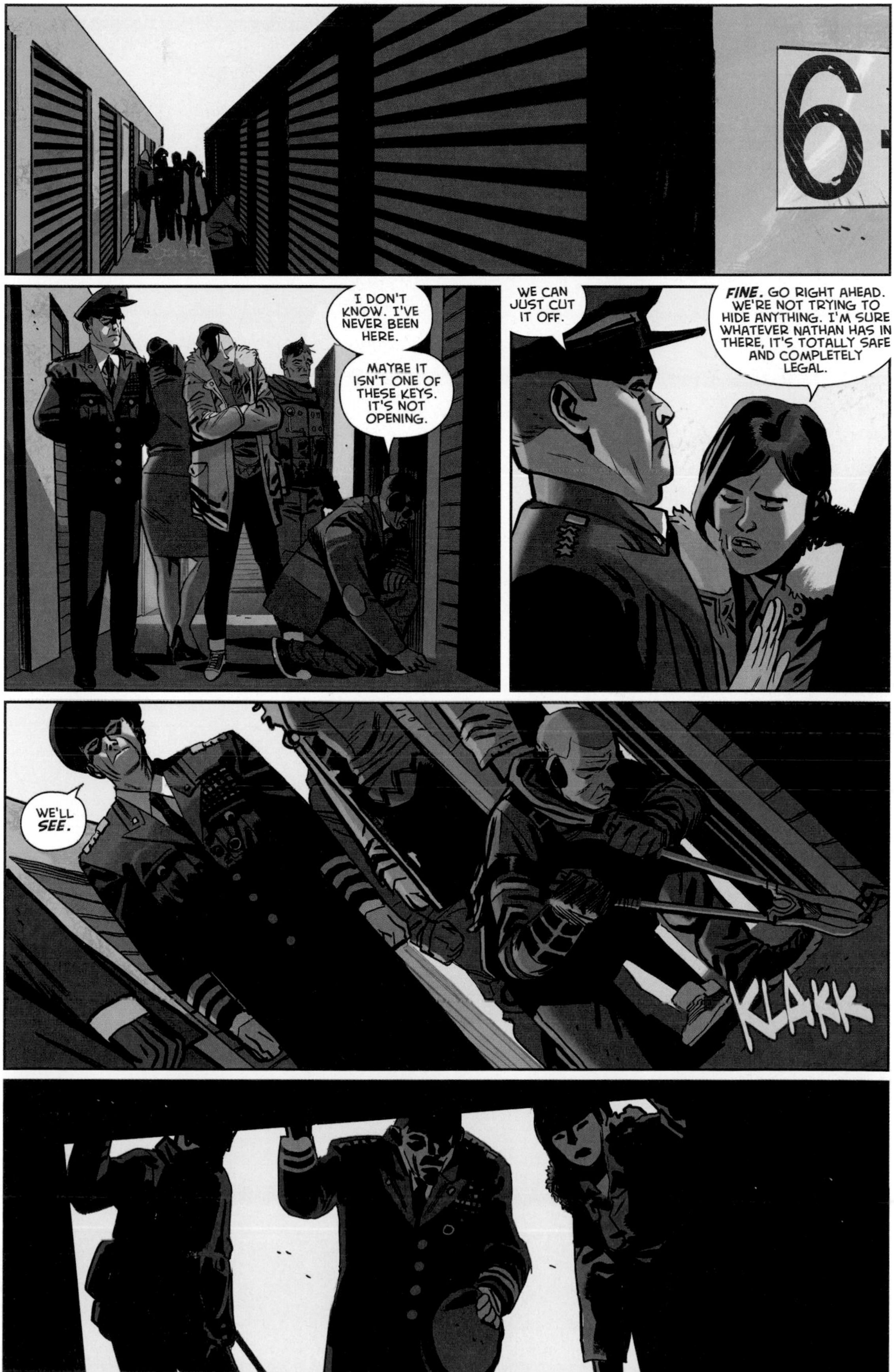

I DON'T KNOW. I'VE NEVER BEEN HERE.
MAYBE IT ISN'T ONE OF THESE KEYS. IT'S NOT OPENING.
WE CAN JUST CUT IT OFF.
FINE. GO RIGHT AHEAD. WE'RE NOT TRYING TO HIDE ANYTHING. I'M SURE WHATEVER NATHAN HAS IN THERE, IT'S TOTALLY SAFE AND COMPLETELY LEGAL.
WE'LL SEE.
KLAKK

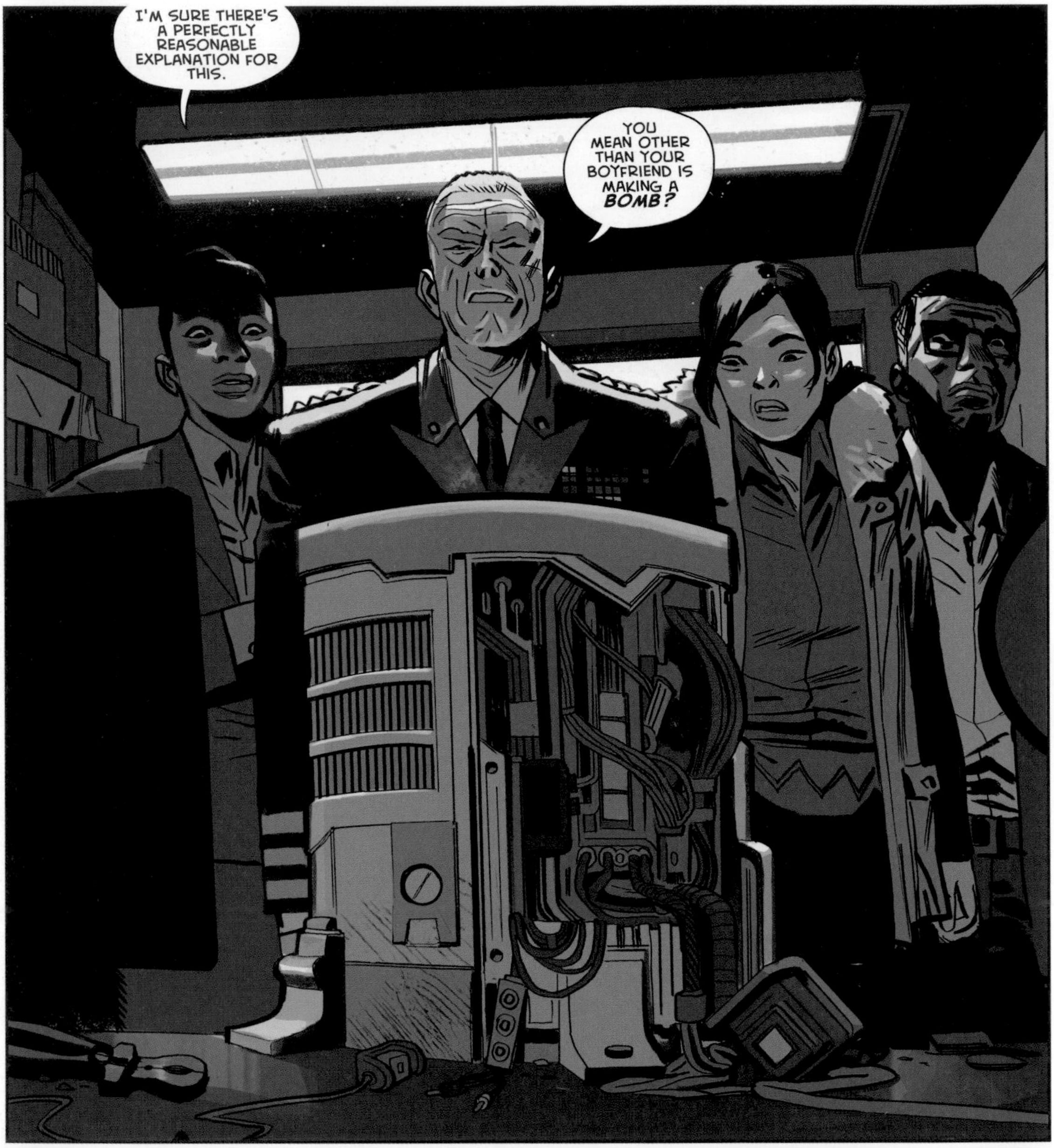
I'M SURE THERE'S A PERFECTLY REASONABLE EXPLANATION FOR THIS.
YOU MEAN OTHER THAN YOUR BOYFRIEND IS MAKING A *BOMB?*

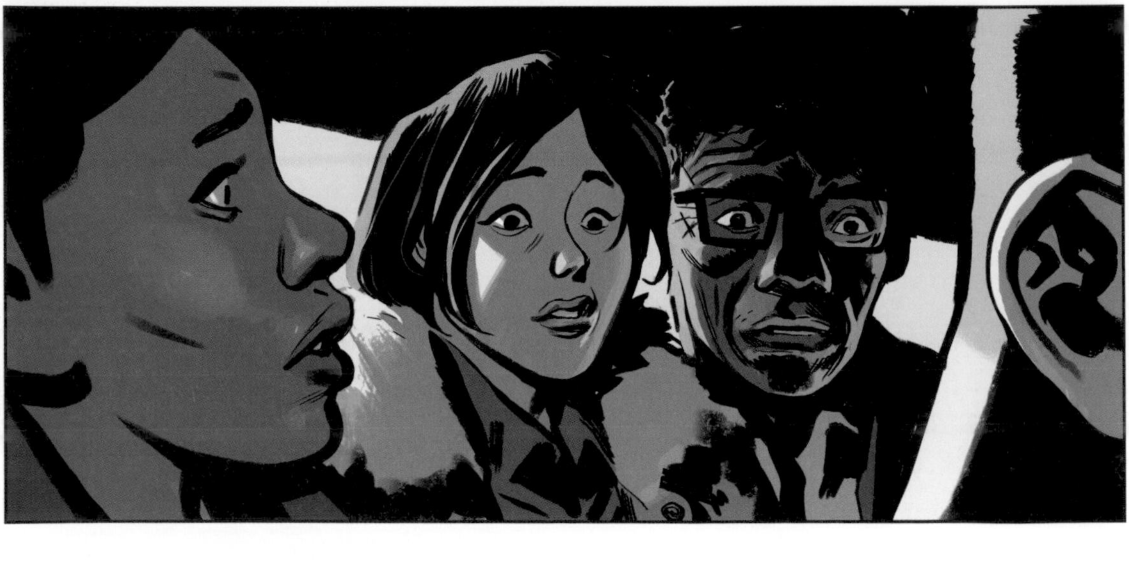

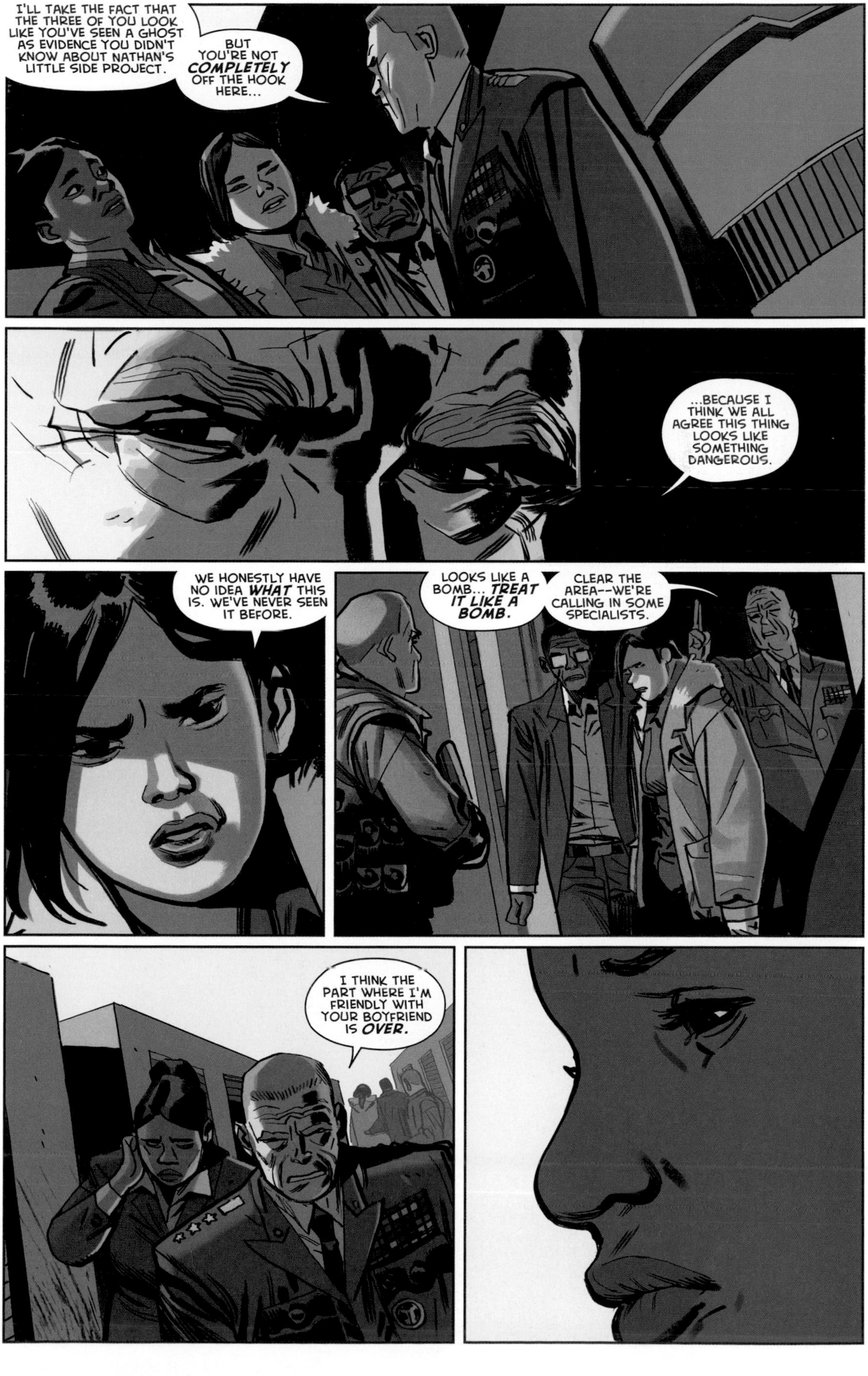
I'LL TAKE THE FACT THAT THE THREE OF YOU LOOK LIKE YOU'VE SEEN A GHOST AS EVIDENCE YOU DIDN'T KNOW ABOUT NATHAN'S LITTLE SIDE PROJECT.
BUT YOU'RE NOT COMPLETELY OFF THE HOOK HERE...
...BECAUSE I THINK WE ALL AGREE THIS THING LOOKS LIKE SOMETHING DANGEROUS.
WE HONESTLY HAVE NO IDEA WHAT THIS IS. WE'VE NEVER SEEN IT BEFORE.
LOOKS LIKE A BOMB... TREAT IT LIKE A BOMB.
CLEAR THE AREA--WE'RE CALLING IN SOME SPECIALISTS.
I THINK THE PART WHERE I'M FRIENDLY WITH YOUR BOYFRIEND IS OVER.

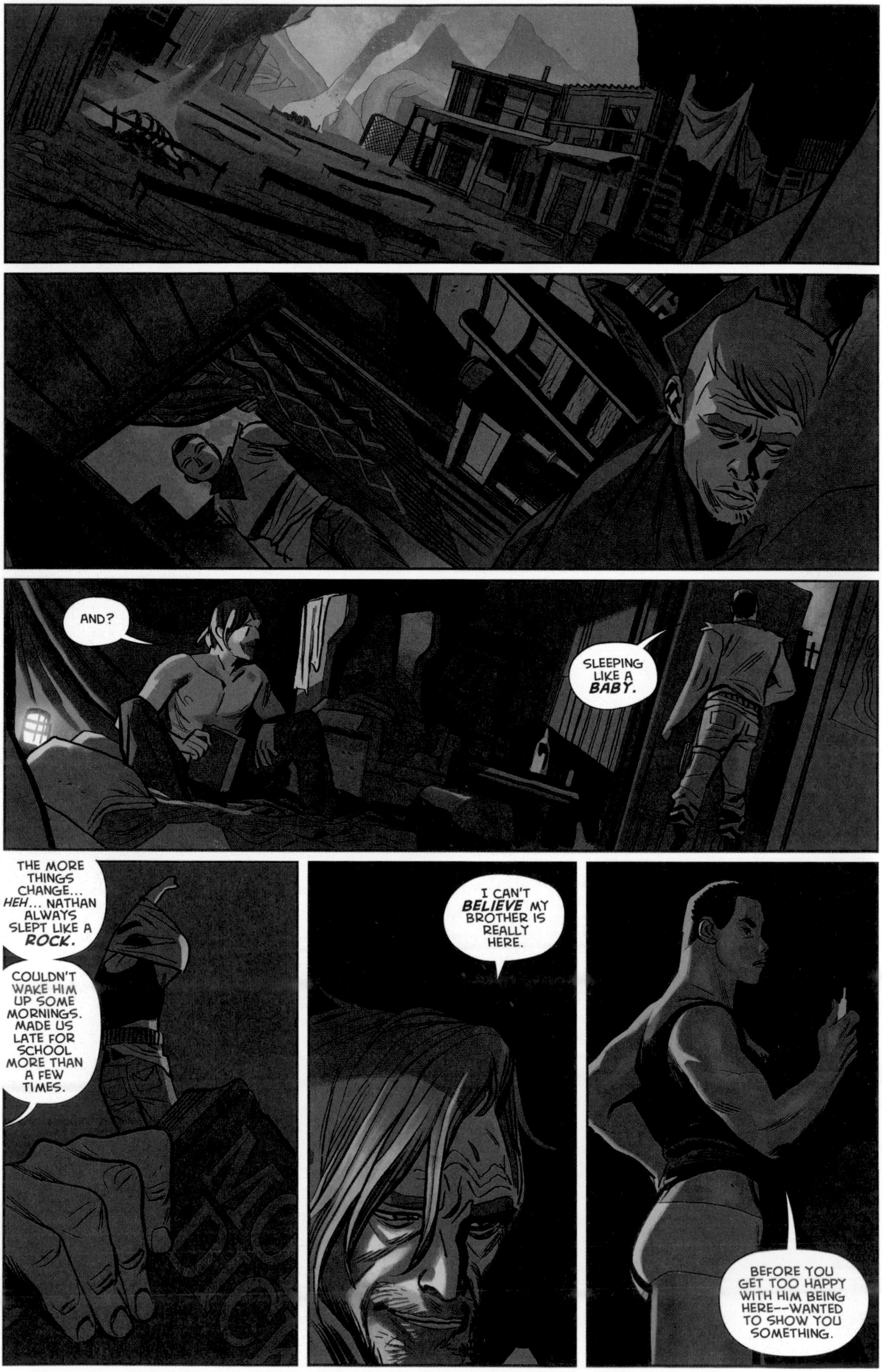
AND?
SLEEPING LIKE A *BABY*.
THE MORE THINGS CHANGE... *HEH*... NATHAN ALWAYS SLEPT LIKE A *ROCK*.
COULDN'T WAKE HIM UP SOME MORNINGS. MADE US LATE FOR SCHOOL MORE THAN A FEW TIMES.
I CAN'T *BELIEVE* MY BROTHER IS REALLY HERE.
BEFORE YOU GET TOO HAPPY WITH HIM BEING HERE--WANTED TO SHOW YOU SOMETHING.

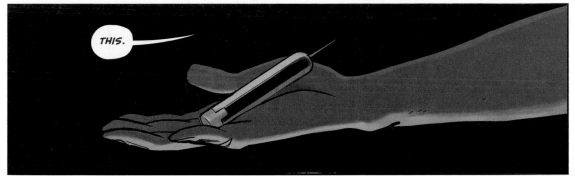
THIS.

WHAT IS IT?

GOT IT FROM *KEITH*. THEY HAD A RUN-IN--YOUR BROTHER TRIED TO SHOOT HIM WITH IT. IT'S WHAT SENDS PEOPLE BACK, APPARENTLY.

THAT'S WHAT HE'S BEEN SHOOTING OUR PEOPLE WITH.

THIS LITTLE THING? I CAN'T EVEN BEGIN TO IMAGINE HOW THIS WORKS.

I KNEW MY BROTHER WAS A SCIENTIST-- *BUT THIS*-- HE MUST BE A DAMN *GENIUS*.

DO YOU *TRUST* HIM?

MY BROTHER AND I... WE'VE ALWAYS HAD A *COMPLICATED* RELATIONSHIP, BUT HE'S NEVER GIVEN ME REASON NOT TO TRUST HIM.

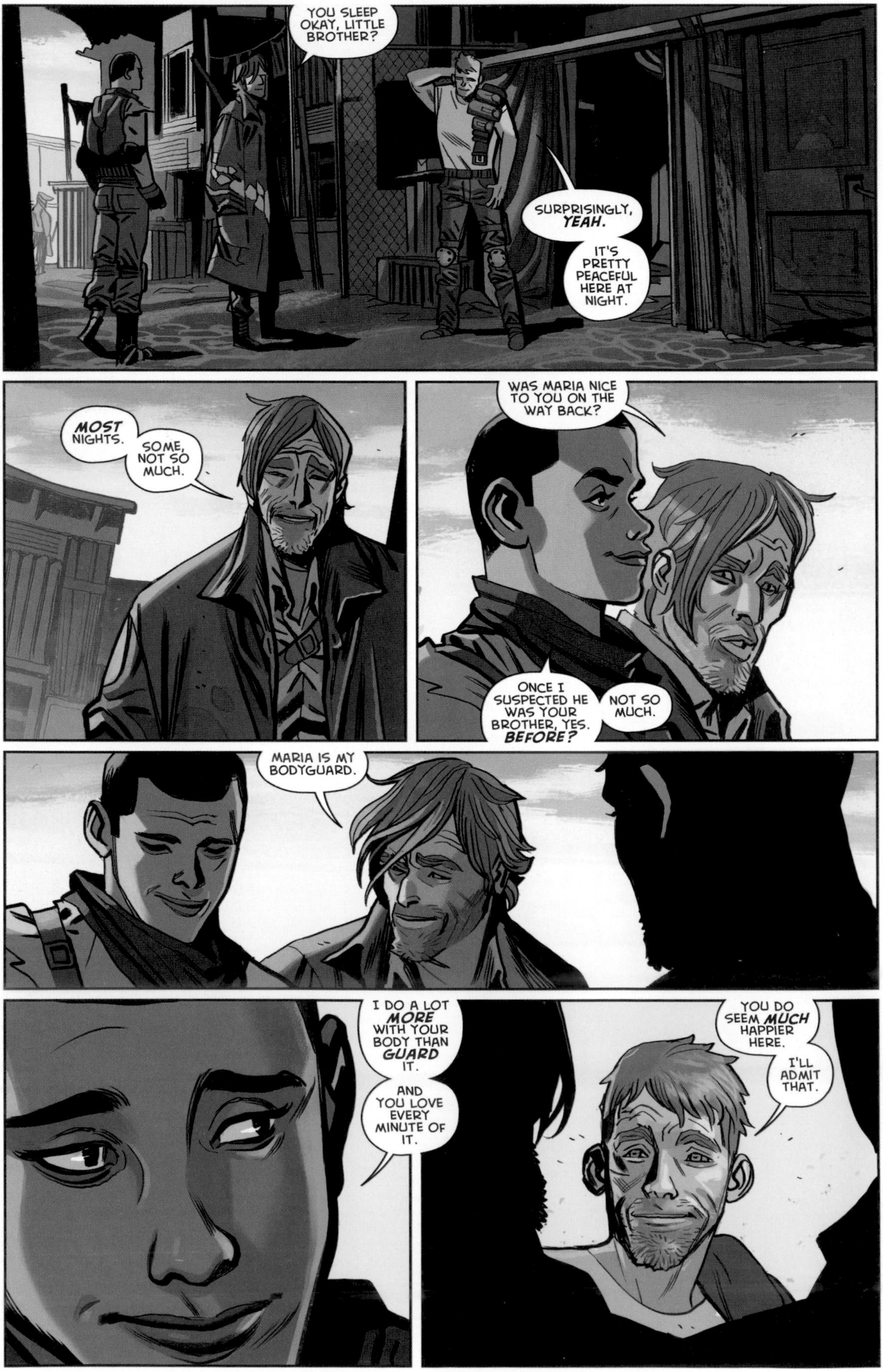
YOU SLEEP OKAY, LITTLE BROTHER?
SURPRISINGLY, YEAH.
IT'S PRETTY PEACEFUL HERE AT NIGHT.
MOST NIGHTS.
SOME, NOT SO MUCH.
WAS MARIA NICE TO YOU ON THE WAY BACK?
ONCE I SUSPECTED HE WAS YOUR BROTHER, YES. BEFORE?
NOT SO MUCH.
MARIA IS MY BODYGUARD.
I DO A LOT MORE WITH YOUR BODY THAN GUARD IT.
AND YOU LOVE EVERY MINUTE OF IT.
YOU DO SEEM MUCH HAPPIER HERE.
I'LL ADMIT THAT.

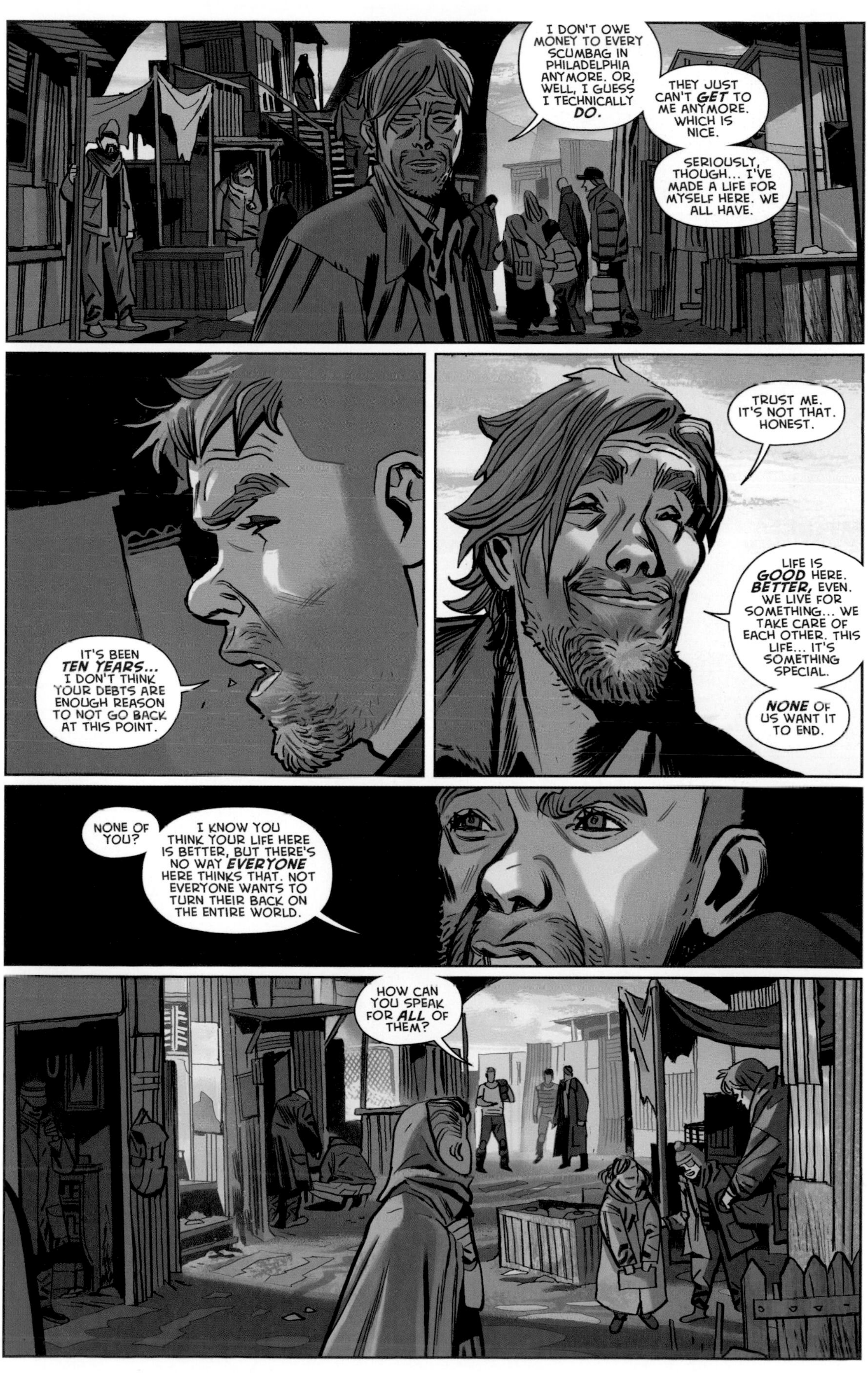
I DON'T OWE MONEY TO EVERY SCUMBAG IN PHILADELPHIA ANYMORE. OR, WELL, I GUESS I TECHNICALLY *DO.*
THEY JUST CAN'T *GET* TO ME ANYMORE. WHICH IS NICE.
SERIOUSLY, THOUGH... I'VE MADE A LIFE FOR MYSELF HERE. WE ALL HAVE.
IT'S BEEN *TEN YEARS...* I DON'T THINK YOUR DEBTS ARE ENOUGH REASON TO NOT GO BACK AT THIS POINT.
TRUST ME. IT'S NOT THAT. HONEST.
LIFE IS *GOOD* HERE. *BETTER,* EVEN. WE LIVE FOR SOMETHING... WE TAKE CARE OF EACH OTHER. THIS LIFE... IT'S SOMETHING SPECIAL.
NONE OF US WANT IT TO END.
NONE OF YOU?
I KNOW YOU THINK YOUR LIFE HERE IS BETTER, BUT THERE'S NO WAY *EVERYONE* HERE THINKS THAT. NOT EVERYONE WANTS TO TURN THEIR BACK ON THE ENTIRE WORLD.
HOW CAN YOU SPEAK FOR *ALL* OF THEM?

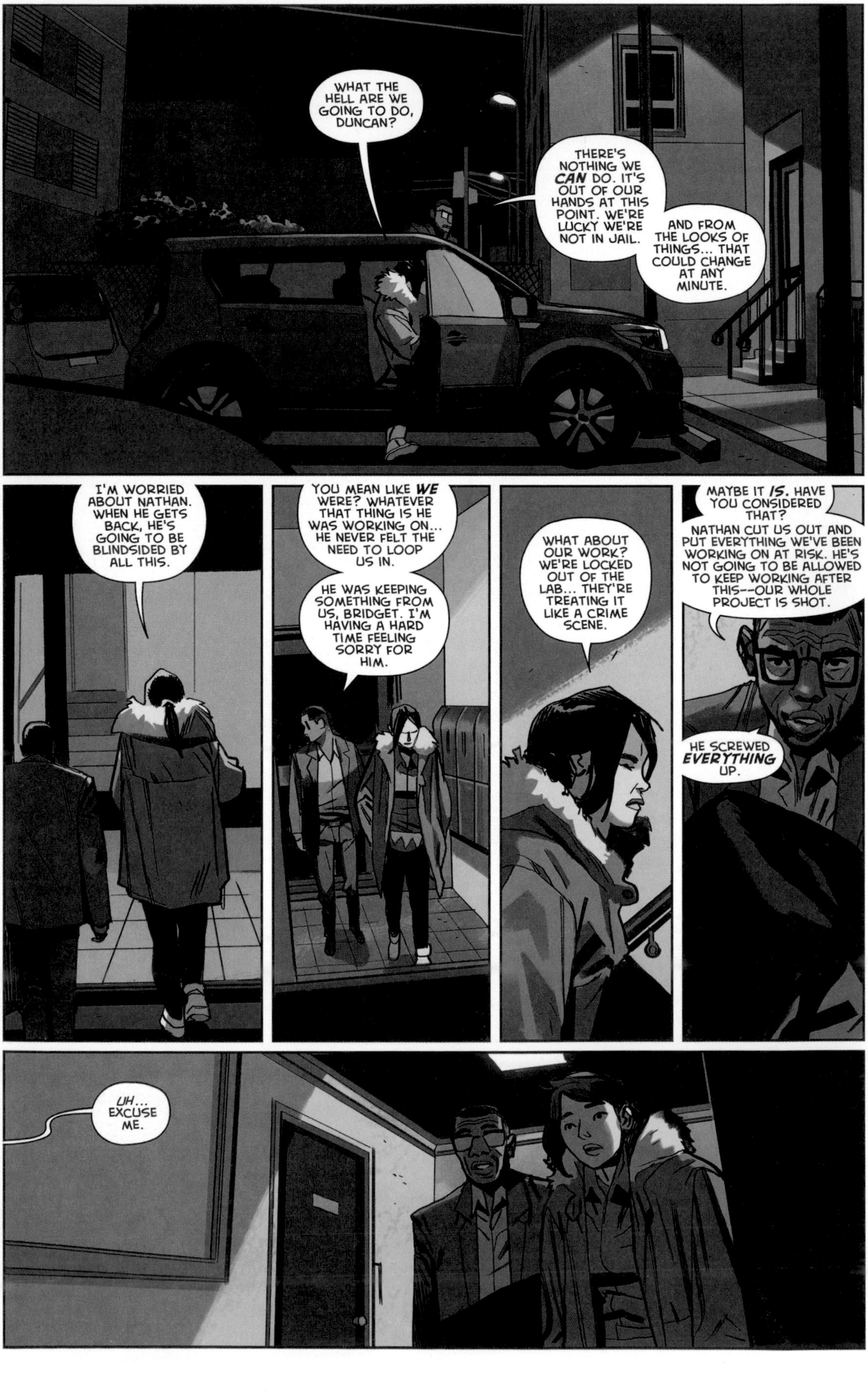
WHAT THE HELL ARE WE GOING TO DO, DUNCAN?
THERE'S NOTHING WE CAN DO. IT'S OUT OF OUR HANDS AT THIS POINT. WE'RE LUCKY WE'RE NOT IN JAIL.
AND FROM THE LOOKS OF THINGS... THAT COULD CHANGE AT ANY MINUTE.
I'M WORRIED ABOUT NATHAN. WHEN HE GETS BACK, HE'S GOING TO BE BLINDSIDED BY ALL THIS.
YOU MEAN LIKE WE WERE? WHATEVER THAT THING IS HE WAS WORKING ON... HE NEVER FELT THE NEED TO LOOP US IN.
HE WAS KEEPING SOMETHING FROM US, BRIDGET. I'M HAVING A HARD TIME FEELING SORRY FOR HIM.
WHAT ABOUT OUR WORK? WE'RE LOCKED OUT OF THE LAB... THEY'RE TREATING IT LIKE A CRIME SCENE.
MAYBE IT IS. HAVE YOU CONSIDERED THAT?
NATHAN CUT US OUT AND PUT EVERYTHING WE'VE BEEN WORKING ON AT RISK. HE'S NOT GOING TO BE ALLOWED TO KEEP WORKING AFTER THIS--OUR WHOLE PROJECT IS SHOT.
HE SCREWED EVERYTHING UP.
UH... EXCUSE ME.

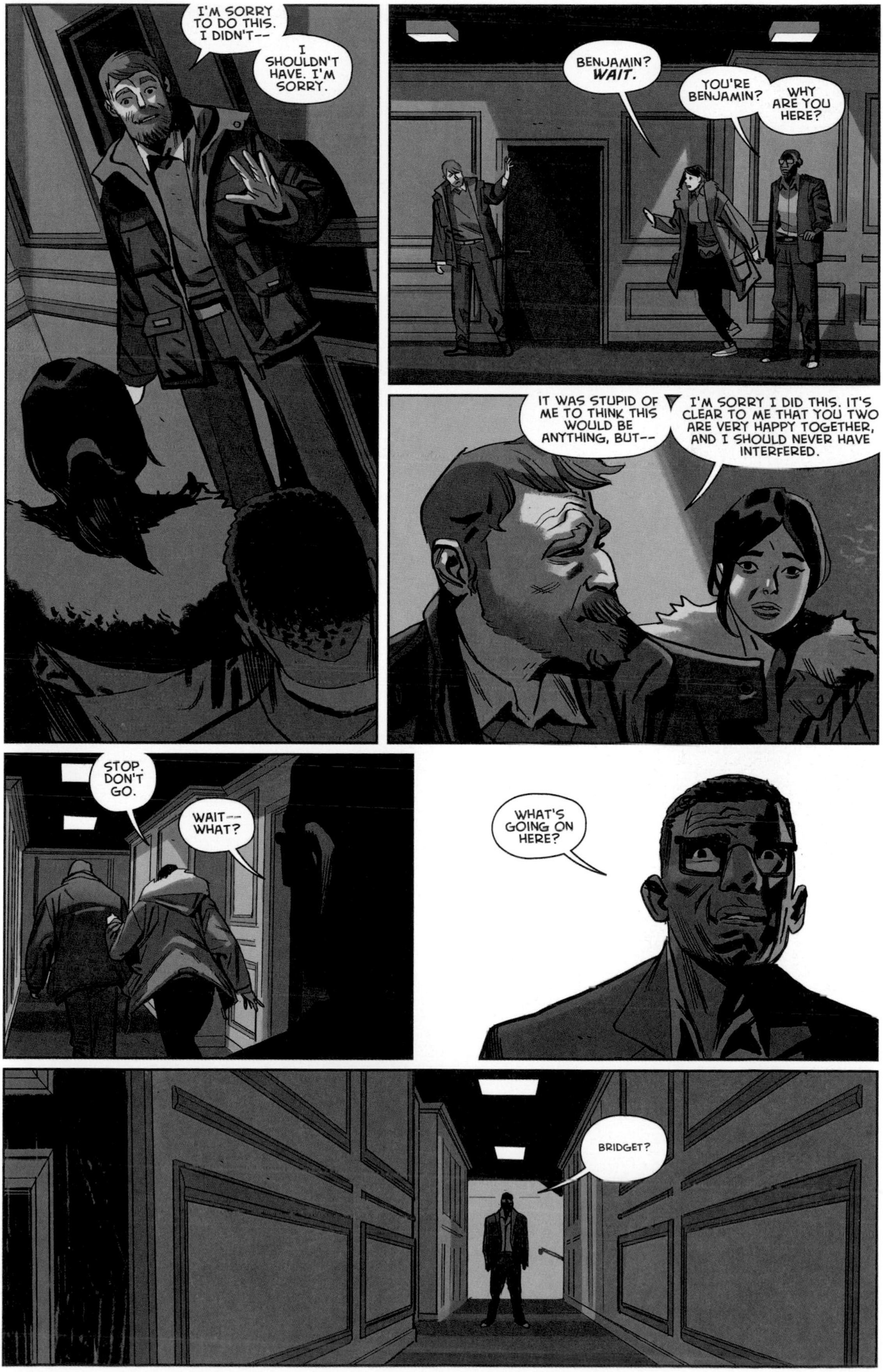
I'M SORRY TO DO THIS. I DIDN'T--
I SHOULDN'T HAVE. I'M SORRY.
BENJAMIN? WAIT.
YOU'RE BENJAMIN?
WHY ARE YOU HERE?
IT WAS STUPID OF ME TO THINK THIS WOULD BE ANYTHING, BUT--
I'M SORRY I DID THIS. IT'S CLEAR TO ME THAT YOU TWO ARE VERY HAPPY TOGETHER, AND I SHOULD NEVER HAVE INTERFERED.
STOP. DON'T GO.
WAIT-- WHAT?
WHAT'S GOING ON HERE?
BRIDGET?

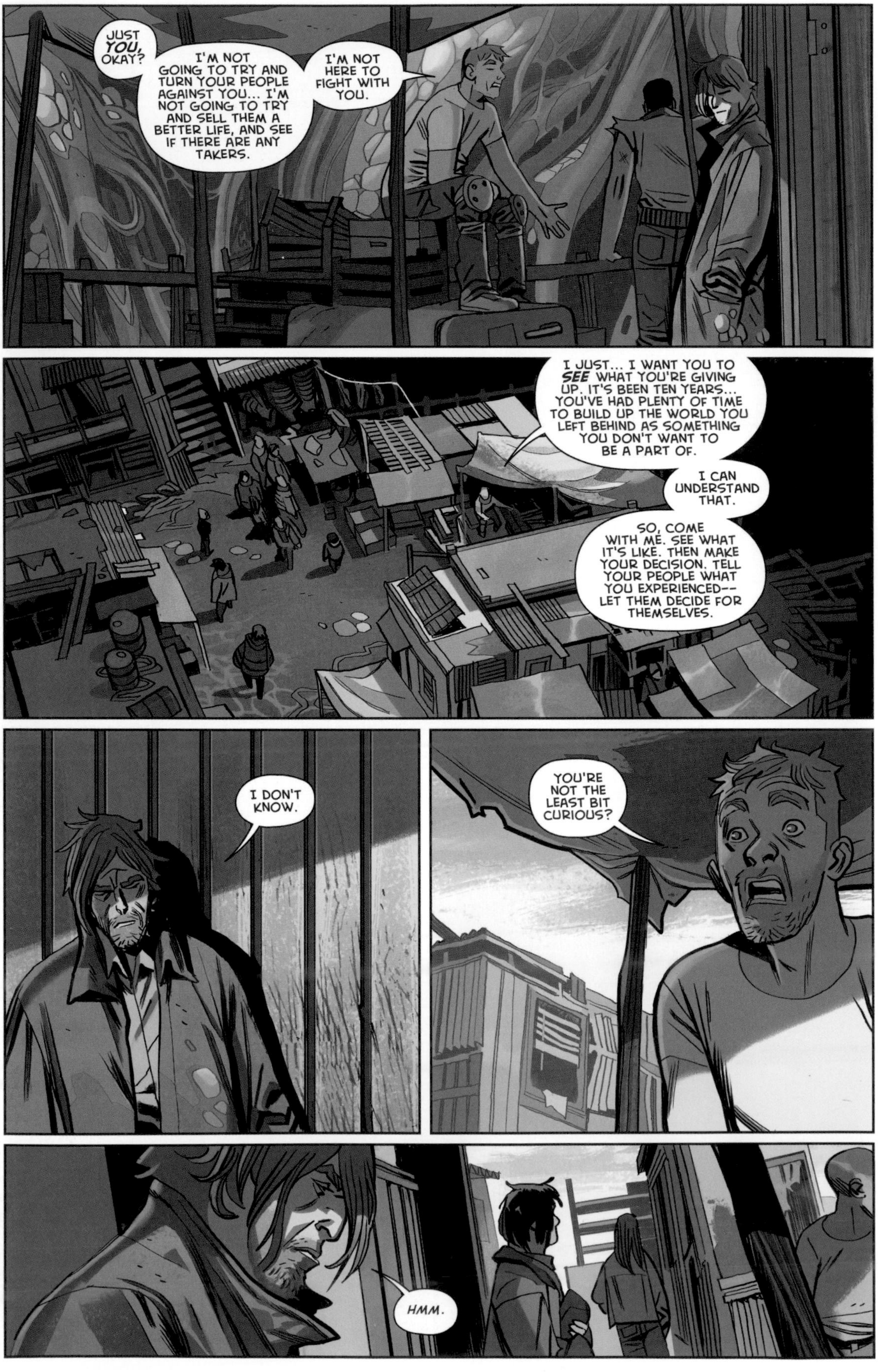
JUST YOU, OKAY?
I'M NOT GOING TO TRY AND TURN YOUR PEOPLE AGAINST YOU... I'M NOT GOING TO TRY AND SELL THEM A BETTER LIFE, AND SEE IF THERE ARE ANY TAKERS.
I'M NOT HERE TO FIGHT WITH YOU.
I JUST... I WANT YOU TO SEE WHAT YOU'RE GIVING UP. IT'S BEEN TEN YEARS... YOU'VE HAD PLENTY OF TIME TO BUILD UP THE WORLD YOU LEFT BEHIND AS SOMETHING YOU DON'T WANT TO BE A PART OF.
I CAN UNDERSTAND THAT.
SO, COME WITH ME. SEE WHAT IT'S LIKE. THEN MAKE YOUR DECISION. TELL YOUR PEOPLE WHAT YOU EXPERIENCED-- LET THEM DECIDE FOR THEMSELVES.
I DON'T KNOW.
YOU'RE NOT THE LEAST BIT CURIOUS?
HMM.

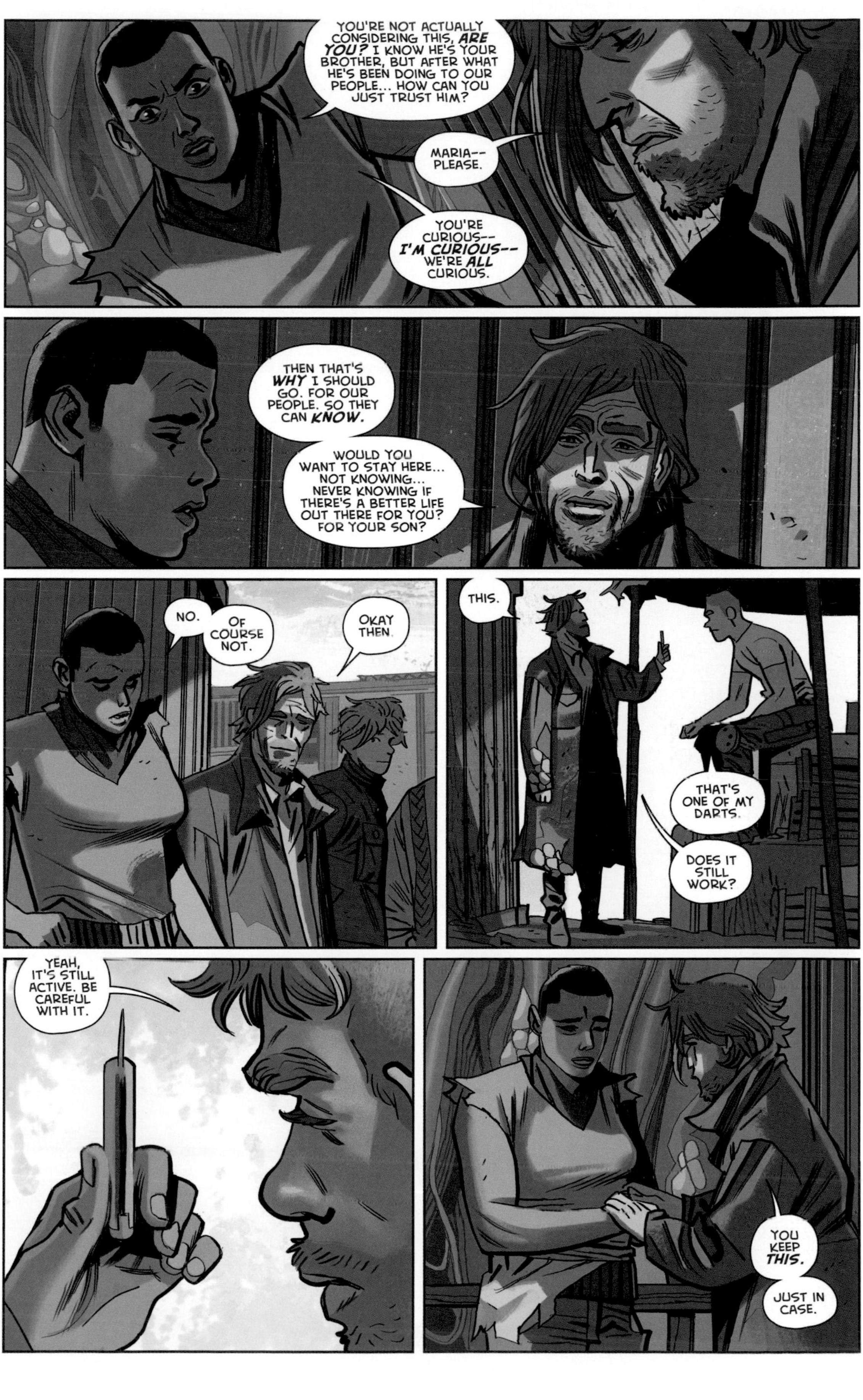
YOU'RE NOT ACTUALLY CONSIDERING THIS, ***ARE YOU?*** I KNOW HE'S YOUR BROTHER, BUT AFTER WHAT HE'S BEEN DOING TO OUR PEOPLE... HOW CAN YOU JUST TRUST HIM?
MARIA-- PLEASE.
YOU'RE CURIOUS-- ***I'M CURIOUS***-- WE'RE ***ALL*** CURIOUS.
THEN THAT'S ***WHY*** I SHOULD GO. FOR OUR PEOPLE. SO THEY CAN ***KNOW.***
WOULD YOU WANT TO STAY HERE... NOT KNOWING... NEVER KNOWING IF THERE'S A BETTER LIFE OUT THERE FOR YOU? FOR YOUR SON?
NO.
OF COURSE NOT.
OKAY THEN.
THIS.
THAT'S ONE OF MY DARTS.
DOES IT STILL WORK?
YEAH, IT'S STILL ACTIVE. BE CAREFUL WITH IT.
YOU KEEP ***THIS.***
JUST IN CASE.

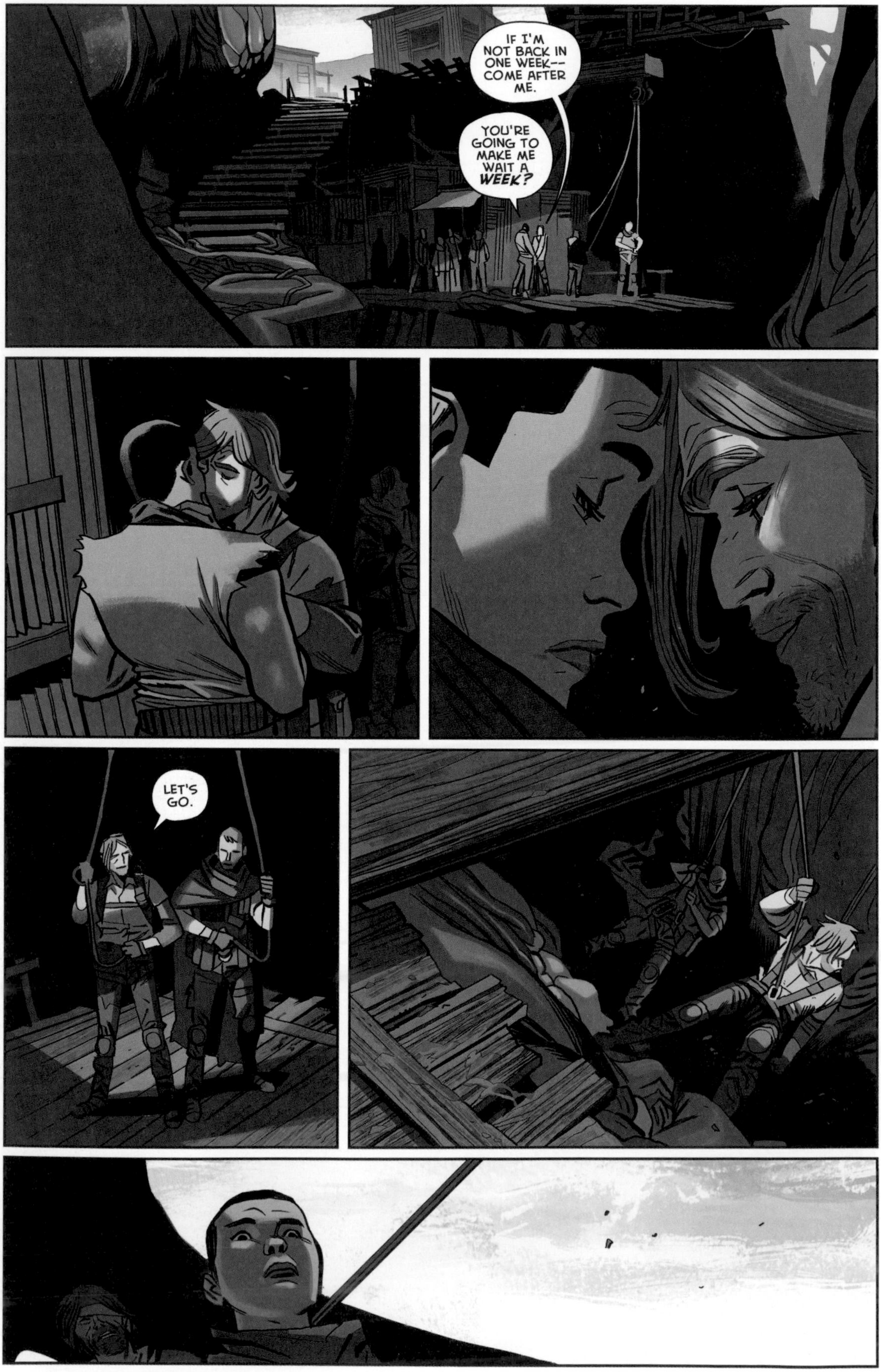
IF I'M NOT BACK IN ONE WEEK-- COME AFTER ME.
YOU'RE GOING TO MAKE ME WAIT A WEEK?
LET'S GO.

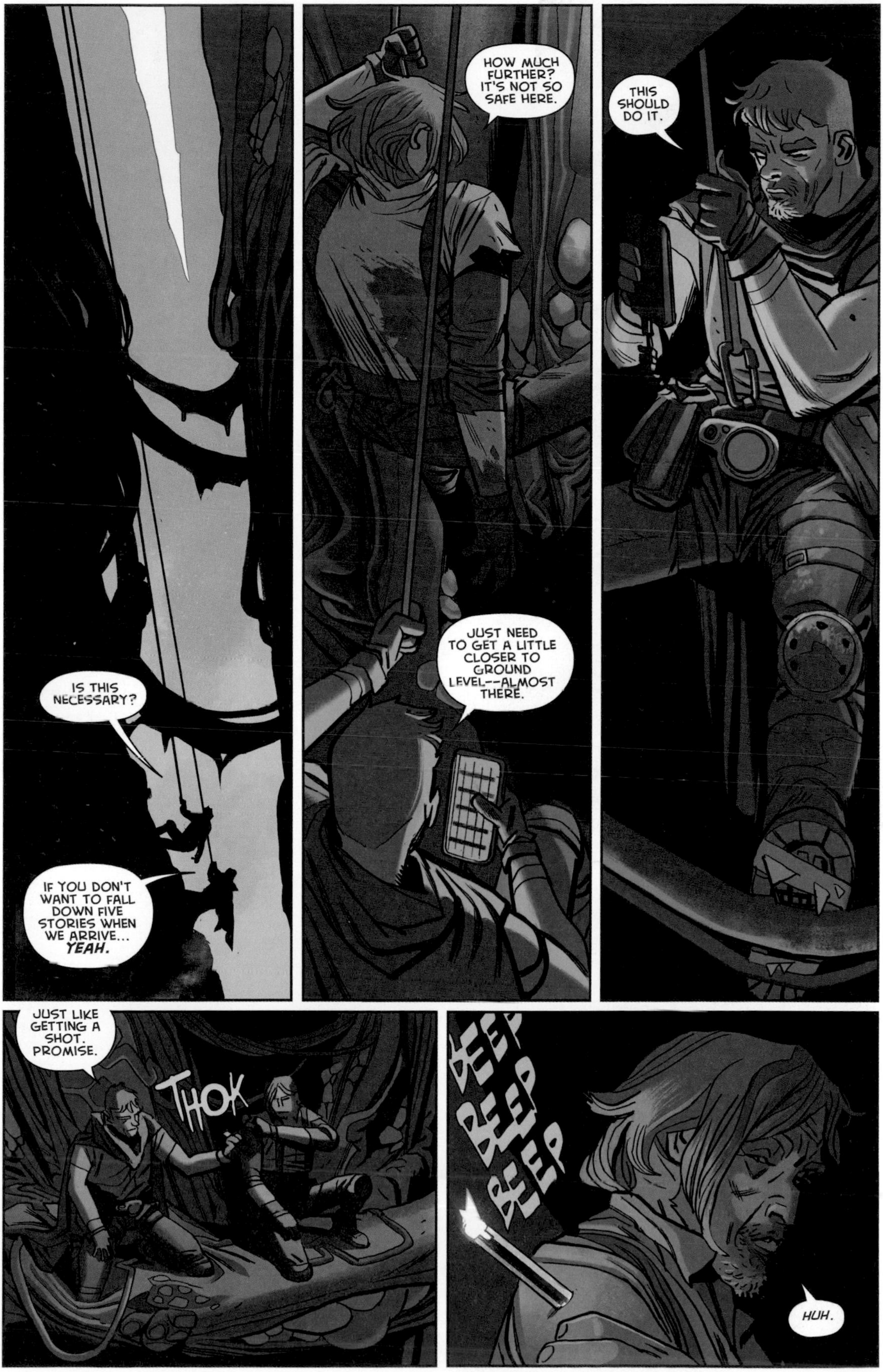
IS THIS NECESSARY?
IF YOU DON'T WANT TO FALL DOWN FIVE STORIES WHEN WE ARRIVE... YEAH.
HOW MUCH FURTHER? IT'S NOT SO SAFE HERE.
JUST NEED TO GET A LITTLE CLOSER TO GROUND LEVEL--ALMOST THERE.
THIS SHOULD DO IT.
JUST LIKE GETTING A SHOT. PROMISE.
THOK
BEEP BEEP BEEP
HUH.

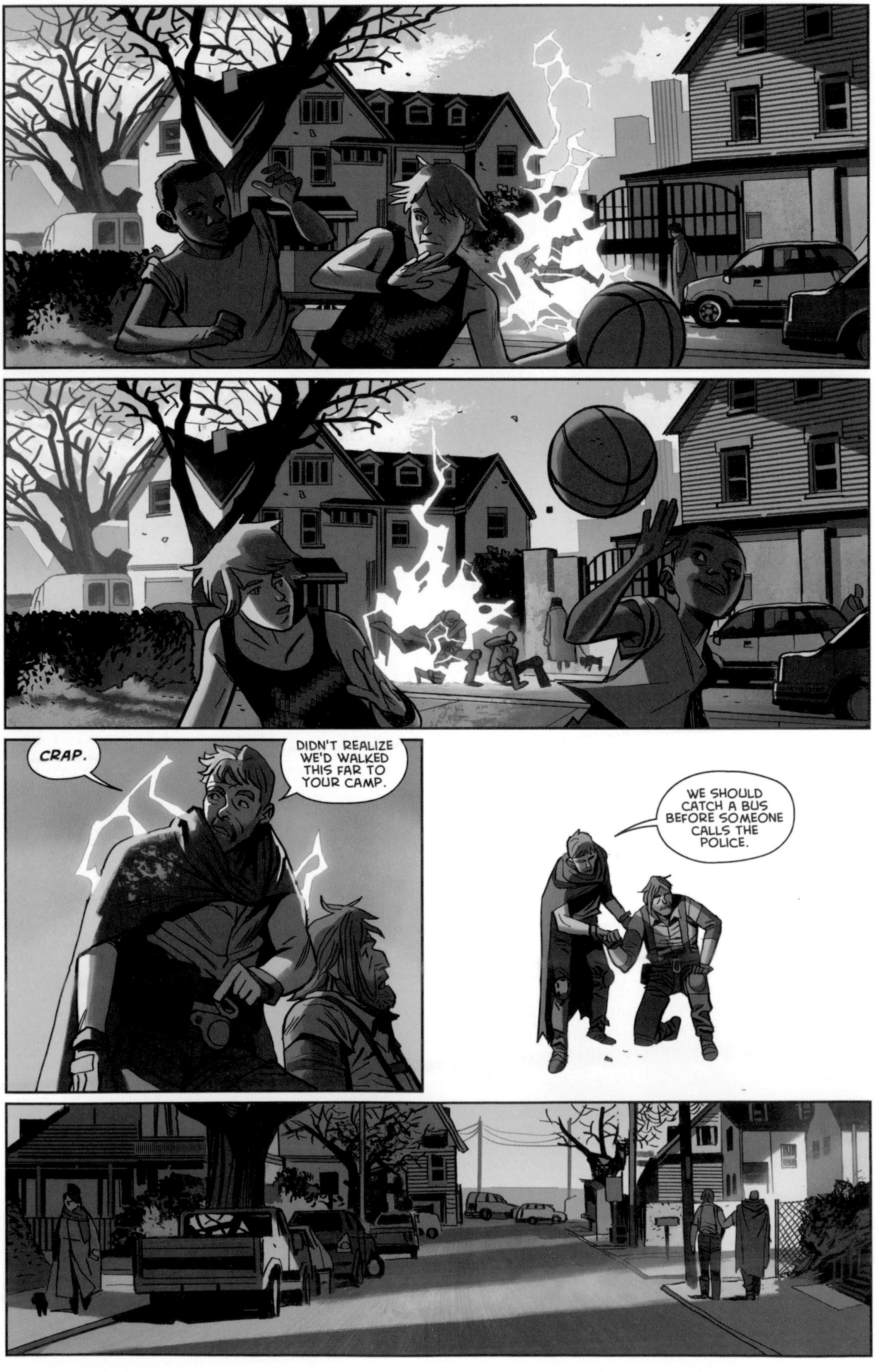
CRAP.
DIDN'T REALIZE WE'D WALKED THIS FAR TO YOUR CAMP.
WE SHOULD CATCH A BUS BEFORE SOMEONE CALLS THE POLICE.

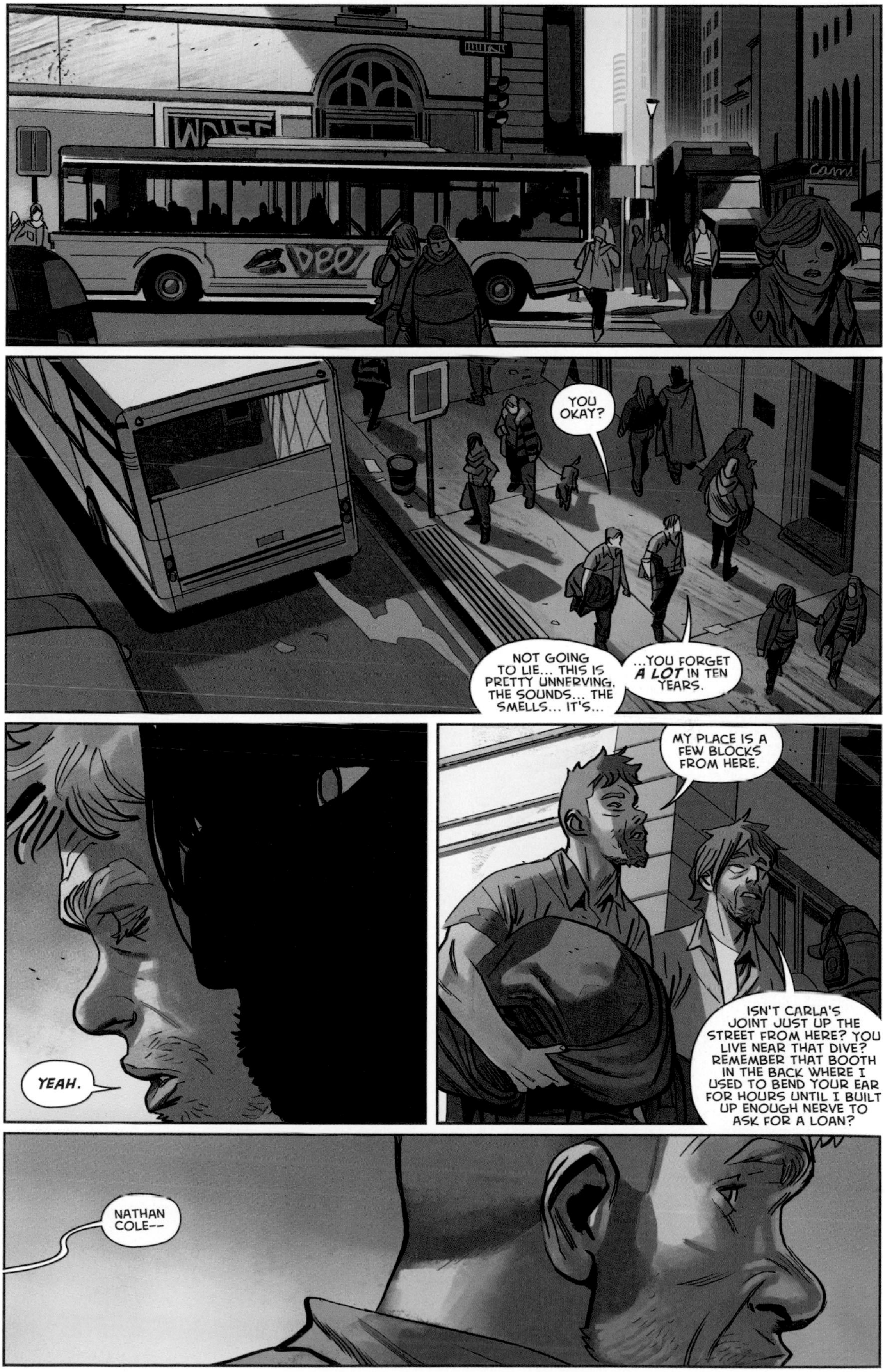
YOU OKAY?
NOT GOING TO LIE... THIS IS PRETTY UNNERVING. THE SOUNDS... THE SMELLS... IT'S...
...YOU FORGET A LOT IN TEN YEARS.
YEAH.
MY PLACE IS A FEW BLOCKS FROM HERE.
ISN'T CARLA'S JOINT JUST UP THE STREET FROM HERE? YOU LIVE NEAR THAT DIVE? REMEMBER THAT BOOTH IN THE BACK WHERE I USED TO BEND YOUR EAR FOR HOURS UNTIL I BUILT UP ENOUGH NERVE TO ASK FOR A LOAN?
NATHAN COLE--

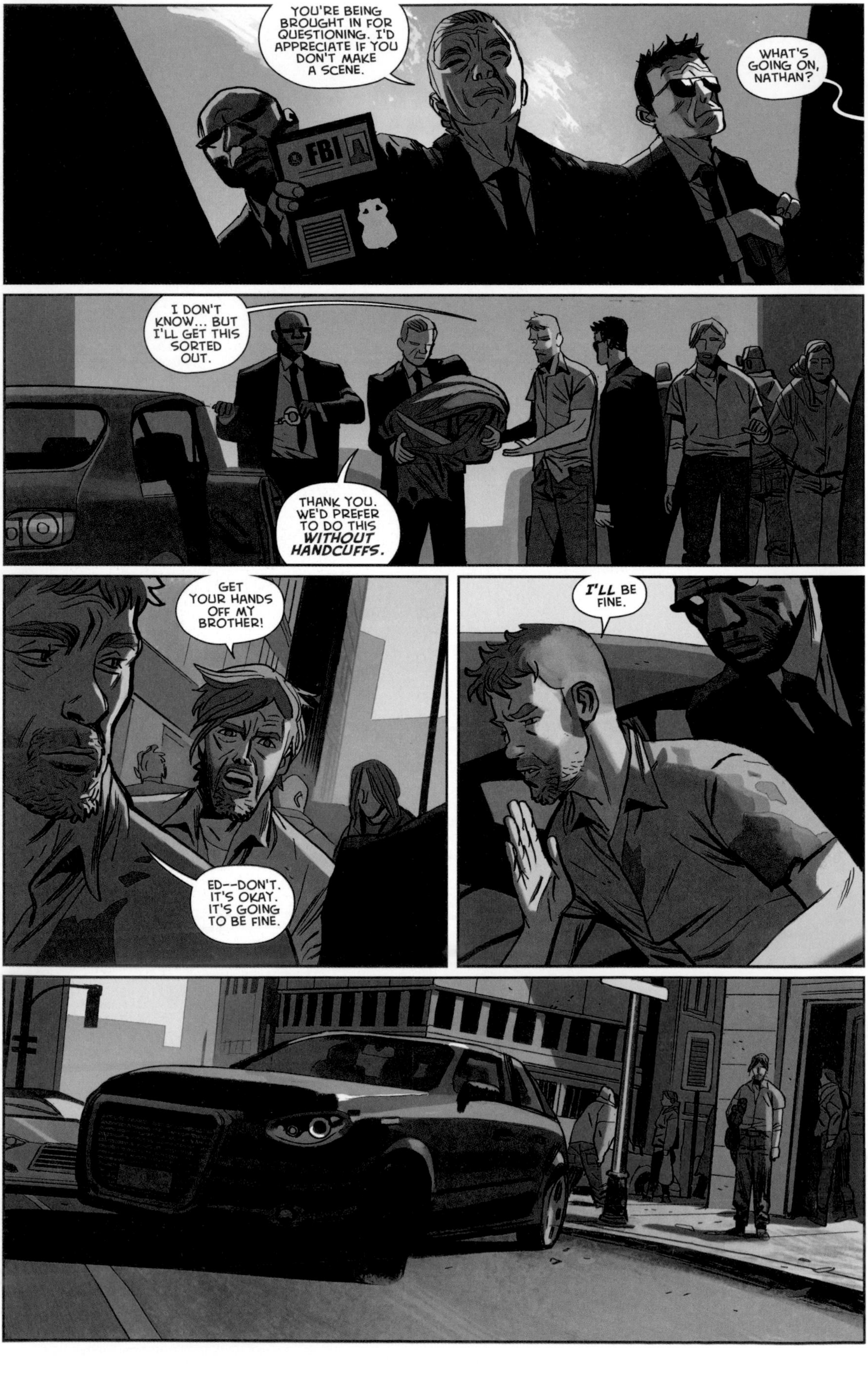

YOU'RE BEING BROUGHT IN FOR QUESTIONING. I'D APPRECIATE IF YOU DON'T MAKE A SCENE.
WHAT'S GOING ON, NATHAN?
FBI
I DON'T KNOW... BUT I'LL GET THIS SORTED OUT.
THANK YOU. WE'D PREFER TO DO THIS *WITHOUT HANDCUFFS.*
GET YOUR HANDS OFF MY BROTHER!
ED--DON'T. IT'S OKAY. IT'S GOING TO BE FINE.
I'LL BE FINE.

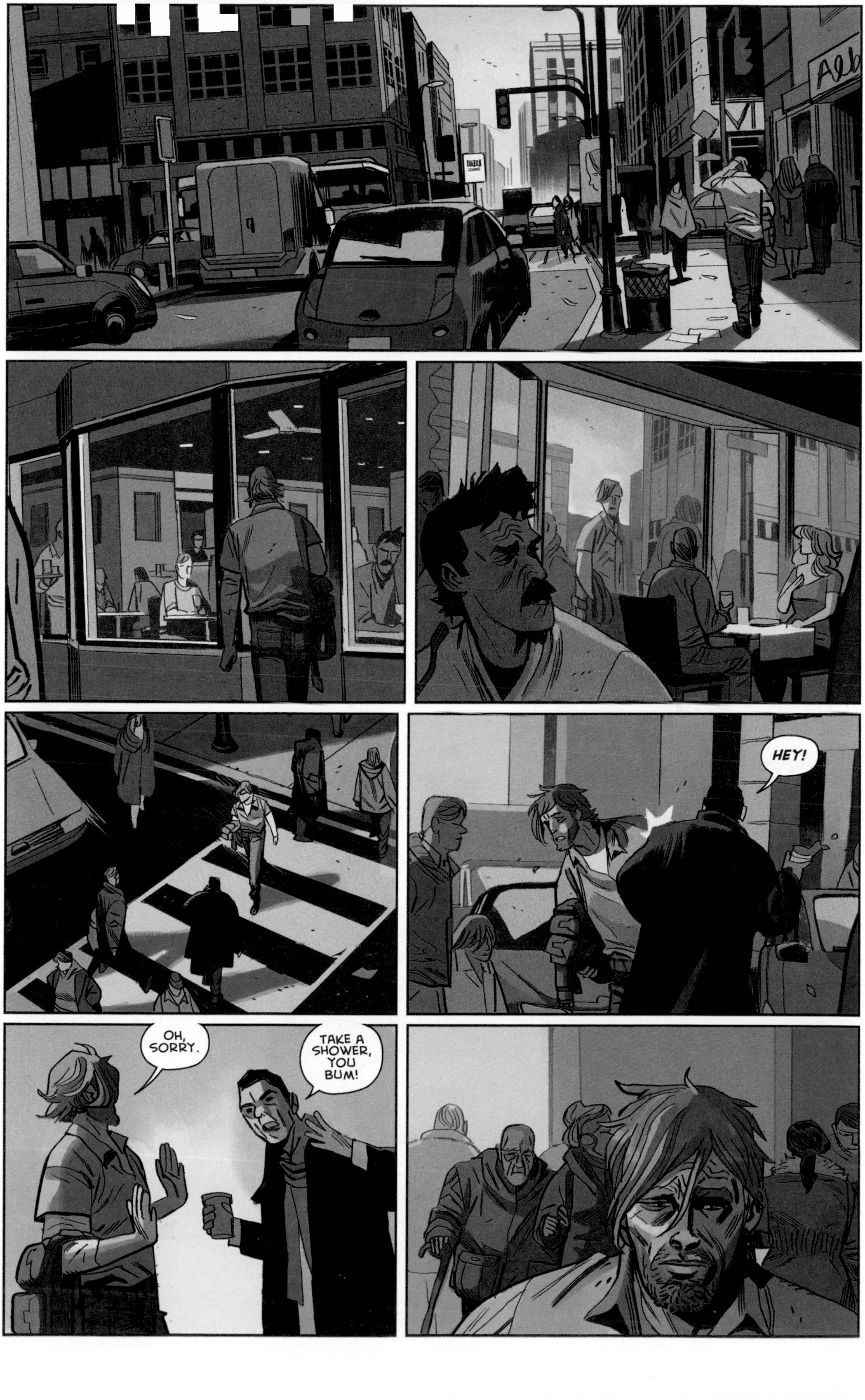
HEY!
OH, SORRY.
TAKE A SHOWER, YOU BUM!

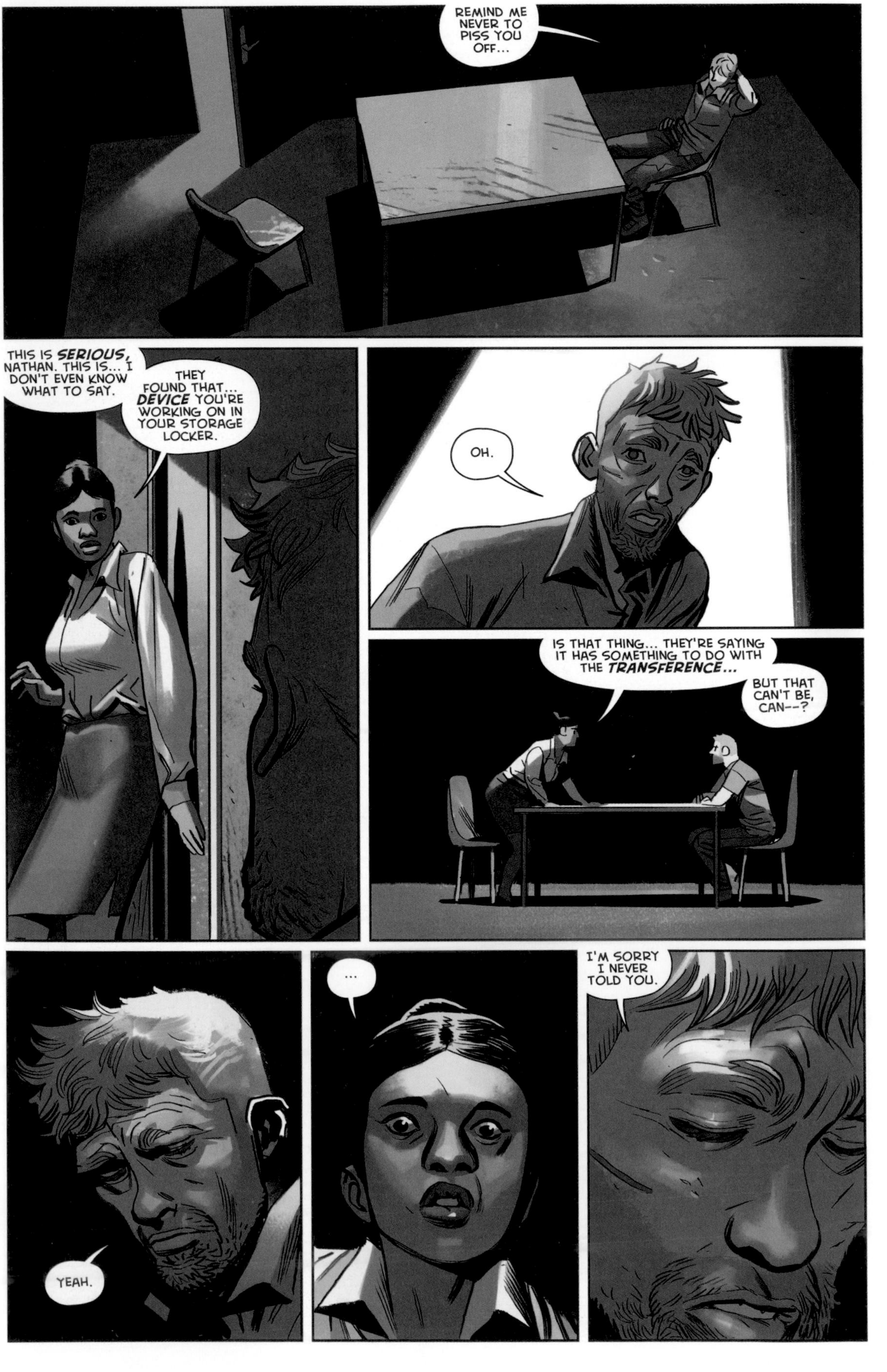
REMIND ME NEVER TO PISS YOU OFF...
THIS IS SERIOUS, NATHAN. THIS IS... I DON'T EVEN KNOW WHAT TO SAY.
THEY FOUND THAT... DEVICE YOU'RE WORKING ON IN YOUR STORAGE LOCKER.
OH.
IS THAT THING... THEY'RE SAYING IT HAS SOMETHING TO DO WITH THE TRANSFERENCE...
BUT THAT CAN'T BE, CAN--?
YEAH.
...
I'M SORRY I NEVER TOLD YOU.

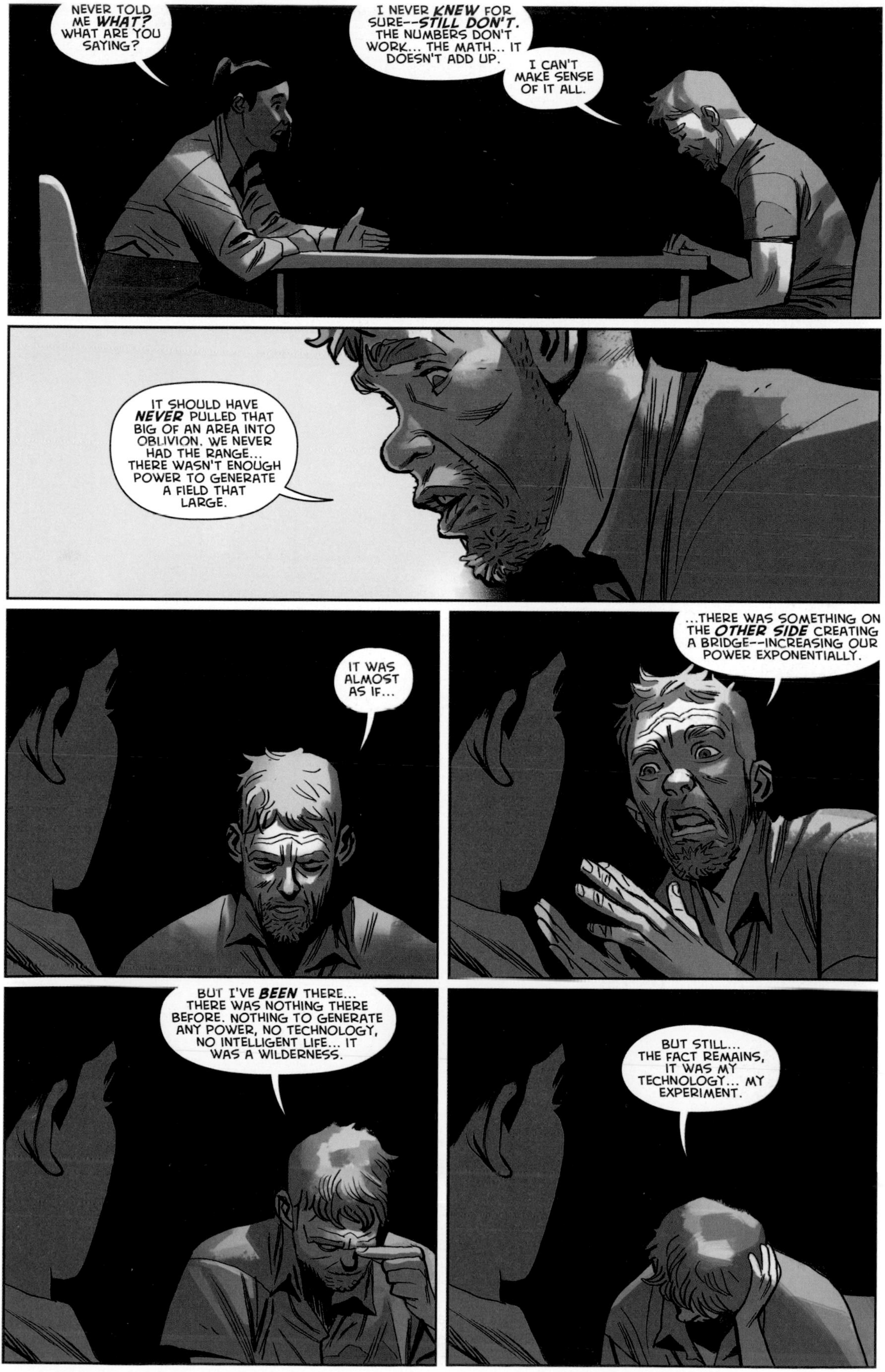
NEVER TOLD ME WHAT? WHAT ARE YOU SAYING?
I NEVER KNEW FOR SURE--STILL DON'T. THE NUMBERS DON'T WORK... THE MATH... IT DOESN'T ADD UP.
I CAN'T MAKE SENSE OF IT ALL.
IT SHOULD HAVE NEVER PULLED THAT BIG OF AN AREA INTO OBLIVION. WE NEVER HAD THE RANGE... THERE WASN'T ENOUGH POWER TO GENERATE A FIELD THAT LARGE.
IT WAS ALMOST AS IF...
...THERE WAS SOMETHING ON THE OTHER SIDE CREATING A BRIDGE--INCREASING OUR POWER EXPONENTIALLY.
BUT I'VE BEEN THERE... THERE WAS NOTHING THERE BEFORE. NOTHING TO GENERATE ANY POWER, NO TECHNOLOGY, NO INTELLIGENT LIFE... IT WAS A WILDERNESS.
BUT STILL... THE FACT REMAINS, IT WAS MY TECHNOLOGY... MY EXPERIMENT.

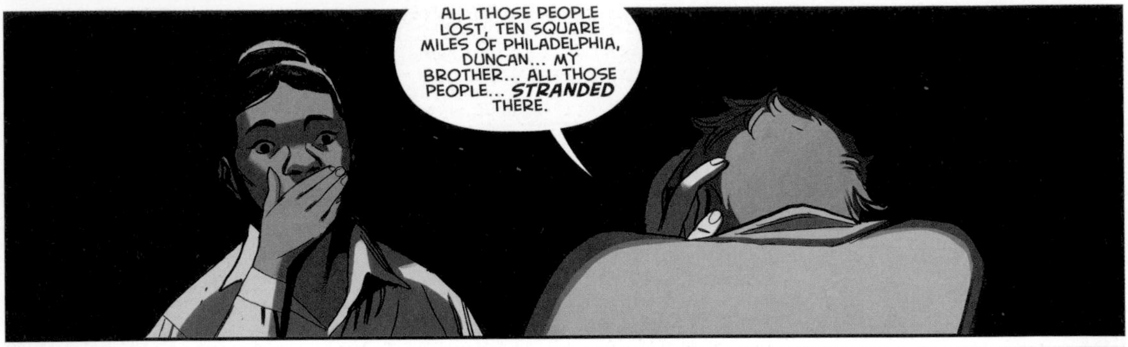
ALL THOSE PEOPLE LOST, TEN SQUARE MILES OF PHILADELPHIA, DUNCAN... MY BROTHER... ALL THOSE PEOPLE... STRANDED THERE.

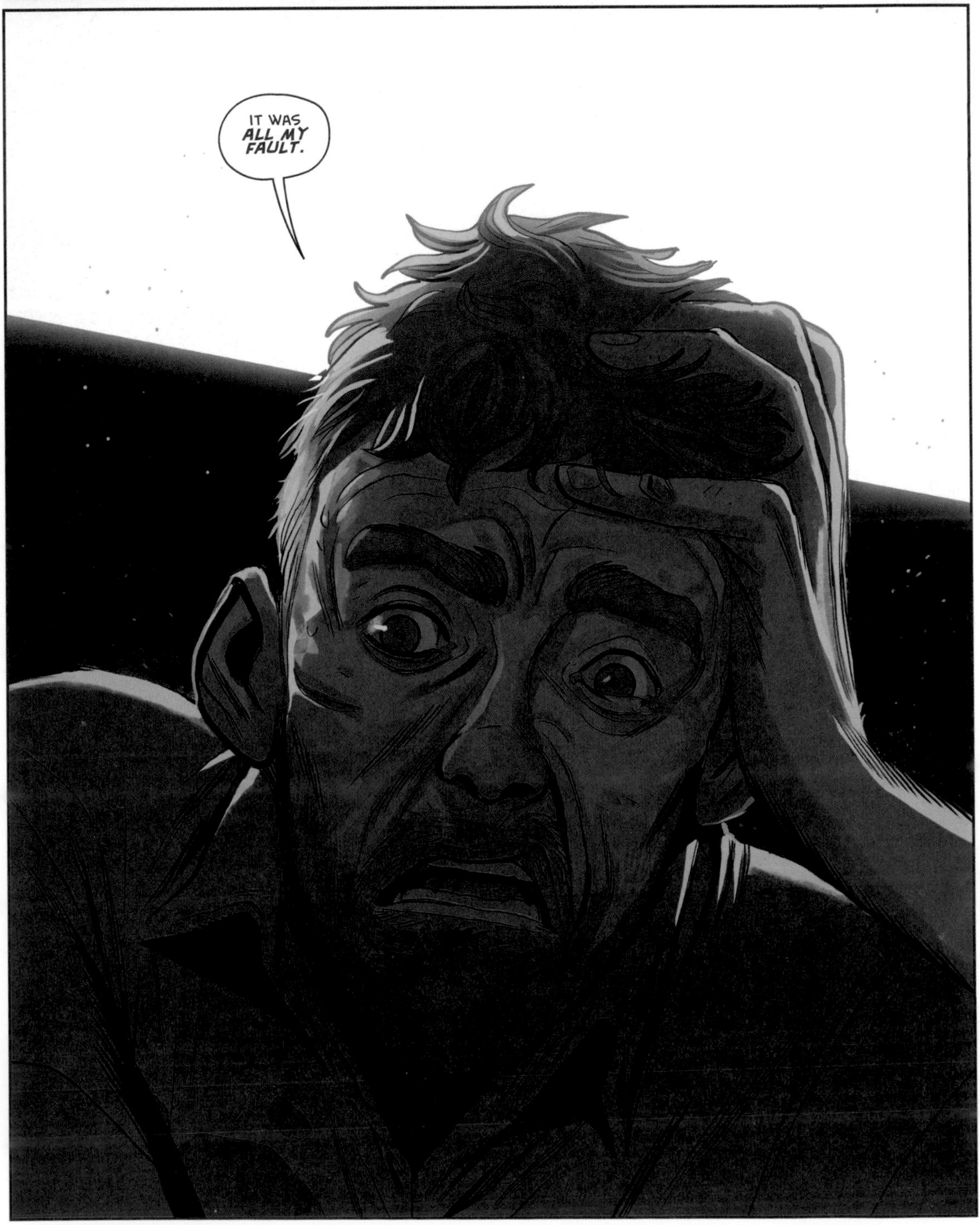
IT WAS ALL MY FAULT.

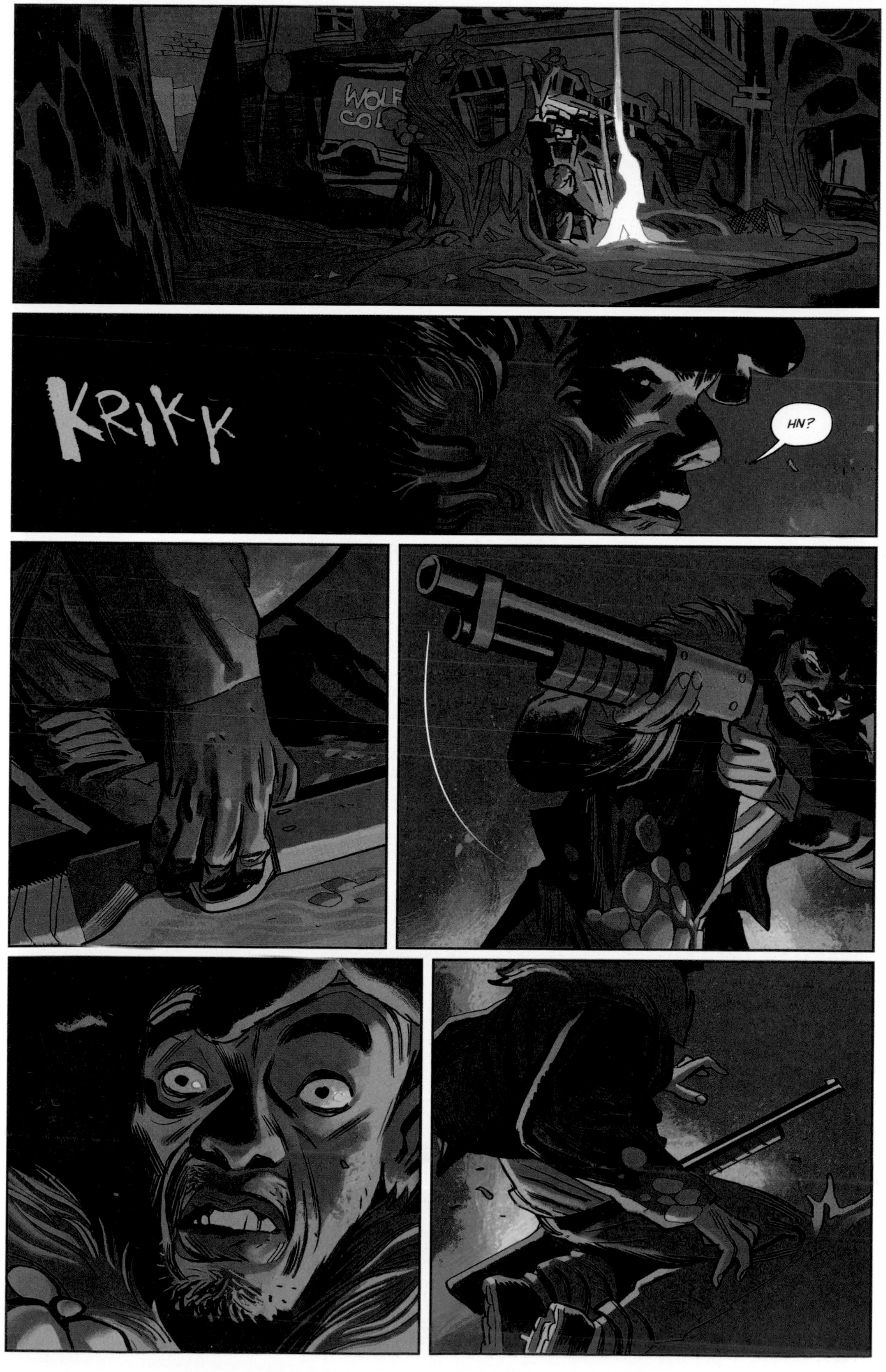
KRIKK
HN?

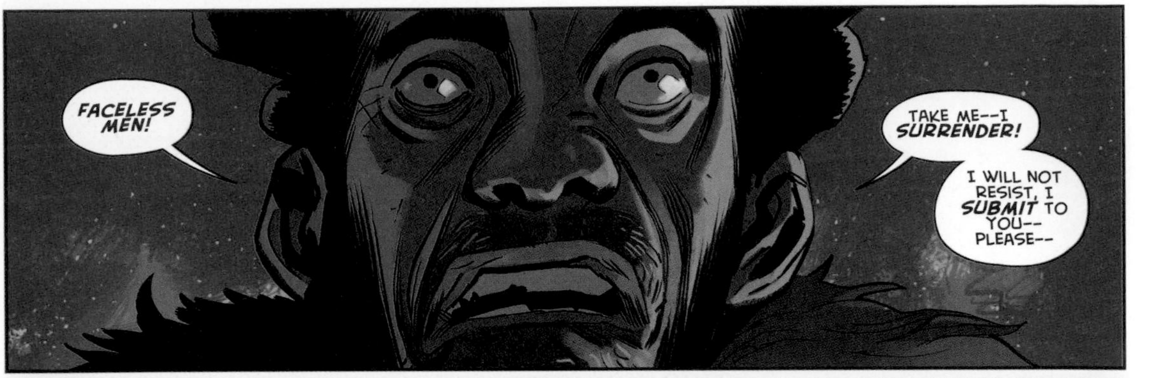
FACELESS MEN!
TAKE ME--I SURRENDER!
I WILL NOT RESIST, I SUBMIT TO YOU-- PLEASE--

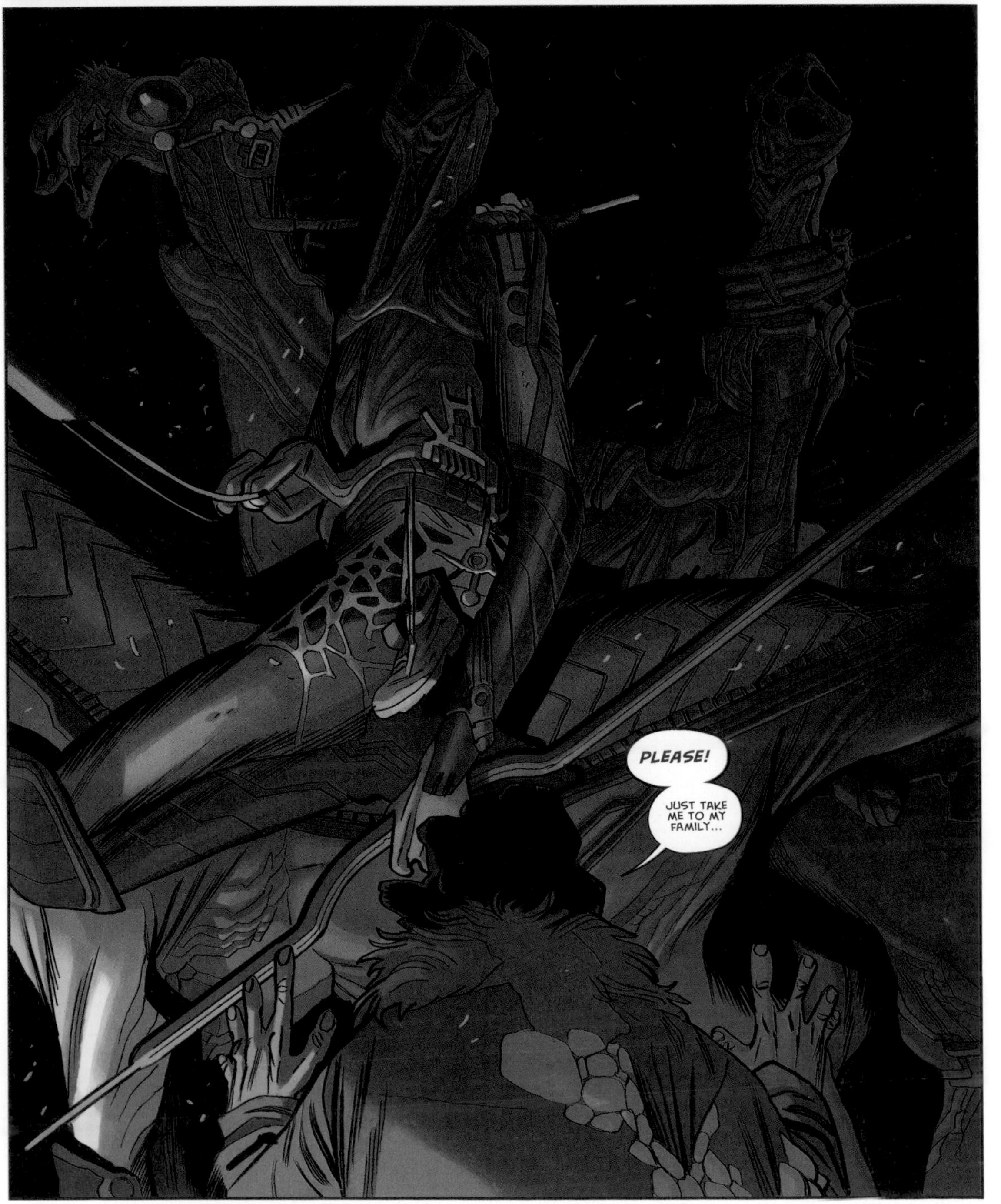
PLEASE!
JUST TAKE ME TO MY FAMILY...

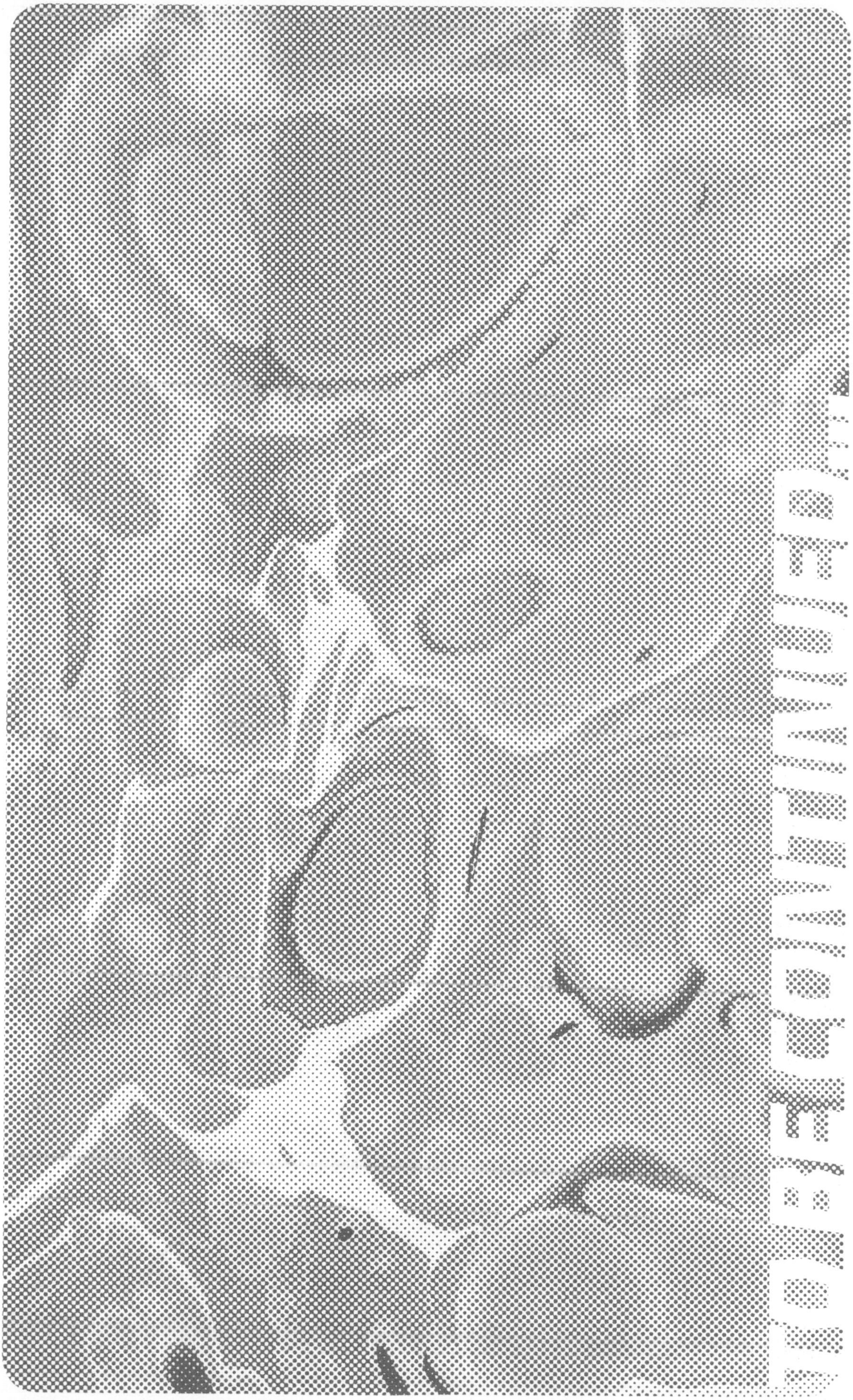
TO BE CONTINUED

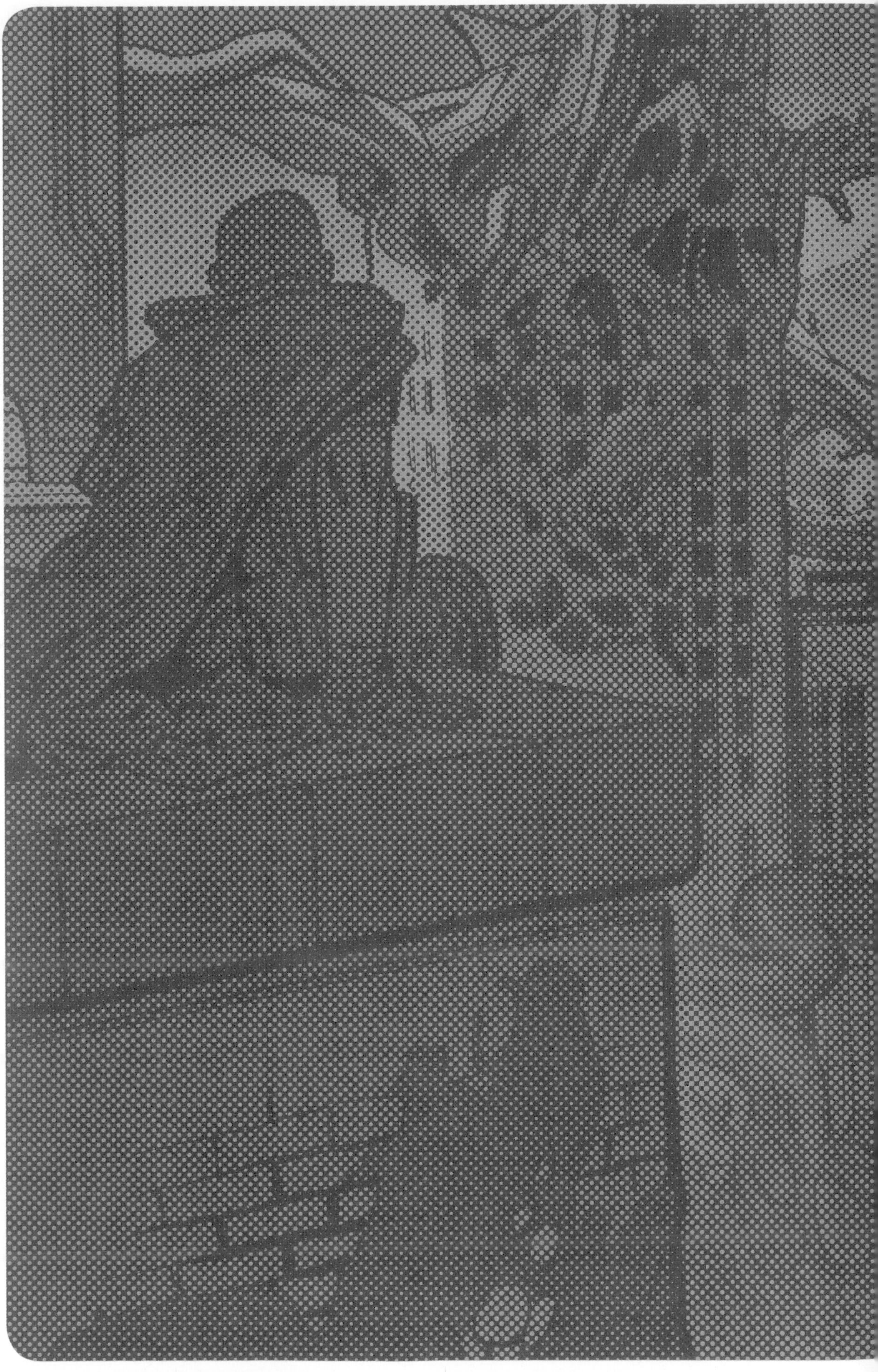

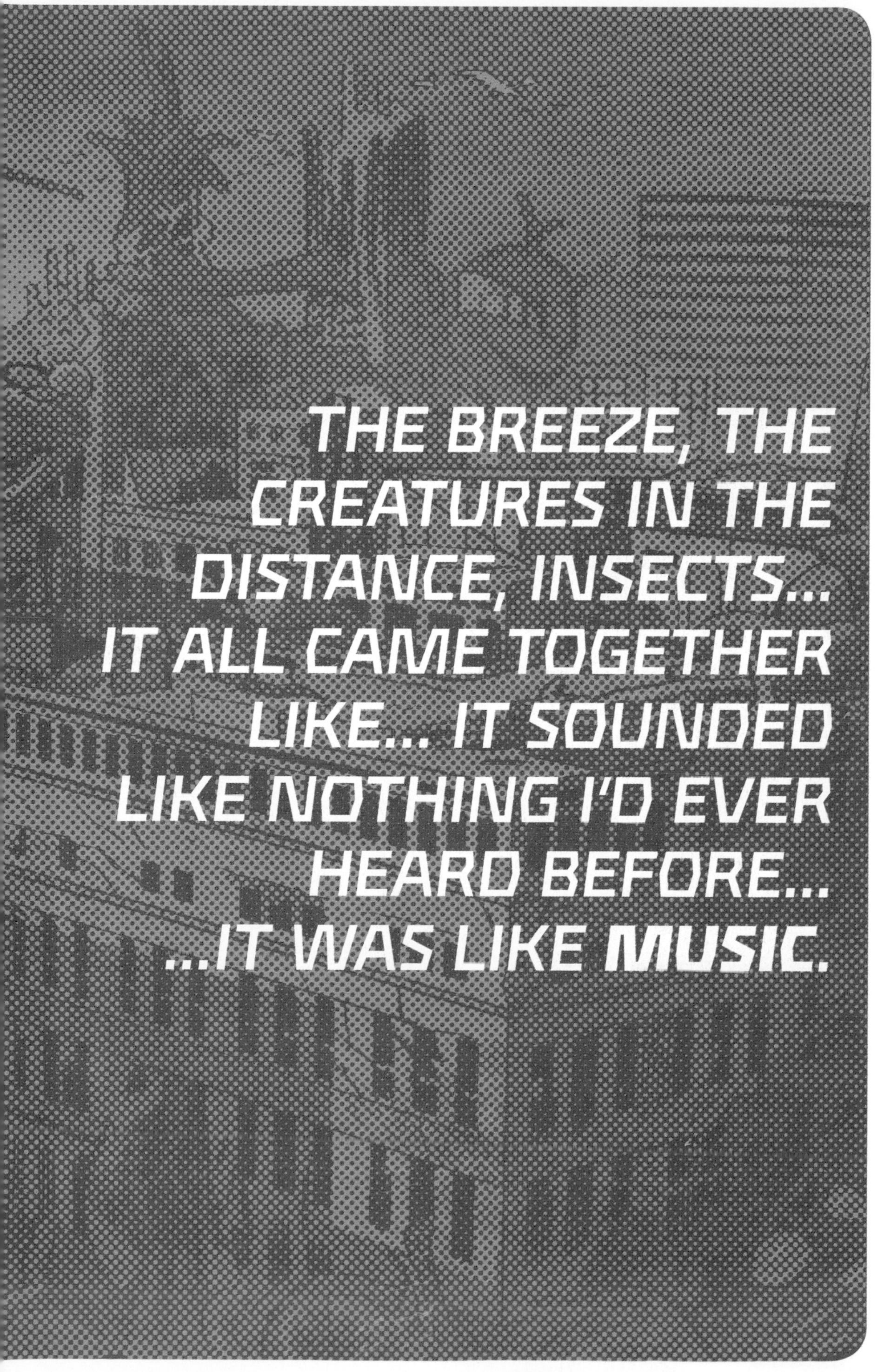
THE BREEZE, THE CREATURES IN THE DISTANCE, INSECTS... IT ALL CAME TOGETHER LIKE... IT SOUNDED LIKE NOTHING I'D EVER HEARD BEFORE...
...IT WAS LIKE **MUSIC**.

FOR MORE TALES FROM ROBERT KIRKMAN AND SKYBOUND

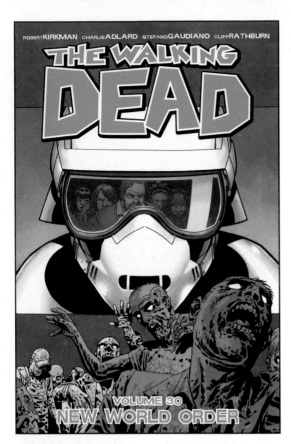

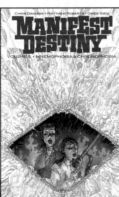